Praise f

Amber Perry's colonial American debut is a stirring story with high drama, romance, and suspense aplenty. From lovely cover to satisfying conclusion, *So Fair a Lady* will win romance readers' hearts!

-Laura Frantz, Christy Award finalist and author of The Colonels' Lady and Love's Reckoning

Amber Perry's debut novel brings to life the days before the Revolutionary War in vivid detail. This fast-paced, historical romance will appeal to colonial enthusiasts and inspirational readers alike.

- Stacy Henrie, author of Hope at Dawn (Of Love and War, Book 1)

A tender Colonial love story, *So Fair a Lady* will sweep you back in time to a nation's turbulent beginnings where love and loyalty wages war against two men ... and the one woman who has captured both of their hearts.

-Julie Lessman, award-winning author of The Daughters of Boston and Winds of Change series.

Heartwarming, suspenseful, adventurous, and romantic ... everything I love in a novel! Amber Perry's elegant prose and deep characters will transport you to pre-Revolutionary War America where tensions were high, betrayal was common, and love blossomed in the most unexpected places.

-MaryLu Tyndall, award winning author of the Escape to Paradise series

When I opened *So Fair a Lady*, I had no idea the emotional turmoil I would endure as I joined Eliza on her tumultuous voyage from her genteel home, through unspeakable heartbreak, and swoon-worthy happiness, all the way to The End. Amber Perry creates a world so real, so intense, that the reader forgets the realm around them and falls down through time into the chairs set in front of the warm fire, ready to join the characters as they try to make sense of the turbulent world around them. This is 'seat of your pants', 'did he just kiss her like that?' reading!

-Jennifer Z. Major,
www.talesfromtheredhead.blogspot.com

Book 1
Daughters of His Kingdom Series

By, Amber Lynn Perry

So Fair a Lady
By, Amber Lynn Perry

ISBN-13: 978-1497518407
ISBN-10: 1497518407

Cover Design by Tekeme Studios
Cover Photography by Danyell Diaz Photography
Interior Layout by Castle and Lynnette Bonner of Indie Cover Design – www.indiecoverdesign.com

Published by Liberty Publishing

CreateSpace Edition

Author/publisher information and contact:
www.amberlynnperry.com

Dedicated to all humble seekers of truth.
May you find it, and may it make you free.

Rejoice, the Lord is King!
Your Lord and King adore!
Mortals, give thanks and sing,
And triumph evermore.

~Charles Wesley

Chapter One

Boston, 1773

Don't leave us, Father, we need you!

Eliza Campbell tried to keep her fingers from trembling as she tenderly stroked her father's arm and watched him struggle to breathe. Her heart withered, and she stared out the partially open window of the large upstairs room, praying. *Lord, how will we live without him?*

The early October sun spilled into the bedchamber, imparting the loamy fragrance of autumn. Large cotton-like clouds dotted the pale sky, while a cardinal floated across the breeze and into a clump of orange-colored maples.

A beautiful day.

Far too beautiful for Father to die.

Eliza mopped his brow and smoothed away several strands of his brown hair, guarding her tears. He was only fifty—a skilled physician in the best years of his life. Eliza shuddered. Though she knew God always worked in wisdom, she couldn't see why He would take Father from them now.

Outside the window, the view across the swaying fields of grasses looked the same—peaceful, welcoming, joyful. But without Father this home, this place that had always brought so much happiness, would never be the same. The dreaded consumption that plagued him for so long, would now take his life. The gray color of death painted his lips and small beads of sweat dotted his forehead. They could only try to comfort him and wait for the end.

Sitting opposite Eliza on the large four-poster bed, Kitty knit her fingers and blinked. Large tears rolled down her porcelain cheeks, and thick dark-auburn curls pulled free from their pins, giving testament to her constant vigil. A sob escaped her lips and Eliza instinctively reached for her younger sister's hand and squeezed. *I won't fail you, Kitty. I won't.*

"Kitty?" Father gasped for air. "Will you . . . fetch me some more cool cloths?"

She straightened and patted her tears, trying to smile. "Aye, Father, I should have thought of that myself, forgive me. I shall return directly." She crunched her apron in her fingers and nodded at Eliza before darting out of the room, her light step echoing down the stairs.

Eliza scooted closer to Father and gulped down the painful lump of sorrow in her throat. But it wouldn't budge. She propped the pillows around his neck and back, but Father still winced with every rise and fall of his chest.

Lord, please be with me. I need thy strength.

"Eliza . . . listen to me." Father wheezed as he spoke.

"Yes, Father, I'm here. I'm listening."

He swallowed. "Behind you . . . on the mantel, underneath the candlestick is a letter." Father stopped and tried to inhale what little air he could. "Go . . . retrieve it."

Eliza shook her head. "I don't want to leave your

side even for a moment. I—"

Father inched his hand across the bedding and gripped Eliza's fingers. "Get it. That letter is of . . . great importance."

Eliza opened her mouth to protest, but snapped her jaw closed. No need to cause Father any added discomfort by her disobedience. "As you wish." Slowly, she moved from her perch at his side, careful to watch him should he begin another fit of coughs.

She removed the folded paper from underneath the heavy candlestick atop the wooden mantel. The paper was crisp and the seal fresh, as if he had just written it. But he couldn't have. She'd been at his side for almost two weeks. When had he composed it? What information could it possibly contain that was so important?

Father turned his head on the pillow. "Aye, that is it." He paused, his lungs wheezing. "That letter . . . is for your eyes alone. No one . . . not even Kitty can know what it reveals."

Peering at the empty doorway, Eliza quickly took her position at his side. "What do you wish me to know that Kitty cannot?" Thank heaven her sister hadn't yet returned with the cloths.

"You are ready for the truth, but Kitty . . . she is too headstrong . . . she must learn of it in God's time." Father blinked slowly.

Eliza forced a smile on her lips, while her insides twisted. Father had turned delirious. Kitty was only three years behind Eliza's twenty. And yes, she may be headstrong at times, but she was mature and stable. Surely she could . . .

No. Best to leave this alone and change the subject before Kitty returned. "I promise I shall do my best to care for Kitty, to protect her and give her everything she needs. I shall try and raise her the way you would have me."

Father moved his thumb across Eliza's hand, providing comfort even in his last moments. "I know of your fears, my dear. What happened with Peter . . . was not your fault."

Her chest constricted. Of course it was her fault. She opened her mouth to speak, but the crowd of emotions in her throat blocked her words.

Father's tired gaze reached around Eliza's shoulders like a tender embrace. "There is plenty of money for you and your sister to live on . . . do not worry." He paused, his shoulders quaking as he coughed. "Focus on the letter . . . it is vital. I want you . . . to know the truth about me."

Eliza pressed her teeth into her lip and tucked the mysterious note into her skirt pocket. What truth? Was he trying to say he'd been hiding something? Surely he knew not what he was saying.

"How is he?" Kitty rushed in, her arms laden with rags and a large pitcher of water.

"Worse."

"I was afraid of that." After wetting a cloth, Kitty quickly took her place at the other side of the bed and patted the damp cotton rag against Father's forehead.

The weight of her responsibilities crushed what strength Eliza had left. Clinging to the last thread of hope within, Eliza pinned a weak smile on her lips to let Kitty know that all would be well. Though of course, it would not. They had no real family to speak of and would be alone in the world if not for Samuel. Thank the Lord he would be there for them.

"My daughters. . ." Father's eyelids flickered, his chest barely moved.

No!

Eliza couldn't breathe. It was upon them. The moment she'd feared for months. Eliza's gut cramped and her eyes burned. *Dearest Lord, he cannot leave us, please do not take him!*

"My spirit . . . will strive with you." Father's mouth barely moved, his voice no more than a whisper. He lifted his gaze to Eliza's. Somehow, in these last moments, his eyes cleared and penetrated into the raw chambers of her heart. "Find the truth . . . find the truth."

The light left his face and his last breath hissed from his mouth.

Numb, Eliza stared, unable to move.

"Father!" Kitty draped herself over his limp form, her body shaking as she wept.

Eliza's chest constricted as she stared at the lifeless form on the bed. Father, her greatest confidante, friend and hero had returned home to God. He still smelled of coffee and sweet tobacco. His body was still warm to the touch. Yet, he was gone.

His last words hung heavy in the air. *Find the truth.*

She covered her face. What truth?

Clutching his limp hand, Eliza blinked away the blur in her vision as she set her mouth in a determined line. She clasped his fingers tighter. *Whatever truth you want me to search for Father, I will find it. I promise.*

The vacant alley was darker than usual, adding to the shadows that littered his heart. Thomas Watson peered up at the black sky, his hands shaking. How much longer could he endure this? He jumped at a rustling sound along the cobblestone and almost dropped the folded paper into the puddle at his feet.

Someone was watching him.

It couldn't be . . .

His breathing stopped. He froze.

Or could it?

Had the worst finally happened? Had the Sons of Liberty discovered his treachery and followed him here? Tonight's meeting at the tavern around the corner would begin any minute—any one of them could easily witness . . . .

Please no, Lord. My friends must never know what I've done.

The hairs on the back of his neck stood on end as he clenched his eyes shut. The sooner he left Boston and started his life over again in Sandwich, the sooner he could leave his terrible past behind him.

He jerked again at a rustling sound. A rat scurried out of a pile of refuse and ran into the dim moonlight before disappearing around the corner. Thomas exhaled and raked his hand over his head.

Blasted rat!

Breathing still labored, he stared at the brick wall across the narrow alley. Paranoid. That's what he was—that's what two years of being blackmailed would do to any man. He crunched the folded paper in his fist as the tall, dingy walls closed in. How could he refuse the British, only to have Daniel imprisoned and dear Clara and the children sent to live in the streets? Impossible.

The blood slowed to a halt in his veins. But what about liberty? Hadn't he pledged his life to that very cause? How could he stand before God at the judgment day knowing that he had been such a coward? Robert Campbell would be ashamed.

At least he never knew.

Forgive me, Lord. Please forgive me.

"You have the information, I trust?"

Thomas jumped at the sound of Samuel Martin's voice, then quickly widened his stance, holding his arms at his sides. His muscles strained. Martin approached, his crimson uniform taking on a foreboding shade of black, while the tiny bits of light from the street flickered off his buttons.

Inhaling a deep breath, Thomas pushed out his chest and raised his chin. The sour odor of rotten fish drifted on the sea breeze and bit his nose. He fought the urge to laugh. Was that foul smell from the wharf or simply Martin's cologne? Either way, the stench suited him.

Without wasting a second, Martin reached out, wiggling his fingers. "Watson, you have the information, do you not? I should hate to have to make good on my promise if you don't."

"Promise? You mean your threat."

Martin's eyes narrowed. "Do you have it?"

Thomas's anger boiled but he said nothing, only handed over the crumpled paper. He clenched his jaw in an effort to hold back the dagger-like words that threatened to erupt.

"Well, Watson." Martin's voice sounded far too relaxed as he unfolded the paper and looked it over. "I know you will be most pleased to hear that my superiors are extremely grateful for the information about the Sons of Liberty that you have so kindly supplied." He chuckled and smiled, the faint light gleaming off his teeth. "You're country thanks you—your *king* thanks you."

Thomas clenched his fists so hard his knuckles cracked. "I have no king. Massachusetts is my country."

Martin gripped the sword at his side with one hand and jabbed his finger in Thomas's chest with the other. "Watch your words patriot, or you will find yourself in the pillory for speaking treason!"

"You don't frighten me."

Martin sneered. "I have you right where I want you, Watson. And you will do what I say, or your cousin and his family will—well, you know the rest."

Standing to his full height of six-foot-two, Thomas gauged his opponent who stood an easy three inches below him. His muscles flexed and his chest pumped. Martin may appear impressive in uniform, the sword at his side might be long and razor sharp, but Thomas's shoulders were broader, his arms more powerful. More than anything he wanted to feel the crack of Martin's square jaw as he sent his fist into it.

At that moment another Redcoat emerged from the shadows. Thomas jerked. Where had he come from?

"This had better be urgent." Martin hissed when the man reached his side. "Can you not see that I am busy?"

The man made a quick bow at the waist. "Please forgive me, Captain. You've requested to be informed about any changes in Robert Campbell's condition."

"Aye, and?"

The soldier cleared his throat. "He passed away earlier today, sir."

The ground under Thomas's feet rippled. His lungs seized and he bit the inside of his cheek to conceal his reaction to the blinding news. *Dear Lord, no!*

Even in the faint light Thomas saw Samuel pale as his features dropped. Was the man upset? Surprising. Yet . . . Thomas reconsidered. Robert had been beloved by the Tories in town, especially the lobsters. It was no wonder Martin would want to know of his passing.

"Thank you." Martin cleared his throat. "That will be all. You are dismissed."

The other soldier looked Thomas up and down as if he were a pile of rubbish, bowed, then took his leave.

Martin turned back to Thomas, his shoulders pulled back. "Two weeks. Two weeks and then I will be done with you. Meet me here at the regular time. I will send one of my men to give you the assignment."

He tramped out of the alley, leaving Thomas in a deafening quiet.

Robert was gone.

The terrible truth settled into his bones. Thomas had known the end was near, but the wrenching loss shredded his heart with unspeakable pain. He shuffled backward and thumped against the side of the tavern, shoving his hands through his hair. His throat tightened and he closed his burning eyes. The dank, salty air around him thickened as his grief swelled.

After several moments of bitter silence, with his head bowed, he shuffled out of the alley and stopped in front of the tavern. He stared at the ground, mindless of the sights and sounds of Boston that usually served to cheer him. Memories of Robert's compassion, wisdom, and fearless strength both warmed and haunted.

Suddenly, a large hand smacked him on the back,

jolting him out of the abyss and into the present. "Cousin!"

Thomas straightened and exhaled a sorrow-filled breath before trying to smile, but nothing came to his lips. "Daniel. 'Tis good to see you. As always."

Daniel grinned, revealing the gap between his two front teeth. "I'm very pleased to see you as well, Thomas, there is much of importance we must discuss tonight, 'twould not be the same without you." Daniel Williams flashed a disarming smile, which reached out and worked as a balm to the sorrow Thomas kept hidden. What a good man he was.

What would he say if he knew the truth of what Thomas had done? No. Daniel should never know. It was better that way.

Thomas looked into the window of the bright tavern at the few familiar faces of the other Sons of Liberty. Robert's voice rang in the chorus of his memory— *"Our greatest desires are worth every sacrifice, Thomas. And this cause? This cause is the future. It deserves everything."*

Daniel's bass timbre broke the silence and his tone lowered. "After today's news about Doctor Campbell, I wasn't sure whether you would come. I know how much he meant to you—how much he meant to all of us."

"Robert would want me here."

Daniel nodded, his head lowered in respect. "Aye, I believe you are right. I've never met a man with more courage and faith." He moved aside to make way for a group of soldiers on the street. He lowered his volume another degree. "Robert had family, did he not?"

"Two daughters."

"Have you been acquainted?" Daniel walked toward the tavern door.

"No," Thomas said, following. "He did speak of them often. I know he loved them dearly."

"What will they do now?"

"I cannot say. I remember something about an aunt, but that is all. I fear they are quite alone in the world."

Daniel opened the door and motioned for Thomas to enter first. "God will keep them. He loves all His children, but I believe He holds a special place in His heart for His daughters."

Daniel's wisdom reached into Thomas's grief, blanketing it with a measure of peace. He gave a polite half-smile and stepped into the busy tavern. *Please bless Robert's daughters, Lord. Send someone to help them in their time of need.*

The air in the glowing room mounted with the pleasing aromas of ale, salty stews, and savory puddings. A gentle hum of voices bounced between the walls and lent a feeling of welcome camaraderie.

The two of them approached the long table in the back. The conversation between the six other men became clear as the group nodded their greetings.

Reverend Bassett, wearing a black jacket and breeches that contrasted his white hair, leaned forward and rested his twined hands on the smooth wood of the table. "I have been informed there is a traitor in our midst."

All the blood in Thomas's limbs stalled and his heart refused to beat. *They know.*

"A traitor? Whatever are you talking about?" Daniel neared and pulled up a chair.

The Reverend continued, his tone grave. "Aye, indeed. Someone in this group is withholding vital information."

Daniel motioned for Thomas to sit, but he couldn't move.

"It seems that you, Mr. Rucks," Reverend Basset continued, "have gotten engaged and have yet to inform any of us of such a fact."

The men at the table burst into laughter while Mr. Rucks's boyish face turned a dark shade of pink. Congratulations bounced around the table while Thomas tried to find his breath. They hadn't been talking about him. Thank the Lord.

He sat next to Daniel and closed his eyes. His recent past had to be laid to rest. In two weeks time, after his last meeting with Martin, he would escape Boston and start anew in a place where no painful memories could haunt him—ever again.

Chapter Two

"Stay with me, Liza, until I sleep." Kitty tried to appear brave, but the sheen in her eyes told Eliza more than Kitty would ever admit.

"Of course I'll stay with you."

Eliza tucked the heavy blue and white quilt around her sister's slim body. The fire crackled, casting gloomy shadows across the walls. The weight of her new responsibilities pressed upon her like a snow-capped mountain and the helplessness that shadowed Kitty's once bright features deepened the heaviness.

"Liza? What do we do now?"

Eliza shook her head. She'd been contemplating the same question since Father's death four days ago.

"God will help us, Kitty. I know He will." She brushed a few strands of dark auburn hair from her sister's porcelain face. "Aunt Grace will continue check on us from time to time, and we can always turn to her for help now that Bess and Jed are gone. We don't need servants anymore, we know how to run this home."

"I suppose we do."

"I *know* we do. I haven't the least bit of concern in that respect. However, we will have to rely on Providence now more than ever I believe."

"Aren't we supposed to feel His strength in times

of trial? I don't feel anything but sadness. Where is He, Liza?" Kitty's tears brimmed again, begging for an answer.

Eliza tried to smile. "He's with us, Kitty. He's with us." She wiped Kitty's tears. "He will not leave us comfortless. He's promised us that. We must do as Father always taught us to do. We must trust Him."

Kitty's mouth lifted in a tight half-smile, then she turned away on her side. Eliza massaged Kitty's shoulder and stroked her arm, praying.

Lord, I am lost. Carry me through my grief.

When Kitty's breathing slowed and her face at last was peaceful, Eliza got up and tip-toed down the stairs. The sun drifted downward and although weary in both body and mind, Eliza couldn't sleep.

Once in the parlor, Eliza paused and swept her gaze across the lonely room. The furniture and modest decorations within the sturdy two-story home were the same, yet they lacked luster and their usual welcoming nature. The dwindling fire in the fireplace pleaded for stoking, and Eliza complied, occupying her fatigued mind for at least a moment.

While she poked at the charred wood, a whisper warmed her ears. *The note.*

Eliza straightened and a trickle of shivers spread over her. She turned around, half expecting Father to be standing there, his eyes twinkling. But the room remained vacant. She inhaled through open lips. *Aye, the note. Thank you, Father.* With the funeral and all the visitors they'd had since Father's passing she had yet to experience a moment of quiet. Until now.

She opened the small wooden box on the table next to Father's favorite chair and retrieved it for the first time since the evening he died.

Pressing it to her chest, she turned and stared

with longing at the small family portrait above the mantel. Of the five happy faces gazing back at her, only two still lived—she and Kitty. A shudder rattled down her back and she moved her tearful eyes away.

If not for me, one more would still be living.

Her body chilled. She had to escape before the memories devoured her. Stepping through the cozy parlor toward the backdoor, Eliza passed Father's study. The entry to his favorite space enticed her to come and surround herself with happier memories. She reached for the handle, then froze. Her fingers lingered only a breath from the cold brass. What was she thinking? She couldn't do this. The joyful memories would only remind her of all she'd lost.

Eliza tried to swallow, but the rock in her throat thickened. A storm within her chest released its thundering power and she ran to the backdoor, out of the house and down the meadow behind her home. Slumping into the tall grass, Eliza wept. Her chest and limbs tightened as she buried her face into her skirt and wailed, a long hollow cry.

When her tears turned to hiccups, she wiped her cheeks and broke the seal of the letter. Surely Father's words would comfort her.

Dearest Eliza,

I have not energy to write much, but a few lines will suffice.

Here is the truth; I am not a Tory as I was believed to be. I am a member of the Sons of Liberty and have been acting as a spy for these four years and was not free to speak of it to anyone.

Forgive me for not disclosing the truth. However, this must remain a secret, so as to keep the other spies in safety. Do not tell Kitty. I fear that she is not yet ready to know such things. Let it come to her in God's time. But I could not die without you knowing the truth of my actions and beliefs.

I am weary, and cannot write more, but will issue this last word of caution. You must beware of Captain Martin. He is not a man to be trusted.

Find the truth, my daughter. Have courage. The cause of freedom is most vital. The future relies upon us.

Forever,
Your Father

This could not be. This could not be!

Eliza's hands shook, her lungs seized.

Her father was a traitor.

"Eliza?"

Samuel!

Eliza shoved the note in her skirt pocket and turned to meet her comforter. Her pulse hammered and her mind reeled from the words she'd just read, but the gentleness in Samuel's soft blue eyes reached through the pain and cradled her quivering heart.

"I thought I might find you here." Always the gentleman, Samuel assisted Eliza to her feet. His tender gaze draped around her like a blanket of sun-kissed flowers. His warm, spicy scent enveloped her and she lost herself in his strong embrace.

Father had to be wrong about Samuel. Of course he was a man to be trusted. Next to Kitty, Samuel was all Eliza had left in her life.

The horrifying contents of Father's note settled deep in her soul and her body trembled from the shock. She buried her face in Samuel's crimson uniform and gripped his back.

Father had raised them to love and serve the king—to honor and respect him. How could he have lied all these years?

She clung to Samuel even tighter. Oh, how she needed comfort. And if anyone could comfort her, it was Samuel.

In all the years Samuel knew Eliza, this was the first time he'd ever seen her beautiful brown eyes puffy from crying.

She wept so, that his own eyes were hot with tears. Her arms wrapped around him, tightening the rope of affection that circled his heart. How he longed to take away all her pain and grief, and replace it with love. If only he had been able to leave his duties sooner, she may not have been alone and weeping for so long.

Stroking her back, Samuel spoke in hushed tones. "Not to worry, my love. Cry as much as you need."

Over time, her sobbing subsided and turned to periodic sniffling. He rested his mouth against her lacey cap, taking long breaths, savoring the rose scent that always followed her.

Eliza pushed away and wiped her tears. Without delay, he reached into his pocket and pulled out a handkerchief.

"Thank you," she said, accepting his offering.

He moved away a strand of tear-matted hair from her face. Her dear, sweet face. Then, tipping her chin upward, he forced her to look at him.

"Forgive me for not coming back until now. I tried my best to get away, but they kept finding new ways to keep me busy."

Eliza lowered her lashes. "Your work is important. I understand." She dabbed at her cheeks again. "How did you know I would be here?"

He grinned. "This is your favorite spot when you want to be alone, is it not? Who knows you better than I?"

With tender hands he cupped her face. Brushing her soft skin with his thumb, he soaked in the beauty of the woman he loved. The small delicate mole on her left cheekbone enhanced her bewitching features and he swelled with longing. Samuel loved every blessed thing about her. She was meant to be with him—forever.

"Are you feeling any better now?"

She looked away and clutched the paper she'd tucked into her skirts. His muscles tightened. Something wasn't right.

"What's troubling you, Eliza? Has it to do with that paper you were reading?"

Her chin shot upward and her eyes were wide for only a second before she glanced down, refusing to meet his gaze.

"'Tis only a note from Father. His last words to me." She pressed her lips together and drew in a long breath through her nose as if straining to remain composed. A slight breeze whispered past, making small tendrils of hair caress her cheek as she spoke. "I'm simply struggling with my grief."

Samuel's heart pinched. He moved his hands to her shoulders and lowered his tone. "This may seem sudden, Eliza, but I must be allowed to speak openly."

She raised her eyebrows. "Of course."

He let out a long sigh before continuing. "'Tis no secret how much I care for you. With your Father now gone, you and Kitty will need the care and influence of a man and I am willing—I *want* to take care of you for the rest of my days, Eliza. Please let me." He paused and took another breath. "I want you to be my wife. I love you."

His hands numbed as he waited for her reply. They'd talked of marriage many times but he'd never officially declared his feelings.

Eliza's blood rushed to her face. That must be a good sign. She must love him in return.

A stabbing thought struck his brain. Then again, perhaps she didn't.

Samuel stumbled over his words. "I'd ask for your Father's blessing, if he were here, of course. But I feel certain he would approve."

She blinked wildly for a moment, and gripped again at the fabric of her dress. Her breathing increased, but when she said nothing his heart pounded, a sinking sensation pushing down into his gut.

"Do not you agree, Eliza?"

Eliza opened her mouth, but closed it again without a sound, then looked away. The soft muscles of her jaw flexed as she gazed toward the house.

The silence continued and he couldn't stop the cannon blast of nerves shooting off in his gut. "Well, what do you say?"

She pulled from his gentle grasp, ripping his heart from his chest as she distanced herself. He could see a far-off stare in her eye. Why hadn't she leapt with joy at his proposal, as he'd believed she would? They were meant for each other, she must know that. They loved each other. Of that he had no doubt.

Something kept her from accepting him.

He pleaded with his eyes. "I know a soldier's life isn't always suitable for one's spouse, but if you will have me, I promise to give you every possible happiness and fill every need."

"What of . . . what of the patriots? What if they . . ." She shook her head and pressed her lips into a thin line once again.

"What of them? Why should anyone give a dog's ear about the patriots? 'Tis not a woman's place to be concerned with such things, Eliza."

She flung her gaze to him, a fleeting question darting across her face, but she replaced it the next second with another reluctant smile. "I . . . I suppose you are right."

He placed a hand on his sword and looked over his shoulder across the small bay, toward the city of Boston. "If those bumbling patriots believe they can fight and win even one battle against our army they're more brainless than I imagined."

Turning back to her, Samuel frowned. "Why are you suddenly so concerned with them?"

The orange sunset crowned Eliza's dark hair like a halo. A tight grin fanned her face before she answered, speaking to the ground. "Well, there is much going on—'tis in all the papers. And, I'm . . . I'm worried. What if, what if the conflict escalates?"

He straightened. "Even if it does, which I doubt, I don't see why that must interfere with our plans to marry." Samuel took her hand and tugged her closer. "I love you, Eliza. That's all that matters. Besides, you can't take care of Kitty by yourself. I can take that responsibility. Please let me."

Eliza tensed and drew back. "You don't think I

can care for Kitty? She's practically a woman herself, I don't see why—"

"Eliza." Samuel sighed and tipped his head to the sky with a groan. "My words betray me, 'twas not what I meant. I simply know of your fears and I want to help ease them." Ignoring the warning that sounded in his mind, he lowered his head in a long, slow movement, until his lips touched hers with a feather-lightness, igniting a raging blaze within. He pulled away, his heart crashing against his ribs. "You will marry me. I know you will."

Her dark eyes rose to his and beckoned for more. He bent to kiss her again, but she placed her palm on his chest.

"Do you really believe the patriots are fools? Maybe they—"

"Eliza!" His patience snapped and it took mounds of strength to keep his voice even. He'd just kissed her and that was all she could think about? "I've only now confessed my love to you—offered you my life. Why are you so consumed with political matters? Are you trying to kill me with waiting?"

She looked away and her shoulders slumped.

"Forgive me, Eliza, but I must know your answer—'tis too painful for me otherwise. I've waited for years for this moment—don't deny me now." He dipped his head and scolded her with an intense stare. "As I have said, 'tis not a woman's place to be concerned with politics. I shall be the one taking care of such things. All that matters is our love."

She studied her feet and wrung the handkerchief in her fingers, still not answering.

The ugly question hopped from his mouth. "Do you not return my love?"

She paused and took a long breath before meeting

his gaze. "Samuel, please." The look in her bottomless eyes killed his last hope. "I care for you a great deal, you know that." Moving closer, Eliza reached up to stroke the lapel of his jacket. "I cannot accept. Not right away."

Her words stung the same as if she'd slapped him across the face. He rubbed his jaw. She couldn't be serious.

Eliza put the handkerchief to her mouth for a brief moment. "It's too soon after Father's death. I'm sorry, Samuel." She covered his hand and circled it with her thumb, but the tender motion did nothing to soothe his wounded pride.

"I don't understand." Samuel grabbed her by the shoulders again. "You can't tell me no, Eliza. We are *meant* to be together."

When she made no reply he did the only thing he could think of. He leaned forward and before she could move away, he pulled her body against his, capturing her mouth with his own. Her warm, soft lips sent liquid passion through his veins. Her gentle curves intoxicated him, and when she didn't pull away he strengthened the kiss until her slight arms wound around his neck. So she did love him!

He could have kissed her until the sun set and rose again the next day, but that would have to wait. Samuel lifted his head as masculine pride welled through him. She couldn't kiss him like that and *not* love him. "Say you'll marry me, Eliza. I need to hear you say it."

She put her hand to her mouth as her eyes darted back and forth between his. "Samuel." Her voice quivered. "I know . . . I know it seems like the right time for marriage, but for me, it is not."

He blinked. She couldn't be serious. But she was.

Her eyes found his and the struggle in her lovely face nailed his boots to the ground. “Father has just now been buried and I am overwhelmed with grief. I cannot accept—not right now.” A tear trickled down her cheek. “Forgive me, Samuel. I know you’ll understand. I don’t want to hurt you.”

Samuel tried to hide a bitter laugh. He’d never been more hurt in his life. He ground his palm into the handle of his sword. What a fool he’d been. How could he have imagined she would accept a proposal now? Of course she needed more time.

They remained silent as he gathered his thoughts and tried to suppress the whirlwind of emotions coursing through him.

“I understand.” He brushed her cheek and leaned toward her again. “There’s no one in this world for me but you. I would wait forever.”

Samuel pulled Eliza against him, the touch of her body fogging his brain like wine. He needed one more kiss, just one more. He moved his lips across hers, over her cheeks and up to her ear, inhaling once again her sweet, womanly scent.

He whispered low, hoping his breath sent a warm tingle down her neck. “You belong to me, Eliza Campbell.”

Eliza pulled away, staring at Samuel, and clutched the soft fabric of the neckerchief at her chest. A spray of gooseflesh coated her arms. Such a kiss should only exist between husband and wife. *Dear Lord, forgive me.*

Samuel smiled, his crystal eyes shining as he

scanned her face. He pulled his shoulders back, accentuating his strong frame under his perfectly tailored uniform. Keeping his clear gaze on her, he backed away a few steps, then bowed, turned and walked through the field, around the house and out of sight.

She stilled and brushed her mouth with her fingers.

Three kisses! And not all polite kisses to be sure. He'd wanted to make his feelings so clear, that she could not misunderstand his intensions. She knew him well enough to know that.

She gripped the handkerchief tighter. No, she did not misunderstand.

They had spoken of marriage and their future together many times, so his proposal was not entirely unexpected. But how could she accept? Her hands still quivered. She gazed at the sky that had turned from orange to purple, as several stars decorated the heavens. Hugging her arms, she started toward the house, the long blades of grass whipping against her skirts as she walked.

There was no question in her mind that she would have accepted Samuel, if not for Father's letter. As much as she wanted to dismiss the warning, it resounded in her ears. Yet again, she tried to brush them from her memory. Father had to be wrong. And even though she didn't truly love Samuel, her feelings were strong and might grow stronger. They would make a good match and she would be happy enough. Besides, who else could she turn to? Eliza scowled at the ground. There *was* something in Samuel's smile that sat wrong in her belly. How was it she'd never seen it before? Surely it was nothing—just nerves. They knew each other well, and had similar ideals.

Didn't they?

She halted mid-step.

What would Samuel say if she confided in him about Father? He hated the patriots and anyone who spoke against the king. Even though he'd loved Father, could Samuel get past what he had done?

Eliza reached the house. After closing the door, she found a lantern and lit it. The light painted the door and she stared at a large knot in the wood. She'd done the right thing. She couldn't marry Samuel—not right now. Not with this pressing secret that Father and Samuel were enemies.

Resting the lamp at her side, she slumped her back against the door.

Samuel said he could help care for Kitty. He knew how she feared her abilities in that respect, and why. An icy shudder passed over her as the images of that frigid day nine years ago flashed across her mind. She clenched her eyes shut, hoping to squash the dreadful memory. She'd already proven her lack of ability in caring for her siblings—which ended with deadly consequences.

Eliza pushed off the door and dragged her feet across the smooth wood floor. She couldn't shove the realities of life onto someone else forever, as much as she wished to. With Kitty now under her care, she'd *have* to make difficult decisions, even if it frightened her to the very core.

What about marrying Samuel? Would she know the right choice when the time came?

God would provide direction—wouldn't He?

She could only hope.

Chapter Three

"Well if it isn't Tommy Watson!" a jolly, fat sounding voice rang out.

Thomas turned from his work behind the press toward the unfamiliar man who addressed him. Grateful to be taken away from his menial task of setting the type, he wiped his hands on his apron.

"You know me, sir, but I'm afraid I can't say the same for you." He stepped around the machine and moved toward the gentleman. The man grabbed Thomas's hand and shook with gusto as he smiled, revealing large yellow teeth.

"Well, of course you wouldn't remember an old man like myself. Last time I saw you, you were no higher than my breeches." He stopped to straighten his posture and thrust out his chin. "I'm your father's brother, God rest his soul." Swooping off his dilapidated hat, he bowed his head as if trying to show reverent remembrance.

Thomas reserved a bitter laugh and shifted his weight over his feet. Anyone who really knew Father would know he wasn't a man worth mourning.

"Name's George Watson," the stranger continued. "Just came over from England today and I knew I had to stop by first thing to exchange pleasantries with my kin." He brushed the toe of his boot against the floor. "My brother left you the press then, did he?"

"Aye." Thomas made a quick assessment of the man who professed to be Father's brother. Father had never mentioned having any siblings. Then again, he had never been forthcoming about much.

The more Thomas stared at the man, the more it all seemed strangely plausible. George *could* be related. It looked as though this man and Father shared the same unfortunate nose. Thomas tried not to grin. Thank goodness God had not endowed him with the same protrusion.

George's very wide frame took up most of the space in the front of the press, and Thomas detected the distinct smell of both urine and alcohol. Perhaps merely a result of the abysmal conditions travelers were often exposed to on the ships coming to and from. One could only hope.

"Very nice to meet you, George," Thomas said, inviting the man in and closing the door. "I'm sorry to say I never knew my Father had a brother. Will you tell me how you knew he had passed? I'm sure we never sent word to anyone."

George nodded and scratched under his immense arm. "Well, the world may be a big place, Tommy, but still word gets 'round. I only found out about a year ago, which is when I started making plans to come and see America for myself."

Tommy. No one had called him that in more than twenty-four years. Thomas remembered very little of getting off the boat from England—he'd only been four years old at the time. Father had heard great things about America, and brought the three of them to Boston "to make a new life". Now, only Thomas remained—the few happy memories of his family, completely overshadowed by the rotten ones.

"What kind of a son are you? You killed your mother. If you'd do that to her, how will you do anyone else any good?"

Thomas took a cleansing breath to erase the doleful thoughts that darkened his mind and focused on the present. "So, George, what made you decide to cross that great ocean and settle in Boston?"

George laughed. "Well, I needed a new start—there was nothing left for me but gaming debts, you see. So I left all that behind. Left the gaming too. Nasty habit, that." His grin made it seem as though he didn't think the habit quite as "nasty" as he professed. "Anyway, I'm here for a new start like I said. I'm old, but there's good work in me. I'm in need of employment, Tommy—hoped you might want some help."

Rubbing his palm, Thomas peered at the press machine behind him. Could this be God's way of providing for him? He hated the idea of leaving the press—the trade he loved and had worked so many years to build. But he couldn't stay. Not anymore. George needed work and Thomas needed someone to take over. But what did the man know about operating a printing press?

Rubbing the cleft in his chin, Thomas exhaled through his nose. He could only hope the bloated fellow before him had the tenacity to deal with the sometimes tedious work. "This is a small shop and I work alone. No newspaper here. Just contracted work for fliers, advertisements, political pamphlets and the like. However, I have needed some help. Do you have any experience with the trade?"

"Aye, Tommy, I have. Not much, mind you, but enough to get me through until I've learned the rest. I have a lot of weight on me, as you can see, so I was hired as a pressman at a newspaper in London a few years back. The owner never complained about my work." George stopped and played with the tricorne he held in his pudgy fingers. "I'm a good laborer, you won't be disappointed in me I can guarantee you that." He nodded as if to emphasize his words.

Could this really be God's will? Thomas stared out the window as a peaceful presence encircled him like white smoke from an invisible fire. Tingles shot down his arms and he smiled. Did he need more of an answer then that? "Excellent, Uncle. I'm pleased to hire you."

He extended his hand and they shook on the agreement. George pumped his arm up and down, his jowls jiggling from the movement. "Thank you, Tommy. I'm indebted to you."

"Think nothing of it."

Thomas grinned and took a deep breath then gagged on the acidic air. As glad as he was to help, the longer this man stayed in his presence the stronger the oppressive odor became and Thomas was forced to breathe from his mouth. No question—this man needed a bath.

George twirled the hat in his fingers. "Uh, there is one more thing, Tommy."

Ready to finish his work, Thomas walked toward the press. "Yes?"

"I'm in desperate need of a place to stay and I was hoping, being that you're family—"

"Say no more." With a wave of his hand Thomas stopped him mid-sentence. "Of course you are welcome to stay here. I'll show you upstairs. Make yourself at home—feel free to wash up." *Please wash up.*

"Thank you, Tommy. God bless you!" George

picked up the small bag he'd carried with him. Thomas showed him through the back door and up the stairs that led to the modest living quarters above the shop.

"Take your time getting settled before you come down. I'll be here whenever you are ready."

George panted in giant heaves as he made his way up the few stairs. Halfway, he stopped and turned to Thomas. "I say, is there anything to eat? I've been living on the most unpleasant grub—I'm in terrible need of some real victuals."

Thomas stifled a chuckle. This man? Hungry? Never.

"You will find a bit of bread and cheese in the cupboard, but I don't cook much. No wife, you know." Thomas laughed to make light of it, trying to tell himself he liked it this way, living alone, but his heart would never believe such a lie.

"I understand. Never had a wife myself." George laughed for a moment, and then shook his head as if fighting a memory. "Thank you again. I'll be down soon enough, and ready to work." He began his trek back up the stairs, pounding on each step as he went.

As Thomas returned to the press, his uncle's foul smell accosted him anew. He opened the front door of the shop, allowing the cool air to pour in from the noisy street. How had he missed that it was raining?

He paused for a moment and leaned his shoulder against the frame of the door, taking in the view and inhaling the fresh scent of rain. Crowds of people ran in and out of the shops, dodging the streams of water. Redcoats dotted the streets, their muskets in-hand. Carriages bumped over the muddy streets, dogs barked. A young boy darted past the shop door, waving with a wide grin on his dimpled face. Thomas smiled and waved back.

Pushing out a loud sigh, his stomach plummeted to his feet. Shaking his head, Thomas went back to his work. He left the door open, savoring the familiar sounds and smells of his city—his home. He hated to leave Boston. In time, Sandwich would feel like home . . . wouldn't it? Only time would tell.

Placing the minuscule type, his thoughts turned to the dark task that awaited him.

The clock struck noon. Only ten hours left, but he wasn't counting.

One of Martin's minions had come by several days before specifying that his superiors wanted names. Four names of powerful members of the Sons of Liberty to use as "examples" of what happens to patriots who choose to go against the Crown.

How could he possibly do it? Thomas placed the tiny metal letters into the trays as a boundless pit dug into his middle. If the soldiers wanted "examples", why not go after them themselves? It wasn't as if all members of the group kept their involvement a secret.

Plunging the letters in with greater force, Thomas clenched his teeth. The blackmail was perfect. He had no choice but to comply. Daniel's safety and the safety of his family was paramount.

Give Robert Campbell's name.

Thomas's head shot up and his hands froze as God's words dripped over him like the rain that fell outside his door. Would it work? Robert had gone to great lengths to be seen as a trusted Loyalist . . .

The longer Thomas contemplated, the more the plot seemed plausible. Robert was dead, there was nothing the soldiers could do to him—they hadn't specified the men had to be *living*.

Chuckling, Thomas pulled the lever of the press. It might work. It *had* to. He would give them the names of two deceased members of the group along with two phony names. Hopefully that would keep them occupied long enough to allow him to get out of Boston and safely into Sandwich before they realized his fraud and caught up with him. He would have to stay hidden for a while, but no matter. He had everything he needed to make a good start. And God would be with him—as He had always been.

Thank you, Lord.

"Excuse me, sir?"

Blast! Who could be bothering him now?

Thomas looked up and his jaw slackened. His neck heated around his collar, his eyes widened. A woman stood just inside the stoop, the rain trickling off her crimson cloak.

She smiled, and his breath caught.

"Sir?" she asked again, in the same melodic voice.

"Aye, forgive me, Miss." He quickly wrenched off his leather apron. "How may I help you?" He rushed forward, almost tripping on the leg of the press.

"Forgive me." Her gaze moved over his face for a moment before she dipped her chin. "I . . . I was looking for the new bakery and I had been told it was down this street, but I can't seem to find it. Your door was open so I just came in." She looked behind her, allowing Thomas a full view of her graceful neck. "It's silly, I know, having lived here all my life I ought to know my way around town, but it's been a while since I've, well . . . never mind." The woman stopped her endearing ramble as her cheeks pinked. She lowered her lashes but not before Thomas took another long drink of her chocolate eyes.

She bit her lip and he grinned as big on the inside

as he did on the outside. "Not silly at all, Miss. The Arbonne's Bakery is just four doors down. The shingle is poorly placed, anyone could miss it." He moved toward her and pointed down the street.

Their eyes locked for a moment and he inhaled the sight of her gentle smile and clear skin. His heart flipped behind his ribs and he couldn't stop his gaze from combing her from head to foot.

Realizing his ill manners, Thomas bowed at the waist, his eyes never leaving hers. "My name is Thomas Watson."

She made a shy curtsy, but said nothing.

Would she not offer her name? His pulse quickened. Etiquette prohibited strangers from being introduced without a third party. But he was desperate, and in a desperate moment such manners were obsolete. "And will you be so kind as to tell me your name?"

Her face flushed with color, adding to the pink that already decorated her skin. "My name is Eliza Campbell."

Thomas stepped back and straightened. "You wouldn't happen to be related to the late Dr. Robert Campbell, would you?"

A shadow of grief darkened her gentle features. "Aye. He was my Father."

The air in his lungs evaporated and all words escaped him. This magnificent woman was one of Robert's daughters. Somehow he'd figured the Campbell girls would be young and gangly. Eliza was anything but that.

Her lips tightened and her fingers twisted the purse string in her hand. His heart swelled with the knowledge that her grief must be even more powerful than his own. He wanted to give her some kind of comfort, but every word that entered his mind seemed inadequate.

Thomas lowered his voice. "I'm so sorry for your loss."

For a second she didn't respond, didn't acknowledge that she'd heard him. Then slowly, she raised her eyes and offered a polite smile. "Thank you."

An alarming thought suddenly revealed itself and attacked his mind like an armed Indian. Did she know the truth about Robert's involvement in the Sons of Liberty? Most likely not. Thomas's brow knit. Tonight's revelation to Martin could put her in very real danger.

No. They wouldn't hurt women and children. And since there were no living men to capture, there was nothing to fear. Was there?

Eliza turned toward the door. "I thank you for your assistance. I should be going." She stopped as if she were reluctant to leave.

Tell her.

Thomas paused.

Tell her you knew her father.

There it was again. He couldn't deny the voice of God.

Despite his reservations, Thomas stepped forward. "I . . . I knew your father, Miss Campbell. He was a man of great honor, and I admired him very much."

"Truly?" Her eyes searched him with a piercing kind of longing.

Just then, another younger woman came to the door. She didn't enter, but stood on the stoop in the pouring rain.

"There you are, Liza. Forgive me for taking so

long in Aunt Grace's shop, I just—" She stopped and her gaze jumped between them for several seconds before she started up again. "This isn't the bakery, Liza." A mischievous smile spread on her face and Thomas pressed his lips together to keep from grinning.

Eliza turned toward the girl and smiled. "Forgive me, Kitty. I couldn't find it and Mr. Watson was kind enough to point me in the right direction." She took the girl by the hand and led her into the shop. "Mr. Watson, allow me introduce you to my younger sister, Miss Katherine Campbell."

Thomas bowed, realizing how absurd his assumptions about Robert's daughters had been. He should have visited Robert long ago. "Very pleased to make your acquaintance, Miss Katherine."

The young girl offered a polite bow and smiled at Thomas before turning back to her sister, with a grin that dripped with glee. Eliza glanced at Thomas again and his muscles turned weightless. He'd never seen such dark eyes.

"Forgive me for taking so much of your time," she said, pulling her wet cloak tighter around her shoulders. "I must allow you to return to your work."

"Think nothing of it."

She stepped into the rain and Thomas strained to think of something he could say or do to make her stay, but his mind worked at half-speed and nothing satisfactory sprung to life in his jumbled brain.

Before walking away, she peered over her shoulder once more then slipped her arm around her sister. They made their way through the busy, muddy street in the direction of the bakery.

Thomas stood in the doorway like a chunk of useless iron, unable to take his gaze off the two women until they entered the shop.

Miss Campbell. *Eliza*.

She was the kind of woman a man did not easily forget. He released a long breath through his nose. He could only hope she would never learn of what he would do in only a few short hours.

God, please keep them safe. I don't want my actions to cause them harm.

"I'm ready for work, Tommy."

Startled, Thomas turned to see George standing by the press, struggling to tie the strings of the apron around his ample girth.

With a low chuckle, Thomas came in and closed the door, hoping his momentary stupor hadn't been obvious.

"Who was that pretty thing you were drooling over just now? I thought you said you had no need for a wife?" George grinned. A flicker of teasing splashed his voice as he fumbled with the apron ties.

Blast. He'd been caught.

Thomas moved behind the press, donned his own apron then dipped the ink balls in the sticky black goo. "I never said I hadn't a need for a wife, I just said I don't have one at present."

"I see," George said. His squinty eyes brightened and Thomas couldn't help but chuckle once again.

Besides, even if Thomas were interested in someone with eyes the color of liquid chocolate, fair skin, and an unmistakable kindness, she'd never be interested in him in the least. Not after what he had to do tonight. He prayed to God she would forgive him.

Chapter Four

"Liza, who was that dashingly handsome man you were talking with today at the Printer?" Kitty giggled and turned under the covers to face her sister. Eliza stiffened and wished she could feign sleep. That was the last question she wanted to answer.

Kitty poked Eliza in the ribs. "You couldn't stop staring—and don't try to deny it, I saw the way you were looking at him."

Her face burned. She pulled the quilt higher around her neck and gave oceans of thanks for the darkness. Otherwise, her sister would have had added ammunition for her harassment.

Considering her relationship with Samuel, Eliza should never have given a second thought to the breathtaking man. But Thomas Watson had consumed her mind the rest of the day.

She stared at the shadowed fabric of the bed curtains.

Thomas knew Father! How had they met? Did he know Father had been a spy and a member of the Sons of Liberty? What other information could he share with her?

Find the truth.

Her breath caught. Could Mr. Watson help her do that? Knowing Father had lied all those years ate away at her heart like a terrible, writhing worm. She had to know—to search out the truth as Father had admonished her to do.

She told herself that the possible relationship between Father and Thomas was the only reason she had any interest in him. But, more than a few times she'd pushed away the memory of his dark blue eyes, straight nose, and angled jaw. His midnight black hair and the broad set of his shoulders weakened her knees. She tried to forget how his smile and the gentle cleft in his chin gave her goose flesh all the way to her toes.

The sound of his voice, like melted honey, swam over and over in her mind. *"I knew your Father, Miss Campbell. He was a man of great honor, and I admired him very much."*

"Liza, are you asleep?" Kitty whispered.

"Nay," Eliza said, waking from her daydream.

"Well? You didn't answer me."

Eliza exhaled. "I don't know him. I've never seen him before today." She paused, trying to contrive a way to become better acquainted with Thomas so he could tell her something—anything—about Father.

"But you were talking to him? You mean you had never been introduced?"

"His door happened to be open, and since we couldn't find the bakery I slipped in and asked him for directions."

Kitty let out a small breathy laugh. "It seemed like you wanted to do more than that."

Eliza gasped. "Kitty!"

Her sister wriggled up closer to her under the blanket. Eliza imagined the sprite smile on her face. "Your jaw was near to scraping the floor. I'm sure he must have noticed your gawking."

Merciful heavens. Had she been that obvious?

Eliza hoped to deflect the accusations. "Well, I will say he was a kind, generous man, and true, he was very charming, but that's the end of it. Now, let us get some sleep before the dawn comes."

"I suppose you're right. Goodnight."

Eliza rolled on her back and wrapped her arms around her middle under the warmth of the blanket. Now, if only the handsome press owner's face would disappear from her mind, she might be able to sleep.

Thomas couldn't keep still. He tapped his foot and drummed his fingers on the envelope in his hand like a timorous rain. Then he looked up and down the alley for the twentieth time.

The same place, the same cold darkness, but a new feeling of unease and anxious anticipation danced around him.

Where was that wretched Martin? He should have been here and gone by now.

His heart dropped to his feet in the next second when two Redcoats started toward him. He could tell from their size and shape that neither of them were Martin.

"You Watson?" A tall, dark-haired Redcoat approached, his posture rigid.

"Who are you? Where's Martin?"

"I'm Lieutenant Donaldson. Martin's busy. He sent me to get the envelope, so hand it over and we'll be done with it."

Thomas stiffened. This man meant business. For the first time Thomas wished Martin were there instead of these two imbeciles. At least he knew better how to deal with him.

This plan cannot fail, Lord. Please be with me.

Thomas handed Donaldson the envelope, hoping he would take it and be on his way. But the soldier ripped into it immediately, huffing as he read the names.

"Excellent. Come with us." The Lieutenant motioned for Thomas to follow them.

Thomas froze. "What?"

Donaldson talked to his companion as though Thomas were made of cobblestone.

"Martin's orders are to bring these people in immediately. We will go right now. Martin said to take not only the men, but their families as well. These patriots need to be taught what will happen to all those who oppose the Crown."

Thomas choked on his breath as utter shock flooded his limbs. This couldn't be happening!

Lord! What am I to do now?

"As for you, Watson," the tall one continued, "do not think Martin isn't mindful of your involvement. He desires you to be the first to show the people of Boston what comes to anyone who opposes the king."

Thomas flexed his muscles and clenched his fists. *Not a chance.*

The smaller soldier grabbed for Thomas's arm, but Thomas swung with years of harbored rage, knocking him to the ground. The man hit his head on the corner of the building and slumped over, knocked-out. Donaldson lunged, but Thomas dodged left and stuck him from behind, landing the point of his elbow on the nape of the man's neck. The soldier didn't go down, but yelled and yanked at Thomas's coat. Thomas slugged him in the ribs, sending him toppling toward the street, his sword clanking as it hit the ground.

Thomas glanced toward the entrance of the alley, but there wasn't a soul around to come to his aid. Probably better to fight this alone. He swung again, this time punching Donaldson square in the nose. The man flew backward, his head hitting the stone street with a loud crack.

While the two soldiers lay motionless, Thomas reached over Donaldson and searched his coat for the piece of paper. He found it and stood, ready to make a quick escape.

Without warning the soldier revived and grabbed at the paper, ripping it in two as he yelled something unintelligible. Thomas stumbled backward. Donaldson shoved the piece of paper deep into his coat and attempted to get up. He grabbed his head and continued yelling as he fumbled for his pistol.

Every nerve in Thomas's body screamed. He lunged at the soldier, grabbed him by the collar, and slammed his head against the cobblestone once more, rendering him unconscious.

Voices and shouts erupted from across the street. A group of men ran toward him.

With no time to recover the other part of the paper, Thomas fled into the blackness, away from his pursuers. Away from his past.

A lone horse stood tethered by an abandoned building as if God had placed it there just for him. Thomas didn't even think of the consequences of stealing a horse. Without a doubt the punishment for striking a soldier would be much worse indeed, and he needed a horse—desperately. Thomas mounted and rode for miles, out of town and over the small neck of land that connected Boston to the mainland. His lungs burned and his muscles cramped, but he couldn't stop. Thank the Lord the tide was out or his escape would have been impossible. He glanced up at the moonlit sky, then dared a look behind him. The city of Boston receded as he neared the farms and estates on the other side of the bay.

When he reached a safe distance with no one on his trail, he removed the ripped portion of the paper from his pocket and held it toward the moonlight, holding tight to the reins of his heaven-sent mount.

He strained to read the names on the paper and his breath caught. Three names remained—only one name was missing. Robert Campbell's.

Eliza!

Thomas's blood stilled and threatening tingles stung his back. He glanced behind him again and his breathing charged. Because of him, Eliza and her sister were in grave danger. He had to save them—had to get them out before Donaldson followed through on Martin's wicked plan. Thomas had to try and right this terrible wrong. But where did the Campbell's live?

Lord, what have I done?

He jerked his head in front and behind him, straining for any sign that he'd been spotted. Only silence answered. Thomas followed his instinct to continue on this road. He kicked the horse into a faster gait when he remembered Robert's description of his home.

"It's a modest estate on a good piece of land. I built it with my own two hands—chose a perfect spot next to three strong maples."

The words came with staggering clarity—three strong maples.

He kept the horse moving at a steady pace, ready to rein-in at any moment should he happen upon his intended destination. Sweat dripped down his neck and his muscles continued to seize from the pressing anxiety.

How could he convince two women who hardly knew him that they were in danger? With his urgent appeal and haggard appearance he would most likely scare them to death. Only God could make them believe him.

Thomas glanced at the home on his right.

Three maples.

He yanked on the reins and swung off the horse, slapping the animal on the rump to make it race down the road and out of sight. Hopefully the horse's escape would be enough of a decoy to take the soldiers in the wrong direction.

Thomas raced up the steps and pounded on the door.

Please, Lord. Help us to get out in time.

Eliza woke from her slumber to a loud pounding. Had she been dreaming? She rubbed her eyes and lay back down.

Bam! Bam! Bam!

There it was again.

Sleep vanished from her body, replaced by a powerful alertness.

Who would be here at this hour of the night? Whatever their reason, it must be serious.

Kitty still slumbered undisturbed, so Eliza scooted out of bed and grabbed her gray shawl, pulling it around her shoulders.

Her hands shook as she lit a small candle. The

pounding intensified. She walked down the cold stairs in her stocking feet, her heart hammering with furious percussion.

"Who is it?" Her uneven voice betrayed her.

"Miss Campbell, 'tis Thomas Watson—the man from the press. This is *very* urgent. I must speak with you."

Mr. Watson? The man she'd just met earlier today? Her heart jumped to her throat. What could he want?

Eliza hesitated only a second before opening the door. The moment she took in his appearance, a fearful shiver pierced her like a razor-sharp arrow. Sweat dotted his face and his eyebrows were pinched. His cravat lay haphazardly on his chest, untied and spattered with blood. The shoulder of his coat was ripped and several buttons were missing from his waistcoat. Mud stuck to his shoes and stockings.

"What's happened, Mr. Watson? Are you all right?"

"There's no time to explain, Miss Campbell. You and your sister and in serious danger. You must leave right now." He rested one hand on the doorframe, panting as if he'd just run all the way from Fish Street.

Eliza couldn't move.

Danger? Impossible. What kind of danger?

She shook her head. "Mr. Watson, it's the middle of the night, I'm sure this can wait—"

"Please Miss Campbell, listen to me!" He took her by the arm and led her inside, glancing over his shoulder into the street. His strong fingers injected fear into her already rigid body. The urgency in his eyes froze her like an icy storm.

"You must leave this house. Now. Wake your

sister, grab your necessities, and come with me. There is not a moment to spare."

Eliza gripped her shawl even tighter and stared at him. Somehow, deep within, she knew he spoke the truth.

She straightened. "I'll just be a moment. Wait here."

Without another glance she left him in the entryway and dashed up the stairs.

"Kitty! Kitty! Get up!" She shook her sister, who slept as sound as the dead. "Katherine Campbell, wake up now!"

Kitty rubbed her eyes, looking perturbed at the interruption. "Liza? What are you—"

"I can't explain." Eliza grabbed the quilt and threw it off her. "Grab your clothes and shoes. We must leave immediately. We're in danger." She pulled clothes out of their chest of drawers and stuffed them in a small bag.

Kitty's face scrunched. She jumped off the bed and began gathering her own clothes. Neither of them spoke, focused on the task. Once their necessities were gathered, they quickly slipped into their shoes before racing back down the stairs.

Thomas stood alert in the open doorway as if waiting for someone. He turned with a jerk when Eliza and Kitty entered, before taking another quick glance outside, and shutting the door. The only light in the room came from the moon outside and the one candle that Eliza still held in her hand. The eerie glow hung around them like a haunting apparition.

"Do you have any food?" Thomas asked. "If you can get it quickly it would be wise to bring with us."

Kitty voiced Eliza's exact thoughts. "Where are we going? What's happening?"

No one answered her.

"Aye, we have a few things." Eliza moved swiftly into the kitchen and snatched some bread and four apples, placing the items in another small satchel. She bumped her elbow and dashed her foot on the leg of the table as she fumbled with the bags over her arm and candle in her hand.

Hurry.

She knew God's voice when He spoke.

Hurry!

Eliza picked up speed and raced into the main room.

"I hear horses!" Thomas said in a loud whisper, yanking the candle from her hand and blowing it out. "We can't use the front door. Is there another way?"

"The back!" Eliza's stomach pulled in knots.

She held tight to her sister's cold hand as Thomas followed close behind. They moved careful and quick around furniture and through doors until they reached the back porch.

Racing down the steps, they plunged headlong into the soggy field for only a few paces when they heard shouts coming from the front of the house.

"Get down!" Thomas yanked on Eliza's arm to stop them.

They slid onto their stomachs, and lay shoulder-to-shoulder facing the house. The cold, wet earth oozed around Eliza's body, soaking the front of her nightdress and pinching her skin with its chill.

From their position in the tall grass they saw lanterns ablaze. Two soldiers stomped through the house, turning over tables and chairs, yelling for Robert and spouting commands to one another.

The world around Eliza spun. She tasted blood as she bit her lip, trying not to cry out, and peered at

Thomas. His eyes were pinned to the house as if his vision alone would impale the intruders. His jaw ticked, tangible rage pluming with every exhale.

She glanced next at Kitty who stared wide-eyed at the scene before them, tears tumbling down her face. Eliza placed her arm around Kitty and pulled her tight, stroking her sister's arm. *I must keep my sister safe. No matter what happens. I will not repeat the mistakes I made with Peter.*

No one said a word until the soldiers left the house. Still yelling as much as before. They were down the road and out of view before Eliza turned to Thomas once again.

"Mr. Watson—I . . . I don't know what to say." She spoke low, straining to keep her emotions from spilling out of her eyes.

Kitty cried in quiet bursts, her voice pinched. "Who were those men? Why were they looking for Father?"

"I want to answer you and I will," Thomas said before Eliza could speak. "Right now we must find a safer place to hide. I have a feeling the soldiers will be back."

Eliza nodded. "Where are we going?"

Kitty began again, hugging her arms. "Can't we at least go inside and get out of these wet clothes?"

"No." Thomas shook his head, still whispering. "I don't want to risk it. We cannot know when they'll return. We will have to make our way down this field perpendicular to the road." He pointed over their backs. "That way we may avoid any additional riders. I have a cousin that lives not two miles from here. We can take refuge there for a while before we continue our journey."

Continue our journey? Where in heaven's name are

we going?

Thomas pushed up, then rested on his heels. "We won't be able to stay long. Let's get moving."

The girls looked at each other for a moment, communicating without speaking. The courage in Kitty's eyes buoyed her own.

Eliza turned to Thomas and rested her fingers on his arm. "Thank you, Mr. Watson. We'll follow your lead."

She jerked her hand away when she realized what she'd done. She should never have touched him in such a way. What would possess her to do such a thing?

Thomas's eyes smiled as he got up slow, looking with obvious caution in the direction of the house. He motioned for them to rise and placed a finger over his lips.

Eliza's nightgown was wet, cold, and smeared with mud. It stuck to her figure to such a degree that she was nervous to get up. She struggled to get to her feet from her prone position, pulling the cloth away from her body to stay modest. Thomas reached forward and helped her to stand, then did the same for Kitty. He picked up the bags of clothes and food, and gestured for them to walk ahead of him, but somehow he fell in step next to Eliza.

She wrenched her head back and gazed at their home. A powerful scream built within her throat, but she held it back. Every step pressed a vice ever tighter around her aching soul. Where were they going? What had happened to make them come after Father? How did Thomas know they were in danger? When would they return?

Despite the frightening emotions that raced through Eliza's trembling body, a single concern possessed her: *keep Kitty safe.*

They walked in silence. The night air sliced through her damp gown and she shivered, but did her best to ignore the biting cold. Noticing that Kitty hadn't grabbed any kind of covering, Eliza shrugged off her shawl and placed it around her sister.

"Hold this tight around you. You need to stay warm."

Kitty looked at Eliza, fresh streams of tears drumming over her cheeks.

"I don't understand, Liza. What's going on?" Kitty remained calm when she spoke but the sadness in her voice ripped Eliza in half.

She wanted to tell her about Father's actions—to erase some of the fear and doubt, but thought against it. Father had told her to keep it from Kitty, and though Eliza couldn't understand why, Father had his reasons. She believed—hoped—that he knew best.

"We'll understand all of this soon enough." Eliza wrapped one arm around Kitty's shoulders and the other around her own waist so she could pull away at the fabric that continued to cling to her. "Mr. Watson has already protected us once. I feel certain he's leading us to safety."

"You're shivering."

"I'm fine, Kitty." Eliza smiled and squeezed her tighter. "We'll be all right if we continue walking."

A welcome warmth suddenly enveloped her. Eliza turned to see Thomas beside her, placing his jacket around her shoulders. "I don't need it," he said. "I've just had a long run." The caring in his deep voice warmed her as much as his coat.

Eliza had been raised to employ perfect manners, but at the moment every proper response fled from her mouth. Nodding her thanks, she pulled it tighter around her shivering frame.

Thomas dipped his chin in return with a half-smile, which made her own mouth lift upward. He was a true gentleman. Such chivalry was difficult to find, not even Samuel had ever—

Eliza inhaled a sharp breath. Samuel! Did he know of this? She pressed her fingers to her lips. No, he would never have allowed this to happen.

"Are you all right, Miss Campbell?" Thomas touched her elbow, his dark brows arching down.

She pulled his coat tighter and nodded, unable to make any sound emerge.

"We'll be there soon," he said.

Eliza retreated into her thoughts. Once Samuel found out about what had happened he would be furious. She had to find a way to get word to him and let him know they were safe.

Wherever they were going, Samuel would find them. She knew it.

Chapter Five

"He did WHAT?" Samuel boomed at Donaldson who stood before him, browbeaten and bleeding.

"Sir, there was nothing we could do—"

"There's always something you can do!" Samuel stopped him before he could say any more. "Where's the list?" He held out his hand to the two soldiers as they exchanged nervous glances. "Well?" His voice escalated.

Donaldson handed him the small ripped paper, pulling his shoulders back. "This is the only name I got, Captain. Watson grabbed the other piece and got away before . . ."

Samuel snatched it from Donaldson's hand.

His face burned and his heart refused to beat. *Robert Campbell.*

"NO!" He shouted and crumpled the tiny paper, throwing it into the dying fire behind him. He rested his fists on the table, breathing hard.

Donaldson continued. "We followed your orders and went to Campbell's to apprehend him, but no one was there so we—"

"You didn't."

Donaldson raised one brow. "Those *were* your orders."

Samuel's fury turned white-hot. They'd been to the house?

Eliza!

If they'd so much as touched her he'd kill them with his bare hands.

"How could you be so foolish?" Samuel marched around the table. "I could have you punished for this! How would your miserable mother and sisters survive then, Lieutenant?"

Donaldson straightened, an air of suppressed disdain lurking in his tone. "We were simply *following your orders*, sir."

Samuel backhanded the inferior soldier, grabbed him by the lapels, and yelled in his face, spitting as he spoke. "You fool! Robert's dead!" Pushing the man away Samuel grit his teeth. Donaldson touched his mouth, examining the new bit of blood on the back of his hand.

"Besides that," Samuel continued, "everyone knows Doctor Campbell was a Tory."

Samuel turned away and gazed into the embers in the small fireplace. There were whisperings about Robert's involvement with the patriots, although Samuel never entertained the vile rumor. He knew everything about Robert. They had shared the same ideals and beliefs—hadn't they?

Gripping the bottom of the table, he yelled with all his might as he flung it across the room and sent it crashing into the wall. The two subordinates straightened, their eyes wide.

"Ready my horse," he barked. "Now!"

Donaldson's mouth hardened and his eyes narrowed for less than a second before he turned to his companion and motioned to the door, then slammed it behind them.

Samuel pulled on his coat, grabbed his pistol, and fastened his sword at his side. If Eliza needed rescuing of any kind, he would be prepared.

Not five minutes later he was astride his gray gelding and riding full-speed toward the Campbell's. His mind struggled to grapple with what Donaldson had reported.

They'd already been there? The house was empty? Not possible.

Eliza and Kitty must be there—likely they were hiding, no doubt scared out of their wits.

Those fool soldiers. He should never have entrusted them with such a task. Samuel wanted to beat them senseless. And he would, just as soon as he knew his love was safe.

When he reached the house and found the front door open, his concern jumped fifty notches. Leaping off his horse, he ran into the house, calling for Eliza.

He strained all of his senses as he took in the scene before him.

The house lay in shambles.

What had happened? The sight of the overturned tables and chairs, the broken glass, turned his chest to stone.

He searched the parlor, the kitchen. Someone had been through the house in a hurry and left evidence of their escape.

"Eliza! Eliza!"

He stopped breathing, hoping to pick up even the tiniest sound. Since the bottom floor held no clue, he bounded up the stairs two at a time, calling for both girls as he explored the small room first, then the larger.

The view in front of him forced his stomach to his throat. His heart thumped against his ribs as he shoved his fingers through his hair.

The quilt had been thrown off the bed, and

articles of clothes were strewn around the room. The doors to the armoire were wide open and the moonlight cast a phantom-like glow making the hairs on the back of his neck stand on end.

They'd been kidnapped. That much was clear. But who had done it and why?

"Eliza!" he yelled again, panic flooding his voice.

His mind whirled at such a pace his thoughts couldn't keep up. He ran down the stairs and out the doorway to his waiting horse, intent on heading back to question the soldiers further.

Suddenly he stopped. A frightening realization fit together in his mind like the pieces of a puzzle box. The autumn air grew thick around him as he formulated what must have happened.

It was Watson.

Watson must have known Robert well, if indeed they were both members of the same traitorous group. There *was* that time he'd seen Robert enter the print shop . . .

Yes. It made sense now. Robert may have told Watson he had two daughters and that Samuel was in love with one of them.

Watson planned to use Eliza as leverage.

Samuel gripped the sword at his side and cursed at the sky.

He leapt onto his gelding and raced back to town. The trees and houses whizzed by him at the speed of his whirling mind.

Watson must have planned to only release the girls if Samuel promised not to follow through on the blackmail. Well, not only would he follow through, he would see to the torture and imprisonment—even death—of Thomas Watson.

Samuel figured the press would be closed up tight. It was.

He didn't even bother to knock. Kicking the door in, he barked at the four other soldiers he'd brought with him to begin searching. Their torches lit the room like monstrous fireflies.

"I'm heading upstairs. Yell for me if you find anything," Samuel said.

As he headed to the back door, a man's large frame filled the emptiness, a wide-eyed look on his round face.

"What's the meaning of this?" The man demanded, his quivering voice a laughable companion to his shaking jowls.

"Who are you? Where's Thomas Watson?" Samuel stood in front of the fat man, looking down at him.

"I'm . . . I'm George Watson, sir. Tommy's uncle." George scanned the space with a bewildered stare. "Tommy's not here. He . . . he never came back from whatever it was he said he had to do this evening. I fell asleep. The first night in a long while that my bed's not been rocking back and forth." He chuckled, while his thick fingers massaged each other and his eyes darted between the soldiers moving about the room.

"You're saying you haven't seen him since earlier this evening. Are you sure? And he hasn't been here?" Samuel had no patience for this. He wrenched George's arm. "Don't lie to me."

"No, sir. I wouldn't lie to you. I haven't seen him since."

"Take him." Samuel motioned to Donaldson who

stood nearby.

Donaldson nodded and moved forward.

"What? Me? I'm innocent!" George's voice edged an octave higher. "I just arrived yesterday. Is this the way you soldiers treat a fellow Englishman?"

Samuel leaned into the man's meaty face and grumbled. "All I know is that you are staying in the home of a man who's just kidnapped two young women. A man who this very night assaulted soldiers in His Majesty's Army and fled the city. I'm not about to take any chances."

Two of the soldiers took the terrified man by the arms and struggled to get him out the door as he dug in his heels and tried in vain to yank free from their grip.

"Guard him until I get back," Samuel ordered.

"Aye, Captain. Where are you going now?" Donaldson asked.

Samuel mounted his horse once again. "There's one more place for me to try."

He headed there in haste.

Thomas peered up at the sky through the canopy of branches. Thank goodness for the moonlight. Without it, their two-mile journey would have been impossible.

He exhaled and shook his arms at his sides. How could he think clearly when his emotions were pulled so tight? Every barking dog, every snapping twig, zapped his raw nerves and made his muscles cramp. No doubt the soldiers were on their trail. And if they weren't already, they would be soon.

Thomas walked in front of Eliza and Kitty to be sure the path was even and that no hidden attacker lay in waiting. He peered over his shoulder as the desire to provide and protect consumed him. His companions huddled together, both for warmth and comfort, he supposed. Thomas's stomach rolled and he gazed once again at the sky. What could he have done differently to save them from such a fate? Why hadn't God intervened?

He couldn't dwell on the thought. God worked in wisdom—even though Thomas didn't always see it.

The three of them trudged on. Behind him, Eliza's gentle voice drifted around him like bird-song as she consoled her sister. He fought the urge to slow his step and walk beside her. That would be too familiar a gesture, and walking in front allowed him to keep a more protective position. She spoke again, whispering something to Kitty and Kitty whispered back.

Thomas strained to hear Eliza's hushed answer. "I'm sure we will be home before too long. Mr. Watson knows what he's doing."

The trust in her voice made his confidence wobble. He had no idea what he was doing. The faith and bravery that nestled inside that petite woman astounded him. She didn't even know him and here she was, placing their lives in his hands. A woman of such courage was a rare commodity.

As they passed into a clearing, his cousin's moonlit cabin came into view. A mixture of relief and added dread kneaded his already weary muscles. He approached the dwelling, scanning the area around him, cautious of any onlookers. Urgency poured into his gut and he waved at the girls to stay close to him.

He pounded on the door just as he had at the

Campbell's. He didn't worry about waking the children as he might have at any other time. They would no doubt be up and running for their safety in a matter of minutes, just as the three of them were doing now.

Peering into the window, Thomas cupped his hand over his mouth as he spoke into the glass. "Daniel! It's me, Thomas! Let us in!"

A candle flickered through the house and the door swung open.

"Thomas!" Daniel said, sleep glazing his eyes. The nightcap on his head tilted, revealing mussed hair. His gaze absorbed Thomas and the two wet and shivering girls behind him. "What's happened?"

Before Thomas could answer, Daniel moved to the side and waved at the three of them to enter. They crowded into the small cabin as he shut the large door and locked it.

"Before you say anything Thomas, let me wake Clara and dress. It looks as if the three of you could use some care."

Daniel put the lantern on a rough-hewn table in the center of the cabin and entered the room where his wife slept.

Thomas turned to Eliza, who continued to shelter Kitty. "Daniel is my cousin. He'll be able to help us, and the two of you can get out of those wet clothes before we leave again."

Eliza gave no expression when she nodded. What must she be thinking?

Daniel reentered, dressed in a shirt and breeches, followed in close order by his wife Clara. The telltale roundness in her middle caused her to hobble as she walked.

Clara's dainty eyebrows rose at the sight of the

midnight guests and she went to work straight away, keeping one hand on her belly.

"Daniel, start some water to boil, please."

Daniel grunted in agreement and went to the fire.

"I'm sorry to wake you, Clara," Thomas said.

She grinned. "This babe was keeping me up as it is, kicking and tumbling. You have nothing to worry over."

Thomas tried to smile back, but he could only nod. He glanced at Eliza and Kitty who still huddled together, taking in their surroundings.

"Thomas, have a seat here while I look at your wounds." Clara motioned to the chair in front of her.

"I don't have any—"

"Sit down, before I decide not to be so kind." She winked and Thomas slumped into the chair with a grin and teasing kind of growl that made her smile widen. Clara continued, "Do you ladies have any extra clothes? You must be a block of ice in those wet nightgowns."

"We do." Eliza's voice was clear, but soft.

"Good. You may take them into our bedchamber there and change while I clean him up."

Eliza and Kitty hurried into the strange room and closed the door, eager to rid their shivering bodies of the icy clothes.

"Let me help you, Kitty." Eliza emptied the bag onto the disheveled bed and filtered through the articles to find what belonged to Kitty.

Through the door Eliza could hear the heated voices in the next room.

"Thomas." Daniel's voice was deep and powerful. "What's going on?"

A deafening pause followed. Eliza and Kitty stared at each other, bracing themselves for the reasons of the evening's nightmare.

"I'm ashamed to admit this." Thomas stopped, and Eliza heard a chair scrape across the floor. She helped Kitty wriggle out of her sticky, wet nightdress as he continued, "I've put you all, and Robert Campbell's two daughters, in danger."

"Those are Doctor Campbell's girls?" Daniel asked.

"They are."

Kitty flipped her head in the direction of the door. "How did they know Father? Were they his patients?" She whispered as Eliza pulled her chemise over her head and down her body.

"Shhh. Let's just listen." Eliza fumbled with the laces of Kitty's stays as she did them up. Her heart palpitated against her chest and she strained to keep her anxiety from showing. She prayed her faux air of strength and calm was believable, at least to Kitty.

Footsteps tapped across the floor. "I was approached several years ago, not long after I joined up with the Sons of Liberty, by a British soldier who asked me to divulge information about our group—what we talked about, what we planned to do, and so forth. But I refused."

The girls shared confused glances, before Kitty helped Eliza out of her own muddy gown.

Thomas continued. "Not long after I'd refused his futile offer, he approached me again—this time telling me if I did not comply they would not only hurt me, but you Daniel, and your family as well. The details of which I wish not to speak of."

Kitty slapped a hand over her open mouth and Eliza gasped. Dear Lord! How dreadful.

"They blackmailed you?" Daniel's voice was quieter now, but threaded with hate. Eliza could well imagine the anger that lined his sturdy face.

"Thomas, I'm so sorry," Clara said. Her heavy step moved across the floor followed by the sound of sloshing water.

"'Tis I who should be sorry. I should have found another way."

Eliza's stomach dropped to her knees and she crossed her arms as Kitty struggled with the laces on her stays. How could any soldier ever do such a thing? She breathed deep as indignation soared from her feet to the tips of her hair. Wait until Samuel discovered this. He would be furious and bring the culprit to a rightful punishment.

"So, what happened tonight? Why are you and Robert's daughters in danger?" Daniel pressed.

Eliza and Kitty slipped into their dresses and helped each other button and lace their last bit of clothing into place while Thomas explained the rest of the tragic tale.

"Tonight was to be the last night they would ever ask for information and they wanted names."

He stopped talking and the girls froze.

"Names?" Kitty whispered.

"Shhh." Eliza put her finger to her mouth.

Thomas went on. "There isn't time to explain it all, but one of the names I gave was Robert's. Knowing he was dead, I knew they couldn't hurt him. I didn't know they'd go after his family until it was too late."

Kitty slumped onto the bed and covered her face. "Father was—no, he couldn't be. It's not true."

"We'll talk of it when we are safe, Kitty." Eliza bit her cheek, recalling her own shock when she'd learned the same about Father. "Remember, we must hurry. Mr. Watson says we are still in danger."

Kitty nodded, all color draining from her face.

When Thomas spoke again his usually confident voice was lined with defeat. "It's only by the grace of God I got to their home in time."

At that moment, Eliza and Kitty emerged, dressed in their modest homespun. Thomas glanced over his shoulder, the looks on their innocent faces drilled holes in his gut. Shackles of regret pinned him to the floor. He had hoped to explain all of it with the girls in the same room, so as not to appear as though he attempted to hide anything from them. But with time as precious as it was, he'd had to explain while they dressed. He knew they could hear through the thin walls. Hopefully that was enough. He could give them the details as they journeyed the rest of the way. God willing, they wouldn't blame him.

Clara finished with Thomas and turned toward her husband. "I'm going to wake the children."

Thomas rose, placing his hands on the back of the chair. He met Daniel's strong gaze with one of his own. "I wanted nothing more than to protect you and your family." The muscles in his jaw twitched as he gritted his teeth.

Daniel came forward, placing a hand on his shoulder. "Do not blame yourself. Clara and I both knew when we joined this cause that there could be consequences. We also knew that it's a cause worth fighting for—worth dying for, Thomas. I know you feel the same." He paused and let out a long sigh. "The soldiers will come here next."

"That's my fear." Thomas flung a quick glance behind him. Kitty's eyes grew wide again, but Eliza remained stoic.

At that moment Clara teetered in, with a small sleeping boy over her belly. A young girl followed behind, rubbing half-shut eyes.

"I'll load the wagon." Daniel went to a large chest in the corner. "We will go to your uncle's." He pulled out a shirt, waistcoat, jacket, breeches, and stockings, then tucked them under his arm.

"We can't take the roads, Daniel, it will be too dangerous." The resolve in Clara's voice reverberated through the room. "We'll walk the back way."

Daniel's loving gaze swept her face. "Clara, you can hardly walk as it is."

Raising up on her toes, Clara kissed his cheek. "I'll be fine. 'Tis only 5 miles. Besides, God will put the wind at our backs. I must get dressed now. We need to leave as soon as possible." With that she disappeared into the room.

Daniel turned to Thomas, thrusting the clothes he'd gathered into his chest. "You'll want to get out of the clothes you have on. Those should fit you. You can use the children's room to change."

When Thomas emerged, changed and warm, Eliza and Kitty were dawning cloaks that Clara had just handed to them.

"These are old, but they should keep you warm enough," Clara said.

Eliza placed the cloak over her shoulders and raised her eyes to meet Thomas's gaze. The strength and determination in their dark depths failed to cover a veil of fear. His muscles hardened as fresh resolve seeped into his bones. He would keep them safe. No matter what.

"We must go," Daniel said, dousing the fire.

"I've a cloak and hat for you as well, Thomas." Daniel pointed to a peg near the front door and Thomas took it.

"You haven't said where you three are going," Daniel asked.

Before answering, Thomas glanced at Eliza and Kitty. Would they go with him? Did they have a choice?

He let out an audible breath before speaking. "We're going to Sandwich."

No reaction came from either Eliza or her sister. That must be a good sign.

"What will you do with your press? You can't simply leave it, can you?"

Thomas shook his head, remembering George's genuine nature and his surprising knowledge of the trade.

"I've done all I can with what little time I had. I believe God has provided yet again in that regard. Though it kills me to leave it."

Daniel nodded. "He has provided and He will continued to do so." He wrapped the young boy in a blanket, picked him up, and placed his head on his shoulder.

Clara tightened the cloak around the young girl before taking her hand. "God speed, Thomas."

"God speed." Thomas's throat grew tight with words he wanted to say, but couldn't.

A storm roared within him and he shuffled forward as if prodded on by invisible angels. They needed to get on their way.

"It will be too risky to send word to one another, at least for a while," Daniel said. "When it's safe, I promise to let you know we are well."

Daniel's voice was thick with emotion as he faced the girls. "Your father was a remarkable man. I count it an honor to have known him. No doubt he watches over you, just as God will always do."

"Thank you, sir." Eliza's voice cracked and her eyes swam with tears. Kitty looked away and wrapped her arms around her middle.

Daniel opened the door and Thomas nudged the girls forward as they began their weary trek into the starry blackness.

Chapter Six

Samuel reached the Williams' cabin and kicked in the door as he had done at the press. A deserted home greeted him and the glowing embers in the fireplace mocked. He was too late.

Blast!

He yelled, slamming the side of his fist into the door-jam. "Fool!"

They'd been here, no doubt. The small room bore witness of a hasty departure. A bloodied rag lay suspiciously on the table. The trunk in the corner sat open and exposed. In the smaller room a set of men's clothes were flayed about. They belonged to Watson. The jacket, ripped at the shoulder, had spatters of blood on the collar. So did the shirt. He remembered Donaldson's mangled face and shook his head.

Stomping to the largest bedchamber, he absorbed the scene and stopped in his tracks. There, on the edge of the bed were two nightgowns, folded, one on top of the other. The fronts of each were wet and covered in mud. He bent over and picked them up, caressing the lace.

Eliza, what has he done to you?

Samuel sat on the edge of the bed and buried his

face in the neck of Eliza's nightgown. He closed his eyes and breathed in deep. Her rose perfume graced his nose under the earthy tones of the mud and laughed at him. If he'd only gotten there sooner.

As much as he despised Watson, he had to give him credit. The man had brains. He'd planned this. And planned it well.

Where were they?

Shaking his head, he talked to the fabric. "Eliza, please forgive me."

He got up, taking the gowns with him, and left the empty cabin.

"I'll make this up to you, Eliza. I promise," he said aloud. "I'll find you. And then I'll make Watson pay."

Sandwich was sixty miles south of Boston.

Sixty miles. Eliza had never walked that far in her life. And certainly not with angry Redcoats on her heels. Pushing away the pit in her middle, she reminded herself again that Samuel would help them—he would call off the hunt, just as soon as she could get word to him.

The stars began to fade, and in a few short hours the morning light would sprinkle down through the canopy of leaves. For now, it was still dark. A light misty fog enveloped them, the cold seeping through her clothes and biting her skin. She inhaled the crisp, clean scent of freshly fallen leaves, trying to chase away the exhaustion in her weary muscles. By now they'd been awake and walking for hours. The sound of the crunching ground under their feet droned on and on. Eliza wanted to roll into a ball and sleep for days. Her legs already screamed in pain and hellish blisters germinated on the backs of her feet. But they continued on without resting, without speaking.

They stayed off the main roads and trails, just as Thomas had said they would do, and so far they hadn't seen a soul. He insisted that if they moved quickly, the journey would take no longer than three days.

The thick forest, with its tall trees and billowing foliage, allowed for little moonlight, and Eliza prayed God would break with tradition—just for today—and send the morning sun several hours early. The darkness of the trail forced her to take cautious steps as they climbed over fallen logs and stepped around large boulders that jumped out at them from the shadows. They continued for several more hours—or what seemed like it, making Eliza wonder if they were actually going forward or only traveling in circles since the view around them never appeared to change.

Eliza glanced at Kitty, then Thomas. She suspected her sister's mind raced, as her own did, at what they'd both heard Thomas confess hours before.

Careful to remain inconspicuous, Eliza peeked at him while they walked, just as the heaven-sent sprinkle of morning light began to illuminate their path and the chorus of chirping birds accompanied their steps. She pulled her lip between her teeth. It wasn't his fault they were now running for their lives. That responsibility rested on Father. If he had not joined the Sons of Liberty, then Thomas would not have been forced to use his name when the soldiers demanded it. Blackmail was a vicious thing.

Kitty hadn't spoken a word. She walked with her head bowed, arms clutching her stomach. Eliza wanted to speak with her, to comfort her, but she needed time. That was Kitty's way.

Eliza ignored the pain in her heels and kept her mind busy. If she didn't, her feet would murder her. Thankfully, no one spoke. It allowed her to think. What kind of cruel person would resort to blackmail? She'd noted the humiliation in Thomas's voice, the shame. But he had done everything for the welfare of those he loved—there was no shame in that.

His kind and caring nature showed in all he did. Eliza took note of everything, though she warned herself not to. He walked ahead of them, searching out the safest and easiest path and offered a strong hand to them when crossing a bumpy patch of earth. Every so often he peered over his broad shoulder to inquire about their welfare. No doubt he was just as tired and hungry as they, but he didn't show it. The smile in his dark blue eyes remained vibrant with every passing mile. He was the kind of man that—

Eliza quickly blinked away her thoughts. She didn't even know the man. Such notions must never be entertained. Not when Samuel had proposed. He deserved an honest answer—one she wasn't ready to give.

Another immeasurable amount of time slipped by as they plodded across the leaf-matted ground before Thomas stopped. "Let's rest here a while. I believe it's safe for us to stop and rest."

Splendid gold and red maple leaves decorated the floor of a small clearing in the trees. Brave blades of grass struggled to poke their pointed heads from underneath the colorful blanket. The sunrise dusted orange light like a celestial cloak to warm them. Both girls found a soft pillow of ground devoid of mud on which to sit.

Heaven! Never had it felt so marvelous to stop moving. Eliza closed her eyes and rested her head on the tree behind her, trying to ignore the throbbing at the backs of her feet.

"Don't get too comfortable."

Eliza's eyes shot open at the closeness of Thomas's soothing voice. He crouched next to her, resting his arm on his knee.

With Thomas so close Eliza could plainly see dark rugged whiskers beginning to appear on his face. Her heart stopped.

He tipped his chin toward the sky. "Now that it's getting light, I'm going to go back about half a mile. I need to make sure the soldiers haven't discovered our trail—if they have, we'll need to put fire in our feet."

"You don't think they are following us, do you? Really?"

"I'd like to think they aren't, but Redcoats don't give up easily, so we have to be stronger and smarter than they are. Which isn't hard to do, thankfully." He chuckled and looked around, but didn't get up. "You seem to be holding up well, I'm impressed." His eyes smiled, then grew serious. "How are you doing?"

She swallowed. His sincerity and honest inquiry made her feel warm and safe—protected. Taking a quick glance at where Kitty rested a few feet away, she sighed, grateful her sister had managed to fall asleep in so little time.

"I'm well, thank you. How far do you suppose we've traveled?"

He rubbed the cleft in his chin. "About ten miles."

"Ten miles," Eliza repeated. Fifty more to go. Her feet would never make it.

"Will you be all right here while I'm gone?"

No. Eliza pulled the cloak around her neck. "Of

course."

As he moved, ready to get up, the words in Eliza's heart found their way to her mouth before she could stop them. "Mr. Watson, I . . . I understand time is of the essence, but I must know. How well did you know my Father?"

With a gentle smile he sat on the ground a polite distance from her, picked up an auburn leaf, and played with it in his fingers. "I knew him quite well. Very well, in fact." He paused and motioned toward Kitty. "We can talk for a moment. Let her rest."

Eliza sat up straighter. "How did you meet him?"

He pulled the dying leaf apart at the veins. "I joined the group three years ago. Your Father had already been part of them for some time."

"You mean the Sons of Liberty?"

He tipped his head toward her and she could see the sparkle behind his eyes when he answered. "That's right."

Eliza moved her gaze down. She reached into her skirt pocket and retrieved the note she had kept with her since the moment she'd read it in the field. Fingering it in her hands, she tried to keep her voice smooth. "My Father always said it was more dangerous to be a Tory. He attended to men who'd been tarred and feathered for staying loyal to the Crown, he had meetings with Hutchinson himself—he couldn't believe people would be capable of going against King George." She stopped and clutched her stomach. "And now to know that he was a member of such a group, a group that would violate property, cause riots, and hurt any human life . . . I don't understand it."

She looked at him, studying his face as her mind raced to put together the words that jumbled in her brain and she squeezed the paper until her fingernails bit into her palm. "I've seen your Liberty Tree. I've seen the soldiers hanging in effigy. I've seen the signs and posters promoting your cause. Father was a good man. He taught us to love and serve our king. How could he align himself with a group that does such horrific things?" Her voice quivered, as did her chin.

Thomas looked down at the leaf in his hands, then back up at her. "Do you believe that every member of His Majesty's Army is upstanding and seeks for the good in all he does?"

She lowered her eyes, smoothing her thumb over the paper.

"Well, it is the same with the members of our growing group. I certainly could never tar and feather a man, and neither would your Father. But there are many who hold the same political beliefs—they strive for liberty and freedom—yet cannot bridle their passions and let their anger get the best of them."

Eliza shook her head. "I'm afraid I'll never be able to come to a full knowledge of why Father did what he did. Why he believed what he believed."

Thomas pointed at the note as if he knew exactly what it contained, and somehow that knowledge alone massaged away the tension in her heart. "God will help you find the knowledge you are searching for." He tossed aside the remains of the sheered leaf. "Your Father always acted with wisdom and responsibility. I'm sure he would never have done what I did. He would never have betrayed the cause of liberty. He risked everything for it. I'm also certain he'd hang me for putting you in danger the way I have." Thomas spat the words as if they were bitter gall.

Wrapping her arms around her knees, Eliza laced her fingers to keep from touching him. She longed to show him comfort, to assure him she held no ill feelings.

"None of what's happened to us is your fault, Mr. Watson. 'Tis all my Father's doing. Had he never joined the group you would never have felt to use his name. I know you did it to protect your family from harm."

Thomas chewed on the inside of his cheek for a moment, then turned to her. "Would you like to know the first thing your Father said to me?"

Eliza jerked back and blinked. "Of course."

"At my first meeting, your Father approached me before anyone else and shook my hand. After introducing ourselves to one another he said, 'I'm doing this for my daughters, Mr. Watson. Why are you here?'"

Eliza's throat closed and her eyes filled with tears she could not contain. They slipped past her lashes and splashed her cheeks. "He never raised us that way, you know." She shoved back her emotions and carefully returned the note to her pocket. Looking over at Kitty, Eliza dotted the moisture from her cheeks. "I never knew his true feelings until after he died. Neither of us did. I wish he would have told me." She swiped at a tear with the back of her hand. "So, Mr. Watson, why *were* you there?"

He tossed her a fleeting grin before his expression turned somber. "Those of us in the colonies are treated like second class citizens. Our king robs us with his taxes and we have no proper representation in Parliament. Our lives will never be the same if we continue to let King George dictate his will at every delicate whim."

Thomas looked in front of him into the mass of trees. "I was there initially for the welfare of my business. I've dedicated my life to my press, small though it may be. I could not much longer continue with such oppression. Through the years I have come to see the importance of the cause for the entirety of the colonies. We must be allowed to represent ourselves and live our lives separate from the king's constant oppression."

His eyes latched with Eliza's. "What do you think about it all?"

Eliza could hardly believe the question. Her mouth dropped open. He cared about what she thought—what a *woman* thought about politics? Samuel believed it wasn't a woman's place to discuss it, and even her own father had never spoken to her in this way. She stuttered. "I'm . . . I'm not sure what to think about anything anymore."

Thomas's mouth bowed upward as he slipped his masculine hand over hers. She lifted her watery eyes, the intense loneliness of seconds ago evaporating at his touch.

"You'll come to know in time, Eliza. God will show you."

The low resonance of his voice sliced through her and his gaze seemed to be memorizing her face. Her breath stuck in her lungs and her muscles froze.

He'd used her first name! It sounded so good when he said it.

She pondered his words. Yes, she did believe God would show her. But would she have the faith to follow whatever it was He revealed?

The intimacy of the moment heated her cheeks. Eliza pulled her hand away and rested her back against the tree once again. Samuel's face flashed across her mind. What would he have said to her at that moment? He certainly would not have asked her what she thought about it all.

Silence enveloped them and she cleared her throat. "You better get going if we're to start again soon. We'll be here when you get back."

His face brightened in a smile that stopped her heart and he gave a quiet laugh. "I'm delighted to hear it." After that, he was gone.

She watched until his tall form vanished from sight. Within seconds, her body surrendered to a welcoming sleep.

Samuel glared at Thomas's uncle who slumped in the corner of his small headquarters. The room had smelled a bit unpleasant before—from dirty soldiers, smoky fires, and stale air. Now it reeked.

Even though the temperature of the room was cold, the man dripped with sweat. His fat legs were spread out in front of him and his swollen hands were tied with thick rope and lying across his bulging stomach. His fingers twitched.

Samuel slid a chair across the hardwood floor and sat only inches from his prisoner.

"Now, George Watson. If you find any value in your miserable life, you will tell me everything you know."

George's small black eyes rounded. "Sir, please! I know nothing. I tell you honestly. I came to port just yesterday. Tommy offered me a job. I was looking for work, you see. I needed to escape my gaming debts so I—"

"Shut up!" Samuel slapped him across his face. "I know Watson had a plan and I know you're part of it!"

"I swear by all that's holy, I know nothing!"

"Where did he go? Tell me now!" Samuel leaned in closer.

The man stuttered, beads of sweat trickling down his face. "All I know is that he had to meet someone last night. He said, 'Take care of the press, Uncle.' And then, he left."

Samuel's heart pumped pebbles of hot coals into his limbs. He leapt from his chair, launching it into the wall with the backs of his legs. George whimpered, shrinking into the corner as far as his large body would allow.

"You can't tell me that this was an accident, that it wasn't planned! He wanted to get away from here, away from me!"

Samuel stomped away from George and clenched his fists at his side to keep from punching the door—or the man. He started to speak quiet, but his volume rose to a fierce thunder. "That man took my future bride and I want her back! If you don't tell me where they are, I believe a stint in prison will relax your memories."

George's hands shook. "No! No, please! sir, if I could tell you, I would—"

"I won't be forced to listen to such drivel. Donaldson!"

The door to the next room swung open and the Lieutenant entered.

"Yes, Captain?"

"Donaldson, help this smelly beast into his new accommodations." Samuel knelt down and drew close enough to see George's black pores. "Welcome to America, Mr. Watson."

Donaldson hefted the heavy man onto his feet and attempted to plow him out the door when the man turned back to Samuel.

"Wait! Wait! I did see something."

Samuel glared. "Well, what is it??"

"There . . . there was a girl."

Chapter Seven

"A storm is approaching. We must quicken our pace if we are to find shelter before the rains descend." Thomas looked behind him at the girls when he spoke. He didn't want to worry his companions, but he couldn't ignore the facts. They still had at least forty more miles to go.

The clouds collected into a thick, gray mass, and a breeze played with the canopy above. Diffused daylight brightened their path, but did nothing to warm their bodies as the scent of impending rain swirled around them.

Thomas glanced back again at his fellow travelers. He couldn't have picked two more compliant females if he'd tried. Kitty had not said three words together. Thomas allowed himself another peek at the eldest Miss Campbell, and tried to quell his growing curiosity. Every moment that passed testified of her unmistakable strength and noticeable charm.

"If it rains, will we be able to find any shelter?" Eliza called from behind her sister.

"I know of a place where we can rest, but we likely won't arrive there until nightfall."

"You know of a place? Have you been this way before?" Eliza asked.

He helped the ladies over a fallen tree obstructing their way. "I knew I would need a place where I could make a new start for myself, and I chose Sandwich. I've traveled there many times—I've even built myself a modest home over the course of about a year." He thought of his new home, his hope for a good life getting swallowed up in their uncertain future. What were they to do when they got there? When would it be safe for Eliza and her sister to return to Boston?

"Mr. Watson, you believe we must go all the way to Sandwich with you to remain out of reach of the soldiers who were looking for my Father? For us?" Eliza's tone relayed her apprehension.

Just then Kitty slipped on a mossy stone and landed on her backside with a surprised yelp. Eliza helped her up before Thomas could offer assistance. The young girl burst into tears and buried her face in her hands. Eliza rested her sister's head on her shoulder and stroked her hair, whispering comforting words in her ear before sending a quick glance at Thomas.

His guilt squashed him like the pounding of his press. He prayed God would guide him and help him keep these trusting women from any additional harm. His father may have thought he was good for nothing, but he planned to prove him wrong.

"Are you all right?" Eliza stroked Kitty's arm.

"No, I'm not all right!" The girl who had been silent the entire trip, now exploded into a whirlwind of tears and fury.

"Kitty, please." Eliza tried to console her, but Kitty wouldn't allow it.

She pushed away from Eliza and unleashed her frenzy at Thomas as she got to her feet. "What are Eliza and I supposed to do when we get to Sandwich, did you think about that, Mr. Watson? We have nothing more than the clothes on our backs. You have been preparing for this. You have a home waiting for you! We have nothing!" She crumpled against her sister again and muffled her sobs with her hands.

Thomas froze, a wicked helplessness moving like a cold vapor through his muscles. The weight of their situation resting on his shoulders now increased a hundred fold.

Kitty was right.

He hadn't prepared for this. How could he? He gripped his fists. He'd make it up to them—make things as easy as possible for them once they got to safety. *God, help them understand why this had to be done.*

"Kitty," Eliza cooed. "Mr. Watson did his best. We are safe because of him. What else could he have done? Remember, God is overall and He will provide. He already has."

Kitty appeared uninterested in being placated. She pulled the hood of her cloak over her head and continued walking. After only a few steps she spun around again, her voice more subdued, but the tears kept coming.

"And *you* knew about Father! Why didn't you tell me? How long have you known? Don't you think I have a right to know?"

Eliza threw a fleeting glance at Thomas, as if requesting some kind of help, but he could only stand, mouth agape. He'd never had much experience with females—much less crying ones—and this drama only mystified him more.

"I haven't known for long." Eliza moved toward her sister with an outstretched hand, as if Kitty were an injured animal. "I only learned of it after he died. He didn't want us to get hurt and—"

"Well, we nearly did get hurt, did we not?" Kitty's face scrunched again as she struggled to hold back a sob. "Here we are, in the middle of nowhere. Cold, hungry, aching from exhaustion and about to be drenched from head to toe!"

She wept again, this time falling to her knees. Eliza rushed to her, holding her in her arms until her crying came to a quiet end.

Eliza turned to Thomas, a caring smile gracing her rosy lips as she silently mouthed, "I'm sorry."

Thomas came near, hoping Eliza could read the apology in his face. "'Tis my fault. I take full responsibility."

Kitty lifted her head and wiped at her tears. The anger from moments ago evaporated more with each word. "Forgive me for such a display, Mr. Watson. 'Tis not your fault. Our father is to blame. If not for his actions we'd never be in this position. He should have stayed loyal to the Crown, like he always taught us to do!"

Eliza wiped her sister's glistening cheeks with tender fingers. "We cannot change the past, Kitty. Father said to trust God, and that's all we can do. That's what we must do."

"You are right. I suppose I'm overcome and I'm losing hold of my senses." Kitty studied the fabric of her cloak. "I do trust in God, but 'tis clear I must work on developing my faith."

Clutching Kitty's hand, Eliza's voice appeared to heal like a physician's balm. "God knows we all must develop more faith, Kitty. I do not think ill of you, and I'm sure Mr. Watson feels the same."

"Most certainly." Thomas used as much gentility in his voice as he could. "If we can but journey another few miles, we'll have shelter and be able to rest. Do you think you can make it?"

"I believe I can." Kitty kept her eyes down and nodded, then stood and pulled away from her sister's embrace.

Eliza walked next to Kitty, her arm around her sister's drooping shoulders. Soon Kitty announced she needed to be alone, and sped up, walking in front.

As they put more miles behind them, the gray sky released its torrent, and Thomas's fears unearthed. They were soaked to the bone. The sound of the rain drummed so hard it drowned out the sound of their steps. By the time they reached their temporary haven, the girls were dripping wet and so weak they could hardly stand.

"This is it. Welcome home." Thomas pointed into the dry, dark cave, grateful to be able to provide something to help ease their burdens. Beautiful moss decorated the house-sized rock and thick trees stood as imposing sentinels around it.

"I've stayed here many times in my travels to and from Sandwich. It's as if God put it here just for us. There's ample of room for all, plus ten more, so make yourselves comfortable."

Thomas strode in, flipping off his sopping cloak, and placed it over another rock to drain. The two girls followed him inside, cautious, as if the cave were home to dangerous dragons.

He chuckled. "Don't worry, no one lives here."

"There aren't any . . . animals?" Eliza took teeny steps forward, but stood straight as if she didn't want her apprehension obvious. The attempt was endearing.

Thomas couldn't hide the mirth in his voice when he answered Eliza's sweet and innocent question, as he reached for the satchel she'd been carrying. "You mean, bears?"

"Bears?" Eliza jerked back, her hands at her neck.

He winked and stepped closer, removing the bag from her grasp. "Well, there is a family of bears that live here, but not to worry. They are visiting relatives in Providence and won't be back for another week."

Kitty smiled and giggled from her place along the wall as she took off her cloak, but Eliza still appeared nervous.

He decided to change the subject. "I put a pile of wood in here last time I traveled through, in preparation for a just such a situation." He reached into a generous opening at the side of the cave, pulled out a substantial pile of dry wood, and built a castle-worthy fire.

Both women stood around the roaring blaze, their gowns not as wet as their cloaks had been, thank the Lord. Eliza searched the satchel of food, and gave a small bit of bread to Kitty, then held out the other piece to Thomas.

"I'm too tired to be hungry," she said.

At that very moment her stomach growled. Thomas couldn't help but laugh.

She placed a hand over her middle and looked away.

Thomas used his hands to mold her trim fingers around the morsel. "You eat it. I can't have either of you going hungry. We still have a long journey ahead of us."

Eliza's grateful brown eyes spoke volumes and she sat down next to her sister in front of the fire, nibbling at her meager meal. She glanced up at Thomas, looking ashamed to be eating when he wasn't. Could she be any more charming?

"Ladies, when you're done with your feast, I'd suggest trying to get as comfortable as possible and sleep as much as you can. This will be our last real shelter before we get to Sandwich."

The sisters nodded and started talking in hushed tones to one another. Kitty devoured her portion of the bread and lay facing the fire, her arms crossed over her chest for warmth.

Thomas watched as Eliza moved to lay behind Kitty, as if to shield her back from the cold. She rubbed Kitty's arm up and down from behind to keep her warm.

Thomas's heart wrenched and a pulsing desire to keep Eliza warm dashed through him. Did she never think of herself? She should be in front of the flames as well, or she might catch a dangerous chill.

Within only a few minutes Kitty slept, but he could tell from the way Eliza moved restlessly on the hard ground that she was not sleeping.

"Are you doing all right, Miss Campbell?"

She poked her head up and her lips lifted into a tired grin. "As fine as I can be."

How enticing she looked. Her rosy cheeks and round dark eyes shimmered with the glow of the fire. The dark strands of hair around her face curled slightly, kissing her cheeks. As much as he wanted to keep her warm for the sake of her health, he feared his nearness to her would drive emotions within him that he didn't want to have.

"Will you be warm enough?" he said.

She stood, rubbing her hands together. "Now that Kitty is sleeping, I think I'll lay in front of the fire as well. If I don't, I'm not sure how I'll survive through the night." She gave a tiny laugh as if to lighten the heavy mood and moved around the fire, holding her long heavy skirts with one hand until she found a comfortable position on the dirty cave floor on which to lay.

He breathed a sigh of grateful relief. At least now he didn't have to worry if he should try to keep her warm. The fire could do that.

"Thank you for being patient with us, Mr. Watson. Sleep well." The melody in her voice caused his stomach to float.

"Thank you, Miss Campbell. Goodnight."

When she closed her eyes, he let his gaze travel over her. She lay on her side and he marveled at the perfect slopes of her shoulders, her waist, her hips. This woman was not only caring, courageous, and selfless, she was bewitchingly beautiful. He never knew such a person existed. If he were ever to marry, she would be . . .

He shook his head and exhaled. She had a life in Boston to return to, and his home would be in Sandwich. This episode would be but a small chapter in the book of her life.

Thomas looked out the large opening of the cave, hoping to clear his foggy brain. The heavy sheets of rain still drummed only feet away from them, and the darkness of the approaching evening thickened.

Please Lord, stop the rain so we can move at a more rapid pace tomorrow.

The next leg of their journey should be the easiest. Yet he couldn't shake the nagging feeling that the worst was yet to come.

The next morning, promising sunlight broke through the leafy mosaic and shimmered on the diamond-like droplets that rested on the foliage outside the cave.

Eliza woke with a start at an unusual noise. Her eyes widened, her heart refused to beat, and she tried to muffle a scream. She stayed motionless, too afraid to move, to breathe. Eliza's blood drained from her face and she tried to rouse her companions without frightening the horrid creature, afraid at any moment it would attack.

"Kitty! Thomas!" she squeaked, staying still.

Neither of them moved.

She called for them again, louder this time. Thomas jerked and grabbed at the pistol underneath his side. He stalled for a moment, looking back and forth before his body shook with a bellowing laugh.

Awake and giggling, Kitty rested on her elbow next to Eliza. "Liza, how do you always attract those creatures?"

"This isn't funny! Why isn't it moving? Get it off of me!" Eliza squealed.

Her plea only made Thomas laugh harder.

How could they possibly find humor in this? "Please! Get it off of me, one of you. Why doesn't it just leave?" Eliza covered her mouth and breathed through her fingers while the large gray squirrel stared at her from tiny black eyes.

"Allow me to rescue you from this dangerous attacker, fair maiden." Thomas reached over and shooed the animal from its perch on Eliza's lower leg. It scampered away as Thomas continued chuckling and wiping tears from his eyes.

He winked and his smile softened, but not enough to soothe the waves of Eliza's embarrassment that crashed against her. She sat up straight and pressed her hand to her chest as she tried to calm the rapid thumping of her heart.

Thomas pointed out the cave with a tilt to his voice that announced his teasing. "You could have been killed."

His winsome smile almost took away the shame. Almost. "I'm glad you were both so entertained." She stood and brushed off her stiff skirts, attempting to appear as casual as possible.

Kitty continued her playful snicker. Despite her humiliation, Eliza couldn't help but be grateful. God knew her fear of those wretched creatures—as ridiculous a fear as it was. Perhaps He'd sent it there to simply bring a smile to Kitty's face. If that were the case, it was well worth the terror.

Thomas stood and looked over at her as he slipped his pistol back in place at his side. A jovial smirk spread across his handsome mouth.

"So, you don't care for squirrels, I take it." He flashed his straight white teeth when he laughed again.

"Oh no, she doesn't." Kitty answered, standing and brushing off her skirts as well.

Pursing her lips, Eliza sent her sister a look that said, "*That's enough*." Wisely, Kitty complied, but not before her face bloomed into another taunting grin. Eliza started to walk out of the cave when Thomas called after her.

"Where do you think you're going?"

She looked at him with cocked brows and lowered her chin. Did she have to say it and complete her utter humiliation?

His face reddened. "Oh, well . . . don't go too far."

She nodded and walked out, hearing from behind her the two of them laughing and discussing the hilarity they'd just witnessed.

Mortifying! She buried her face in her hands as she walked.

That dreadful display wasn't the kind of thing she wanted anyone to witness, let alone the dashing press owner.

She couldn't explain why she cared about his opinion of her—or why the thought of never seeing him after this turmoil ended made her insides tie in knots. But it did. Within a few short weeks, or sooner, after Samuel heard of this and came to their aid, she'd likely never see him again.

When she returned to the cave, Thomas and Kitty were donning their dry cloaks and Eliza quickly did the same.

"Do we have everything?" Thomas asked as he looked around.

"I believe so. Then again, we didn't come with much." Eliza shrugged and winked at Kitty to show her good humor was repaired. At least that's what she wanted them to believe.

Kitty massaged her stomach. "Liza, I'm . . . I'm . . . oh, never mind, forgive me."

Gripping Kitty's hand, Eliza looked her over. "Are you all right?"

She shrugged. "It's nothing." Just then her stomach groaned and Kitty's cheeks reddened.

Eliza frowned and squeezed her hand. "Kitty, I'm so sorry I didn't bring more."

"'Tis not your fault."

Thomas stepped forward, his large frame silhouetted against the bright mouth of the cave. "I've stored much food, so you can have your pick of goods when we reach Sandwich."

Ignoring a hunger pang of her own, Eliza straightened. "See? We'll be eating like King George before you know it. We best get going, should we not?" She followed Thomas out of the cave with Kitty close behind.

After several more hours of torturous hiking over rain sodden earth, Eliza stopped and leaned her hand against the rough bark of an old tree. Oh, the pain! The quick rest allowed her to take some of the weight off her feet and legs, but doing so did little to ease her discomfort. She'd nearly bit her lip in two as she tried to keep from groaning.

Thomas must have heard her stop. He turned around, worry shaping his features as she attempted to pry her shoe from her foot.

"Are you all right?"

Eliza bit her lip harder. *No.*

When she didn't answer he called for Kitty to stop.

"What is it?" he asked again. The concern in his velvety tone made her legs even weaker.

He came close and Eliza choked back a cry when her skin peeled away from her heel as she removed her shoe. The large blisters had long since broken and her shoes rubbed her stockings into the raw flesh on the backs of her feet. Blood stained her white stocking and the inside of her shoe, a shoe made for appearances, not functionality.

Thomas crouched beside her and tenderly reached for her foot. "Why didn't you tell me?" He lifted his eyes to hers. "May I look at it?"

Eliza nodded, hesitant for him to touch her, but somehow she couldn't refuse.

Kitty came near, her mouth pressed with concern.

"How are your feet, Kitty?" Eliza asked, suddenly worried her sister might be suffering the same as she.

"They hurt, but I'm all right." She leaned closer.

"Eliza, you're bleeding!"

"It doesn't really hurt. Don't worry." Eliza worked a tone of confidence in her voice that she could only hope was believable.

Thomas performed the polite examination, his masculine fingers so gentle that the pain in her foot faded at his touch.

"You should have told me, Miss Campbell." He shook his head and Eliza tried to guess his meaning. Was he upset with her? Worried? "I'm not sure there is anything we can do until we get to Sandwich." He kept his hand around her ankle for a moment longer than necessary before looking up at her again.

Her lungs froze.

She pressed her teeth around her bottom lip again, but this time for a different reason. She placed one hand over her middle, attempting to still the flurry of butterflies that were multiplying with rapid succession.

"I'm sorry," he whispered. His soothing voice evaporated the world around her. In a quick, smooth motion he removed the cravat from around his neck, and bent down to tie the fabric around her foot—fabric that was still warm from being so close to his skin.

She relaxed her hands at her side and tried to keep her breathing even when he gingerly finished doctoring and slipped the shoe back on her foot.

He stood and towered over her, squinting his eyes. "Are you sure you'll be fine? I can carry you if needed, at least for a while."

Yes. I mean, no!

"No, thank you. I'll be just fine. I promise."

Thomas looked at Kitty. "How are you holding up?"

"As well as can be expected, I suppose."

Thomas put his hand at Eliza's lower back and gently nudged her onward. For some reason he felt the need to walk beside her. Perhaps he thought she would have to be carried after all. She would rather die before that happened, and prayed that God would help her appear healthy and normal so not to attract unwanted attention. The last thing she needed was to be swept-up in the strong arms of the handsome man at her side.

She exhaled, blowing away the unwanted imaginations.

Kitty began to snicker and looked over her shoulder. "Oh, Eliza you should have seen yourself this morning." She laughed aloud this time as she walked ahead.

Eliza stole a swift glance at Thomas. She could see the hint of a smirk raising his lips.

"You know, Mr. Watson. Eliza has always been a very good sport." Kitty giggled again. "She is afraid of many things. We teased her mercilessly growing up."

Eliza didn't really mind laughing at herself, but she feared where the course of this conversation might venture, so she spoke up. "Thank you, Kitty. That's quite enough."

"Oh no. Please go on. You have me exceedingly curious now."

Eliza jerked her head toward Thomas. Disbelief took possession of her. He grinned back and gave her a playful wink, as if he were enjoying this all too well.

"Aye, let's see," Kitty said, obviously feeling playful as she slowed her pace to walk closer to them. "Hmmm . . ." She cocked her head to one side and squinted her eyes as if trying to think of something specific, but couldn't quite place it. Her act helped to relax the heavy mood and Eliza let a small humming laugh escape her throat.

"Eliza's afraid of water, heights, spiders, bees, and as you witnessed this morning, she is deathly afraid of squirrels."

Kitty's gaze followed Eliza, as if to explore how far she could take her story. Eliza pinched her mouth, raised her eyebrows, and shook her head, but the reprimand went unheeded.

"Oh, you must continue. You have me baited now." Thomas's winsome grin widened.

Without losing a second, Kitty cleared her throat and started into the story that Eliza secretly prayed she would never share. "One day, Eliza and I were enjoying a marvelous autumn afternoon in front of the house under the maples. The sky was a lovely blue if I remember right, dotted with the puffiest clouds."

She stopped, as if waiting for Eliza to concur.

Eliza glared, willing her sister to stop, but she did the opposite. "We decided to make beds out of the crunchy leaves, and we reclined on our backs, finding shapes in the clouds for hours on end. Eventually, the musky smell of the leaves and the warm autumn sun lulled us to sleep."

Kitty's giggle grew until she couldn't even continue.

Thomas slipped a questioning glimpse toward Eliza, and she smiled in return but her face burned.

Kitty went on between titters. "The next thing I remember is a hair-raising scream. I sat straight up and heard Eliza repeating, 'Help! Get it out! Get it out!' Father rushed out of the house . . ." Kitty had to stop again to release another fit of giggles, and wiped her eyes. "Apparently, while she'd been sleeping, a squirrel climbed up her skirts and somehow had gotten lost. What a sight! Her legs were flailing, her skirts were flying, and all the while the screeching of the little creature could be heard from under her clothes!" Kitty burst out laughing again and used her arms to imitate the scene.

Thomas could no longer suppress his obvious amusement and his robust laugh bounced on the air between them. Reliving the memory Eliza too burst into the laughter she'd been attempting to repress, basking in the joy of the moment as they temporarily forgot their weighty pressures.

Kitty calmed, wiped the happy tears from her eyes, and sighed. "Oh, it was wonderful." She gazed at her sister, her head cocked with a joyful swoop on her mouth. "I'll never forget it as long as I live."

"When did this memorable incident occur?" Thomas asked.

Eliza stopped laughing and froze, her features dropping. She shook her head at Kitty and narrowed her fiery gaze. Kitty had better not . . .

Kitty's smile expanded and occupied her entire face. A thud of dread socked Eliza in the gut and she closed her eyes.

"Last year," Kitty said. "Just about this same time, I do believe."

Thomas snapped his head toward Eliza, his eyes wide. A grin expanded his lips as he spoke. "Really? Just one year ago you were romping in the leaves and finding shapes in the clouds?"

Eliza's face heated until she knew her cheeks were as red as the leaves at her feet. No use in hiding it now. Her embarrassment had tripled, and there was nothing she could do about it. Better to accept it, than try and hide it.

"Yes, it's true," she said, walking to try and keep her embarrassment at bay. "I know it seems childish. And, I suppose I shouldn't allow myself to be frightened by a woodland creature, but so it is."

She pinched her mouth into a thin smile and marched ahead, exhaling plumes of chagrin through her lips. What must Thomas think of her now? The sooner she got back to Boston and away from this handsome stranger, the better.

Chapter Eight

"This is madness!" Samuel barked, leaving the damp, smelly prison yard. He slammed the door behind him and yanked at his cloak. The cloudy skies above matched his mood.

Donaldson marched to keep up with his feverish pace.

Samuel kicked a bulbous rock that blocked his path. "All I know is that Eliza stopped by his press that morning. To what end?" he yelled, raising his arms. "The man has no other information to offer? I don't believe it!"

Donaldson only nodded, but said nothing. That was fine. Samuel wouldn't have wanted to hear anything anyway.

Walking down the crowded street to his meager office, Samuel pushed through the door, still talking. "Watson lured Eliza there for some reason, and that George fellow knows why but he isn't saying."

"I'm sure you're right, sir."

"Of course I'm right!"

Samuel removed his hat and cloak and whacked them on the peg by the door. Donaldson followed his lead, like the loyal puppy he was.

"Eliza is an innocent pawn in Watson's wicked game." Samuel paced the room. He removed his sword and pistol from his side and dropped them on his littered desk. The papers and maps reminded him of the duty he owed his superiors, but he pushed the twinge of his conscience aside. Eliza waited for him to rescue her from capture. What could be more urgent?

Donaldson crouched by the soot-covered fireplace as he built a royal blaze.

"Have you nothing to add? No ideas to offer?" Samuel snapped.

The muscles in Donaldson's jaw flinched. "What would you have me say, sir?"

Samuel plunked into the hard chair and ran his fingers across his scratchy face. What a nightmare. "Lieutenant, I want you to tell me again everything that happened."

Donaldson pushed off his knees, his face shadowed. The pinch to his voice gave testament to a buried disdain. "I've said all there is to say, Captain, and you've heard it dozens of times—"

"I don't care!" Samuel slammed his fist on the desk. "I'm missing something. Start from the beginning. And when you're finished, you and I will come up with a plan on how to find that wretched Watson before the week is out."

How could any woman be more charming?

Thomas turned weightless as he watched Eliza and Kitty walk side-by-side several paces ahead of him, whispering to one another. He'd never met a woman like Eliza. She wasn't afraid to have fun and enjoy life, as the story of her playing in the leaves demonstrated. That alone made her increasingly alluring.

Her open nature, strength, and the fact that she had "fears" made her all the more real to him. In his past acquaintances with women, he had noticed they tried to be too perfect—in their manner, their dress. They denied any faults or impurities, trying to be something or someone they weren't.

Not Eliza.

He tried not to stare at her, but where else would he look? And with her back to him, she wouldn't be made uncomfortable, so he indulged his aching eyes. Several brown locks of hair bounced and danced around her neck as she walked. His appetite for knowing more about her deepened. They had to talk about something as they walked the last fifteen miles, why not her? Kitty would no doubt be all too pleased to comply.

"Miss Katherine?"

Both girls turned.

"Aye?" Kitty answered.

He stifled another playful grin as Eliza shyly turned forward again and kept walking.

Kitty stopped and fell in step with him. "What is it?"

"You have laid before us a . . . uh . . . lovely display of your sisters, well, weaknesses." He coughed to clear his throat and peered at Eliza, hoping to see her reaction, but she kept her face forward so he continued, "Why don't you expound a bit, and this time tell us her strengths. Her likes and dislikes."

At that comment, Eliza tilted her head in a quizzical manner, peeking over her shoulder. Thomas could make out the distinct presence of a grin and he floated over the bumpy path as excitement flickered within him.

Kitty beamed at the request.

"My dear sister is talented at many things," she said, lifting her chin. "But there are two things that stand out in my mind at which she is proficient."

"Go on, please."

"Her primary strength is recitation and readings." Kitty stopped talking for a moment and released a soft breath as if recalling a precious memory. "After our mother passed, Eliza would read and recite poems before bed to help me feel less lonely. She performed Shakespeare most of the time and would do all the parts for me, from all the plays—she's incredibly gifted."

Kitty no longer held even the slightest hint of teasing in her tone. Under her breath she whispered, "I miss those days."

Thomas allowed a broad smile to cover his face—a smile that matched the hidden one in his heart. "Well, that is very impressive and I do hope your sister will pleasure us with her talents one day."

"Eliza is also excellent with people," Kitty said. "She understands them, and always thinks of others before she thinks of herself. She can discern people in a way most others can only dream of."

"Oh, Kitty, you flatter me," Eliza announced over the gentle slope of her shoulder. "I'm not that good with people."

Kitty lowered her head and tucked a length of hair behind her ear. "Well, you're that good with me. And a few other people, I've noticed. If only you could have used those discerning skills before a certain handsome young man proposed."

Eliza stopped mid-stride and whirled around to face her sister. Her fiery eyes were wide as she stared at Kitty, her lips pinched white.

Both Thomas and Kitty halted where they stood. Eliza's gaze shot poisonous darts at her sister and Thomas stepped back, not wanting to get caught in the crossfire. Kitty's features flattened and her shoulders dropped.

Attempting to process what Kitty had unwittingly divulged, Thomas stared at one sister, then the next.

Eliza was engaged?

His heart sank for a moment, before he talked himself back to reality.

What was he thinking? He didn't even know Eliza. His responsibility for them would end after he brought them safely home when the hunt was over—which is the way he wanted it, certainly. But his mind whirled despite his vigorous efforts to stop it until curiosity got the better of him.

"You're engaged?" The words splashed out.

Eliza looked back at him, gifting him with a tiny sparkle in her doe-like eyes. "No. I am not engaged."

Thomas released a long breath he hadn't known he'd been holding and continued walking, pretending her answer didn't matter to him. Because it didn't.

His mind drifted away until all he could hear was the crunch of the ground beneath his feet. Right now, back in Boston, some man was no doubt searching for the woman he loved. He must be worried about her—frantic. Any man would be.

Who was this . . . suitor? Did she miss him?

Lengthening his stride and pounding his feet a little harder than necessary, Thomas shook his head. He had no hold upon her heart and he didn't want to. It was better that way.

Much better.

The sun relaxed low in the October sky, fashioning long skinny shadows as its caramel light bounced through the trees and across the quilt of red and gold hues that draped the surrounding hills.

After another day of ceaseless walking and another night suffering the elements, Eliza prayed with every painful step that they would reach their intended destination before her burning legs buckled beneath her. Thomas believed that the Redcoats would close in on them if they didn't continue moving, so they journeyed as fast as their weary bodies would take them. The continuous scraping sensation against her heels made her hands shake and she promised her bleeding feet that once they reached Sandwich, she would never walk again. For the rest of her blessed life.

As she trudged across the soggy ground, crunching leaves with every step, her thoughts somehow always found their way to the man at her side. And the man that wasn't. Thomas and Samuel were similar to a degree. Both were handsome, strong in body and mind, and cared for those around them. Each held strong to their beliefs and were valiant in their respective causes.

Then again, the two men could not be more different.

She lifted her skirts to avoid a stagnant puddle and stepped around it. Still, she would like to believe they could be friends. After Samuel learned what Thomas had done in protecting them, how could they not be? But her conscience told her that despite their common interest in keeping her and Kitty safe, those two men would be enemies.

Eliza peeked at Thomas who walked a few paces ahead, his cloak draping his broad shoulders, and her insides performed a pirouette. She had to put a hand on her middle. She shouldn't be thinking about him, studying the lines of his face when he wasn't looking, memorizing the color of his hair and the shape of his smile. Not when Samuel waited on her answer.

But she couldn't help it.

Such close proximity to undeniable masculinity and gentleman-like manners made it impossible to focus on anything else.

A grin teased her lips at the memory of the mysterious emotion that had flitted across Thomas's face when she'd said she wasn't engaged. What was it? Surprise? Amusement? Whatever it was, it vanished as soon as it appeared. What made her think he cared about such a thing? She and Kitty were nothing more than a responsibility to him. It would serve her well to remember that.

"Good news, weary travelers." Thomas stopped and turned. "We are very near to Sandwich now—only about two miles. But before we make our way straight into town, I need to make sure it's safe and that no Redcoats are there, already looking for us."

"What would you have us do?" Eliza asked.

"I need you to wait here. I won't be long. I promise to return before sundown."

Kitty laughed and sat beneath a large oak, closing her eyes and resting her head against the trunk. "I'm more than happy to rest. My only concern is whether my legs will be able to move again once they've stopped."

Both Eliza and Thomas chuckled and exchanged shy smiles.

His gaze pinned her feet to the ground. A nervous excitement bubbled in her chest and suddenly she didn't know what to do with her hands. She looped them tight around her waist.

He came to her, standing closer than he ever had before. His eyes, pools of deep blue, roamed her face and Eliza's lungs refused to function.

His low, honey-like voice melted around her. "Will you be all right while I'm gone?"

Eliza forced her lashes upward and her heart patted wildly against her ribs. The lines around Thomas's caring eyes deepened, causing her legs to grow weak. Why did he have to be so kind?

"We'll be just fine. Thank you, Mr. Watson."

He lingered, still searching her face. The world around Eliza slowed as she lost herself in his nearness.

Without warning he moved away a step and looked around.

Eliza did the same, shaking her hands at her sides. How silly to get absorbed in such a moment. She must be more weary than she thought.

Looking around, Thomas gave instructions. "Stay in this spot until I get back. If for some reason you should need me, follow this path through the trees and it will lead you into town."

Eliza nodded.

"Tell Kitty as well, before she sleeps, in case anything should happen."

"I will. Don't worry." Eliza hoped he caught her reassuring tone, instead of her doubt. "We'll be fine."

He looked back at the trail before once again turning Eliza's insides to mush with his penetrating stare. "I wish I didn't have to leave you, but I can't take any chances and lead you into danger. You're sure you'll be all right?"

Eliza nodded. "I promise."

Thomas took long strides along the familiar path, trying to put the feathers in his stomach to rest. Eliza could cast quite a spell. The closer he got to town the harder he tried to focus on something—anything but her.

He chuckled. His good friend Doctor Nathaniel Smith would surely have a good laugh when he found out Thomas was now in charge of caring for two women. He'd prepared to provide only for himself. Now, at least for the near future, he had Eliza and Kitty to think about.

Eliza.

The memory of her gentle features and the song of her laugh formed a grin on his lips. Then another memory took the stage of his mind and he couldn't stop his fists from forming. Who was the blackguard who had asked for her hand? Did he even love her? Did she love him? If she did, he was a fortunate fellow indeed.

Just as his foolish imaginations began to run away with him, he rounded the last corner and his home came into view. Checking around the outside and inside of the house to see that all was safe, Thomas exhaled a heavy sigh of relief. Before he went into town he walked through each room, inspecting it and making a quick inventory of all he had, and the things he may need now that he had two women to care for. They would at least require clothes of their own and whatever other mysterious items a woman's needs demanded. Scratching the back of his neck, he huffed. He'd have to think of what to do about that ...

He took another moment and looked around him. Masculine pride welled like a rising sea. This was a good, solid home. One he crafted and filled with his own capable hands. The parlor was small, but nothing to scoff at. The large fireplace sat agape, ready to devour the pile of logs that was stacked behind the house. Upstairs were two fair sized rooms, each with a feather bed and a chest of drawers. What would Eliza think of—

He stopped and shook his head again, harder this time. Fool. She would think nothing of it compared to the fine home she'd lived in all her life—the home she would return to when this horror ended.

Thomas left and quickly made his way to town. Bustling markets, shops, and taverns dotted the street. Men and women milled about, paying him no attention whatsoever. His arms and hands relaxed somewhat and it was only then he realized his fists had been clenched.

Upon seeing no red uniforms, he ventured deeper into the small city, continually reminding himself that Eliza and Kitty should not be left alone any longer than absolutely necessary.

As he walked down the main street, a new mercantile shop beckoned him. He halted and peered through the window. How could he resist? His chest and shoulders buzzed with the urge to hurry, but he resisted. The women needed supplies. He strode in, intent on buying fabric for Eliza and her sister. Time was valuable, but he hoped this small offering would be well received. They would want to make themselves new dresses and it was the least he could do for all the trouble he'd caused them.

The proprietor helped him pick out all the items the girls would need for their craft, since Thomas had no idea about the tools a woman used for sewing.

"What fabrics would they fancy?" The stout old man asked from behind the counter.

Thomas ran his fingers through his hair and shrugged as he stared at the stack of various colors and patterns. A laugh bubbled through him. "I haven't the slightest idea."

"Well," the man continued, winking over his spectacles. "May I suggest this lovely purple batwing or this soft blue floral? These fabrics seem to be popular with the ladies in town."

Thomas nodded, his shoulders suddenly lighter. "I'll take it."

When he left the shop, the bundle of fabrics and accouterments under his arm, a familiar voice called to him from behind.

"Thomas! Greetings to you, my good friend!"

Thomas stopped and turned. A large smile warmed him from his face to his feet. "Nathaniel!"

The tall, broad-shouldered doctor met Thomas with friendly eyes, his suit immaculate as always. Nathaniel's wide smile, brown hair, and chiseled features attracted countless women, but it was his indomitable personality that men and women alike admired and were constantly drawn to. He and Thomas shook hands before exchanging a hearty embrace.

Nathaniel Smith knew Thomas just as well as anyone. In fact, at times Thomas believed Nathaniel knew him better than Thomas even knew himself.

"I never received word that you were coming to town. What brings you back this way?" Nathaniel asked. "I hadn't expected you for some time." He raised one brow and his mouth tipped sideways as he glanced up and down Thomas's clothes. "Have you been sleeping in the dirt, or did you just forget to change your clothes for a week?"

The attempt at humor couldn't penetrate the thick anxiety covering Thomas's usually amiable nature. He didn't answer, only tightened his lips. Nathaniel was the only person he'd confided in about Martin's blackmail, and his friend's trust had been a source of strength and encouragement more than a few times.

Nathaniel stopped with a jerk, his eyes widening. "Something's happened—I can see it in your face." He lowered his voice and peered up and down the street. "Perhaps it would be wise for you to stay with me while we determine—"

"Things have changed slightly since we last talked," Thomas said.

Nathaniel tilted his head. "Continue."

"I'm already behind schedule as it is. I have only a few seconds to explain." Thomas moved out of the street beside the mercantile. Nathaniel followed close behind.

"I'm not actually here alone." Thomas motioned to the package under his arm. "I have two women traveling with me."

"Really?" Nathaniel whispered back, raising the corners of his mouth and slapping his hand on Thomas's shoulder. He looked at him, his white teeth shining through his smile. "I can't wait to hear this. I have a feeling it's going to be good."

Chapter Nine

The two sisters lounged on the damp ground under a few gnarled oaks. Eliza's legs throbbed as she massaged them, carefully avoiding her injured feet. She'd attend to them later.

Thomas left hours ago. The daylight began to fade, but still the sky was bright enough to illuminate their surroundings. She could only hope he would return before the light disappeared completely, forcing them to walk the last two miles in the dark.

"How will we know when it's safe to go back home?" Kitty asked, her hands resting in her lap.

Eliza could hear the fear in Kitty's voice and pumped strength into her own. "I don't know. I've been wondering the same." She paused and continued kneading her legs. "God will provide. He already has. I know He sent Mr. Watson to protect us. I'm going to try and send word to Samuel as soon as possible. I'm certain he'll—"

Eliza stopped, the hairs on her arms stood rigid. Something rustled in the trees and bushes in front of them.

She looked at Kitty to see if she'd heard it too, but the relaxed appearance on her sister's tired face told her she hadn't. Thank the Lord.

"He'll what, Liza?"

"Oh, nothing. I don't even remember what I was

saying. Not to worry, Kitty. Just rest." Eliza focused on her breathing, attempting to calm the rapid beat of her heart.

They were being watched.

Every nerve in Eliza's body jolted, making her stomach roll. She looked around, realizing the sky had darkened almost entirely now. The remaining light waved farewell at the edge of the faraway horizon. Night was upon them—and they were alone. An ominous feeling ballooned around her, thickening the air and making it hard for her to breathe.

The heavy, ragged footfall drew closer.

"Stand up." Eliza whispered at Kitty.

"What is it?" she asked as Eliza pulled her to her feet.

Just then, two large men emerged from their covering in the bushes. They were sailors—not soldiers. And from the way they swayed on their feet it was obvious they were drunk.

Eliza pushed Kitty behind her, her protective instincts working at a zealous pace.

The taller of the two men inspected them, a lecherous smile crawling over his scruffy face, while the other looked around them.

Kitty clutched the back of Eliza's cloak and moved closer.

"What are you two pretty ladies doing out here in the dark? You alone?" The tall one walked closer and sneered, chuckling.

"No." *Forgive me for lying, Lord.* "Our brother will be back any moment."

Her voice shook as much as her legs. She hoped they didn't notice.

Kitty found Eliza's hand. Gripping it with ferocious strength, she whispered into Eliza's ear.

"What do we do?"

"Pray."

"What will they do to us?"

Eliza could only grip Kitty's hand tighter, for answering such a question would make Kitty faint dead away.

The lanky sailor crept nearer. "Your brother is a fool to leave you out here, in the middle of a dark, scary forest all by yourselves." He gave a dramatic frown, followed by a nauseating smile, exposing what few teeth were left in his mouth.

The second man closed in. "This must really be our lucky day, Roy." His slurred speech oozed lasciviousness.

Roy chuckled. "It must be, Lee." His voice was deep and his breath so foul Eliza had to bite her cheek to keep from gagging.

Her racing heartbeat drummed from her head to the ground beneath her feet. She knew what they wanted and the thought made the forest swirl.

Lee limped over to Kitty and yanked her from behind Eliza, then pet her arm up and down. The terrified look on Kitty's face made tears burn in the back of Eliza's eyes. *I cannot fail her, Lord. I cannot fail her like I did Peter. Please help me.*

"We've been needing some company." Lee chuckled and glanced at Roy, then turned his ugly face back to Kitty. "You're not scared of two lonely old sailors like us, are you?"

Dear Lord, have mercy! Help me protect Kitty!

Eliza reached over and squeezed her sister's arm, keeping her eyes on the criminals in front of them. Releasing her grip on Kitty, Eliza walked closer to them, smiling as enticingly as she knew how. Bile surged in her stomach and threatened to escape her throat but she willed it away.

"Should we be scared?" she answered, looking up at the tall sailor.

"Eliza, what are you—"

Eliza interrupted her sister with a brief warning glance over her shoulder.

"Not in the least, little lady." Roy stepped forward, closing the last few inches that separated them. He slipped his lanky arm around her waist and pulled her to him. "You're that kind, are you?" He sneered, then gave a low rumbling laugh.

The other man went toward Kitty who stood frozen, her face stark white.

"No!" Eliza cried, her voice betraying her cover. She prayed for composure and took a few deep breaths. "Not her. You can do what you like with me, but leave her alone."

"There's two of us and two of you. Why would we do that?" Roy asked, holding her tighter and moving his possessive hand down the side of her body.

The acrid odor of ale and the stench of urine from his clothes assaulted her. Eliza's stomach lurched at the feel of his body near hers.

Summoning every ounce of quaking courage within her, she moved her hand up his chest and pouted. "Can't we just have all the fun? I don't feel like sharing."

Water welled in her eyes. The only way to keep Kitty safe was to distract these sailors with herself. *Anything to keep Kitty safe.*

Eliza peered at Kitty. Her sister remained motionless, her eyes round and dripping tears.

"I don't care if you don't, Lee," Roy said.

"I'd rather not have to fight to get what I want anyway."

Eliza tasted acid in her mouth. She was sure she would retch at any moment. She pleaded with the Lord to send Thomas back right away—before her life changed forever.

Roy moved closer, sniffing her neck then letting out a long whistle. He bent down again and whispered in her ear. “I’m looking forward to this.”

Both men howled with delight.

Roy pushed her ahead of them. They walked a few paces into the darkness of the trees, talking of such vulgar things Eliza knew she would go to hell just from hearing them.

I only want to protect Kitty, Lord. And I am willing to suffer anything for her, but please, please don’t let them do this!

“You going stay here and wait until we’re through?” Lee stopped and laughed, turning to where Kitty had been.

She was gone.

Faster!

The feeling that had haunted him for the past several minutes, now came with greater fervency. Hollowness settled in his gut and his leg muscles tensed.

Go faster!

Thomas couldn’t ignore the terrible anxiousness any longer. He ran. Something wasn’t right. He needed to get back to them. The package he carried under his arm scolded him. If only he’d waited to buy the fabric, he could have been there by now.

The impression came yet again and he quickened

his pace, jumping over logs and ducking under branches as he flew across the path.

Soon the sound of someone running reached him. And the sound of crying. His heart leaped into his throat.

Only the slightest sliver of light remained, leaving the forest around him dark. He could barely make out the silhouette of someone coming toward him.

"Mr. Watson!"

"Miss Katherine!"

Her terror-stricken face, evident even in the dim light, sent chills over his body.

"Mr. Watson! Mr. Watson, help us!" She cried and reached for him, her fingers gripping him like ropes of iron.

His back and arms cramped as he grabbed her by the shoulders. "What's wrong? What's happened?" He looked around and his breath caught. "Where's your sister?"

She trembled under his fingers, so winded she could hardly speak. "They have her! They have her!"

"Who? Soldiers?" He gripped tighter.

"Not soldiers. Two men . . . they took her . . ." Kitty tried to continue, but couldn't.

"Where did they take her?"

She pointed in the direction of where they'd been waiting.

Thomas gripped her elbow and ran, his heart pumping so fast his ribs shook.

It took less than a minute to reach the place he'd left them earlier that day. There was no sign of Eliza. Or anyone else.

"Liza!" Kitty cried, wrapping her arms round her.

Thomas scanned the area, searching for anything that might give him a clue, but he saw nothing.

A piercing scream split the air sending an icy shiver over his back. When it came again another second later both he and Kitty dashed in the direction of the sound.

In seconds, the horrifying scene came into view.

Eliza lay on the ground, one large man crouching in front of her, while a second knelt behind her, his knees on her outstretched arms, holding her down. The fat savage by her legs fumbled with her skirts as she struggled to get free. He cussed at her to keep quiet and stay still.

Thomas's body nearly split in two as hot rage shot down his spine. He dropped the package and burst into the small clearing. Lunging at the larger man, he yelled with barbaric volume. His veins pumped fire. He plowed into the fat man's torso, sending both of them flying and landing in a tangled heap.

The man's meaty build flexed beneath Thomas's body. The attacker fought back, but his efforts were vain. The sorry excuse for a man didn't stand a chance. Not after what he tried to do to Eliza.

As Thomas prepared to strangle the assailant, Eliza screamed again. This time, two octaves higher. Keeping his hands on the fool's neck, he whipped his head around and saw the other man stretched out on top of her. Eliza tried to wrench away, but her attacker pinned her down.

Thomas pounded his fist into the sailor beneath him with the force of cannon fire. The crack of the man's jaw met with a terrible wailing and he stopped fighting to hold his face.

The other stranger grabbed a knife from the side of his belt and yelled as Eliza continued to writhe.

Bolting toward the struggle, Thomas skidded on his knees and lunged for the weapon, but the boney man turned toward Thomas at the last second, brandishing his dagger. Thomas stopped the man's arm with his hand just before the blade sliced his cheek.

Eliza struggled to free herself from underneath the fighting men, but was trapped beneath their weight. Thomas squeezed the man's wrist and twisted it with all his strength in an effort to make the man drop his knife on the ground.

The sailor's grip didn't loosen. But his stance did.

Before Thomas could stop him, the man pitched and fell forward with all his force onto Eliza, his knife slicing into her abdomen.

She screamed. A terrifying, ear-splitting sound.

Thomas froze.

Without thinking, he shoved the man off Eliza, the knife following him onto the ground. He grabbed the weapon, slippery from Eliza's blood, and plunged it into the man's chest.

A guttural moan ballooned around them before the soldier quivered and flopped motionless against the ground.

Thomas couldn't stop shaking. He just killed a man. *Forgive me, Lord. I only did it to protect us all.*

The fat one, whose jaw Thomas had broken, yelled something heinous as he stumbled about in the dark, away from the scene and out of sight.

Thomas flew to Eliza's side. Kitty did the same with uncontrollable sobs.

"Liza! Liza! Wake up!" she said, kneeling by her sister's bleeding body.

"Eliza!" Thomas crouched over her. *Dear God, please help her!*

She groaned and tried to push him away.

"Eliza, it's me, Thomas. I won't hurt you." His

voice cracked. His limbs shook.

Eliza's body went limp. Her head rolled to the side and her arms flopped to the ground.

Thomas reached for the lifeline in her neck. A soft beating nudged his fingers. *Thank you, Lord!* He pulled away to check the rest of her.

Her hair had come undone and lay tangled across her neck and face. Her cloak was missing and the skirts and petticoats she wore were ripped.

He touched her body, talking to her in gentle tones as he worked to find where she had been injured. A warm liquid pumped from her torso through her stays.

"Is she dying?" Kitty wept.

"I don't know." He ripped the bodice of her dress and using the same knife, cut off her stays.

Kitty knelt beside him. "What are you doing?"

"I need to stop the bleeding." He rent a large section of Eliza's already tattered petticoat and wrapped it around her tiny waist, then carefully placed his own jacket around her shoulders for warmth. He prayed the bandage would hold back the surging flood long enough for him to get her the proper care she needed.

Please, Lord Almighty. Don't let her die!

Thomas picked up Eliza as carefully as he could manage. "We must get to town as quickly as possible. I have a friend who is a doctor he'll . . . he'll know how to help her." *I hope.*

He continued to speak to Eliza as they dove through the dark, though he knew she couldn't hear him. Her slender, limp body rested in his arms and an animal-like urge to keep her alive raged through him. Eliza's limbs and head flopped and swayed with his movements. Was she already dead? No. She couldn't be. God wouldn't let her die. Not now.

"Miss Katherine, tell me what happened. Who were those men?"

She started crying again at the question and took several seconds to answer. "I don't know. They came from nowhere." She wept louder. "Eliza knew right away what they wanted. She . . . she offered herself, to keep them away from me."

Thomas prayed like he'd never prayed before. *Lord, please spare this remarkable woman.*

They reached the clearing that led to his house just as his legs were ready to burst. Once on the stoop, he kicked open the door. Racing up the stairs, he plowed into the largest room.

He placed Eliza on the bed as if she were made of glass.

"Whose house is this?" Kitty asked, shaking.

"It's mine."

"Yours?"

"There's a candle on that table over there in the corner," he said. "Light it and bring it here."

Kitty obeyed and soon the glow of the lantern crawled over the bed and across the floor, revealing Eliza's gruesome state. Her dress was covered in dark red fluid from her legs to her neck.

He took the lantern from Kitty's trembling hands and set it on the stool next to the bed. The poor girl stood motionless, her hands assuming prayer position.

Thomas took her by the shoulders, speaking firm, but calm. "Kitty, I need you to keep constant pressure on Eliza's wound until I get back. Do you understand?"

Her eyes bulged. "Where are you going? You can't leave us here. She could die!"

"If I *don't* leave, your sister *will* die! I need to get the doctor."

Kitty looked ready to faint, but nodded and did as instructed.

Thomas reached Nathaniel's in mere minutes and explained the horror as they ran back to the house.

When they returned, Thomas found Kitty just where he'd left her. She sat on the bed next to her sister, pressing a wad of cloth on Eliza's wound. Kitty's hands and arms were covered in blood.

"How is she? Has she moved? Has she said anything?" Thomas questioned, taking quick strides to the bed.

Kitty only shook her head, tears still pouring over her face.

Thomas looked at Eliza's pale features and feared for the hundredth time that she wouldn't make it through the night.

Nathaniel flew to the other side of the bed and began his examination, taking over Kitty's job of covering the wound. His face scrunched and he mumbled something under his breath as he touched Eliza's neck.

"What? What is it?" Thomas snapped.

Nathaniel didn't answer.

"Well?" Thomas stepped closer.

Nathaniel untied the wrap around her middle and ripped open a large slit in her bloody chemise. The sound of the tearing fabric made Thomas shudder, remembering the sound of the dagger piercing her flesh.

He stared for the first time at the hole in Eliza's belly. The gash looked smaller than he'd imagined, but it bled like it was ten times its actual size. Nathaniel pressed a fresh wad of cloth into it.

Thomas clenched his fists. This should never have happened. He should have been there. He should have kept her safe.

Again Nathaniel mumbled, then turned urgent eyes at Thomas. "Help me get her out of these bloody clothes so I can tie a proper bandage around her."

Thomas's face slacked.

"Get over here! This is no time for modesty, Thomas. It will be safer for her if we both lift her," Nathaniel commanded.

Thomas didn't move. This might be life and death, but he still couldn't do such a thing.

Nathaniel shook his head and growled. "You." He pointed at Kitty. "Get over here and help me."

Thomas moved out of the way, then turned his face to the wall, running his trembling hands over his hair. "Is she dying?"

No answer. Nathaniel instructed Kitty when to lift Eliza, when to lay her down, and how to help him tie the bandages.

"Nathaniel! Answer me!"

"Thomas, she needs a shirt. Now." Nathaniel's voice remained calm but acute.

Thomas flew to the dresser, careful to keep his gaze away from the bed, and yanked out one of his own. Keeping his gaze to the floor, Thomas held the shirt to Nathaniel.

Nathaniel snatched it from his hand. "I wish you wouldn't worry about propriety at a time like this."

Thomas ignored him and continued staring at the back of the room, biting the inside of his cheek and praying.

"She's decent, Thomas. You can turn around now."

Thomas spun on his heel, holding his breath.

Eliza wore his shirt and a blanket covered her lower half. Her hair remained disheveled and her sweet face looked gray. Blood still covered her chest and neck.

"I'm still waiting for an answer, Nathaniel. Is she dying?"

"I don't know!" Nathaniel shot back, holding Eliza's wrist between his fingers. "Only time will tell us that. Though I will tell you it could have been a lot worse. It appears that the knife missed her vital organs, otherwise there would be no hope for her at all."

Thomas remained at the end of the bed, staring at the painful sight before him. He turned toward Kitty who stood near the table in the corner, her bloodstained hands covering her face as she cried.

"Nathaniel, that wound was deep. Why didn't you stitch it?"

"I could have, but I chose not to. Stitches can sometimes make such injuries worse. As it is you'll have to monitor her wound carefully, and often." Nathaniel wiped his red hands on another cloth. "It's better to leave it as it is."

"Tell me what to do." Thomas's voice shook when he spoke. All attempts to remain composed failed.

"Try and stop the bleeding. It's not flowing as forcefully as it was, from the looks of things, but she is by no means out of danger. She cannot afford to lose any more blood."

Nathaniel rose, his mouth tight.

"What is it? Tell me!" Thomas yanked on his arm.

Nathaniel glanced at him, his eyes holding a critical edge. "She needs our prayers."

He walked away from the bed and lowered his voice. "I shouldn't give you false hope. I can't pretend that her situation isn't very grave. These types of wounds don't . . . they don't . . ."

He didn't finish. He didn't have to. Thomas knew exactly what he meant. The news came as little surprise, but it still made his knees buckle.

Nathaniel continued, staring at Eliza. "If she develops a fever, or the wound begins to look gangrenous, call for me at once. If she—I mean, *when* she wakes up, keep her in bed as long as you can. Try to give her broths and other fluids to keep her strength up. Change the dressings as often as necessary."

Thomas blinked and nodded in response, trying to keep the whirlwind of emotions from stealing the last bit of strength from his limbs.

With a gentle squeeze to Thomas's shoulder, Nathaniel softened his words. "You did your best, Thomas. It's not your fault."

Thomas clenched his teeth and exhaled loudly. "They tried to have their way with her."

Nathaniel growled low. "Did they succeed?"

Running both his hands over his head, Thomas peered at Kitty before answering. The poor girl looked tortured, her entire body shivering.

"I don't know, though I feel certain they didn't. But the fact that they tried, that they were so close . . ." He blinked his burning eyes. "If I'd have been there this never would have happened." He breathed harder at the memory of those men on top of her. Killing that man didn't seem like a harsh enough punishment.

"Did they get away?" Nathaniel asked.

"One of them did. I killed the other."

Nathaniel's hands flopped to his sides and his jaw dropped. "You did what?"

"I had to." Thomas strained to keep the volume out of his voice. "He tried to kill me and may have even killed Eliza! What choice did I have?"

Nathaniel wagged his head and wiped his palm over his eyes. "I'm not blaming you. Anyone would have done the same, but you know what this means, don't you? That man's body will be found, and when it is, people will be looking for who did it."

"I don't care. My only concern is to keep Eliza and her sister safe, at any cost."

"If you're lucky," Nathaniel continued, "the other man will simply move on and you can lay low to avoid the soldiers, just as you intended to do. But if he doesn't, and he tells of this ordeal, you might have to stay in hiding much longer than you thought."

With a groan, Thomas looked at the ceiling. Nathaniel was right, but at this moment that was the least of his concerns.

"I'll return in the morning," Nathaniel said, patting his arm.

Thomas moved his gaze to the dying woman in his bed. "Will she make it 'til morning?"

Nathaniel whispered his answer. "Pray, Thomas. Just pray."

Pain remained constant.

Eliza tried to move, tried to escape the agony, but something held her motionless. She wanted to cry out for help, but her mouth refused to move.

Where is Kitty? Is she all right?

The agony surged through her again—pulling, ripping, charging.

Then, she felt nothing. A sweet peaceful rest enveloped her.

Suddenly the war for life plunged upon her again. Then nothing.

Am I dying? Lord, I'm not ready to die!

Quiet commotion surrounded her, and she sensed a devoted presence always at her side. But nothing could calm the storm of misery that raged within her.

She burned, then shivered. Her muscles convulsed as if to crush her very bones.

She had to give up. How much longer could she fight a losing battle? Finally, her strength surrendered.

In a slow, easy motion, all her pain and worry evaporated into a beautiful calm. She opened her eyes and realized that every ounce of misery had gone from her body.

Next to her bed stood Father. He looked young and strong. Not like he had when she'd seen him in his last moments, so weak and thin. A radiating light surrounded him, and when he smiled, a peaceful warmth burned in her chest.

The longing for his nearness crashed upon her. She reached for him. He took her hand, the love in his eyes penetrating her from head-to-toe. Eliza started to get up, to be next to him, to embrace him, but he leaned forward and placed his hand on her shoulder.

"Your mother and I miss you, dearest. And Peter too. However, your time has not yet come."

Eliza tried to speak, but the words she formed were silent. Peter? Peter missed her? Did that mean he'd forgiven her for what she'd done? She shook her head in confusion.

Father smiled. The tenderness from his gaze once again pierced her heart. "You are not responsible for Peter's death. Do not deride yourself for decisions of the past. God called him home. It was his time. Now you must give God your pain. He will carry it." He gripped her hand tighter. "Eliza, be wise. The choices you make for your future are paramount. God's work for you is not finished, my dear. You have much yet to do."

Again Eliza opened her mouth, ready to protest, to break loose a flurry of questions. What choices would she have to make? What work did God have for her to do?

Father kissed her fingers then released his hold and stood straighter, and it was then Eliza realized she could see straight through him. He smiled. "We will be with you, waiting for you, my sweet. We love you."

No! Don't go, Father, please!

He winked, the way he used to do when he couldn't give Eliza the answers she wanted. "Follow your path of peace, Eliza. Follow what you believe."

I don't know what I believe!

His tenor voice wrapped around her as the vision of him disappeared. "Find the truth, and the truth shall make you free."

No, Father, don't leave me! She tried to call after them, but no sound emerged. She wanted to raise her arms and reach for him, but her heavy limbs remained still. *Let me come with you!*

"Noooo!" She heard someone from a great distance. "Eliza, no!"

The voice was familiar, strong and knowing. So why did it sound so desperate? Powerful fingers wrapped around her shoulders. The voice continued its plea for her to stay.

"Liza, please! You can't leave me. I need you!" Another voice, more familiar than the first, rang with anguish.

Just when she thought her soul could rest and her war with death would cease, the torture fell upon her once again. But before it consumed her, she drifted into a blissful sleep.

"No! Eliza, no!" Thomas choked on his words, frantically feeling for a pulse.

Nothing.

Her chest no longer rose and fell. He leaned in, hoping to feel a slight movement, or hear the soft beating of her heart.

She can't die! Lord, please!

Kitty sat on the other side of the bed, begging the Lord to let her sister live.

After two days of tireless care-giving both he and Kitty were exhausted and their emotions unhinged. This was the moment. The moment where Eliza would live or die.

Thomas held her by the shoulders as he sat next to her lifeless frame. He looked into her white and vacant face, powerless to do anything more for her. Except pray.

"Eliza." He spoke quiet, still gripping her shoulders. "I don't know why, but I believe God has led you into my life." His throat swelled and tears trailed down his face and dripped from his chin. "If you live, I promise to make up for all the ways I've failed you."

Clenching his eyes shut, Thomas willed away the tears that continued to form and struggled to slaughter the words that rang in his head. *"You killed your mother, Tommy . . ."* He couldn't live knowing Eliza had died under his care.

As he prayed, the arms of the Lord wrapped around him. *Nothing has happened that I have not blessed. Have faith.*

Thomas shook his head. What about the soldiers chasing them? What about the men who did this to Eliza?

All things work together for the good of those who love me. Vengeance is mine.

A soft moan floated to his ears. His eyes shot open and the hope he'd been suspending draped around him like the arms of an angel. Eliza's head moved slightly and she let out another small whimper.

"Eliza!" Kitty breathed.

He locked his gaze with Kitty's red-rimmed eyes.

God had given them a miracle.

Eliza was going to live.

Chapter Ten

Samuel walked by the bustling wharf, studying the map of Boston in his hand as they went door-to-door, still hoping that somehow luck would turn in their favor. Two more soldiers followed behind him and Donaldson, muskets on their shoulders. Rain pelted Samuel's face and a fierce wind struck his back. Boats of every shape and size bobbed in the choppy waters only three yards away. The mid-Autumn storm worked against him, just like everything else did.

"Are you sure you've checked this side of town well enough?" He yelled at Donaldson over the roaring gale before looking at the two other men. "This is a large city. They could be anywhere." The tension barreling through him carried into his tone. "You can't honestly make me believe that there are no signs of them at all!" Where was the passion that used to surround him—the drive that kept the world afloat? It seemed as if everyone and everything around him lacked the one thing he truly needed. Determination. Was he the only one who cared what happened to Eliza?

"We have done our utmost," Donaldson replied, holding his hat to his head as the wind tried to snatch it. He looked irritated, but held whatever reservations he had within him. Smart man. "Of course we will continue to look for them, but I do believe all of the men you've put to work have checked every building and home in town. We've worked morning and night, Captain. We'll find them, sir. I know we will."

Samuel grunted as cold drops stung his face, his neck muscles twitching. He crunched the map in his fingers. "I did everything I could to get any usable information out of Watson's supposed uncle, but the man is as dumb as he is fat. And now I've been forced to let him go. What a waste."

Samuel pointed at the next house and then to the soldiers behind him. They nodded and marched forward to do his bidding. He turned back to Donaldson as the wind yanked at his cloak. "I want you to tell Officer Clark and the other men to go north and search in Salem."

"Excuse me, sir."

Irritated, Samuel spun to see Clark standing behind him, his boyish face looking dwarfed under his dripping white wig. "Clark, where did you come from? You're just the man I wanted to see. I need you to—"

"Pardon me, Captain, but—"

"But what?" Samuel barked.

Clark refused to meet his gaze. "Major Stockton wishes you to meet him at his quarters, sir."

"Why?"

"Something about the rebels. He says it's urgent."

Blast it! It was always about the rebels. Didn't Stockton know he was dealing with them in his own way? Watson was a rebel of the worst kind. Why did he have to be bothered with these things now? Eliza's faraway cries kept him up every waking minute. He couldn't rest, couldn't think clear until she was found. And now he had to be interrupted with this?

"Tell him I'm on my way."

Clark turned, but Samuel stopped him. "When I'm done there, meet me in my office. I've got an assignment for you."

With a sharp bow, Clark headed into the wind toward the other side of town.

Turning once again to Donaldson, Samuel continued, pretending he hadn't had to endure the untimely interruption. "After my meeting with Stockton, you will come with me. I can't stay in this blasted town any longer or I'll run mad."

Donaldson held his mouth rigid as if he were trying to hold back a retort. "If I may, Captain. Where will you and I be going?"

Samuel squinted his eyes into the pelting drops, looking past the endless boats and beyond the rolling hills. "We're going south."

Thomas stayed by Eliza's side day and night, hardly taking any time to care for his own basic needs. Eating was a trial. Sleeping was a burden. Every move she made, every sound that escaped her pale lips made his heart leap, hoping that maybe today would be the day she would open her brown eyes and look at him.

The autumn weather sent cool rains that pounded without end, increasing Thomas's sense of helplessness. There was no bright sunlight to warm the cold that seeped not only through his clothes, but through his heart. No happy rays to bring cheer to a cheerless place. He wanted nothing more than to take Eliza's pain for her, to turn back time and do things differently.

Kitty offered to relieve him, at least for an hour or so, but he declined. He was the cause of Eliza's pain, and insisted that he would be the remedy. She would wake any day now, he was sure of it, and prayed for it without end. When that blessed moment arrived, he wanted to make sure his face was the first thing she saw.

A few times Eliza called out, delirious with pain. She developed a fever not long after her attack, just as Nathaniel feared. One minute, she was hot as fire. The next, a pool of sweat. Thomas never experienced anything so terrifying.

He mopped her brow endlessly and moved the few strands of dampened hair from her soft face. His moments alone with her gave him ample time to observe the shape of her eyes, the length of her lashes, the perfect curve of her lips. He found himself mesmerized by the delicate mole adorning her cheekbone and noted how it intensified her beauty.

His face flushed every time her wound needed dressing. Even though she always remained properly covered, her shape and form under the coverings could not be denied. The bleeding had stopped and thanks to proper care and healing herbs, no gangrene or other illnesses assaulted her.

"Kitty?"

Thomas jerked forward at the sound of Eliza's dry voice and cupped his large hands around her trim fingers. "Eliza, 'tis I, Thomas."

She didn't open her eyes, only moved her head from side-to-side and called for Kitty again.

He leaned in closer, wanting desperately to stroke her face. Instead, he held his hands tighter around hers to keep from caressing her soft skin. Doing such a foolish thing would only increase his already budding feelings. Feelings he shouldn't have.

"Eliza, it's Thomas. What do you need?" He spoke low, hoping it would help calm her distress.

Her eyebrows pinched into a deep V, her breathing erratic. Thomas held his breath. She must be in a great deal of pain.

Keeping his grip on her hands, he looked over his shoulder and called toward the open door. "Kitty! Eliza is calling for you!"

Within seconds, Kitty's light step raced up the stairway.

When she rushed to the bed, Thomas released his grip on Eliza and sat back in his chair, reluctant to give up his perch. Kitty sat on the bed and held Eliza's hand just the way he had done.

Her frantic gaze washed over her sister. "Liza. Liza, I'm here." She touched her face. "You're safe now, don't worry. What do you need?"

Eliza's feature's relaxed and her head slumped into the pillow, her body engulfed again by sleep.

Kitty patted her sister's fingers and moved away from the bed. She stared, her lips thin, her eyes blinking away glistening tears.

The thrill of hearing Eliza's voice nourished Thomas's weary soul with a much-needed boost of hope. But such hope refused to linger when reality shuffled near. He should have let Kitty be at Eliza's side. She needed her sister, needed to hear her voice and know that Eliza wanted her.

"I'm sorry." Thomas stepped forward and rested his hand on her arm. "She'll wake again. I'm sure of it. Would you like to sit by her for a while?"

Kitty looked up. Her mouth formed a small O and she exhaled. "I would indeed. Thank you."

Thomas motioned for her to take the chair. Once seated, Kitty leaned into the bed like a cold child leans toward a fire.

He backed up, taking slow steps before turning around and heading down the stairs. There were many beneficial things about taking a break. He could eat, clean up, and maybe even sleep.

But he did none of those things.

Thomas slumped into his large upholstered chair in front of the blazing fire and wiped his hands down his face, trying to locate the source of his turmoil. It was a miracle she'd spoken, let alone survived such an attack. So why must his stomach ache and twist?

How selfish he'd been. He'd wanted to be by her side when she awoke, but of course Kitty deserved that right. However, he promised himself, he wouldn't give up his position at her side permanently. He had a right to be there, of course, seeing as how it was his duty to see she was cared for.

Thomas pressed out of the chair and walked to the fire, resting his hands against the mantel. Why was there still such emptiness within him? Why the gnawing in his gut? He shook his head and exhaled through his nose as he accepted the root of his angst.

It was Kitty's name Eliza had spoken.

Not his.

Chapter Eleven

Eliza stirred. The pain in her middle burned and the ache vaulted through her entire body. She needed water.

Pulling open her heavy eyelids, Eliza tried to focus on what surrounded her. A dark wood beamed ceiling, a candle on a table near the far wall, fire crackling in a small fireplace. The smell of warm air mixed with a fresh cool breeze danced in the room around her. Heavy, comforting blankets covered everything but her arms and head.

With great effort she turned her gaze. On one side of the bed, several feet from where she lay, was a wall with a large window. Rain dripped a kindly rhythm from the slightly open pane.

She eased her head in the other direction. A male figure slumped in an uncomfortable-looking position in a chair beside the bed. His chest moved up and down with deep breaths and his eyes were closed.

What happened? Why was she in bed? Suddenly the overpowering need for water accosted her again. When she tried to speak only a frail murmur emerged.

Her lids dropped again, feeling heavy and scratching her eyes. As if from afar, a gentle voice spoke.

"Eliza?"

A large gentle hand swept across her head.

"Did you say something? What do you need?"

She couldn't respond. It took ages to gather enough strength to raise her eyelids a second time. When her vision finally cleared, she focused on the bluest eyes she'd ever seen. The familiar face hovering over her carried a worried-like smile.

An extra ounce of strength stormed through her at the realization of who stared back at her—his touch so caring and his voice so soothing.

Thomas.

She tried to smile, wanting to show her gratitude for his company, but again the extreme thirst that plagued her begged for relief.

"Water." Her voice sounded so hoarse she didn't recognize it.

Thomas jumped to his feet, going to the pitcher on the back table. He returned seconds later, water glass in hand.

"Let me help you," he said.

The melody of his deep, resonating voice reached into her and stroked away another layer of fear and confusion.

He tucked his hand under her head and lifted her just enough as he held the cup to her lips. She reveled in the feel of his gentle strength.

The sip of liquid coated her dry throat, chasing away the bitter palate in her mouth.

Thomas lay her head back down and placed the cup on a small stool at the side of the bed. The lines around his eyes deepened as he smiled, massaging away the worry etched into his face.

Her eyes followed his every feature. The dark whiskers on his cheeks and chin were long, enhancing the perfect shape of his jaw. Deep shadows under his eyes gave testimony to his constant vigilance. His thick black hair, still dutifully tied behind his head, peeked around his shoulders. If she wasn't so weak the temptation to reach up and test its softness might have been too much to overcome.

"Mr. Watson?" Again the need for water scratched her throat. "May I have another sip?"

He grinned and nodded, then repeated the assistance just as before and this time she emptied the entire glass. Never before had a glass of water been equivalent to pure heaven.

"Thank you." Her voice was still strained but it sounded more like her own.

"Of course."

Thomas breathed heavy as if he was trying to expel some kind of emotion. Eliza knew she'd been the cause of his sleepless nights and an all-consuming blame shook at her conscience.

"Mr. Watson, I'm so sorry."

Thomas straightened. His handsome face softened and he moved the chair closer to her bed. "First of all, please call me Thomas. I think we've been through enough to forego that kind of ceremony."

If she'd had enough strength, she would have laughed. "All right, Thomas." Somehow his name lifted off her tongue as if she'd said it all her life. And she liked it. She was liable to like it too much.

"Second," Thomas continued, "you have nothing for which to be sorry. I should be the one apologizing. Everything that's happened has been because of me."

The gentleness in his gaze and the intensity of his words made her stomach weightless. Eliza hardly knew what to say. It wasn't his fault. No one could have predicted what would happen.

"You look like you haven't gotten much sleep."

His eyes twinkled. "No, I haven't. Thanks to you."

Eliza lifted the corners of her lips in return. "I'll try and be more considerate next time."

She stopped. A surging panic raced over her. Where was Kitty?

"Kitty? Is she all right?" The words burst from her lips.

"She's fine." Thomas motioned with his head toward the open door. "In fact, she's been at your side most of the day. She's been busy caring for you as well, and has been *almost* as worried for you as I have been." He winked, before his tender gaze traveled over her face.

Eliza's weariness suspended as his stare turned the color of twilight.

"Where is she now?" Eliza tried to stay on subject and ignore the ridiculous thoughts that raged through her weary mind. She was simply too tired to think straight.

"She's downstairs making breakfast."

"How long . . . how long have I been sleeping?"

"Ten days."

Ten days. It felt like ten months.

"My stomach hurts." She went to touch it, but he stopped her hand.

"Be careful." He reached forward, his gentle fingers held hers for a moment longer than necessary before he laid her arm back by her side.

"Do you remember anything? Do you remember what happened?" The low timbre of his voice soothed her so. She didn't want him to stop talking.

Eliza inhaled little breaths and looked up at the

ceiling, trying to piece together the broken bits of memory. The heavy fog in her brain gathered again and nothing clear emerged.

"Only bits and pieces."

Thomas's head bowed and the muscles under the stubble on his face flexed. "I'm nearly positive they didn't take advantage of you." He kept his chin down and cleared his throat. "Am I right?" His eyes popped up with his last question and he swallowed.

The fatigue that toyed with her muscles made it impossible to stay awake, but she could tell from Thomas's impatient demeanor that he was desperate to know.

"Not to worry. I am safe." She formed a weak smile on her lips as the exhaustion pulled her deeper into the bed.

Thomas exhaled with an audible huff as a visible load lifted from his shoulders. He leaned back in his chair and smoothed his hands over his head. Did that mean he cared? He must surely or he would not have done all that he had in her behalf.

She surrendered to the assault that ravaged her body and closed her eyes. Thomas would never have feelings for her. She was nothing but a burden. Besides, Samuel was surely looking for them even now and would find them within the week. And once Samuel learned of the treatment Thomas had received he would find that wretched soldier and have him punished.

Blissful sleep drew around her like a curtain of black fog, while visions of a handsome face, kind eyes, and a generous spirit floated in her memory.

Though she may be nearly engaged to Samuel, there couldn't be any harm in dreaming about Thomas.

A smile twitched on her lips. No harm whatsoever.

They traversed twenty-five miles, searching every boarding house, every tavern.

Samuel hated how long it took. Almost two weeks passed since the night he found her missing. In his dreams Eliza called to him, and each day he awoke with renewed strength and resolve. Eliza's love pulled him to her. He would find her. No matter what.

His head throbbed and his muscles pleaded for mercy. He and Donaldson ate little and slept even less. Donaldson didn't complain, though Samuel saw the weariness in the gray circles that fringed his eyes. His reluctant companion had no choice but to obey orders. The man was a soldier and should expect to be tired and hungry.

They entered a small wayside town with only a few shops and a dreary looking tavern.

"We'll stop here for the night," Samuel said, dismounting. "Find a place to stable our horses and I'll order a hot meal."

"Right away, Captain." Donaldson also alighted off his horse, then led the animals away.

Inside the small tavern, several lanterns glowed and the few patrons looked up at him with indifference as he entered. An empty table near the back called to him. He wanted to be alone.

Samuel removed his cumbersome cloak and hat, then slumped into the hard chair, feeling almost grateful for the musty, sour air that filled the dingy room.

A circular woman with white hair approached his table.

"How can I be of service to you, sir?"

"I'm in need of a room and a hot meal for myself and another soldier."

Just then Donaldson entered, looked around the nearly empty establishment for only a moment before spotting Samuel.

"The horses are taken care of, Captain," he said, as he neared the table.

The old woman twisted her mouth in disgust as if she thought two British soldiers could only mean trouble.

Donaldson took off his hat and cloak. He nodded to the woman then took the chair across from Samuel, emitting an exasperated huff as he sat.

"We have only a Shepherd's Pie." The woman slanted one brow. "I do hope that will be satisfactory."

"That will be sufficient." Samuel's impatience mounted higher.

The woman put a hand on her large hip and turned to leave.

"And as I said—" Samuel stopped her with his comment and she turned back. "We'll be needing a room for the night."

"I heard you the first time," she snapped. "You're in luck. We've only one room left, but it's yours for the customary price."

Donaldson turned to her as she marched away. "Thank you."

Samuel leaned forward. "Don't thank her. You're a soldier. She should be thanking us for what we sacrifice for selfish colonists like her."

Reclining in the chair, Donaldson played with a bent fork that lay on the rough-hewn table. His lips tightened. “Did your mother never teach you about etiquette? She looked like she could use a kind word. I’m simply glad to be in a warm place, awaiting a warm meal, and a warm bed. That is all.”

“Well, don’t get used to it.” Samuel rubbed his aching knee. “It’s only for one night. We’ll be on the road again in the early morning.”

His companion poked the fork into the wood as his jaw muscles flinched. “Aye, Captain.”

At that moment the wrinkled woman tottered over to them with two large chargers overflowing with a sumptuous spread, each topped with a thick slice of bread.

Samuel hadn’t realized how ravenous he was until the smell of the juicy meal made him salivate.

He peered at Donaldson whose eyes were as large as the chargers themselves.

The innkeeper plunked the plates down. “I’ll be back with a jug of ale for you.”

The two of them devoured the delicious food as if it was the first meal they’d ever eaten. And their last.

Samuel was so consumed by his need to eat that he almost didn’t notice the man who staggered through the door.

“Greetings, Lee,” the innkeeper said, stepping away from the large fire in the back of the room. She wiped her hands on her stained apron.

“Good evening, Mrs. Langdon.”

“Where’s Roy?” she asked.

The fat fellow looked around the room and put a hand to his jaw.

Samuel swallowed his bite and rested his fork.

“He’s, uh, he’s not here.”

He sat at an empty table. The innkeeper poured him a large mug of ale. He gulped with greedy pleasure, then used his hand to dab his mouth.

"Truth be told, we ran into a few pretties a while back and . . ." The sailor looked around the room again. He locked eyes with Samuel and stopped talking. Casting his gaze back to Mrs. Langdon, he took another long drag out of his mug. "He's already at the wharf."

The woman's eyes narrowed and she tilted her head. She looked at Samuel, then back to the sailor.

"I see."

She went back to her chores by the fire, before seeing to the few other patrons scattered through the small room.

A few pretties? Samuel's pulse began to race. Could he have seen Eliza?

Samuel shook his head at the foolish thought and took another bite of food. Of course not. The low-life could be referring to any number of women.

Samuel took a swig of drink and gazed back at the sailor who leaned into the long table where he sat.

What am I thinking? I have to question him. Samuel had promised to explore every avenue, every path that could possibly lead him to his love. Eliza was in danger. She needed him to save her, to bring her home. He could only imagine the horrors she was being forced to endure. No doubt she prayed night and day for him to rescue her. It may be a gamble, but he had nothing to lose.

"Stay here." He pointed to Donaldson, scooting his chair away from the table. "I'll be right back."

Donaldson nodded and went back to his meal.

Samuel's heart punched his chest as a new hope built within him. He'd been inspired by this kind of optimism before, only to have his excitement dashed into pieces. This time, he believed that somehow luck would be in his favor.

When Samuel approached, Lee slid his face upward. "I have nothing to say to you." He sneered before turning back to his own large meal.

Samuel gripped the sword at his side to try and extinguish the embers that sparked at Lee's comment. "I'm looking for a young woman who's been kidnapped. I overheard you saying that you 'ran into a few pretties', as you put it. I need you to tell me about them."

The man didn't look up. "What's it to you?"

Samuel inspected the sailor. His stature was large, but more from fat than muscle. He picked at his food and only spooned the soft potatoes. That's when Samuel noticed that one side of his face was dark purple and swollen to a considerable size. His jaw was broken.

Standing taller, Samuel shifted his weight to the other foot. "Did you not hear what I said? A woman's been kidnapped. Two women to be exact. I need to know if perhaps the women you saw are the ones I'm looking for."

The sailor cranked his neck toward Samuel again, his face a tangle of hatred. "Sounds like you're a fool to me. Going after every wind of chance. Those *pretties* could have been anyone. How could they possibly be the ones you're looking for?"

Samuel's patience went bone dry. "Tell me now!"

"What's in it for me?"

Glaring, Samuel imagined all the glorious ways he could torture this man to get him to talk. He kept his answer simple. "You'll have the satisfaction of doing a good Christian act."

Lee laughed even louder now, then growled and swore under his breath as he put his hand to his enlarged jaw. "I want something in return for telling you what I know."

Samuel's own jaw ticked. "Such as?"

Lee's gaze went to Samuel's belt. "I want your pistol."

"Are you saying you want a hole in your head?" Samuel's arms twitched with raw anger at the gall of the man.

"No," he stated, before swiveling in his seat. He faced Samuel with scowling eyes. "I want your pistol. No pistol, no statement."

Blast!

Samuel clenched his fists and snarled. He couldn't arm the man and wouldn't be used by him either. His nostrils flared as he considered his options. Of course, he could always take the gun back after he'd gotten the information. Then again . . .

He scowled at the snarling sailor as his confusion and boiling anger reached excessive heights.

Another inner voice called like a wild animal in his brain. What if this man said nothing useful? What if he played him for a fool? But again, what if he did help? What if this man did know something that could lead him to his beloved?

He had to take the risk.

Samuel reached at his side and produced the weapon.

A glutinous chuckle emerged from the sailor as his fingers laced around it. "Perfect."

"Now tell me!" Samuel demanded, leaning in.

The man shoved the pistol into his belt and turned back to his meal. "I saw two women."

"I know that much already. What did they look

like? When did you see them?"

Lee looked up with a lecherous grin. "A bit over a week, I'd say. They looked like sisters and were far too beautiful for their own good. Dark hair and eyes. Soft skin . . ."

A storm surged in Samuel's muscles. The man's description was ambiguous but a nagging feeling told him it was Eliza. The thought of this man's hands going anywhere near her made Samuel strong enough to break every bone in the sailor's worthless body.

He grabbed the mug out of Lee's hand and whacked it against the man's already injured jaw. Lee flailed, falling out of his chair and onto the ground with a thud. He cried out like a wailing child and grabbed at his face.

The few other patrons scattered through the tavern jumped in their seats.

"You touched her?" he roared. "Get out! All of you!" Samuel motioned to the wide-eyed spectators.

"You can't tell them to leave!" Mrs. Langdon bellowed. "This is my—"

"I'll do as I please!"

At that instant Donaldson was at his side. Samuel whipped around, still holding the mug in his hand.

"What would you have me do, sir?" Donaldson's gaze dashed between Samuel, the man on the ground, and the mumbling crowd.

"Escort these lovely people outside and stay with them until I come to get you."

The room emptied as the patrons bumped between tables and chairs before scrambling out the front door.

"You too!" Samuel shouted, pointing at the innkeeper.

She glared, then huffed and mumbled fighting words under her breath. Donaldson ushered them out, prodding the small group like livestock and slammed the door behind him.

Silence swelled and matched the emptiness in his heart. Only the sailor's moaning and the crackling of the fire oscillated in the quiet room.

"You blackguard! You touched her!"

The man started blubbering. "Don't hit me again! It's not what you think!"

"Then you better begin talking. I've a mind to arrest you for assaulting a woman!"

Samuel crouched down and lifted Lee to his feet by his coat. He shoved him onto the table and pounded the mug down so hard the remaining drops of liquid sprayed out.

"You have three seconds!" Samuel thundered, leaning over him.

"All right!" Lee cried. He spoke as if the words couldn't come out fast enough. "They were alone when Roy and I found them. The older one said their brother would be back for them any minute, but we could tell she was lying about something. A few seconds later the man did arrive and started handling them rough, telling them they needed to get going and to stop cavorting with strangers. When we tried to help the poor girls, the man attacked us."

Samuel released his hold. That didn't seem like Thomas, but then again neither did kidnapping. "Go on."

Lee lifted onto his elbow from his semi-reclined position on the table. His clothes were covered with food. "Roy got out his knife to protect himself, but the man turned it on him. Killed him. I saw it with my own eyes."

Samuel straightened and thinned his eyes. "This man killed your friend? Was it he that broke your jaw?"

"Yes, sir." Lee still trembled.

"Is that all? Did you see where they went?"

"No. But that's not the worst of it."

Samuel's stomach dropped to the ground. What could be worse?

"Well?"

"In the ruckus, somehow the girl, the oldest one, she was stabbed too."

His stomach lurched from his feet to his throat. Eliza had been stabbed? Impossible. It was too horrid to be real.

"I don't believe you."

"It's as true as I'm living."

"Where was this?" Samuel asked.

"Two miles north of Sandwich."

Samuel looked away quickly doing the calculations in his head. From where they were it was about another thirty-five to forty miles away.

He took a step away from the table and ground his teeth.

This story had holes. How did he know this man was even telling the truth?

He didn't.

What was worse, he still didn't know if the woman was in actuality his Eliza. He could spend all this time following another dead trail and lose precious time.

Lee groaned when Samuel increased the pressure of his grip. "How well did you see these girls? Was there anything unique about them, any distinguishing features?"

"It was past sundown so there wasn't much light."

Lee turned his head and squinted his eyes. "I didn't see much of the young one, but the other girl had a small mole right here." He pointed at his left cheekbone and Samuel nearly vomited.

He pushed the man back down on the table and wrenched the gifted pistol from his belt, speaking only inches from the man's swollen face.

"Thank you for your help, but I'll be taking this."

Lee didn't seem to care. He cupped his cheek and lumbered off the table, then sunk into the nearest chair.

Samuel hurled out the door and into the shivering group.

He yelled at Donaldson. "Get the horses. We're leaving. Now."

Chapter Twelve

As the days passed and the decorated trees relinquished their dressings, Thomas could sense that Eliza continued to gain strength. He stayed at her side as much as he could, while still allowing Kitty her share of the care-giving.

Never had such a task brought more fulfillment. He helped her with every sip of broth, every small bite of bread. Ever so slowly, she spent more time awake, spoke with less strain, and even made a few attempts at teasing him. Her chocolate eyes, so round and deep, seemed to brighten more everyday. He pretended not to notice all the times she peeked at him when she thought he wasn't looking. Had he imagined the traces of longing that often shrouded her charming face? Perhaps.

She lay quiet most of the time, eyes closed, her chest making lazy movements up and down as she breathed. When she slept, Thomas read by her side, not wanting to disturb her, but ready at any moment to help should she need him.

A gentle tapping sounded on the front door downstairs.

Thomas stood from his perch, placed his book on the chair, then took quiet steps down the staircase.

He opened the door, already knowing who came to call. "Come in, Nathaniel. Good to see you."

"Good day, Thomas," Nathaniel boomed as he removed his cloak.

"Quiet, my friend, Eliza's sleeping."

Putting a finger to his lips, Nathaniel nodded.

Kitty hurried in from the kitchen, drying her hands on a checkered cloth. She bobbed her head and curtsied.

Thomas covered his mouth to keep from chuckling. He'd wondered how long it would take her to make an appearance. She always rushed in when Nathaniel arrived, and Thomas had a difficult time disguising his amusement. It was obvious Kitty found Nathaniel charming by the way her cheeks blushed and how quiet she was around him, when most of the time she had plenty to say.

Nathaniel bowed in a playful manner, making sure to keep his volume minimal. "Mademoiselle." He looked up and flashed his winning smile.

Thomas rolled his eyes.

Kitty's face flushed as she made another quick curtsy. She flashed an impish grin at both of them and went back to the kitchen, towel in hand.

"Don't play with her, Nathaniel." Thomas didn't say more until he was sure Kitty was out of earshot. "You'll break her heart before she has a chance to give it to you. Besides, you're too old for her."

"I'm not playing with anyone. And who are you calling old? I'm only a few years older than you." Nathaniel kept his eyes on the kitchen door and sighed before he shook his head and straightened. "I have to be myself, my friend. I can't help it if my good looks and charm makes those of the fairer sex swoon in my presence."

A grin he could not contain overtook Thomas's face. "Your humility amazes me."

"It should. With such a face one would expect a certain degree of pride, but I like to treat even a common looking fellow like yourself with the highest respect." He chuckled and pat Thomas on the back, then quickly turned solemn. "How's the patient? I know you said she's asleep, but I need to see how she's healing. Would now be all right?"

"Of course." Thomas motioned for Nathaniel to lead the way. "She's improving all the time, I'm happy to say."

Nathaniel let out a slight chuckle. "I bet you are happy."

"What do you mean by that?" Thomas protested, grabbing his arm and stopping him mid-stride on the stairs.

"Nothing." Nathaniel painted a look of bewilderment on his face. "But, I've been meaning to ask you, how would you feel about me, say, taking her around town once she's feeling up to it?"

A sudden fire burned inside Thomas. The muscles in his face began to twitch as he shot Nathaniel a glowering look. How dare his friend make such a comment?

Nathaniel tried to suppress a large grin. "That's what I thought." He laughed under his breath.

Thomas relaxed a bit and attempted a small grin of his own as his pulse cooled. "You're asking for trouble."

Nathaniel slapped him on the back with a loud smack, then whispered into his face. "It's too easy to ruffle your feathers, Thomas." His eyes lit with mischief. "Don't worry, I know you saw her first."

If only that were true. Thomas remembered all too clearly the fact that someone had already proposed to Eliza.

Thomas followed his friend the remainder of the way up the stairs and into the room. He planted himself in his usual spot while Nathaniel sat on the bed next to his patient.

After a small examination that could be done while she slept, Nathaniel took her hand and stroked it ever so gently. "Miss Campbell? Miss Campbell, it's Dr. Smith, I'm here to assess your condition."

Thomas drummed his fingers on his thigh. Nathaniel had better keep everything professional. Why did he have to look at her with such tender eyes?

After another few seconds of agony, Thomas pushed his friend aside. "Let me do it."

Nathaniel stepped away and raised his hands, a laugh dancing in his expression. "By all means."

Thomas glared and shook his head at Nathaniel before turning his attentions on Eliza. "Eliza, wake up."

Thomas touched her slender shoulders, trying to ignore the pleasant warmth of her skin through the linen fabric of her clothing. He stroked her arm, gentle but still firm enough to wake her. "You can sleep again in a few minutes, but the doctor needs to speak to you. He wants to see how you're healing."

Listless, she opened her eyes and turned her gaze at him. He didn't miss the immediate sparkle that flashed over her face when she saw him, though he pretended it didn't cause his heart to beat faster. He removed his hands from their place and got up from the bed, giving Nathaniel more space.

"Sorry to wake you." Thomas smiled. "Doctor Smith is here."

He stepped away and inhaled a deep breath to blow away the quivering in his chest. How did her eyes always do that to him?

Eliza nodded, looking more tired than usual. Worry gathered across his brow. He'd begun to believe she was doing well, but maybe she wasn't improving after all.

"Good afternoon, Miss Campbell." Nathaniel sat on the bed and folded his hands on his lap.

"Good afternoon, Doctor." Eliza's gentle voice was once again weak and hoarse.

"'Tis good to see you awake. How are you feeling? How is your pain?"

"It seems to be getting better all the time. Still tender."

Nathaniel dipped his head. "May I have a look at it?"

She nodded and moved her arms to her sides, working the blankets away from her when she froze, a shock of red lacing her features. Looking away, Eliza crossed her arms.

"Is something wrong, Miss Campbell?" Nathaniel asked.

She licked her lips before she answered. "Thomas? Could you leave us for a moment, please?"

"Certainly." He nodded. The request was reasonable enough. But why did she want him gone? He helped her every day.

He walked out and closed the door behind him. Their voices were muted behind the door and though he was tempted to lean into the wood that separated them, he thought better of it.

Downstairs, the menial tasks Thomas employed to keep his mind occupied while he waited for Nathaniel to come down proved worthless. He stoked the fire, checked the stack of logs, even brought in a few more from the back of the house before he realized his list of things to do was frustratingly short.

He checked on Kitty in the kitchen. She smiled from her position, kneeling near the fire. Thomas relaxed a bit. At least one of the girls was none the worse for wear. Kitty appeared to have gotten over the shock of the events and seemed content, despite the tribulations, though he'd noticed her pinched lips and quiet huffs any time he or Nathaniel mentioned anything about the patriot cause. If that was her only complaint, she'd done a good job at hiding it.

He left the kitchen and turned back to the parlor, taking his place by the fire. Another ten minutes of trying to occupy his jumbled mind nearly killed him. His nerves jumped like a rowdy army of frogs. What could be taking so long?

Finally the tapping of Nathaniel's shoes resonated in the stairway. Thomas almost jumped from his breeches.

"Well?"

Nathaniel ignored his question, a solemn shadow veiling his face. "It's really a miracle she lived, Thomas. A true miracle."

"Is she all right? She looks more tired. I'm worried."

"I know you are, Thomas." Nathaniel turned and slouched in the largest chair in front of the fire. "You and Miss Katherine have done very well caring for Eliza and I'm sure she'll make a full recovery."

Relief flooded Thomas's rigid muscles. He exhaled long through his mouth and brushed his hand over his hair. "You don't think she's too fatigued? She's not too pale?"

A sparkle of mischief lighted Nathaniel's eyes and a chuckle escaped his throat. "She's fine."

"What's so funny?"

"Nothing."

Thomas lowered his voice as he leaned toward Nathaniel. "Why did she ask me to leave? I've seen her wound a hundred times. Doesn't she know that?"

This time, Nathaniel burst into a full-blown guffaw. "Oh, Thomas, my boy, you are in deep, aren't you?"

Jerking back, Thomas stiffened. "What are you talking about?"

"You care for her. Don't try to deny it."

"You didn't answer my question." Thomas tilted his head toward the ceiling and let out a heavy sigh. He refused to give credence to such an inane suggestion.

Nathaniel continued his aggravating behavior. "What question?"

"Why would she ask me to leave? It's not as if she's ever been indecent. Kitty and I have always made sure to keep her properly covered."

Nathaniel stood, laughing again. Thomas wanted to kick him, literally, out of the house.

"I can't honestly say." Nathaniel pulled his ankle over his knee as he nestled back into the patterned chair. "My assumption is, now that she's more aware of what's going on, it's probably embarrassing for her."

"Embarrassing?" Thomas protested. "Then why isn't she embarrassed to have you looking at her?"

Nathaniel cocked his head and lifted one eyebrow. "Need I explain? I'm a doctor. It's different. She only sees me occasionally and she knows this is my trade. But you, you're here all the time. And knowing that you will be so close in such an intimate way—"

"Nathaniel." Thomas spoke through his teeth to keep from shouting. "There's nothing intimate about it." He cooled his growing fury with several cleansing breaths.

"It can seem intimate, if you care about someone."

Shaking his head, Thomas grit his teeth and stared into the crackling flames.

Nathaniel's chair creaked and suddenly Thomas felt his friend's hand on his shoulder. "You may not have feelings for her, but I believe she might have feelings for you."

Thomas's jaw gaped open and he flicked his gaze at Nathaniel.

"See, did I not tell you?" Nathaniel laughed, but without his usual teasing. "You can't hide anything from me. I know you're falling in love with her."

What? Impossible. Thomas released a light laugh and moved his focus back to the fire. Falling for her? No. Cared for her? Yes. Maybe even more than he wanted to admit, but he was not falling in love with her. He couldn't even if he wanted to. She had a man waiting for her, and a much better life in Boston to return to.

But could Nathaniel be right about her feelings for him? His friend was always keen on those kinds of things.

Thomas shifted his weight and rested one hand on the smooth wood of the mantel. True, he'd seen the added spark in her gaze, noticed how she often found a reason for him to stay with her—just to talk. Surely there could be plausible explanations for all of that.

And of course his reasons for wanting to be with her were perfectly normal. He was responsible for what had happened and he wanted to make sure she would be all right. That was all. Nothing more.

"I'm correct, am I not?" Nathaniel's taunting tone returned, yanking Thomas from his daydream.

"No. You're not correct. Not this time."

Thomas continued staring at the orange flames popping and juggling heat in front of him. He'd have to work extra hard at keeping his distance before his feelings burned as hot as the fire before him.

"Not correct, you say?" Nathaniel walked toward the door and jested in a loud voice as he walked out of the house. "Oh, we'll see about that, my friend. We'll see about that."

Chapter Thirteen

The hazy autumn sunset filtered through the open curtains in Eliza's cozy room and the bronze fire in the fireplace performed a welcoming dance. She drew in a long breath, savoring the scent of clean air that mixed with the musky aroma of colored leaves. Thomas had gone out briefly to get a few more supplies from the doctor, and promised to only be gone an hour. It was still very dangerous for any of them to be out, but sometimes it could not be avoided.

Alone, Eliza moved her hand across her belly. The wound continued to heal, thanks to God's mighty hand and the good care Thomas and Kitty tenderly provided. She peered down at her toes and wiggled them under the quilted blanket. When she finally got out of bed, would her legs even remember how to walk?

Her soft giggle echoed through the room. Oh, how she wanted to get out of that bed. Yet, how many days on their journey had she vowed that she would never walk again when they got to Thomas's home?

Her breath caught and she smoothed her fingers over the fabric at her neck.

Thomas.

His name sent a burst of flower petals showering

down her skin. Here she was in his home—in his bed—wearing his shirt. Eliza's mouth went dry and her cheeks scorched from the inside.

She glanced at the door. How long would he be gone? His absence created a loneliness as deep as the well at their Boston home. She shook it off. Silly woman. She only cared for Thomas in a grateful way—just as anyone would care for the person who nursed them back from the very edge of death.

It would be best to keep occupied while he was away. Otherwise, she might spend her time counting the minutes until he returned.

"Kitty?" Eliza called. She hoped her sister could help her freshen up seeing as she'd really only had simple sponge baths since her harrowing ordeal.

Kitty stepped up the stairs, wiping her hands on a blue and white-striped apron. Eliza smiled at the picture of domesticity that entered her room. She'd prayed with earnest that God would help Kitty accept their unusual situation and be content until things went back to normal. It looked like her prayers were working and she gave silent thanks for the miracle.

"You're looking even more lively today than yesterday." Kitty's smile encompassed her gentle features. She sat on the bed then lounged on one side, resting on her elbow. "Wasn't it a glorious day? And the sunset is exquisite."

"Oh, it is. I love autumn most of all." Eliza gazed out the window at the orange clouds waving above the line of trees. "How are you holding up? I'm not too much of a burden, am I? I feel so guilty. I need to be doing my share of the work."

Kitty reached out with her available hand and massaged Eliza's calf. "I am finally able to do something in return for all the years you've sacrificed for me, Liza. You're never a burden. It's a blessing for me to serve you."

The genuine love in her sister's eyes nourished the already growing lump in Eliza's throat. The Lord truly was all-loving and all-powerful. He'd kept them safe despite such danger, Kitty was content and Eliza was alive. What more could they ask for?

"I do have one request, Kitty," she asked with a smirk on her lips.

"Anything."

"I want to get up. I mean, really get up. Maybe take a few steps around the room. I need to get out of this shirt, wash my body and hair, and get into something that's fresh and clean."

Kitty's eyebrows dipped down. "I don't think Thomas would approve."

A smile played across Eliza's lips. "Yes, but Thomas isn't here. Is he?" She practiced her best pathetic look and batted her eyes. "Please?"

"I concede." Kitty launched off the bed with a youthful spring and bounced out the door. "Who doesn't like a bit of danger in their lives? For surely we shall be in danger should Thomas find out." She winked. "I'll get the water and be right back to help you."

She returned not five minutes later, bucket in hand, holding several towels and a clean garment under the other arm.

"Alright." Kitty peeled back Eliza's coverings. "Don't move too quickly. We don't need Thomas coming home and finding you on the floor."

The caution was well advised, for simply sitting up straight caused considerable pain and the room began to spin.

"I suppose you're right." Eliza gripped the edge of

the bed. "I'll just sit here. No use in over doing things."

"Good idea." Kitty's face relaxed as she moved Eliza's legs to the side of the bed. "But now that you're up, let's wash you and get you out of that shirt. I'll avoid your bandages since we just changed them."

Eliza slipped out of the shirt she'd worn for who knew how long and quickly covered her chest with her arms.

Kitty giggled. "Don't worry, I closed the door and he won't be home for a while yet."

Eliza nodded, although the thought of him returning home while she was so exposed made her grip her arms even tighter.

"You're lucky I already had water on the fire, so this is warm. Why don't you let me wash your neck and arms first, then I'll work through that mess of tangles."

The mere thought of it was heavenly. "Thank you, Kitty. That would be wonderful."

Over the next thirty minutes the girls acted as relaxed as they would if they were in their own home. They talked and laughed, allowing themselves to be blissfully lost in conversation. Kitty left the room for a moment to grab another clean towel and left the door open when she returned.

She helped Eliza into one of Thomas's clean shirts, pulled her long, wet hair from her back, and plaited it into a perfect braid. "Why are you blushing, Eliza?" Kitty asked as a smirk toyed with her mouth.

Eliza knew her sister well enough to detect the crack in her voice that meant she was teasing. She'd hoped Kitty wouldn't notice the color in her cheeks. Wearing Thomas's shirts seemed far too intimate, and she shouldn't like it. But she did.

"I'm not blushing, Kitty."

Her sister laughed out loud and pointed out the window. "Then why is your face red as the leaves on that tree?"

Eliza pinched her lips together, hoping if she ignored the comment her sister would change the subject.

"I think you like Thomas," Kitty said, as she continued working with Eliza's hair.

Eliza blinked with a quick laugh. "I do not like Thomas. Not in that way. He's kind and generous and I appreciate all he's done for me, but that is all."

"I don't believe you. I see the twinkling in your eyes when he comes into the room. I see how you try not to smile too big when he looks at you."

"I have no idea what you're—"

Just then the door opened and closed downstairs.

The girls froze and shared panicked expressions. They scrambled to get Eliza back in her usual position before he saw her.

Too late.

Eliza's stomach collapsed. Thomas's tall frame dominated the empty space in front of the open bedchamber door.

"What are you doing?" His blue eyes were dark and worry dug itself deep into the muscles of his jaw. He hadn't taken the time to remove his cloak and the long black fabric accentuated the dark of his hair and made his shoulders seem as wide as the doorframe.

Eliza sat still, trying not to be overcome by the fluttering in her middle. Kitty too must have felt like a child who'd been caught in the middle of mischief, for she remained motionless.

"I just wanted to get cleaned up. Is that such a crime?" Eliza wore an easy smile, hoping to massage away the frustration in his face.

He shook his head like a father with two disobedient children, wiped off his cloak, and hung it over the chair by the table in the corner. “I leave you both for a moment and here you are trying to kill yourself all over again.”

“It’s not as bad as all that, Thomas. I’m getting better.”

Eliza tried lifting her legs back onto the bed to show her improvement, but she winced as a shooting pain gouged into her stomach. Thomas rushed to her side. He put one arm around her shoulder, the other under her knees, and lifted her back to her usual position.

His face was much too close, the musky scent of his clothes much too inviting. His warm breath on her ear made her own breathing difficult.

Eliza’s gaze moved to Thomas’s face as he propped the pillows behind her. He stilled when their gazes locked, only inches apart. His eyes transformed into sparkling sapphires and for a moment the world around her dissolved.

“You just took another year off my life, Eliza.”

His rich masculine voice sent a ripple of pleasure flowing down her skin and the compassion in his eyes made her heart stop beating. Why did he have to be so kind? Didn’t he know what it did to her?

He looked away too soon, shaking his head. “Don’t try anything like that again.” His reprimanding tone returned full-force.

The longing look she’d savored from his gaze just seconds ago disappeared. She chewed on her lip. It was all for the better, she supposed. Eliza intertwined her fingers in her lap as he got up. He motioned for Kitty who came and helped pull the quilt over her.

Kitty winked as she tucked the blanket around Eliza's legs and waist. Eliza pursed her lips and shot daggers through her widened eyes. Kitty smiled bigger and gathered the pail, towels, and dirty garments, then left the room.

Eliza bit her lip once more and pretended not to notice Thomas still standing by the bed, staring right at her.

Thomas clenched his jaw. How could they have attempted something so incredibly foolish? He wanted to give Eliza the scolding she deserved, to tell her he hadn't saved her life just to have her start acting rash and putting herself at risk again.

But he couldn't speak. All thoughts escaped him but the scent of the rose-perfumed soap that had circled him when he'd been only inches from her freshly washed hair and the thought of how feminine she felt in his arms. Her silken locks, all smooth and still wet from its wash, rested around her shoulders in a tight braid. The clean clothes she wore—his clothes—draped over her flawless curves. Her skin had more pink to it now, and if he wasn't mistaken, that pink color was deepening.

Was she blushing? Her chin was tucked and she focused a great deal of attention on her fingernails. He held back a smile, remembering Nathaniel's words. Did she really have feelings for him? Shaking his head again, Thomas tried to remember what it was he had been so frustrated about.

Eliza shot him a quick glance before once again studying her fingers. "How did things go in town?

Did you get everything you needed from Dr. Smith?" Her satiny voice floated in the air and caressed his weakening walls of resistance.

Thomas took his usual seat by her side and tried to focus on her question. Why did she have to be so innocent, so alluring?

"Nathaniel's been a God-send. We can't risk being seen at the market, someone might be able to identify us. Especially after the plight with the sailors. I got some more food supplies. And something else. I'll be right back."

The nerves in his stomach swirled like leaves in the wind. He went downstairs to fetch the fair-sized bundle he'd dropped downstairs and bounded back up the steps like a giddy schoolboy. There shouldn't be any reason for his nervousness. It wasn't as if it was an inappropriate gift. Not really. Just a token of his gratitude for her patience and forgiveness.

He placed the package on her lap and watched as she fingered the twine with apparent apprehension.

"You needn't get me anything, Thomas."

"Oh, it's nothing really." Thomas answered, sitting back down to ease the nerves in his legs. "It's actually for both you and Kitty."

Eliza's dark eyes darted between him and the package a few more times before she opened it. Slow and deliberate, she untied the small bow and pushed back the wrapping. Thomas kept his gaze on hers and stamped at the rising anticipation in his chest. What would she think of it? Would she like it?

Her lips parted and she sucked in a tiny breath. Thomas felt light as a thread of silk. That was just the reaction he'd been hoping for.

Her delicate fingers caressed the lavender colored day-dress.

Thomas yearned to see the expression in her eyes, but she didn't look at him. She continued examining the gift, lifting it higher and smoothing out the wrinkles in the skirt.

Finally, she moved her face toward him. The gratitude in her eyes along with the small smile that pushed at her lips revealed her feelings. Thomas couldn't retain the wide grin that spread across his face and deep into his heart. The nervous leaves in his stomach blew away with her pleasing reaction.

"You like it?"

She laughed, breathless. "Oh, yes. It's lovely, thank you." She looked away and lowered her voice. "But you know it's far too intimate. How can I accept such a gift?"

He figured she would say as much. "Very easily, Eliza. The only dress you had was ruined. So, as I see it, you have no choice. You have to accept it."

Eliza peered at him from the corner of her eye and appeared to be pressing away another winsome smile.

Thomas pointed at the light-green dress that still lay in the package. "That one's for Kitty. And there are two . . . two nightgowns for you both as well. And, well, all the other things you will need." His face burned and he cleared his throat.

Eliza's countenance brightened. She must have noticed his obvious embarrassment.

"Thomas, you've done too much. How will we ever repay you?"

"Well, I wish I could say I picked it out myself." He moved his chair closer to the bed. "I *had* bought you and Kitty some fabric when I came to town the day that . . . the day you were attacked, but I dropped it along the way in my hurry to, well, anyway . . ." He stopped, and searched for another way to explain it. "I gave Nathaniel some money and asked him to pick up some dresses. I'm not sure how they'll fit, so I had Nathaniel purchase what things you'd need to take them in."

"They're simply perfect." She smoothed the dress again, stroking the fabric, then turned to him. Her eyes narrowed and she tilted her face down as if she might lecture him. "We will repay you, Thomas. Once we get home—after this madness has ended, this ridiculous search for all of us—I promise to make it up to you."

He leaned forward. "I don't want anything from you, Eliza. I take full responsibility. And I won't argue with you about it."

She sighed and for several silent seconds looked at the wall in front of her. "No. 'Tis all Father's doing. We've been over this before." She remained motionless, only blinking her eyes.

He looked down at his hands and massaged his palms as he worked out what to say.

Lord, how can I help her see that Robert did what he thought was best? How can I help her see the importance of our cause?

As he stared downward, his gaze slipped to the worn copy of Cicero resting on the small stool. It was the book he'd been reading while he kept vigil at her side those many days on end. A book Robert had given to him.

He picked it up. "Have you read this?"

She studied the tired, leather-bound copy of The Republic and The Laws.

A curious spark rested in her question-filled eyes. He wiggled the book, hoping she would take it.

"You're reading Cicero?" She laughed and took

the book in her slender fingers. "I didn't know you're a scholar."

Thomas grinned and relaxed in his chair. "I'm not. But your Father was."

"Yes, he was." Her voice was so quiet he almost didn't hear her answer.

Thomas pinned his eyes on her. "I knew nothing about politics when I joined the Sons of Liberty. All I knew was that I didn't like the oppressive nature of the British government." He stopped for a moment, remembering the many happy times he and Robert had talked hour after hour. The man was like a Father to him—a real and loving Father. "About a year ago, he gave me that book."

He nodded toward the worn article in her hands. Eliza's mouth formed a small O and her eyes widened. Then the sadness returned and she shook her head with tiny movements, her delicate eyebrows dipping down. "Why would he tell you all these things? Why would he open his heart and his beliefs to you and never tell me anything about what he truly believed?"

Her eyes glistened and Thomas's gut pricked. He knew Robert loved his daughters and wanted only the best for them, but how could he make her see it?

He leaned forward in his seat. "I believe that he must have taught you more than you think he did. He didn't always feel this way. He came to the truth of things a little at a time, like we all do. Since he was known and loved by the British he had to keep up his appearances, even after he inwardly renounced all for which they stood."

Eliza tightened her full lips into a long thin line. "I still don't know why he couldn't tell me. I'm his daughter."

Thomas expelled an exasperated breath and cupped his hand over his mouth. He hadn't wanted to make her upset. "Why don't you read this book while you *stay in bed.*" He emphasized the last bit with a touch of teasing hoping to get her to smile. "Your Father treasured this book. You may understand more about him and about what he believed in—and why he did what he did—after you've read it. When you come to understand the truth of it, Eliza, the truth will make you free."

Eliza jerked up at Thomas's words. That was what Father had said.

Her heart beat like the pounding of an Indian drum and the hairs on her arms pointed straight up. She wanted to know more. Truly. She wanted to believe her Father hadn't kept his secret for lack of faith in her.

But Samuel had said a woman had no place in politics. And maybe that's what her Father had thought as well. Maybe that's why he'd never told her, along with wanting to keep her safe.

She swallowed timorously at the question on her tongue. "I heard a woman has no place in politics."

Thomas grinned. "Politics is for everyone." He tilted his head. "Who told you that? Certainly not your Father?"

"Oh, no. Samuel did."

"Who's Samuel?"

Eliza released a heavy sigh, raising and lowering her shoulders. "He's the one who proposed to me. I asked him once about all of this and he told me it wasn't my place. He's a Captain in the British Army and he feels very strongly about these things." She pulled her braid over her shoulder and tightened the white ribbon at the end. "He is a very determined man, so I didn't argue with him on that point. But, I knew I couldn't accept him until I had more time to come to terms with all of this. And study it out, as Father told me to do."

Thomas's face went white. "What was his last name?"

Eliza raised her brows at his pointed question. The terrified look in his handsome face made her grip her braid. "Who? Samuel?"

He stilled and stared at her, his voice a hoarse whisper. "What was his last name?"

"Samuel's just an old family friend. I've known him for years—"

"Tell me, Eliza." Thomas rose slowly, with a darkness behind his gaze that turned his eyes into a terrible stormy blue. His fingers curled when he asked again. "What was Samuel's last name?"

"Martin. His last name is Martin."

Chapter Fourteen

Thomas didn't stop, didn't look back. He walked straight through the cold to Nathaniel's home. If he didn't talk to someone he would explode.

Darkness settled on the trees and houses around him, amplifying the heaviness he now carried. If he thought his load was oppressive before, it now crushed him.

The situation was a thousand times worse than he'd imagined. Samuel was not merely looking for him, he was looking for the woman he loved, the woman he hoped to marry. Samuel would no doubt kill him if he found where she was. He wouldn't even have time to explain he'd done it to protect her—from him!

A violent revolt brewed in his stomach. He shoved his fingers through his hair and growled as he contemplated this disaster. Not to mention how the thought of that man and Eliza being married made his lungs burn. Thank goodness she hadn't given him an answer yet. And he hoped when she did, the answer would be no.

He stomped across the soggy ground, splattering mud as he went. Samuel Martin. What a rat. Did she have any idea about him? Did she know what he was really like and what he had done? She couldn't possibly know or she wouldn't esteem the vile man as she did. The question burned in his skull. Should he tell her? Would she even believe him? He reached Nathaniel's darkened house and settled on a conclusion. It was best not to say anything to Eliza. At least not now. Maybe never.

Thomas pounded on Nathaniel's door harder than usual. When it didn't open instantly, he pounded again.

Finally the door flew open. Nathaniel's initial look of concern intensified when he saw who waited on his stoop. "Thomas, what's wrong? I thought you were going to break the door down." His banyan hung open revealing his rumpled nightshirt and a pair of breeches he'd obviously just pulled on.

Thomas didn't wait to be asked in. He pushed past his friend and walked straight into the main room. Nathaniel closed the door and followed him with the candle.

"Please, come right in. And don't worry about the mud on your boots, I'll clean it up."

Consumed by every terrible scenario, Thomas could only glare at his friend's attempt at being jocular.

"Are you going to tell me what's got you so riled? Or would you prefer to simply continue glaring at me while I try and guess your distress?" Nathaniel set the candle down on his oak desk and went to the large stone fireplace. "Did Eliza not care for the gifts?"

Thomas paced for another moment, clenching and relaxing his fists, breathing deeply through his nose. How could he form the words? They were too odious to speak.

After stoking the fire, Nathaniel leaned against his desk and folded his arms across his chest. "Out with it."

Using an army's worth of fortitude, Thomas forced his legs to stop moving and glared at the floor, speaking through gritted teeth. "It's Samuel."

"Samuel? What are you talking about? Who is Samuel—*the* Samuel?"

Thomas could tell his friend tried to make light of it, but that only reddened his anger. He hit his fist on the mantel. "Nathaniel this is no time to be trivial. Eliza just informed me that Samuel Martin—the very same man who blackmailed me—is the man who proposed to her." He wiped his hand across his face and looked up at the ceiling, before letting his arms drop heavy at his sides. "She says she's known him for years. You know what this means, don't you?"

Nathaniel's expression dropped. He exhaled deeply then closed and opened his eyes again while his voice remained low. "He'll be frantically looking for her, as well as you. Did you tell her about him?"

"No."

"Why not?"

"I can't. Not right now. I need to sort this out first."

Another rapping on the door shot through the silence of the room.

"Who could that be?" Thomas asked, irritated.

"I don't know. But in case you haven't heard, I am a doctor, so I do get people coming to my home at all hours of the day and night."

The pounding continued and this time a muted voice behind the door ripped through the air.

"Doctor Smith, this is Captain Samuel Martin. I must speak with you on a very urgent matter. I order you to open this door immediately!"

Thomas's blood evaporated in his veins. Impossible.

Nathaniel's face turned pale and his jaw flopped open. "What?" he whispered.

The knocking pounded with the same rhythm of Thomas's beating heart. Neither of them spoke. Nathaniel motioned wildly for Thomas to stand flush with the end of his large bookcase on the side facing away from the door. Thomas slid his large body in the almost too tiny space between the bookcase and the wall and held his breath. He hoped his shoulder wasn't visible. The bookcase was deep, but possibly not deep enough.

The pounding escalated, and so did Samuel's demands. Thomas could hear Nathaniel's casual sounding footsteps as he walked across the room. As the light of the candle followed him toward the door, Thomas was shrouded in black.

The door creaked open. Thomas closed his eyes and didn't stop praying, his hands pressed firmly at his sides. The thudding of his pulse rang with such force he feared it echoed clear as cannon fire.

"What took you so long?" From the loud jangle of swords and the sound of stomping boots that entered the house, it was apparent Samuel was not traveling alone and every parcel of air vanished from Thomas's lungs.

"Forgive me, Captain. How may I be of help to you?" Nathaniel's voice remained even. The door latched shut.

"I am searching for two woman. Eliza Campbell and her younger sister Katherine. I have reason to believe they have been kidnapped and brought this way. A source tells me that a young woman was stabbed near Sandwich in the past several weeks and I'm afraid she might have been the victim. Being that you're the nearest physician, I reasoned you might know something about it." Samuel's voice grew more intense the longer he spoke.

Thomas practiced breathing in and out as he waited for Nathaniel to answer. How in heaven's name had he learned all of that? He clenched his teeth. Hearing Eliza's name come out of Samuel's mouth made Thomas's stomach roll.

"This is imperative, Doctor," Samuel boomed. "I need to know now! I believe she might have been brought here. *Did you treat her*?"

Nathaniel stayed quiet for another moment, making Thomas's extremities go numb. His throat seized and needles of panic pierced him from head to foot. *Say no, please say no!*

"Yes, I did."

Thomas bit his cheek and stared at the black ceiling above him. *Nathaniel, what have you done?*

"When? Did she live? Is she still in town? I'm desperate to find her." The consuming worry in Samuel's voice gave testament to his feelings for Eliza. Thomas swallowed another lump of anger that lodged in his throat. Eliza was far too angelic to be tangled up with such a man.

The rustling of boots, the rattling of swords, and the hard breathing of the men grew louder. Thomas tried to inch closer to the wall but there wasn't any way for him to fit any more snug than he already did. If Samuel came much closer . . .

"Go on, Doctor!"

"Yes, I treated her not long after it happened."

Samuel muttered a curse. "And?"

"She did live, for a few hours. Undoubtedly you know how grave stomach wounds can be. It's almost impossible to survive such trauma."

A dreadful silence followed. "I don't believe it. It

can't actually have been Eliza." Another long silence. "Can you tell me . . ." Samuel's voice cracked. "Can you tell me what she looked like? Did she have any features that make her stand out to you? I have to know if that woman really was Miss Campbell."

"She had brown hair and brown eyes. I do remember she had a small mole on her left cheekbone, but nothing else stands out to me. She was extraordinarily beautiful."

"Oh dear God, it was Eliza." Samuel's boots shuffled against the wood floor. "Was there anyone traveling with her? Was she alone?"

"No. Her sister was traveling with her. And there was a man, he claimed to be their brother."

Thomas looked up, biceps flexing. Did he have to reveal everything?

"What did this man and the sister do? Did they bury her here?" Samuel's dark voice was laced with venom.

"No. I don't know where they went, but they took her with them."

Samuel cursed again under his breath. "Come, Donaldson."

Donaldson! He was the one who'd attempted to take Thomas when all of this began. Thomas clenched his fists so hard he winced. This could not be happening.

"What are you going to do?" Nathaniel questioned.

"That man has committed copious crimes for which he must stand trial. Worst of all, he has kidnapped the woman I love, and now he is responsible for her death! Not to mention the fact that he killed another man who tried to help her escape him. What am I going to do? I plan to find him. Then kill him."

The door opened again, letting in a stream of cold night air that scraped its way up Thomas's body. *How in the world could he possibly know about what happened? And what's worse, he thinks I killed her!* His hands trembled and he pressed his teeth together until his jaw ached.

The other sailor.

Nathaniel ushered the soldiers out of the room, bidding them goodnight. "I'm sorry I couldn't be of more help."

As Samuel and Donaldson prodded out of the house, Thomas could hear his enemy speaking loud and coarse to his companion. Soon their voices trailed away as they walked down the street, most likely toward Newcomb Tavern.

Thomas's mind whirled, ferocious as a late-summer gale. How long would they be in town? How in heaven's name would he get safely home to the girls? They couldn't be left alone for a second.

The lock clicked in place and Nathaniel's steps beat against the floor as he stomped back to the study. Only then did Thomas ease out of his hiding space, realizing for the first time how tense his muscles were.

"How in the world could he know all of that? And to think that I—" The words tasted so bitter he couldn't speak them. "Could this get any worse?"

Nathaniel shook his head and looked in the direction of the door. His jaw ticked. "I don't honestly think it can. I have a feeling you'll have to find a way to enjoy that house of yours. You won't be leaving it for quite some time. Not until those two have left town. And even then . . ."

Thomas whirled toward the fire, his emotions

scorching any bits of reason left within him. He turned to his friend, blinding anger pummeling him. "Why did you have to say she died? Why did you have to identify her so perfectly?"

Nathaniel stood taller and stepped toward Thomas, slamming the candle on the desk. "I was put on the spot. What would you have me say?" He walked to the large chair behind his desk and sat with a disgruntled humph. He threw his hands in the air. "If I had to do it over again, I would probably say something different, but there's nothing I can do about it now."

Thomas disposed an ounce of his misplaced indignation and redirected it at a more appropriate recipient. Samuel. "He will not stop until he's found me."

Both men remained mute, absorbed by the towering obstacle. Nathaniel's tapping foot against the hard floor matched the rhythm of Thomas's own nervous shuffling across the length of the study.

"While there are soldiers in town you'll not be able to leave your house."

"We've established that," Thomas said over his shoulder.

"Since you haven't been in town regularly anyway that won't be much of a problem. However, I suggest making your situation appear as far from the truth as possible—just in case people start asking questions."

A spark of something flashed across Nathaniel's eyes. Thomas grumbled. His friend was about to say something that would shock him.

"What is it, Nathaniel?"

"You need to allow people to think you are married to Eliza."

The impact of Nathaniel's statement produced

the same effect as if he'd been shoved. "Pardon me? How in the world would that make any bit of difference?"

Nathaniel tried to pull down a mischievous smile that tugged on his lips. "Well, that way if anyone asks questions about 'that man in the house at the edge of town' I will have some substantial story to tell them. You're newly married and your wife is recovering from a miscarriage or something so you are at her side day and night. I won't use your real names, of course. That way you can eliminate any scrutiny that you might otherwise have to endure. The soldiers will be looking for someone who is unmarried. People in town will believe anything I tell them. I see everyone, I know everything."

Thomas closed his eyes. *Ridiculous*. But, perhaps his friend had a point.

"I hate to willfully spread lies." Thomas thought for another moment, then laughed with a sliver of acquiescence. "Though the risk is too great otherwise. I suppose you're right."

Beaming, Nathaniel sat straighter. "Of course I'm right." He rose from his chair, glowing with self-satisfaction and came toward Thomas. "All you have to do now is find a way to tell the ladies."

Thomas lowered his head and peered ruefully into the radiating embers.

Nathaniel laid a comforting hand on his shoulder. "I can see that you carry the responsibility very heavily, Thomas. None of this is your fault."

"I have to keep my distance from Eliza—and Kitty—for their own good. The sooner they can get back to Boston, the better."

Nathaniel bumped his back against the wall next to the fire. "Well, seeing as how Eliza will be your *wife*, she may not ever care to leave." His voice bled sarcasm.

Thomas fought the urge to smack him. "I better be going." He walked down the darkened hall toward the back door. Nathaniel followed him through the narrow hallway, the glowing candle painting the walls with light.

"How will you get home? Samuel could very likely still be on the street." Nathaniel asked.

"I'll go the back way."

Thomas reached the door and put his hand on the cold handle, but before he turned it Nathaniel touched his arm.

"Since you'll be in sequestered from now on, I'll be by more often. You can tell me what you need. The supplies, food, etcetera. If it's all right with you, I'll be by tomorrow sometime to hear how the girls take the news."

"What news?" Thomas spat.

Nathaniel's jeering tone relaxed Thomas's startled nerves. "The news about your *marriage*. What else?"

"You are allowing people to believe that you and I are married?" Eliza could not believe the words that poured from her mouth. More than that, she could not believe the flutter of pleasure that spun behind her heart at such a shocking proclamation.

Thomas leaned against the table and gripped the oak with his palms, drumming on the bottom of it with his fingers.

"Yes," he answered. "Knowing that they are still looking for us makes this a useful cover." His harsh tone grated against her fragile security.

Pulling a long piece of brown yarn from her shawl, Eliza twisted and untwisted it around her little finger. She didn't know what to say. Thomas had left earlier in such a storm she'd feared she'd done something to offend him. And when it was several hours before his return, both she and Kitty feared something had happened.

And apparently it had.

He'd rushed into the house ten minutes earlier in a burst of cold air and stomped up the stairs to tell them of his dreadful adventure at Nathaniel's.

It was just as they had suspected. Soldiers were looking for the man who had killed the sailor. Now none of them could leave the house for fear of being apprehended. The news came as quite a blow and renewed her harbored fears.

"I'm sorry, Eliza," Thomas said." I should have asked you before, but this has two benefits. It will hopefully make us less likely targets for attention. And, it will be better for your reputation should things get around. I wouldn't want to blemish your good name, or Kitty's. We'll have to stay here for much longer than expected, and none of us can leave the house. Once this is over, I promise to return you to Boston where you belong."

Eliza looked up from her busy fingers. She tried to place an encouraging smile on her face but nothing came. He wanted to get rid of her. What had happened? Before this he'd been warm and caring, but now he was as cold as the ocean in winter.

She tried to press away the rattle of her distracting feelings and fight the marvelous tumbling in her middle. Even though it wasn't a real proposal, her heart leapt as if it were. What was wrong with her? This was no time to be considering such things when their very lives were in danger. She kept her gaze down and shielded her expression. Foolish girl.

"I understand, Thomas," Eliza said, after a minute of dreadful silence. She focused again on the string. "And I thank you for being so forthright."

Thomas let out a loud exhale and pushed off the table with perceptible impatience. Eliza slumped against the pillows.

"I'll leave you now. I know you need some rest," he said over his shoulder as he walked out the door.

Kitty came up the stairs, her expression drawn and arms hugging her chest. She climbed onto the bed next to Eliza and lay on her back. "So, we're to be here indefinitely it seems."

"No, not indefinitely, but certainly longer than anticipated."

"I overhead Thomas's new plan." Sighing, Kitty gripped Eliza's hand. "At least this unfortunate arrangement has been made more enjoyable by your pseudo nuptials. I think it's a marvelous idea and certainly gives me plenty to tease you about." She winked as her lips quirked in a wry grin.

Eliza squeezed Kitty's fingers before pulling her hand away. "I don't find it funny."

"I can't see why not." Kitty rolled off the bed, closed the door, and began changing into her nightgown. "And please don't misunderstand me. I don't mean to make light of something so serious. But this budding romance brings a much needed bit of brevity to an otherwise dreadful circumstance." She giggled as she finished with the three small buttons on the front of her gown. "Thomas is very nice, and you have to admit, ridiculously handsome."

Yes, Eliza could admit that. But she wouldn't. She

rested her head behind her on the sweet smelling pillows and gazed at the ceiling. Kitty needed to stop reading her beloved Shakespeare and getting such silly ideas in her head, then perhaps they could be done discussing this once and for all.

But still, Thomas's honey-smooth voice, his broad shoulders, and a smile that reached into Eliza's soul, flooded every thought. Samuel's nearness had never made her heart react the way Thomas did.

The memory of Samuel's three kisses floated around her mind. Nothing. No butterflies. No longing for more.

Her breath flickered. What would it be like to kiss Thomas? She placed a hand over her mouth and tried to shake away the enticing thoughts. How could she even entertain such a notion? Grabbing the yarn she once again started circling her finger. Thomas cared nothing for her. This temporary situation would last only a few more weeks. After that she and Kitty would be home and safe from the terrible wrong that hunted them. That was for the best. Thomas only did this out of the duty he felt he must fulfill on their behalf.

I'll do well to remember that. But the pit that tunneled within her stomach told her such a task would be impossible.

Eliza's eyes shot open and she gripped the fabric at her chest. She choked on her breath and worked to calm her erratic pulse. *Dreadful nightmare.* The cold air was silent, only the sound of Kitty's soft breathing whispered through the room—a drastic contrast to the terrible screams that still wailed in her head. Memories from long ago lived fresh in her mind like an ever-blooming bush, ready to share the tragedies of the past whether she wanted them or not. The cold, the fear—all so real, made the hairs on her arms shoot up. If only she had done for Peter what was best. If only she had *known* what to do.

Eliza placed her palm over her face and shook her head. It had been over a year since her last bout with such dreams, and here they were again to haunt her. Father's words tried to squeeze past the dominating thoughts. He'd said it wasn't her fault, that God had taken Peter because it was his time.

Assailed by grief, Eliza pushed back the covers as carefully as she could. She had to get out of bed. She had to get a change of scenery and clear her mind of the deafening cries in her head. Using careful movements, she pulled her legs from under the covers and rested her feet on the frigid hardwood floors. She tugged on a pair of stockings to help shield her toes from the cold, but the thin fabric did little to help warm her. It may be only October, but the temperatures at night bit like January. Gritting her teeth, she pushed off the bed and wrapped the heavy brown shawl around her shivering shoulders.

Every step sent a stab of pain through her belly, and yet the movements brought breath to her limbs in a way she hadn't experienced in weeks. The stairs were hard and noisy. She winced with every creaking telltale step, praying that her jaunt downstairs would go undetected.

Once at her destination, her lips stretched into a wide, mischievous grin. She'd made it, and already the journey down the stairs had been the best medicine she'd received in days. The logs in the fireplace glowed, though no flames ascended. If she were to stay down here for any length of time, the fire would need to be built again, to usher away the creeping chill. Keeping one hand on the rocky fireplace to steady herself, she gazed across the room. The central fireplace dominated the large front area, framed by a beautiful wood mantel. Two inviting chairs rested in front of the fire, and a small table nestled between them. A simple patterned carpet dressed the smooth wood floor. There was little in the way of decoration. The only items were two long muskets mounted above the mantel and the candlesticks and books that relaxed on the lowboy near the wall next to the kitchen.

This home was indeed pleasant, comforting, but it lacked a woman's touch. If this were her home . . .

Foolish girl! This would never be hers. Why would it? She had a home in Boston—a home she loved and missed. Didn't she?

The air that clouded around her pinched at her ears and toes. She looked at the fire, then at the stack of logs resting a few feet away. After the short rest, Eliza gathered her strength. She would be a fool to try and lift anything at all, let alone a heavy piece of wood. But if she managed, the fire would be just big enough to ease away the shivers. Wary of going too fast, she stepped forward and reached for the stack.

"What are you doing?"

Eliza yelped and turned so abruptly at the sound of Thomas's voice that she lost her footing. She flayed her arms behind her to catch her fall. Instead of hard ground, two muscular arms caught below her shoulders.

She scrunched her face and bit her cheek to fight away the pain that ripped through her abdomen.

With a tender hold, Thomas scooped her up and without a word carried her to the nearest chair, then set her down as if she weighed no more than a pillow.

She dare not look at him, though she could feel his gaze burning into the top of her hair. The pain in her side was nothing to the pain her pride had suffered.

"Really, Eliza. Where is your reason?" His tone of rebuke was painted with concern.

Eliza built up her bravery and lifted her lashes. Her lungs froze and she held her teeth together to keep her chin from dropping. Whatever pain she experienced diminished to a low throbbing at the sight before her.

Thomas's dark hair fell just above his shoulders, accentuating the perfect cut of his jaw and the strength of his shoulders. The light blue banyan he wore remained open above the waist revealing a white nightshirt and his solid chest beneath.

She dipped her head again, the glare in his eyes admitting to his frustration.

He walked over to the other chair, and instead of sitting like she expected, he pulled it over the floor, until it was only a few inches from hers. He put three more logs on the fire and stoked it. Then he sat. And stared at her.

Heavens! She froze. What should she do? What should she say? The divine fluttering sensations that Thomas stirred within her had a commanding presence, making them impossible to ignore. *He* was impossible to ignore. Being alone in such circumstances was highly improper. She could only hope Kitty would remain sleeping to avoid being caught in such a situation. Then again, perhaps Kitty's presence would make it easier to get up and leave.

Eliza swallowed the bulging nerves that rose in her throat and did her best to act normal. "I'm sorry. I guess I have lost my reason of late." She paused. "I just needed a change of scenery."

Thomas tilted his head and his eyebrows folded. "Are you alright? What are you doing down here at this time of night?"

The tenderness in his eyes reached out to caress her, releasing innumerable butterflies within her belly, which soon consumed her entire body. How did he do that? How did he make her feel this marvelous? It only made it more difficult to remember she couldn't stay, to remember that this arrangement was a burden to him. Thomas had made that clear with how displeased he was at the idea of being "married".

A terrible loneliness killed the flutters in her chest. She looked into the fire and without warning, the words poured from her.

"I was dreaming about my brother again." She stopped, emotions still skidding down the slippery ravine of her memory.

"You mean Peter?" Thomas asked.

Eliza jolted. "How do you know about him?"

He smiled, and leaned toward the fire, poking it with a stick. The flames rose higher and sparks smacked the air. He sat back in his chair, while the lines around his eyes deepened as he offered a gentle smile. "I heard you calling for him when you were . . . recovering. I asked Kitty about it. All she told me was that Peter was the middle child, and had died when you all were still young. She said you took it very hard."

Eliza searched his caring face, suddenly overcome

with the need to be folded in his embrace and forget all her fears and self-doubt. She shivered and told herself it was more from cold than from anything else. The floor-length nightgown did little to protect from the elements. As if he knew her thoughts, Thomas shot up and fetched a blanket from a small chest at the corner of the fireplace. He knelt in front of her and gently covered her frigid legs. He stalled, gripping the arms of the chair and his gaze traced her face as if she were some exquisite flower. Eliza's muscles tightened and she sucked in a quick breath.

What was he doing? The hunger she'd once seen in his eyes had returned with a powerful craving. He looked at her with such unmitigated desire, her heart nearly beat itself out of her chest.

Suddenly he pushed to his feet, a startled look fleeting across his face. He rubbed the back of his neck then walked to his chair and sunk down without another look.

Eliza forced her gaze to the fire and swallowed to wet her dry mouth.

Thank goodness he'd moved when he did. She'd nearly lost her head and reached out to touch his face. His caring nature and alluring smile nearly toppled her already collapsing barricade of resistance.

She snuck a peek at him as he continued giving his attention to the bright orange flames. The angular muscles in his face flexed as if he were struggling to fight something hidden. Her heart twirled behind her ribs. What if he felt the same as she? Could she possibly bring life to him, the way he did to her?

The sporadic popping of the flames broke the thick silence, helping gather her scattered thoughts. *Come now, Eliza. Be sensible.* She had to keep her distance. Getting close would only make it more difficult when it came time for her to leave.

Thomas wriggled in his chair and sat straighter, keeping his eyes forward. "Would you . . . like to talk about it?"

Eliza's brows rose then lowered again. His tone said he cared, while his posture said he wanted distance. Well, if he wasn't going back to bed perhaps it would be best to talk about it, since he'd asked. They were to be "husband and wife" for a few weeks after all, why not share with him the painful recollection that pricked her memory day and night. It could only help, couldn't it? She crossed her feet and pulled the soft shawl tighter.

"Peter was a joy." She gave a small silent laugh and spoke to her lap, afraid to look up. "He was pure male and let us know it. He wasn't about to let two sisters dress him up and force him to play house."

Stopping, Eliza clenched the fabric in her fingers. "One day in late February—I was eleven at the time, Peter was nine and Kitty seven—we were making snow angels and throwing snowballs, having a grand time. Peter insisted that we play near the large pond at the back of our property behind the meadow." She dared a glance at Thomas. As if sensing her gaze, he turned to look at her, orange shadows swaying across his face.

A smile crossed his features that seemed to reach out to lift her drooping spirit, but she looked away before the tender gaze could trap her heart. She shouldn't need him like this.

After a deep breath to blow away the yearning, she continued. "Father had instructed us specifically not to play near the frozen pond, for obvious reasons, but Peter wouldn't stop begging. Finally, I agreed—so long as he promised to stay away from the ice." Pausing, she licked her lips. "Once at the pond, he pleaded to me, 'Let me get on the ice, just near the edge, I know it will hold me!' I refused to let him, until finally I'd had enough and I said, 'Fine, Peter, but if you fall in, don't tell me I didn't warn you.'"

She picked at a knot in the fringe of her shawl. "I watched him as he walked gingerly across the ice. The farther he went, the bigger his triumphant grin became." The blood drained from her face. "In one terrifying moment he fell in, screaming. I froze with fear. I didn't know what to do. We were so far from the house that no one could hear us if I called out. I thought a thousand things all at once. I should have told Mother and Father where we were going. I should have obeyed Father's rules and I should not have given in to Peter's prodding to go to the pond. I should have never let him get on the ice. I stared in horror at his flailing arms, the ice breaking around him. He continued calling for me to help him, but I was paralyzed. I knew if I went on the ice I'd fall in as well, which would do him no good and it would take too long to run to the house and get help . . ."

A warm hand covered hers. At that moment, she looked up and her breath caught. The lines framing Thomas's masculine brow grew deep and a tiny smile nudged up on one side of his mouth.

Her heart lurched.

He squeezed her fingers as if he sensed she needed strength and wanted to massage a bit of courage into her spirit. "Go on."

Moving his hand back to his own knee, he nodded while Eliza tried not to think how cold her hand was without his. Thomas's desire to help, if that *was* his desire, worked to give her heart courage and her voice found its footing again on a small stool of bravery.

"God must have warned Father, because he appeared out of nowhere. Running with all his might he yelled at Peter to stay calm and that he would get him out. He grabbed a long dead branch and went to the side of the pond where the water was shallow and Peter could more easily reach the branch. Father stomped through the ice until the water reached his knees and he called out to Peter to grab onto the branch. Peter had just enough strength and Father pulled him onto the ice, then lifted him in his arms and carried him to the house."

She raised her eyes toward Thomas. The intensity in his stare drew the rest of the words from her heart like a spring. "I could see Peter shaking from cold, and I know Father must have been freezing as well, but he didn't show it.

"Once inside, Mother and Father got him out of his wet clothes and did their best to stop him from freezing. Mother warmed some blankets and heated water for him to drink. Father never reprimanded us for disobeying. I always supposed he knew how sorry we were. Peter's body warmed quickly enough, and we almost thought he would recover without any trouble. Then he developed a terrible cough. He died two weeks later."

Eliza flung a hand to her mouth when her voice caught. She couldn't cry in front of Thomas. Taking a long breath, Eliza moved to put her hand in her lap, but he caught her fingers in his, this time wrapping both of his strong hands around hers as if cupping her heart.

His grip tightened around her slender fingers. "I'm so sorry."

No longer able to fight the emotions that crashed within, she swiveled in her chair to face him. "By not being more careful, by not knowing what to do, I felt I had cost Peter his life. I promised myself, from that moment on, that I would do my best to care for Kitty—no matter what happened."

"And you have done just that, Eliza." Inching closer, Thomas's deep voice cradled her insecurities, and gave her strength to say all that yearned to be said.

"I promised Father I would not fail him. He asked me to search out the truth. But, I'm afraid that I won't know what the truth is when I find it. Or when I do, I'm afraid I won't have the courage to embrace it. Then, what if I end up hurting Kitty through what I choose to follow? What if . . ."

Thomas brushed a stand of hair behind her ear, silencing the endless stream of words at his touch. "Eliza, you *can* make important decisions and care for Kitty just the way she needs. I've seen you do it. Don't worry about bringing harm to Kitty through choices that you make. You won't. I know you always do your best for her—and everyone else. Leave the rest to God."

He scooted forward on his seat until their knees touched and Eliza's breathing increased with every inhale. What was he doing? His smooth tone dropped low, drawing her closer. "Eliza, you're the most courageous woman I know. I have no doubt you will find the truth. And that you'll embrace it when you do."

Eliza's heart thrashed so wildly it stole the blood from her head. She needed to move away, but somehow she moved closer.

And so did he.

Before she could stop it, he leaned forward and covered her mouth with his own. The cushion of his smooth lips molding against hers sent a thrilling spray of tingles over her skin and a muted squeak escaped her throat.

If this was heaven, she'd found it.

He should stop, but the intoxicating sensation of Eliza's hot breath on Thomas's face dominated him and he could think of nothing else. Nothing but kissing her. The world around him stopped and he moved both hands to cup her smooth cheeks as he continued to taste her lips. She pressed into his kiss, moving her own delicate hands to his face. Sampling the sweetness her mouth was the biggest mistake he'd ever made. Just one would never be enough.

Reluctant, Thomas pulled away, aching for more, but knowing he must stop now or he never would. His rapid breathing matched hers and they stared at each other in bewildered silence while the mischievous fire crackled on, as if glad to be the only voyeur.

Her lips parted, her breath catching, and he wanted to believe she was begging him to lean forward and begin again.

Reality suddenly smacked him across the face. The more probable fact was that she was upset by his forwardness. After all, she'd wanted a friend to talk to, not a lover to ravish her.

Before he could do any more damage, he stood and walked to the fireplace, then dropped two more logs on the dying embers. Trying to calm the raging flood in his veins, he stared and laughed inwardly at the sparks that flew in the air. That kiss had generated sparks a hundred times more numerous than the ones popping before him.

"Forgive me, Eliza," he said, still facing the flames and in as calm as voice as he could manage. "That was dreadfully inappropriate of me."

He looked over his shoulder. Eliza gripped the shawl around her with such intensity, her knuckles were white, her gaze in her lap. An emotion swept across her face as she peered up at him. She looked hurt.

Fool! Now he'd gone and made it worse. Why couldn't he have left his emotions where they belonged? She would be all too glad to get away from him as soon as she could. He must stop allowing his heart to direct his actions instead of his head.

"Don't worry," he said. "Just because we're allowing people to think we're husband and wife doesn't mean I'll treat you as such." He exhaled loud, trying to expel his self-directed anger. "It won't happen again."

Chapter Fifteen

The two weeks following Thomas's bewitching kiss dragged on as if they were two years. That blissful, fleeting moment all but consumed Eliza's mind. There were times when she relived it, springing to life the same beautiful passions she'd relished when his lips had touched hers.

Now, he refused to talk to her, except to offer a muted greeting and hardly even looked in her direction. She couldn't deny the powerful yearning between them and she was sure he'd felt it too. So why did he avoid her as if she was some horrid disease? Samuel's kiss had produced but a single drop of wanting in comparison to the oceans of desire that Thomas swelled within her.

The days were very short now and many of their evenings were spent in front of the fire. Eliza would read aloud while Kitty sewed or mended in the dim light. Thomas kept busy with extraneous tasks far away from their presence.

Eliza craved his closeness, but employed her acting skills and kept aloof. She sent him only tiny smiles when he walked by, pretending she didn't hear him come in the room, forcing herself not to look at him if he joined them by the fire. It took all her strength to not allow her eyes to linger on his kind face, and smile the way he made her want to smile.

One bitter cold evening, Thomas came into the main room and placed a large pile of fresh cut logs near the hearth. He bent and arranged the wood, while the fire made alluring shadows dance across his face. She noticed the evening whiskers that covered his jaw and chin, and how bits of his long dark hair freed themselves from the ribbon that held them in place behind his head.

To her surprise, he started talking. "I've asked Nathaniel to join us for a special dinner on Sunday evening. I hope that will be agreeable to you. I think it would be enjoyable for us to have a little change of pace and celebrate your recovery, Eliza."

What? He'd actually addressed her! She sent a fleeting glance to Kitty. From her wide-eyed expression, her sister could not believe it either. This must be a positive sign. And since they could do nothing but stay in the house every hour of the day, a change would be more than welcome.

So he *had* noticed she was doing much better. Of course he must have, but he'd never breathed a word of it since he had stopped his constant attentions at her bedside.

Thomas turned from his crouched position in front of the pile of logs and peered at both she and Kitty with an arm draped over his knee. If he had thought about her that much, the least she could do was show him her gratitude.

Meeting his gaze, Eliza allowed herself to smile as wide as she wanted. She thought his sapphire eyes filled with longing, but before she could be sure he looked away and turned his attention to Kitty.

"So what do you say, Kitty? Do you like that idea?"

"Yes, indeed! 'Tis a marvelous plan, Thomas!"

Thomas turned back to his task with the wood. "What about you, Eliza?"

Why doesn't he look at me? She pressed her hands in her lap and struggled to keep her voice even. "I'm thrilled as well. Thank you, Thomas."

"Excellent." He got up, and moved his head in their direction from over his shoulder. "I'll be going to bed now. If you stay up, there are plenty of logs to keep the fire going. Goodnight."

He walked away without another word.

An instant emptiness filled Eliza's belly. It was from the nervous excitement. Nothing else.

The next morning Nathaniel made an early visit. He burst through the door without knocking, as usual, carrying a large parcel under his arm.

"Good morning, one and all!" he said, loud and jolly. "I come bearing gifts!"

Kitty's cheeks reddened when Nathaniel winked at her, and Eliza giggled behind her hand.

"Do sit down, Doctor Smith. And please tell us what all this excitement is about." Eliza pointed to the chair closest to the kitchen door.

"Oh, thank you, but I'm much too animated to sit just now."

Thomas came in from the back, a relaxed smile lighting his face. "Nathaniel, what brings you here so early?"

"Nothing particular. I just had a little something for the ladies and I wanted to bring it by." Nathaniel moved to the table between the two large chairs and set his package down. "So did Thomas tell you of my idea?"

"What idea?" Eliza glanced toward Thomas who leaned against the stone around the fireplace with his arms across his chest.

"The idea for a celebration dinner, of course."

Eliza and Kitty exchanged curious glances.

"He didn't say it was your idea. Not that it matters, of course." The rosiness in Kitty's cheeks spread across her face. "We're just happy to have something different and exciting to look forward to."

Nathaniel's eyebrows shot up. He looked mischievous. "Thomas wanted to take credit for the idea himself, did he?"

Thomas rolled his eyes and shook his head with a playful grin, then pushed off the wall and walked into the kitchen.

Eliza's heart slowed and she bit her lip. So Thomas hadn't really been thinking about her. It had been Nathaniel's idea all along.

Filling the hole that dug in her chest, Eliza lifted her chin. She didn't need his attentions. After all, she wouldn't see him when all this was over. Why fret about something so trivial?

"Well, never mind." Nathaniel motioned for them to come closer to the small table where he'd laid the large package.

Eliza sat in the chair and Kitty stood beside her.

Nathaniel spoke louder and pointed his face in an exaggerated manner toward the kitchen. "Thomas is one lucky man! I don't have even one pretty lady at my house, let alone two!" He laughed and looked again at Eliza and Kitty. This time his voice was quiet. "I saw these gowns in the shop downtown and they begged me to buy them. One for each of you."

Eliza's face went slack. He'd bought them gowns? Heavens! How would they ever repay him? "You really shouldn't have, Doctor."

"Think nothing of it."

Kitty pressed her hands against her chest, sending

Eliza a wide-eyed look and mouthed, "Gowns?"

Eliza could only shrug her response before Nathaniel continued.

"Would you like to do the honors and open it, Miss Katherine?" He looked at Kitty and winked again.

She glanced at Eliza as if searching for approval before sprouting a grin that made her face glow and untied the ribbon, quickly unfolding the first gown.

She gasped in delight and Eliza froze. She'd never seen anything so lovely.

"That one's for you, Miss Katherine," Nathaniel said with a lopsided grin.

Kitty held the emerald silk up to her body and twirled, watching the skirt float on the air. Trimmed with delicate gold-colored lace, the dark green gown contrasted beautifully with Kitty's dark auburn hair. Red embroidered roses traced the bodice and the edges of the sleeves.

"Doctor, this is the finest gown I've ever seen. I can't thank you enough."

His voice lowered and for a moment his eyes turned dreamy. "You'll look marvelous in it, I have no doubt." With a quick shake of his head he cleared his throat and the usual gaiety returned to his voice. "And you don't have to thank me. Just promise me you'll make your fabulous carrot pudding on our special evening and that will be thanks enough."

Gratitude for Nathaniel's kindness moved through Eliza like warm steam. She pressed a hand to her chest. How marvelous it was to see such a smile on her sister's face. Her breath caught. Kitty was no longer just a girl of seventeen. These past weeks had changed her forever—into a gracious woman.

Wrapped in the joy of watching Kitty's

merriment, Eliza didn't notice Nathaniel standing in front of her until he spoke. "This one's for you, Miss Campbell."

She turned her head and sucked in a slow breath, her eyes swiftly trailing the magnificent gown from top to bottom. Never in her life had she seen anything so breathtaking.

The brocaded silk gown was dusty pink. Soft cream-colored lace followed the low neckline and around the openings of the sleeves. The stomacher was embroidered with the most intricate cream-colored floral pattern to match the lace, and embedded with hundreds of white beads. Her face heated with the intimacy of the gift. They could never accept. How much must it have cost him?

She looked up, her face glowing like the embers in the fire behind her. A movement caught her eye and she tossed her gaze at the kitchen door. Thomas stood in the doorway, but when her face turned toward him he ducked away as if he hoped to remain unseen.

Her earlier merriment crashed to the floor, leaving her with a rotten emptiness.

Eliza placed her hands around her middle and gripped tight hoping to press away the aching. She fingered the soft fabric. "Oh, Doctor, these gowns are so lovely, but we simply can't accept. They're much too expensive and—"

Nathaniel put his hand in the air, motioning for her to stop. "Not another word." His voice was low and pointed as if he hoped Kitty would not hear. "You can accept them, and you will. You wouldn't want to disappoint someone who so desperately wants to please you, now would you?" Nathaniel whispered with a curious gleam in his eye.

Eliza slanted her head. "I'm sorry, Doctor, I don't understand."

Nathaniel opened his mouth to continue, but Thomas's commanding voice dominated the room.

"So what time can we expect you on Sunday, Doctor?"

Eliza noted the ease with which Thomas averted his gaze. She tried not to want him to look at her, but the desire betrayed her at every turn. She kept her vision at either the ground or the gown and pretended not to notice he was only four feet away.

"Well, since you three can't venture out in society, being that you are hunted by the law," he said with a chuckle, sitting in the chair Eliza had initially offered him. "I wanted to propose a small Sunday service here before dinner. What do you say to six o'clock?"

Thomas nodded in agreement, then looked at both Eliza and Kitty for approval.

"That's a fine idea. I'm glad *you* thought of it," Thomas said, pacing back into the kitchen. "Until Sunday, my friend."

Nathaniel rose and stood in front of Eliza. His pleasing face beamed as if he had a secret. "Sunday will be full of entertainment. I'm looking forward to it."

He whirled around, and went to Kitty before he put on his hat and coat. "You'll look like the royalty in that gown, my dear." He winked at her again, sending the blood into Kitty's face.

The three of them shared their goodbyes and Nathaniel bounced out the door with the same vim as when he'd entered.

Sunday will be full of entertainment. What in heaven's name did that mean? Eliza pushed the comment aside and focused on the other cryptic comments he'd made. If Nathaniel was implying that Thomas had some hand in the planning of this celebratory dinner, she figured the least she could do was wear the gown—just this once—and do her best to enjoy the evening whether Thomas looked at her or not.

Samuel sat in his empty Boston office, his mind blank, staring out his window. Snow fell in heavy clumps, adding to the empty coldness that had taken root inside him the day Eliza disappeared.

The doctor in Sandwich claimed she was dead. The initial shock of it had almost knocked him to the ground. He drowned in the depressing thoughts of a life lived without her.

Still he couldn't believe it was true. Something deep inside told his heart she still lived, despite the doctor's statement. Somewhere in the black, cold November night Eliza waited for him to rescue her.

The power of their love surpassed all tribulation. They reached for each other from the distances and he knew—even now—Eliza was calling for him, just as his soul was calling for her.

The door burst open and Samuel jumped from his chair. The cold air blasted his body as a snow-covered Donaldson stood in the doorway.

Samuel growled, his nostrils flaring. "Well? Close the door."

Donaldson did so and came to stand in front of the desk. "News, Captain."

"What is it?"

Donaldson reached into his knapsack and pulled

out a letter. “I’ve just received word from Clark in Salem.”

A meager hope took shape in his chest as he snatched the paper. “And?”

“He says he’s spotted a man and two women matching the descriptions of Thomas and the Campbell girls just outside the city.”

“When was this?”

“Two days ago.” Donaldson nodded when he spoke, but kept his eyes in front of him and away from Samuel.

“How positive is he that those three are the people we are looking for?”

“Quite positive, sir. He didn’t get a close look, but he said he’s willing to bet his life it’s them.”

Samuel laughed, his irritation growing. “So he’s not positive, but he’s willing to bet his life on it, is he?”

He whirled toward the fire and wanted to beat his own dumb head against the hard wall.

Thomas no doubt paid the sailor and that impudent doctor to make up such a story to keep him off their trail and lead them in the opposite direction. Such a stupid mistake had now cost him weeks. In truth Eliza had been alive all this time and he had been sitting, doing nothing, like a bumbling oaf.

Pushing his hand through his hair, Samuel closed his eyes and shook his head. *I’m so sorry, Eliza.* His anger toward himself and hatred toward Thomas crashed into his lungs.

“Is there a message you would like me to relay to Clark, sir?” Donaldson asked. “What are your orders?”

"No message," Samuel said, grabbing his sword and pistol. "I plan to bring the blackguard in myself."

Chapter Sixteen

Thomas tied his cravat.

Then he untied it and tied it again. His sorry reflection peered back, mocking him.

It still wasn't right.

Frustrated, he yanked it undone and fussed with it three more times until it rested just the way he wanted.

He had been to numerous dinner parties in Boston—ones with many more guests and at homes of great opulence, yet he'd never been this nervous. So why did this menial party at his humble home make his hands fumble over his buttons?

This dinner was intended to be a celebration for Eliza's miraculous recovery and she deserved nothing less. What could be so intimidating about that?

Thomas sighed aloud as he fastidiously tied his hair behind his head with a dark blue ribbon.

Eliza.

She was unlike any other woman Thomas had ever known. He admired her strength, her courage, her humble willingness to admit what she didn't know, and her openness in acknowledging when she was afraid. Her hunger for knowledge was contagious, and supremely attractive.

As he moved his arms through the sleeves of the blue-gray suit jacket that matched his breeches, a realization came alive amid his tangled thoughts. *God has placed her in my life to help her find the truth she needs!* How had he not seen that before? This entire time he'd been trying to do what was honorable by staying away and avoiding Eliza. If he really wanted to help her, he would teach her! He would tell her what he knew about her Father, the things he'd said and the things he'd done. Eliza wanted to know, and might have even asked him if he hadn't been so eager to keep his distance.

Thomas sneered to himself. He was an even greater fool than he'd realized, but there was still time to make it right. He could finally do good for someone for a change, forever dispelling the nagging repetitions of his father's hateful rants.

Now, when he looked in the mirror, he smiled. His stubborn cravat remained in perfect form, as did the rest of his favorite suit.

Yes. Since Eliza would be forced to remain in Sandwich until the search for them ended, he planned to make the most of it. No more hiding, no more silence. He prayed God would help him perform his mission without succumbing to his emotions. Eliza needed his help, not his affection.

Thomas buttoned the legs of his breeches when he heard the front door open and close.

Nathaniel's voice rang through the house. "Greetings, one and all! I am here. The party may now begin."

With a quick chuckle, Thomas worked his feet into his shiny black shoes.

"Hello?" Nathaniel called.

"Coming." Thomas checked his appearance one last time and emerged into the main room. "Sorry. I was just finishing."

Nathaniel whistled in approval and widened his eyes. "Thomas, you look quite dashing. You know you really didn't have to dress up like that for me."

He smiled at his own joke and slapped Thomas on the shoulder.

"You don't look too terrible, yourself," Thomas said as they each took a seat in front of the hearth.

"Well, I donned my best suit as you can see."

Thomas smirked. "I noticed."

"I think this is a wonderful idea of yours, Thomas. I can't figure why you wouldn't want them to know this is all your doing—the gowns and everything." Nathaniel's volume quieted.

Thomas moved his head to peer in the direction of the stairs. "Eliza already feels like she owes me for the first dresses, along with everything else. I don't want her believing she's obligated to repay me for anything." He reached for his shoe and used his thumb to work away a smudge. "I wanted to do something for them. After everything they've been through and for how well they've handled it all, I feel it's the least I can do. So no, I don't want the girls to know. It will make it easier that way when it comes time for them to leave."

"When will you tell her about Samuel?"

Thomas's gut twisted. "I won't. There's no need to tell her."

Nathaniel tilted his head. "No need? I disagree, Thomas. You must to tell her about Samuel. I find it difficult to believe she knows his true nature, and she needs to understand what kind of man he really is. You can't let her go back to him without knowing the truth."

Thomas gritted his teeth and wiped his hand over his mouth. Of course he didn't want to send Eliza back to that snake. *Lord, what am I to do?*

A weighty silence lingered between them before Nathaniel spoke again. "You're becoming attached to them Thomas, whether you'll allow yourself to admit it or not."

Thomas refused to respond. Ridiculous comment. He flicked a vagrant string from his sleeve as Nathaniel continued his lecture.

"Did you know you always refer to Eliza and Kitty as 'the girls?' I think it's endearing, but also reveals your true feelings." Nathaniel's smile bent upward. "Eliza has captured your heart. You can't deny it."

Thomas glared at his friend who only grinned in return.

"You know," Nathaniel said, an impressive seriousness knitting his voice. "They don't have to leave. They could stay right here with you. What life do they have for them in Boston? They've no family, nothing to entice them away from you."

"They have more than you think," Thomas shot back. "Besides, in the end, Eliza may decide she'll marry Samuel after all."

"Don't fool yourself." Nathaniel leaned forward and rested his elbows on his knees. "I've seen the way Eliza looks at you, and her eyes are not those of a woman longing for home, let alone another man."

Thomas exhaled, his shoulders dropping as he did. "I've told you, I will not water the garden of affection." He stood, walked to the fire and rubbed the wood along the mantel. "Although, I have decided to help her learn what she wants to know about her Father—she deserves that. I've already created too much turmoil in her life and I don't want to be responsible for any more."

Nathaniel growled and began to respond, but Thomas continued before he could start. "Let me handle my own affairs, Nathaniel."

His friend slumped in his chair and shook his

head, a disapproving expression clouding his face. "As you wish."

Thomas changed the subject. "Dinner's been ready for a while now. When do you think the girls will be down?"

Nathaniel tilted his mouth, then lifted and lowered one shoulder. "A woman's toilette is a mystery and one I will never pretend to understand."

Thomas chuckled and kicked a renegade stick back into the blaze.

"Good evening, gentleman."

Thomas spun on his heel and Nathaniel jumped to his feet. Kitty had somehow entered without them knowing. She looked like a grown woman in her emerald gown. Her dark hair rested on top of her head in a stunning array of curls, the sparkle in her young eyes the most fetching accessory.

Thomas bowed. She curtsied.

Nathaniel's eyes were wide and he shook his head after a moment of silence. Thomas bit his cheek to hide the grin that pressed on his mouth. He'd never seen Nathaniel lose hold of his composure.

Stuttering, Nathaniel finally spoke. "M-Miss Katherine—Kitty, you must be the most beautiful woman in Massachusetts." He offered a generous bow and quickly took her hand, pressing his lips to her skin.

Kitty's face turned a healthy shade of red. "You can't mean that, Doctor, though I appreciate your compliments."

His features brightened as if he'd recovered his usual charm. "I never say anything I don't mean. And please, call me Nathaniel."

He offered his elbow and Kitty once again ducked her chin. "Thank you . . . Nathaniel."

Thomas glanced back at the stairs, excited nerves leaping in his stomach.

"Is Eliza coming?" After the words escaped his mouth he realized how comical he sounded. Of course she was coming. "I mean to say, is Eliza ready?"

A wide grin washed over Kitty's face, as if she were hiding something. "She'll be down shortly."

Thomas nodded and rested his fidgety hands on the back of the embroidered chair. Nathaniel led Kitty to the other seat and helped her to sit.

At that moment, the dainty tap of Eliza's shoes on the stairs forced Thomas to whirl around.

Nathaniel came up behind him. "Steady, boy."

Thomas clenched his jaw to keep it from gaping and dropped his hands to his sides.

His eyes traced Eliza's dainty form. She was even more radiant in that gown than he'd imagined and her face glittered with the most magnificent smile he'd ever seen. The fitted gown accentuated her perfect curves and impossibly tiny waist. The white lace around the neckline tickled her creamy skin, while the dusty-pink color drew out the rosy nature of her cheeks and lips.

He tried, but he couldn't stop staring. Her hair was curled like Kitty's and wrapped with a delicate ribbon that matched the color of her gown. Her creamy complexion and the velvety look of her long neck were so enticing he had to fight the sudden urge to taste it.

Eliza curtsied low and dipped her head. Upon rising she lifted her lashes and spoke to him in a tantalizing timbre. "Good evening, Thomas."

Thomas's heart beat with such profound strength, it ripped every word from his mind. He wanted to say how beautiful she was. He wanted to tell her he was sorry for keeping his distance when she needed him. Even more than that, he wanted to move his face near hers, and inhale her graceful rose scent deep into his lungs before tasting her lips once again.

Every appropriate response fled his mind as his blood raced around his body. He bowed. "Good evening, Eliza."

"Do my eyes deceive me?"

Nathaniel, back to his charismatic self, pushed Thomas aside and kissed Eliza's hand as he bowed with dramatic flare. "You are even more alluring than Aphrodite herself, my dear."

Eliza smiled again and giggled low in her throat. "You are too generous, Doctor."

"I am too enamored. You and your sister shine like the stars themselves." A hearty grin flashed across his proud face. "Shall we go in to dinner?" He took his place beside Kitty and sent a flashing glance to Thomas, no doubt intended to instruct him to make the most of the moment.

Thomas could kill himself. *Good evening*? That's all he could say?

Eliza's body faced away from him, but she turned in his direction and the rest of her followed, her gown sweeping across the floor.

Thomas closed the space between them, offering his arm. "Shall we go in?"

Her slender hand grasped his arm. "You look very nice this evening, Thomas."

Thomas's tongue dried up in his mouth, shriveling his ability to speak. He could never compete with Nathaniel's theatrical praises. He'd have to just say what he thought. "You're a vision, Eliza."

Her eyes twinkled up at him and her fingers tightened around his bicep.

Nathaniel and Kitty were already seated when Thomas and Eliza entered the eating area.

Thomas almost laughed. They must be quite a sight—dressed in their finery, sitting at a simple table eating a simple meal, but none of them seemed to mind. They acted like life-long friends. Kitty insisted on making the delectable fare herself. The thick lobster soup, along with the fresh bread, tasted even better than it smelled. And Nathaniel made sure to compliment her on the carrot pudding, though Thomas could never figure how his friend liked the stuff no matter who made it.

Eliza glowed. He had never seen her so relaxed and carefree. Nathaniel kept up a lively conversation, sharing stories and telling jokes that kept bright smiles on the girl's faces throughout the entire meal. While the utensils clinked against the fine plates, and the candles sparkled off the glasses, Thomas contented himself with watching, too besotted to even enjoy the food in his mouth. He feasted upon Eliza with his eyes, wishing the evening would never end.

After dinner, and a delicious dessert of apple tansy, the four of them retired to the main room, bringing two additional chairs from the table and setting them in front of the fire. They sang a few hymns and read the story of Christ walking on the water.

After praying, Thomas looked up to find Eliza's eyes focused on him. A modest smile pulled at her mouth, which grew into a palpable longing that painted itself into her sweet face, turning his stomach as light as the first flakes of snow.

He was in grave danger of losing his heart. She was far too sweet, far too real, and far too bewitching for him to stay away.

Tingles of pure joy streamed over Eliza. She'd never enjoyed an evening so much in all her life. Being here with Kitty, and Thomas and Nathaniel made her almost believe she belonged here.

It pleased her to no end the way Thomas looked at her. Since their ill-advised kiss he had paid her little attention, but not tonight. It seemed all the awkwardness was forgotten, and they were back to being the friends they used to be.

Hearing Thomas pray during their small church service startled her. She listened to him ask God to bless this land and to help the Colonists secure their rights and freedoms. He prayed for wisdom, and the strength to go forward in a righteous cause. She couldn't keep her head bowed, no matter how she tried. Thomas spoke to God as if He really did care for their cause, and would help them secure it. In that instance Eliza wanted more than ever to know what Thomas knew—what Father had known. How could she build up the courage to ask him to help her? For that's what she needed, desperately. He had known Father and could tell her what she needed to know. She'd read the book Father had given Thomas and found it fascinating, and at the same time perplexing. But Thomas could help her—if only he would.

Kitty's fidgety fingers drew Eliza's attentions. With pursed lips and how she wriggled in her chair,

Kitty's discomfort stood out like a cardinal in a snow-flocked tree. Why did the talk of the patriot cause give her such unease? Releasing a slight sigh, Eliza dropped her chin again. Father had said she wouldn't take the news well, yet she'd kept silent, so perhaps it would work itself out over time. Eliza could only hope.

A loud "amen" cut through Eliza's inner conference. She refocused her gaze and drank in the perfect male form before her. He looked so strong in his tailored suit, his muscular shoulders and arms filling out every inch of fabric. The color of it brought out the bewitching blue of his eyes and contrasted with the magnificent midnight color of his hair. His masculine face was freshly shaven, and looked so smooth it tempted her to reach out and test its softness.

She tried not to be obvious as her eyes trailed over him, but he caught her and raised his eyebrows ever so slight as a grin tugged at his lips. She ducked her head, the blood rushing up her neck and into her face.

Nathaniel jumped to his feet and removed his jacket, laying it over the back of his chair. "That was an inspiring service, Thomas, and I believe it should be followed by an inspiring bit of entertainment."

Kitty clapped her hands. "Oh yes! What a lovely idea."

"What shall we do then?" Nathaniel asked.

"Why don't we have Liza perform for us?" Kitty said.

Eliza snapped her head toward her sister. "Me?"

Kitty tilted her head. "Yes, like you used to do! I haven't heard you perform Shakespeare in so long."

Nathaniel sat back down. "I have heard tales of

your talents, Eliza. Shakespeare is one of my favorites. It would be a great honor if you'd perform for us."

Eliza turned to Thomas, shooting him a stern but playful glare. "Did you have anything to do with this?"

Thomas attempted to smother a telling grin. "Nothing whatsoever."

She turned again toward her sister. Kitty bit her lip and tilted her head farther as if to say "pretty please?"

Eliza looked around the room tapping her foot, searching for a reason to decline. The last thing she wanted was to make a fool out of herself. "I'd love to, Kitty, but it's been such a long time and I don't have any of my books with me. I really need to freshen my memory before I do anything like that and I'm out of practice on my recitations. I'm sorry, my dear."

"Not to worry." Nathaniel popped out of his chair again and went to fetch a small bundle by the front door. "It so happens that I've brought such a book with me."

Eliza threw an accusatory glance at Thomas. He grinned wide as the horizon, and leaned back in his seat. She couldn't get out of it now. She was trapped. She pinched her lips and laced her fingers in her lap.

Nathaniel came to her chair and held the thick book in front of her. "Your reputation precedes you, Miss Campbell. You must indulge us, please."

Eliza swiped it from him, giving him an exaggerated glare before the grin she hid brightened her face. She rose and stood in front of the fire, trying to ignore the fact that every eye in the room was positioned on her. Thumbing through the book, she struggled to locate a short, dull scene—nothing romantic, nothing dramatic. Something she could easily read without much emotion.

"Liza, do my favorite, will you?"

Eliza pulled her gaze from the book and stared at her sister, shooting fire through the slits in her eyes. Kitty smirked as if she'd had it planned from the beginning. There was no possible way she would read that scene.

"I'm sorry, Kitty. I don't remember what one that is. Besides, I think—"

"Of course you do, silly. It's act two scene two from *Romeo and Juliet*."

Eliza's lungs flattened and her face roasted from within. There was no possible way to do that romantic reading without feeling completely foolish, especially in front of Thomas. Acting it out for Kitty, in their room, when they were younger and with no audience was a different situation all together. She glanced at Nathaniel, then Thomas. Both men smirked and didn't even try to hide the satisfied grins on their faces.

Kitty pleaded again, melting the barrier around Eliza's heart. How could she resist her sister? After all her kindness and patience, after all her caring and with nary a complaint on her lips, Kitty deserved a bit of diversion.

Eliza released a soft sigh. "Alright. I'll read it."

Kitty squealed, and Eliza had to smile. She could do it for Kitty—despite her mischievousness—and forget about the other two.

Thumbing through the book to the section on "plays", Eliza located the requested scene.

"Do you plan on reading both Romeo *and* Juliet's lines?" Nathaniel asked none too casual.

Eliza's stomach lurched and she blinked. What

was he suggesting? She would rather die than read it with Nathaniel. Then again, she would rather be buried alive under a mountain of rank earth than read with Thomas.

Without thinking, she did what she hoped might save her from complete humiliation.

"I suppose I really cannot perform this alone, can I? Would you be so kind as to join me by reading Romeo's lines, Doctor?"

Nathaniel beamed at the invitation and pushed out of his chair. "Why, it would be my pleasure, *Juliet*."

Chapter Seventeen

This is ludicrous. Thomas forced himself to calm his tensing muscles and strained to keep from jumping out of his chair when Eliza asked Nathaniel to read.

Better to have Nathaniel performing with her, that much was certain. The last thing he needed was to stand next to her, to smell her sweet fragrance, gaze into her dark eyes, and feel the warmth of her body radiating only a few inches from his.

No. Let Nathaniel do it. Thomas had never been very good at reading aloud anyway.

While the two performers held the book and reviewed their lines, standing much too close, Kitty leaned over to him from her chair. "Liza does this so well. I can't wait for you to see it. It will be divine!"

Thomas's insides solidified and he didn't know how to respond. "We'll see."

Eliza stepped forward. "Kitty, I remember how you used to like to 'announce' me. Would you do us the honors?"

"With pleasure!" Kitty stood in front of the fire. In her most poised tone she announced the entertainment. "Ladies and Gentleman, *Romeo and Juliet*, act two scene two."

Once she'd taken her seat, Nathaniel cleared his throat and began.

"But soft!"

Even at the beginning of the monologue, Nathaniel made it painfully clear he was no actor. He read flat and stumbled over his words. None of that seemed to bother him or Eliza. She looked at him and smiled, trying hard not to laugh. He chuckled at his mistakes and continued on, sending Kitty an occasional smile.

Thomas sighed, his tense shoulders relaxing into the chair behind him. Maybe this wouldn't be as bad as he'd imagined. So long as things didn't get too intimate, he could sit through it.

When Eliza's turn came to read, her voice floated like a song. The words flowed from her—she became the part. Her eyes filled with longing as she spoke the words. Thomas became so mesmerized he nearly forgot how uncomfortable he'd been to have his best friend reading by her side instead of him.

Thomas looked at Nathaniel. It was apparent she had entranced him as well. His friend couldn't seem to look away, and smiled with more sincerity than Thomas had ever seen from him. When his turn came, his voice dripped emotion—however ridiculous he continued to sound—and he drew Eliza closer.

Suddenly the temperature of the room increased by twenty degrees.

Thomas's mouth went dry and he took off his jacket, but the room was still too hot. He unbuttoned the cuffs of his sleeves and rolled them up.

Eliza and Nathaniel went back and forth, getting more comfortable and more absorbed in their roles. They appeared to be having a marvelous time. Too marvelous.

Thomas's legs burned as if he'd sat on a pile of

ants. He had to use all his endurance not to squirm and move about in his chair.

Twice Eliza had snuck a peek at him between lines, gifting him with a titillating smile. He hoped she didn't notice his uncomfortable writhing and assume he didn't care for her performance, because he did care for it. Very much. Too much.

"I would not for the world they saw thee here," Eliza said.

"I have night's cloak to hide me from their eyes." Nathaniel failed again with miserable cruelty at his dramatic attempts, but he made up for it with flare.

Eliza pressed her lips down as if to try and hold back a smile and accompanying giggle.

Nathaniel moved closer to her as he spoke. She no longer needed the book. It was evident her memory had been refreshed, so Nathaniel held it in one hand, and placed his other around her waist. She moved closer, placed her hand on his chest and gazed up at him. Nathaniel pulled her completely against him.

Thomas gripped the upholstery to keep from bolting out of his chair.

He looked at Kitty, expecting her to be just as riled. She smiled as big as the sky with her head at a slant.

How could anyone be enjoying this?

Eliza smiled up at Nathaniel, a coy slope to her lips.

He drew her closer and lowered his head. "And but thou love me, let them find me here."

Thomas's blood boiled. "That's enough!" He bellowed, shooting out of his seat.

The two actors jumped apart, their mouths agape. Kitty stared with round eyes.

Jaw solid, he walked to Nathaniel and swiped the

book from his hand. “Sit down, you’re terrible. I can’t stand to watch you. It’s my turn.”

Nathaniel raised one eyebrow and dipped his chin. A bold, satisfied grin swept across his face as he took the seat where Thomas had been. “Continue, oh great one.”

Thomas glared at his friend, calculating the different ways he could wipe the smirk off his face, then shuffled into Nathaniel’s previous position. His stomach turned weightless. Palms clammy, his breathing faltered.

This was a mistake.

Eliza’s face shone up at him, sparkling like the stars in the winter sky. The corners of her mouth lifted ever so slight. The orange glow of the fire kissed her supple cheek and made him want to do the same.

He kicked away the dangerous thoughts, and carefully slipped his hand around her tiny waist, relishing the warm smoothness of her gown and spread his fingers across her back.

Her dark eyes widened and she inhaled a sharp breath. In her gaze circled a mixture of nervousness and pleasure as the color in her cheeks deepened to scarlet. He smiled and pulled her body closer to his.

Pure heaven! Perhaps this wasn’t a mistake after all.

Thomas pointed to the words. “Why don’t you start from where you say, ‘I would not for the world they find thee here.”

Eliza bobbed her head in agreement before releasing a soft breath through tight lips. Did she feel it too? The force between them that acted like a heavenly vice, pressing them ever closer?

He almost couldn’t focus when she started

talking. "I would not for the world they find thee here."

Her quiet voice wavered and Thomas reserved a satisfied smile.

"I have night's cloak to hide me from their sight," Thomas said, allowing the deep resonance of his voice to circle between them.

She lifted her eyes to his as a beguiling grin peeked over her lips. Slowly, she traced her fingers up his chest. His heart thumped at a ferocious pace and he had no doubt she could feel it through his waistcoat. The sensation of her hand on his body intoxicated him.

He did his best to keep his sound even. "And but thou love me, let them find me here. My life were better ended by their hate, then prolonged wanting of thy love."

Eliza's breathing quickened, and the red in her face turned an even deeper shade of crimson while her eyes beckoned him closer.

After a moment of luscious silence Thomas cleared his throat.

"It's your turn," he whispered.

She shook her head, and looked toward the book. "Of course. Uh . . . where were we?"

Thomas pointed to her spot.

Eliza turned back to face him, as if fully composed. Her tantalizing voice reached into him and wrapped around his heart. "By whose direction foundest thou out this place?"

Thomas couldn't resist and pulled her closer, heedless of the two spectators only a few feet away. "By love, who first did prompt me to inquire. He lent me counsel and I lent him eyes. I am no pilot; yet were thou as far as that vast shore washed with the farthest sea, I would adventure for such merchandise." He lowered his tone, adding to it a husky vibration.

Eliza froze in his embrace. Her hand on his chest moved higher and pressed stronger.

Neither of them spoke. Neither of them moved.

If they were alone, he would kiss her. He wanted to kiss her. And with passion. Having her body to near to his, seeing her lips parted—so vulnerable and wanting—made it impossible to turn away. He remembered the sweet taste of her mouth and relished in the memory of her breath on his face, the soft brush of her nose on his cheek.

Thomas increased the pressure on her back, making her torso press firm against his. Time suspended around them and the world misted away.

Eliza breathed harder and pushed away, waking Thomas from his blissful state. She stepped back until he could no longer keep his grip on her. A physical pain ached in his fingers as her body left his grasp.

"I . . . I'm getting a bit light headed. I should sit." She blinked rapidly a few times and took the chair next to her sister.

"Oh, Liza can't you just finish, there's not much more," Kitty pleaded, swiveling in her seat.

Eliza looked back at Thomas, her face more flushed than ever. She placed both hands over her stomach and breathed out from the small O in her lips. "No, I'm sorry, Kitty. Perhaps another time."

Kitty gave an exaggerated frown then forced a small grin. "Oh, alright, I understand. You did a marvelous job. No actress could have done any better."

While the girls whispered to one another,

Nathaniel stood and faced the fire, his hands clasped behind him. "That was quite a performance, old boy, I'm impressed. Bravo."

Thomas exhaled, hoping to drive his raging pulse into submission. "I wish I could say the same about you."

Nathaniel leaned his head back, laughing. "What, you weren't impressed?"

Thomas peered back at Eliza. She glanced up from her conversation with Kitty, then turned away again. The memory of her dainty form pressed against him was now burned into his mind forever.

"You have impeccable taste, Thomas." Nathaniel's gaze flitted to both girls, landing on Kitty and lingering, before he quickly turned back to the conversation. "I can see how you have been entranced. How could you not be, when Eliza is so fair a lady. She may be a decoy wife, my friend," Nathaniel spoke low through closed teeth, "but I'd venture to guess she'd be willing to be more."

Thomas rubbed his hand over his face, trying to scrub away his monopolizing thoughts. How could he spend any time with Eliza and not take her in his arms and kiss her with all the passion that swelled within him? At this moment he could easily see Eliza as his real wife—in fact *wanted* it to be so. But it would be better to fight such imaginations. Better for the both of them. She needed to know all that he did about her Father. It was his duty and he must act on his resolve to teach her, despite the risk to his heart.

"Let it go, Nathaniel."

Nathaniel shook his head then turned his back to the fire and spoke loud. "I can't recall the last time I've had such an enjoyable evening among friends."

"Well, we owe this to you, Doctor." Kitty lifted her

chin and pressed her knitted fingers into her lap. "You can't know how much this means to us."

Eliza stood, taking hold of Kitty's hand. "Yes, Doctor. Thank you so much." She moved her eyes to Thomas. "And thank you as well, Thomas."

Her glowing eyes melted him and it took a moment for Thomas to find his voice. "It was my pleasure."

Thomas opened his mouth, to respond, but Eliza continued. "It truly was a magnificent evening, but I do believe it's time for both Kitty and I to retire."

"But the evening's only just begun," Nathaniel protested.

"Liza, must we?" Kitty spun toward her sister, holding her hand to her chest. Silent, Eliza kept her eyes to the ground, when Kitty took her arm. "I should have known. We don't want you making yourself overtired. I guess this is goodnight, gentlemen."

Nathaniel gave Kitty a sweeping bow as they said a quick "good-evening" before the two girls moved toward the stairs. Thomas's gaze trailed Eliza, and just before she disappeared behind the wall, she peeked at him over the curve of her shoulder. Her eyes locked with his and she instantly looked away, stealing Thomas's breath. Then she disappeared up the stairs.

He gripped the chair beside him to keep from floating away. His life was changing and despite his greatest efforts, he couldn't stop it. His fascination with Eliza had mounted into an all-consuming attraction. No—desire.

He dropped into the chair, sweeping his hand up and over his head.

"You look like you want to talk," Nathaniel said.

"Sure, I'll talk," Thomas replied. "I'll talk about anything but Eliza."

Nathaniel choked on a laugh before a somber veil enveloped his features.

"There *is* something I've been meaning to discuss with you—but not in front of the ladies."

Chapter Eighteen

Eliza halted at the top of the stairs. Kitty stopped as well, a puzzled wrinkle on her brow.

"Aren't you coming up?" Kitty asked.

Nodding, Eliza put a finger to her mouth. She brushed her hands in front of her, motioning Kitty to go to the room.

Kitty pursed her lips, waiting longer than Eliza wanted, then obeyed. "Fine. But don't make yourself sick."

Silent, Eliza descended a few stairs, remaining out of sight. What had Nathaniel wanted to keep from their ears? Her conscience told her it was wrong to eavesdrop, but her curious nature won the battle of wills.

"What is it?" Thomas's voice sounded quiet and nervous.

"I know you want to stay away from town—and for good reason, but I want to tell you something I've been planning."

"Planning?"

Eliza heard the rustling of feet and pressed her back firm against the wall, hoping to remain unseen. The creaking of a chair let her know someone had taken to sitting.

"The tension you felt in Boston is just as hot here."

"I know," Thomas said.

"There is much talk of the Tea Act, among other issues. I've been approached by several members of the community and they have invited me to be the leader of a group similar to your Sons of Liberty."

Eliza strained her ears as their voices dropped in volume.

"You've accepted I hope?" Thomas asked.

"Indeed. The Tories in town are causing extreme tension and discord. Those of us who believe in this cause need to band together. The stakes are very great, but the consequences we will suffer if we do not oppose the Crown are too costly—not only financially but personally as well."

Thomas's masculine voice grew deeper. "Nothing could be of more importance."

Eliza held her breath. *What are the stakes? What are the consequences?*

"I've been working for some time now to organize a large political rally. It's scheduled to take place two weeks from tomorrow just before sundown."

"Why haven't you told me this before?" Thomas asked.

"There wasn't much to say, knowing all the stress you've been under. It's not as if you could have helped me."

Thomas hummed in agreement.

The more Nathaniel spoke, the more strength flooded his voice. "Those of us in attendance plan to let our local leaders know where we stand on the issue of taxation. It's going to be a peaceful gathering, but of course the militia won't see it that way. I've just had word this very morning that three hundred people are expected to attend from Plymouth, and even more from Rochester and other surrounding provinces. I'm expecting upwards of eight hundred. With numbers that high, I imagine the British army will send even more of their minions to keep the peace." Nathaniel's voice knotted with poison.

Eliza covered her mouth to keep from gasping. Eight hundred people? Where would they fit such a crowd?

Nathaniel continued. "The rally will begin just before sundown. Wythe will be helping me lead the crowd to the courthouse. Do you know Joseph Wythe?"

More shuffling sounds echoed into the staircase and Eliza stiffened.

"No," Thomas said.

"You'd like him. Strong as an ox and, like you and I, he'd be willing to give his life for this cause. His brother Cyprian owns Newcomb Tavern. Hateful man."

"You mean Tory Tavern?" Thomas asked, with piqued interest in his tone.

"The very same. He's given Joseph his fair share of trials, God knows. At any rate, we'll meet at the south end of town, and God willing, within a few hours we'll have this county acting in the name of the people—not the king."

Eliza recognized Thomas's heavy sigh through the silence. "Sounds like quite an affair. I wish more than anything that I could attend with you, help you in some way, but I need to think about the safety of Eliza and Kitty."

"I know. I tell you not to ask for your attendance, but to caution you. There are already a larger number of Redcoats in the city, and I petition you to use even greater caution."

"How can I possibly use greater caution, I already

stay here as it is—"

"I know, but I have a grinding feeling that somehow something will go wrong and you'll be caught. Just be careful."

"Of course," Thomas said.

"I will continue to check on all of you regularly, as I have been, and help you with what you need. But as the rally draws near you must not—*must not*—come to town."

"I won't." Thomas answered with a small laugh. "Don't worry."

The chairs squeaked again and footsteps moved around the room. "I'll get on my way," Nathaniel said. "Since the girls don't know to whom the praise must honestly be directed, let me thank you, Thomas, for a most satisfying and shall I say, *enlightening* evening."

The blood in Eliza's arms and legs surged faster. This whole celebration had indeed been Thomas's doing all along?

The door opened and she imagined Nathaniel putting his hat over his head as he walked out the door.

"I couldn't have done it without you, old friend. And thank you for keeping my secret." Thomas replied.

"I always keep your secrets, Thomas."

The door closed and the lock flipped in place.

Eliza looked up to the room she shared with Kitty. The candle still glowed, but she heard no movement. Kitty must already be out of her gown and readying for bed. Eliza's curiosity and desire to speak with Thomas pooled in her legs and before any sense of reason could stop her, she emerged from her safe spot in the stairway into the dimly lit main room.

"Thomas?"

Thomas straightened from his crouched position by the fire.

"Eliza. I thought you'd retired for the evening?" The shadows from the fire caressed his chiseled face. His enchanting eyes reached out and drew her to him.

"I did, but . . ." She didn't want to admit to listening in on their conversation but she had to thank him. The words she'd tried to hold back stumbled out of her mouth. "Why didn't you want us to know this was all your doing?"

Thomas folded his arms around his muscular chest gifting her with a teasing half-smile. "You were eavesdropping."

Eliza's face heated. She licked her lips and lowered her gaze to the floor.

"Forgive me," she said gathering enough courage to look at him.

Eyes twinkling, Thomas's lips rose and his shoulders straightened. "I have nothing to say that you cannot hear, Eliza."

He motioned for her to join him in front of the fireplace. Her heart leapt to her throat and she stopped breathing. If she went anywhere near him, she feared the remaining waters in her reservoir of resistance would run dry.

His hand remained outstretched but she couldn't move. "I'll explain to you, if you come stand by the fire. It's warmer over here."

It's true. It is warmer over there. That was her only reason for failing to listen to the warning that thundered in her ears—wasn't it?

Eliza neared and stationed herself by the fire, a safe distance from him. Thomas placed one hand on the mantel, and the other behind his back as he stared into the flames.

"I've put you and your sister through so much, Eliza. I wanted to do something for you—something as a way to thank you for your temperance, but I didn't want you to think you must repay me for any of it." He paused and turned to face her. "When it comes time for you to go, I want you to keep these gowns and the others. It's my penance, I suppose."

"You bought these gowns as well?" Eliza breathed. "Thomas, they must have cost you a fortune."

"Not in the least."

He moved forward and Eliza's stomach flipped upside down. She moved back a step, afraid of what she might do if he stood any closer.

Thomas must have seen the apprehension in her eyes, for his face softened and a tiny smile lifted his lips. "And even if I had spent a fortune, Eliza, I would have considered it an honor to do so."

"We *will* repay you."

"You won't."

"We must!"

He took a step closer, his hungry eyes flowing over her.

As if propelled by invisible cords, she too began closing the distance between them. She willed him to reach out, pull her into his arms and kiss her like he'd done an eternity ago.

Then without warning, the hungry look disappeared and he backed away once again, staring into the flames as if nothing had happened.

Eliza studied the ground, her heart cold. The distance between became a cavern where her emotions echoed off the lonely, towering walls. Maybe he really didn't care. Maybe she'd imagined it all because she wanted it to be so. Maybe the emotions she'd felt between them during their reading had been an act all along.

"Eliza," Thomas said, "I've only ever done what I thought was best—though perhaps not what your father would have done. When the danger is past, I'll return you and your sister to Boston. I promise."

It is clear, then. He doesn't want me.

Eliza swallowed the hurt and blinked back a wave of tears. It made sense she would go back to Boston. They weren't really attached to each other anyway. This wasn't her real home. He didn't want to be shackled with two women for the rest of his life. He'd done his duty in caring for her and Kitty, and nothing more should be expected.

But why did such a thing have to be so painful?

The light in Eliza's sparkling complexion dimmed and Thomas's muscles tensed. He hadn't meant to hurt her. He'd seen the way she looked at him, with the same desire that burned in his chest, but he had to stay focused on what God had asked him to do. He had to ignore his desire for her, and teach her what she wanted and needed to know.

Releasing a weighted breath, Thomas shifted his weight and caught a glimpse of Robert's book on the table between the chairs. His throat thickened. What a noble man Robert had been. If only Thomas could help Eliza to see that Robert truly did everything for the welfare of his daughters.

He picked up the book, turning it over in his hands. "My father was a hard man."

Eliza pulled back, her brows pushing down. As if

unsure what to do or say, she backed into the nearest chair and knit her fingers in her lap.

Thomas faced the fire and rested his palm on the smooth wood in front of him.

"I had an older brother, Michael. He was my Father's pride and joy. Father doted on him, and loved him powerfully, but he saw me differently. Mother died bringing me into this world and Father blamed me for her death every day of my life. When I was a young boy he simply ignored me, pretended I didn't exist. The three of us came to America when I was only four years old and Father opened his printing press. As we matured, Michael said he wanted to grow up and inherit Father's business, and of course Father was thrilled, but I knew Michael cared nothing about the trade. Not like I did. I enjoyed the press, found satisfaction in the work. I felt it in my blood. We both helped in the shop, but Father hardly even recognized my presence. Whenever Father finally did speak to me he reminded me of how worthless I was—telling me I would never do anyone any good—that I was responsible for Mother's death. He already had a son that filled his every dream, what did he need me for? Of course, I did my best to please him. I studied and worked to make myself strong both in mind and body to show him I really could do all the things he claimed I couldn't. I worked hard to show him how much I excelled at the profession, but he never noticed a thing. Nothing except Michael."

Realizing he'd been talking for some time, Thomas stopped and flung a quick glance at Eliza. Her wide eyes and attentive stare reached out, stroking his stiff muscles. He hadn't talked about all of this with anyone—not even Nathaniel knew about his mother. Somehow Eliza made it easy to open even the most tender wounds of the past.

"As Michael got older he formed a blinding attachment to strong drink and women. One day Father found him face down in a puddle of mud behind the press. After Michael died, my Father took to drinking and increased his hatred toward me as if somehow I had been responsible for Michael's death as well as Mother's. He stopped working the press completely and that's when I took it over. He died only a year later, in '67."

Eliza's heavenly eyes swam with tears and her voice sounded thick. "Thomas, I'm so sorry."

Thomas stood straighter, as if an anvil had been lifted from his back. "Eliza, my father never acted as a caring, concerned parent." Quickly moving to the chair beside her, he took her hand in his. "But when Robert—when your father took me under his wing—I knew a parent's love for the first time. I felt what it must be like to have someone care for you so much they would risk everything for you."

Slowly, Eliza's face softened and her mouth opened as if her understanding had cleared.

Thomas carefully chose how to continue. "Your Father was the bravest, most caring man I've ever known, Eliza. And I know that everything he did, he did with you and Kitty in mind. He loved liberty and he understood the importance of rallying for such a vital cause. I'm sure you long to know more about him and what he did, and if I hadn't been such a selfish fool, I would have seen that long ago."

With eyes shimmering from the glow of the fire, Eliza scooted forward and gripped his hand tighter. "I do, Thomas. I want so desperately to know." Suddenly she stood, pulling Thomas to stand in front of her. It took all his strength not to pull her forward and kiss her right there. If only she knew how completely bewitching she was. Her innocence and caring was enough to make any man turn mad.

A smile lit her face. “I’ve wanted to ask you this very thing so many times, but since the accident, and my recovery, and . . . after what happened a few weeks ago between us, I suppose I’ve not had much opportunity until now.”

The way her lips moved when she spoke, the way her chest pushed up and down as she breathed, acted like an opiate in his blood. All he could think about was the imprint of her body against his, the scent of her hair and the taste of her sweet lips. She had no idea what she was doing to him. He cleared his throat and focused on communicating. “I admit, I should have seen your need for it long before now, forgive me. God placed you in my life so I could help you find what you are searching for.” Unable to stop, Thomas moved closer, shrinking the distance between them.

“I believe you’re right.” Eliza stared at him, her eyes never leaving his.

Her cheeks flushed dark pink and her breathing turned rapid. Placing her delicate fingers on his bicep she slid her other hand up his chest. She parted her lips and her eyes closed. She was his for the taking! Thomas smoothed his hands around her warm waist and leaned so close he could feel her breath on his mouth.

What am I doing? Thomas crunched his eyes shut. *How can I take such advantage of her? She needs me as a friend, as someone she can trust. This can only make things more difficult between us.*

It took every thread of strength to curb the

roaring hunger in his chest. Thomas pulled away, trying not to groan from the sheer pain of it. Eliza's eyes slowly blinked open, and the pain he saw there sawed his heart in pieces.

He turned away. *Please forgive me, Eliza. Forgive me.*

The heat from moments ago turned to ice. Eliza wrapped her arms around her chest as an uneasy quiet settled in the glowing room. How she wished she'd never come back down! Oh, why did she have to open her heart to him?

Wisdom told her to march upstairs and forget it. She should shut the window to his affection and build a wall high enough to keep him out forever.

But she couldn't. Somehow she couldn't even find the strength to make her feet unlock from their position on the floor.

Chewing on her lip, Eliza stewed. Well, if she couldn't escape, she might as well say something. Eliza kept her voice low to cover any remaining quiver. "I overheard Nathaniel tell of the political rally."

Thomas peered at her from over his shoulder. "You overheard a lot." A sliver of mirth rippled his voice as one brow tilted up.

Eliza's spine straightened as she tried to forget the pain of moments ago. "I know you said it would be dangerous to attend, but I can't help my curiosity. If my Father can risk what he did surely we can also. I know how much you want to be a part of it as well, and I believe we must be. God protected Father, and I know He'll do the same for us."

Thomas jerked his head back. A chuckle rumbled in his chest, but Eliza could sense his earnest. "Eliza, you know we can't leave this house. As much as I would like to attend the rally, it's far too dangerous."

Eliza took a step forward and softened her tone, releasing her hands at her sides. "If we go to the rally together, in disguise of course, I'm sure we will be safe and no one will recognize us. I believe I could begin to truly understand what Father felt and why he—"

"Absolutely not." Thomas came toward her, lowering his chin. "Neither of us will be attending that rally and that's the end of it."

"But—"

He interrupted her again, this time with a finger on her lips. The feeling of his warm flesh scalded her skin. "You must wipe that foolish notion from your pretty head. I won't have you going anywhere near trouble."

"How else am I to find out the truth? Sitting here and reading about the importance of liberty cannot be enough, surely. I must be involved if I am to understand it. I thought you wanted to help me."

"Of course I do, Eliza, but going to the rally is not the way I'll go about it." He took her by the shoulders and looked down at her as a father would to a child, sending a painful sting down her spine. He continued, his voice heavy. "If you heard everything Nathaniel said, then you would have also heard his warning. Already there are more soldiers in town and we must not risk being found out." His deep voice remained calm, but Eliza's pulse heated at the intensity of his words.

She pinched her lips and lifted her lashes to meet

his gaze. The closeness of him almost untied the laces of her willpower. His blue eyes radiated as they roamed over her face, causing her mouth to go instantly dry.

He brushed a flyaway hair from her cheek, tenderly stroking the skin of her neck with his thumb. What was he doing? The sensation of his skin touching hers sent the most pleasurable tingles chasing up her neck and down her arm. Her lungs halted and she stared into his fathomless eyes.

"We want to avoid trouble, not search it out." The delicious timbre of his voice twined around her. "I'd never forgive myself if anything happened to you."

His gaze traveled to her mouth and lingered there.

Eliza tried to move, but couldn't. This could not be happening. Not again. She froze, wanting—and at the same time, not wanting—him to come closer. She cleared her throat and tried to focus on her words. "How else can I really taste what Father tasted? How better for me to learn what I need to know than to attend that rally—to be a part of it? I want to know why my father betrayed King George. And for my benefit no less!"

A charming smile lifted the corners of his mouth and he moved his lips to her ear. "I'll tell you everything." His low tone trickled through her and settled in her stomach, awakening thousands of butterflies.

Slowly, Thomas released his hold and moved away, then turned and placed another log onto the fire. He acted so casual Eliza almost believed she'd imagined his closeness. He must experience the same storm of longing that pelted her chest. How could he now act as if nothing had happened between them?

She turned to face the stairs, searching for the strength to make her feet move across the floor. Somehow her body was as stuck as her clogged mind. She wanted to believe he cared—that he wouldn't want to rid himself of her when the search was over. She tried not to hope he would ask to her stay and be his 'real' wife, but she saw the resistance in his eyes, and all reason told her such a hope was folly. He was doing his duty—that was all. Caring for her like Father would have wanted him to. Nothing more.

Chapter Nineteen

"Clark, you fool! Because of you, now I've wasted even more time! I should never have listened to you." Rubbing his forehead, Samuel handed the reins of his horse to another soldier and waved him off.

Boston's wintry night sky shrouded the three men as Samuel clenched his fist to keep from pounding the young soldier.

Clark, his boyish face and small frame trembling, shook his head. "I truly believed it was them, Captain. Or I would never have said so."

"Well, your pure motives make everything all right, don't they?" Stupid boy. Nothing would bring peace to Samuel's anguished soul. Nothing except finding Eliza. He would die without her, just as surely as she was dying without him—alone and frightened in some strange place.

Donaldson dismounted and stood behind Clark, his gloved fingers twitching. "What's done is done, Martin. Best to let it go and get back to work."

"Shut up, Donaldson, I'll have none of that from you. I went to Salem on good faith, Clark," Samuel said, jabbing his finger into the boy's chest. "I saw no one that even remotely resembled that barbarous fugitive or my future wife!" He yelled and yanked the lapels of Clark's red jacket, expelling all his anger through his voice and onto the soldier's face. "Not *one*!"

"I'm very sorry, sir." The miserable soldier cowered under Samuel's powerful grip.

"Get out of my sight." Samuel shoved him away.

"Yes, sir." Clark bowed and shot Donaldson a pitiful glance before walking away through the darkness, straightening his jacket.

"He was just following orders." Donaldson repositioned his cloak.

"My orders were to find them—and he did not!"

"Your anger is misplaced," Donaldson snapped, straightening and stepping forward. "Save it for Watson."

Samuel rolled his shoulders back. That Lieutenant thought he knew everything. A vile concoction of rage against Thomas and fear for Eliza mixed in his belly. "You will do well to remember your place, Donaldson. I've lost precious time and I will not be sent on another false errand."

He looked up at the icy, star-dotted sky and released a foggy breath. They'd only just minutes ago returned from his fruitless journey to Salem. If he had been less impetuous, Eliza might even now be safe and wrapped in his waiting arms. He had lost his slipping grasp on reality.

Donaldson's strong voice cracked through the frigid air. "Sir, forgive me, but if I may be so bold. Perhaps she is dead, like the doctor in Sandwich said."

Seething, Samuel breathed fire. "You forget your place, Lieutenant."

The sound of horse hooves pounded the frozen ground, and Samuel jerked toward the sound. Who could be here at this time of night?

Suddenly, upon recognition, Samuel stood at

attention and bowed low. "Captain Curtis, 'tis good to see you. What brings you here at this time of evening?"

Three other soldiers accompanied Curtis, sitting erect on their heaving horses and looking ominous, but Samuel could sense the weariness that drifted from them. They must have traveled straight from Providence from the look of things.

His gut rolled. What could they want with him? Surely something to keep him from his most vital task, no doubt.

Curtis leapt off his horse and strode toward Samuel. His dark eyes were fringed with shadow, and bits of white hair frayed around his face from underneath his hat.

"Martin," he said, nodding. "I need your help."

Samuel stiffened and his muscles twitched. Just as he'd expected. His duties would once again call him away from Eliza.

Blast! "Yes, sir. How may I be of assistance to you?"

Curtis rubbed his hands and motioned to the small building that served as Samuel's Boston office. "My men and I are frozen. May we join you inside? I can apprise you of the details as we warm ourselves."

"Of course." Samuel motioned them forward. "This way." A bit of warmth would do him good as well. He too was bone-cold and could use a few hours in front of a warm fire, if not to thaw his muscles, at least to thaw this brain.

Once inside, the fire popped with annoying gaiety, and Curtis began to reveal his purpose.

"I've just had word that a large political rally is appointed to take place in Sandwich three days from today. There's a large group expected from

Providence, and other surrounding areas as well. There are only a few soldiers in the small town and they will need our help should things get out of hand. We don't want a repeat of 1770."

Samuel nodded and huffed. No one wanted that.

"I need you and five other men to join me there. We have soldiers from other provinces who plan to assist us as well, so we won't be the only military present. If you make haste you can cover the miles in about two days."

Samuel cleared his throat and kept pacing to keep from being consumed by his frustration. He'd already been to Sandwich and back. What a waste!

Curtis continued. "The leader, a man named Nathaniel Smith, has been planning this for some time now, and we hear he is anticipating an enormous crowd."

Samuel halted and jerked his head toward Curtis. "Do you mean *Doctor* Nathaniel Smith?"

"Yes, the very same. Do you know him?"

"Not really, no," Samuel said through his teeth as the doctor's face flashed through his mind and a gurgling hatred bubbled in his stomach.

"We'll have to stay a few days after, just to keep an eye on things until the group disperses, but at that point you'll be free to return here."

Samuel held his mouth together and the muscles in his jaw twitched as he sat back down. *This can't be happening. I've already wasted enough time!*

Curtis stood in front of the fire and reached for the warmth that radiated from the flames. "I've already received authorization. We leave at first light."

Samuel gripped the arms of the chair, fighting the urge to stand and launch it into the fire.

"We'll be ready," he croaked.

Samuel looked up at the ceiling and groaned. He lived for the day he would hold Eliza against him, and beg her forgiveness for not finding her sooner. He could only hope she would understand how hard he'd tried to save her.

Even more, he lived to move Thomas from this blessed world into the brimstone of hell where he belonged.

Thomas slammed his axe into another helpless log.

CRACK!

Chips flew and the severed pieces tumbled to the ground. He grabbed another, then another and continued releasing his pent up emotions into the innocent wood.

Since coming to Sandwich it seemed all he was good for was chopping wood and building fires. He was near to going mad—for more reasons than one. Though, when he allowed his true feelings to emerge, this place was lodging in his heart, and his memories of Boston were becoming just that—simply memories.

What could Boston or even his beloved press ever mean to him without Eliza in his life? This home and his memories with her in it were beginning to overshadow every other thought. Sharing the same dwelling with her was nothing but torture. Never had he experienced such a rush of passion. Not only did her beauty lure him in, her desire for truth and learning—those attributes, along with her humble and teachable nature acted like a Siren song to his lost and lonely spirit.

He bashed his blade into another thick stump. Inside she waited for him to begin their new nightly ritual of discussing politics and other such topics in front of the warm evening fire. They'd done so since the infamous "reading" almost two weeks before, and it was both his favorite and most loathed activity of the day.

Torture. Pure torture. Having to sit across from her, remembering the feel of her soft cheek, smelling the rose perfume lifting from her, hearing the melody of her voice and yet not being able to touch her. It was too much. He had to keep his distance or he would lose focus on what really mattered. Eliza needed him, he had to remember that, and not allow himself to get distracted. One more touch, one more kiss and his heart would be hers forever. That was something that he could never allow. Not when she was planning to return to Boston and the life she'd left there.

He smacked the last log in half with an additional rush of strength and gathered the pieces in his arms, before tromping in the house through the back door.

The conflicting thoughts and feelings that swarmed in his chest as he entered the main room moved up to fog his brain. He kept his gaze averted from the pretty woman in the upholstered chair, dropped the logs onto the floor, and took long inhales to calm his thumping heartbeat.

"Gracious, Thomas," Eliza said, her soothing laugh only making him more unhinged. "You chopped an entire tree, did you not?"

She pushed up from her seat and knelt beside him. "Here, let me help you."

Thomas clenched his jaw and shook his head. He turned to her, intent on telling her she needn't help him. Mistake. Her warm eyes thawed the self-placed wall of protective ice around his heart. She was so close he could pull her to him and . . . he shook his head and turned away, saying nothing.

Silence enveloped the room, and she must have sensed his reserve because she lowered her gaze and rose to her feet.

He peered at her from the corner of his eye. A blush painted her cheeks and she swallowed as if his quiet had wounded her.

"Of course you don't need my help, how silly of me." She took her seat again and picked up the apron she'd been mending, working feverishly with the needle.

Once the logs were stacked in their usual manner against the wall, Thomas stood and brushed his hands across his thighs. He exhaled a hard sigh and took his seat opposite Eliza.

"Where's Kitty this evening?" he asked, grabbing Robert's Cicero off the table that stood dutifully between the chairs.

Eliza didn't look at him. "She says she's tired of listening to our political conversations. She's taken the Shakespeare book upstairs. I imagine she'll have more fun reading romance and tragedy than hearing us discuss our views on government."

Thomas removed his jacket and laid it over the back of his chair before sitting. He crossed one ankle over his knee and tried his best to smooth his ruffled will. *No touching, Thomas. Don't even get close.*

"Well," he said flipping through the book in his hands. "What would you like to discuss first?"

She rested the mending on the floor beside her

chair and scooted to the edge of her seat with her hands in her lap.

Thomas relished in the feel of the enormous grin that flooded his face. Her enthusiasm and excitement never ceased to amaze him.

"I'd like to talk more about the Tea Act."

"Alright," he said, relaxing into his chair.

She licked her lips, leaving her plump lower lip tucked between her teeth before she started again. "Tea is such a part of our daily lives, a part of our culture. Why can't people simply pay the tax? Is it too much money, or is it more about principle than actual price?"

Thomas placed the book back on the small table and rested both feet on the floor. "I believe it's about both," he said. "However, your father always taught me that principle should be our guiding factor in everything. Especially in such issues as this."

Eliza nodded, her eyes begging him to continue.

"The Tea Act, like the others pressed upon us by the king and Parliament, is another way for us to be controlled and manipulated. If we don't stand against it, we don't know where it will end. Robert taught me that we must pursue goodness in all its forms and be courageous enough to stand for the right no matter the cost. He said the pursuit of our righteous desires is worth every sacrifice."

Eliza sighed and stared at the ground, lacing her fingers. Her mouth brightened in a sweet smile as if a happy memory placed it there. "Yes, I heard him say that many times." Her eyes met his. "I saw he wrote that in your book."

Thomas opened to the front of the book and absorbed the treasured words. "Yes, he did."

Both of them remained quiet. Thomas's mind

consumed with the example of strength and faith that Robert had given him, and from the look on Eliza's delicate face, her mind was also thus engaged.

His deep voice split the silence. "He was a man unlike any other, Eliza. I can only hope to someday emulate his greatness."

She stilled and released a quiet sigh as she looked at her laced fingers in her lap. "You already do." She peered at him, a half-smile on her shy face.

Thomas's heart and stomach danced together in his middle. She could never know what those words meant to him.

His face suddenly heated and he realized his embarrassing error in opening his heart to her in such a way. Though his intentions had been pure, it no doubt made him look as though he was bating her for praise. *What a fool I am.*

He shifted in his chair and strained to form some kind of response. Instead of speaking, he rubbed his hands together and grabbed the book again.

"Shall we continue?" he said.

"Please."

Lord, help me to stay focused on the task you would have me do.

All evening Eliza listened, but she didn't hear a word Thomas said. She asked questions but only to keep him talking—to drone out the radiating pain that lingered within her.

Her damaged heart had cracked even deeper at his obvious rejection and made it impossible to concentrate.

Their evening discussions were what kept her alive through the long winter days and yet those same discussions pulled the life right out of her. His nearness and kindness was too much to bear when she knew he cared nothing for her as a woman—only as his duty, as his responsibility.

There had been a time when she'd seen the desire in his eyes, but it died long ago.

As Thomas talked, Eliza's brain whirled. There had to be something she could do to get her mind away from the never-ending pain of longing. She nodded and listened, giving an obligatory answer here and there, while her mind circled, searching for the proper balm for her ailing heart.

Suddenly, an answer flashed across her whirring mind.

She sat straight in her chair, her eyebrows bouncing to the top of her head. *I can go to the rally myself!*

"Eliza?" Thomas said, pausing with a small laugh. "I have a hard time believing my quote from John Locke was that exciting, but you nearly jumped out of your chair. Did you find it that interesting?"

Eliza's face and neck burned. She placed an easy smile on her lips to mask her nervousness, fearing he could see through her. "Oh yes, well, it was interesting but, could you read it again, please?"

He tilted his brow and grinned from the corner of his mouth. "Of course."

Does he suspect something?

He read it again, but still she didn't hear it. Her mind was too busy engineering her masterful plan. She would need men's clothing and a way to sneak out of the house without being seen . . .

What a marvelous solution to her troubling

dilemma.

And the most wonderful part . . . Thomas would never know.

The sun rose with an exquisite overture of delicate lavender. Eliza slipped into her day-dress of the same hue, and twisted her long hair into a bun, pinned it, then moved her cap into place. She pinched her cheeks and brushed the sleep from her eyes.

Though to own the truth, sleep had evaded her thanks to the irritating nervousness that swirled in her stomach. But, despite her restless night, she felt fresh as a spring morning.

Over the past two days, her sly scheme to attend the rally had taken root in her conscience. This particular morning was the first time since the day of the "recovery celebration" that she actually smiled with true zeal. Tonight's rally would prove to be a salve to her aching spirits and allow her to focus on what really mattered: finding the truth of what Father believed, and why.

As mid-day approached, those same nervous feathers of anticipation that lined her stomach, morphed into tumbling rocks. She busied herself with chores and chatted with Kitty about the latest Shakespeare play she'd been re-reading, but such activities did little for her nervous anxiety.

Thomas regarded her with little less than a nod as he passed by through the day, which deepened the chasm in her chest. She pretended not to care.

Minutes stretched to hours.

Finally, the time to act approached and her careful plan took form.

"Kitty," she said, "I'd love to indulge in some of your delicious apple tansy tonight. Would you be so kind as to make it for us, dearest?"

Kitty closed her book and stretched her arms above her head. "I'd be happy to, Liza. How did you know I was in the mood to cook?"

Giggling, Eliza winked. "Aren't you always in the mood to cook?"

"You know me too well." Kitty pushed up from her seat and hummed on her way to the kitchen. "Besides, on these cold nights I'm always looking for a reason to stay close to the warm kitchen fire."

Eliza buzzed from head-to-toe.

Kitty will be busy and out of sight. Now for Thomas.

Through the day, Eliza had secretly removed one log at a time from the large pile that Thomas had brought in that morning, and stashed them in the empty chest that rested near the hearth.

"Thomas?" she called, exhorting herself to sound relaxed.

He entered the room, an emotionless expression in his handsome features. Eliza sighed and stamped-out the hope she'd born in her heart. If only he'd looked at her with at least a hint of a smile.

"We're out of wood again it seems," she said, pointing to the vacant wall near the fire.

Thomas shot a glance toward the once towering pile of logs. "What happened? I chopped an enormous pile this morning."

A tinge of mirth sounded in his voice and Eliza allowed a grin to twitch at her mouth.

He moved his head and looked at her, a tiny

sparkle glittering in his eyes. How she wished he would come close to her and place his hands around her just as he had the night of the reading. But she resigned herself to the truth: he never would.

Eliza cleared her throat as she remembered her purpose in calling him. "It's been so cold, we're burning more wood these days."

A smile lifted one side of his mouth, which in turn lifted her drooping spirit. "I'll go chop some more." He moved toward the back door without another glance and a blast of frigid air let Eliza know he'd gone outside.

The well-known rhythmic chopping ensued thereafter and Eliza flitted upstairs. She reached under her bed and pulled out her disguise. Thomas's extra pair of breeches—which she'd taken from the bottom of the chest—were far too large. Using a sturdy piece of twine, she secured the fabric around her waist, praying it would stay in place. Next came an old shirt and jacket, as well as woolen stockings and a long brown scarf all topped with a heavy black greatcoat.

She took only a second to survey her appearance, pulling her posture back and grinning at her reflection. The clothing hung on her small frame—the greatcoat falling practically to her feet—but there was nothing she could do about it. At least she would be warm.

At that moment her nerves began a rally of their own. What if she was caught? What would Thomas say if he knew she'd gone? What if she put them all at risk? Was this worth it?

She paused, wrapping the scarf around her head. *Maybe this is a fool's errand.*

A small voice of warning echoed in her mind, but

she ignored it. With such a grand disguise, no one would ever recognize her. There was nothing to be worried over. Besides, she would only stay a few minutes—just long enough to absorb the scene and listen to Nathaniel's speech, then she would be home.

She lodged the tricorne she'd swiped on top of her head, peeked out the door of her room, and listened.

Not a sound.

Her feet twitched in her shoes, eager to carry her to an event that would change her life.

Careful not to make the floors creek, she crept down the stairs, listening for the clanking of Kitty's utensils in the kitchen. *Good, she's still busy*. The chopping continued in the back, and a bit of the anxiety she'd harbored skirted free. *I'm going to make it!*

She held her breath and opened the squeaky door, praying Kitty didn't hear. She called to her sister from the partially open door, the majority of her body already out in the cold. "Kitty, I'm so sorry darling, but I'm feeling poorly. I'm heading to bed now and I'll eat your delicious dessert in the morning."

"Alright, Liza. I'll be up before too long." Kitty called from the kitchen.

Eliza dare not respond, in fear her sister might come out to continue the conversation. She closed the door and relished in her newfound freedom.

The cold chased up her nose, and slapped at her cheeks, but the rest of her remained toasty. The fresh winter air smelled of ice and freedom. She wiggled her toes in her shoes and peered up at the cloudy sky, just as lazy flakes of white swung down on the small breeze. Delirious excitement tightened around her.

Thank you, Lord! Please keep me safe. I promise I won't stay long. Help me to find the truth I'm searching for.

Eliza picked up the greatcoat that hung around her legs and dashed toward town like an energetic child running toward an unexplored meadow. The exhilaration pumping through her blood gave her added speed as she neared her destination. An expansive grin spread from her face down to her running feet.

When she reached the edge of town where the main shops and markets lined the streets, a large group had already assembled. Lanterns dotted the crowd, adding an almost festive air as a stream of rally-goers poured in from the small highway that led into the province.

Her eyes widened to take in the scene. Never had she beheld such a sight. Some people carried large poles with a familiar yellow banner. She'd seen the flag with the coiled snake many times in Boston but never so many in one place. Also, the Sons of Liberty's red and white striped flag blew proudly from some poles, as well as the popular "Join, Or Die".

She had seen these flags and cartoons in Boston but always brushed them aside as wicked schemes used by those who betrayed their forefathers and the great King of England. But tonight, they took on new meaning as she mixed with the expanding crowd of proud patriots. What would Father say if he saw her now? Would he be proud of her and how she tried to learn what he'd believed, and loved, and sacrificed for?

Her entire frame tingled and her breathing quickened as she scanned the growing assemblage.

Scattered on the edges of the streets stood numerous Redcoats, all looking formidable and each carrying muskets. Instinctively, she dropped her head and pulled her coat around her neck.

After a time, the gathering became so enormous Eliza could neither make out the front nor the back of the group. Everyone talked and mingled about, awaiting the call to march to Barnstable Courthouse.

The thrill of it all seeped through her chest. How she wished Thomas was here. She wanted him to experience this with her. She knew he'd wanted more than anything to come and support the cause that he and Nathaniel loved so well, but he'd abnegated—for their safety.

She bit her lip and looked down at the muddy snow. *Dear Lord, I don't want my actions to bring harm to Thomas or his cousin's family. Help me to stay hidden.*

The crack of a musket rocked the air and every face in the crowd shot up and turned to the man standing atop a rickety platform.

Nathaniel's voice sang loud and ripped across the freezing air.

Eliza remained motionless and almost floated off the ground.

Raising his fist in the air, Nathaniel beamed. "Fellow patriots! We stand united!"

Chapter Twenty

Thomas whacked the axe harder with every stroke, making an even larger pile than he chopped that morning. Would this chore never end? He'd noticed the temperatures dropping, but hadn't felt it getting quite as bitter as the girls seemed to think it was. They burned more logs in one day than he burned in a month.

He hauled the wood into the house in three massive armfuls. Careful to remain aloof, he looked around the vacant room, hoping Eliza might still be sitting in her favorite chair. Alas, she was not to be seen.

The last two weeks had been a most futile exercise in abstinence. The more he kept his distance from Eliza, the greater his longing became.

But he had a duty to perform. His emotions were not welcome in the equation.

He placed two more logs on the fire and heaved an exasperated breath. He'd done his utmost, expounding to her all he knew and loved about her Father. She relished it all. When she found the truth, she would embrace it, he had no doubt. It warmed him to the depths of his soul, knowing that he was doing what God intended. Thomas loved to watch the spark in her eye and the determined twist that played with her lips when she asked questions. He savored Eliza's every move, and craved the sound of her voice. Her gentle scent found him in even the furthest, most vacant corner of his home.

What would his life be like without her? He wouldn't acknowledge the painful answer.

Thomas peered around the room again. This time of evening Eliza always sat by the fire, mending or reading, but not tonight. Curiosity pricked him and his stomach dropped.

Where is she?

He wagged his head and rolled his shoulders, trying to shake the uneasy feeling. The house wasn't tiny, but it was small enough. Shouldn't he at least hear her and know where she was?

Thomas walked toward the kitchen, expecting to find both women laboring over the fire even though no talking emanated from the warm space.

He tried to squelch his growing worry upon finding only Kitty.

She looked at him and smiled, before moving back to her work at the small table.

He peered around, his fingers tapping his leg. "Smells delicious, Kitty."

Another grin moved across her face, but she didn't lift her head. "Thank you. Liza asked me to make apple tansy again."

Thomas nodded and inhaled the fresh scent of tart apples and nutmeg that billowed through the small kitchen. "Speaking of Eliza, where is she?" He fingered a few bits of peel, then snuck a piece in his mouth, trying to swallow the nerves that choked him.

Kitty wiped her hands on her well-loved apron. "She called down to me earlier. I believe she's already in bed."

"Really?"

She cracked a few eggs and began to beat them. "I noticed she acted a bit anxious today. I hope she's not unwell."

Thomas had noticed the same thing. "I'll go see if she needs anything."

Kitty looked up to give him a quick smile. "Alright."

His blood pumped quicker as he passed Eliza's empty chair. Something was amiss—she hadn't skipped a single evening of discussion since they'd begun, and she never went to bed early. He grabbed a candle and started upstairs.

Eliza's door was closed and no light peeped from beneath the door. Maybe she retired early. He hated the thought of waking her, but his nervous stomach would never allow him to rest until he knew she was well.

He tapped on the door with the backs of his knuckles and kept his voice quiet. "Eliza?"

Nothing.

He knocked harder. "Eliza?"

Still nothing.

He knocked again, then turned the knob and pushed the door open, peering cautiously into the room.

Her small form lay peaceful and still under the blankets.

She must be sleeping. His shoulders dropped and he released a harbored breath, yet his concern remained healthy. Was she ill? He fought the temptation to go to her, to hear the soft whisper of her breath, to feel her brow and check for fever.

Reason reigned and he left the room, closing the door behind him. If he were to be that close to her again, the pull of her nearness might prove too much to resist. He promised himself that if she didn't emerge by morning he would check on her again.

Once downstairs, he picked up the latest Gazette that Nathaniel had brought that morning, dropped into his favorite chair and tried to read.

He couldn't shake the feeling that something was terribly wrong.

Nathaniel raised his hand to silence the cheering crowd. Eliza teetered back and forth on her feet, trying to see between the swaying heads of the taller men surrounding her.

"My good countrymen! We gather together this winter eve to show our collective displeasure." He raised his voice to be heard over the consistent hum. "Those of us here feel the constant and ever expanding oppression of King George."

A thunderous applause erupted. The men around her shook their raised fists and waved their towering flags. All the while, tender white flakes dusted their hats and coats, senseless of the excitement.

"While the king luxuriates in his opulent throne, we strive to live day-to-day, barely able to pay the excessive taxes he presses upon us!"

Again the group exploded into a thrilling cacophony of shouts and cheers. Eliza marveled at the strength and composure of those who had gathered. They were a powerful, even foreboding presence, yet none exhibited anger or unneeded hostility. The nervous feathers that had coated her stomach since sunrise floated away as she grew ever more relaxed.

"His Majesty treats us as foreigners—with disdain and even with brutality! We are a part of England's great and noble empire, yet he seems to think otherwise. So, I would remind you my fellow patriots, Massachusetts is our country!"

Shouts of consensus rang wild through the air, and Eliza couldn't hold back the smile that bloomed on her frozen cheeks.

"We have gathered in this peaceful protest to unite in our noble cause, to give strength and courage to one another as we strive to show our local government we refuse to be so oppressed. Remember, brethren, we serve but one King, and He reigns in the heavens."

Nathaniel's statement struck Eliza like a powerful wind. Father's words resounded in her mind. *"You must always serve your King, Eliza. Love him, and honor him."* Had she mistaken his meaning all those years? Had he been talking of Christ the King?

"We must arm ourselves with knowledge and with the almighty power of God, for He is truly on our side. We must stand for the truth! For the truth shall make us free!"

Another jubilant roar rose in the air. Eliza's breath stuck in her throat. The plea her Father had spoken in that precious vision those many weeks ago, now rushed with striking force into the forefront of her memory. *The truth shall make you free.* Even Thomas had said those very words.

Tears threatened. She covered her mouth with both hands, pressing away the rising emotions. This was the third time the statement had been made. Father, Thomas and now Nathaniel.

Yes! God was her true King. This was what Father had intended for her to know. This is the truth she had been searching for. Armed with this knowledge she would never again be a prisoner to herself or anyone else. All along, Father *had* been telling her what he believed. He *hadn't* kept her in the dark.

Thank you, Lord! And thank you Father for believing in me and trusting me to find what I needed to know.

Nathaniel's resounding cry lifted above the fray and pierced her heart. And from the palpable reaction in the crowd, his words penetrated every other heart as well.

"This Liberty Pole represents our united cause. We must ever strive to be worthy of the blessings of God. We must ever be humble, teachable and courageous enough to accept the challenges and turmoil that awaits us. If we will but stand valiant, God will surely deliver us!"

Eliza raised her head as a tangible weight lifted from her shoulders.

"Let us march!" Nathaniel yelled, with his fist raised to the clouds. "Let us show the leaders of this historic city where their constituents homage lies! They must no longer work under the name of the king, but of the people!"

Nathaniel stepped down from his perch and began his walk toward the other side of town as a thunderous roar exploded. The jubilant crowd followed, clapping and cheering, bouncing their flags and waving their lanterns high in the air.

Eliza reveled in the joy of her personal revelation. The truth did make her free. She was weightless, and walked as if on a bed of flowers.

Father taught her from the beginning. How had she become so confused? It was understandable, she supposed. The political turmoil of the time was such that everything was upside-down. But now she knew, and the world seemed as bright as noonday. She would unite with this cause as Father had done, and by so doing, ensure their prosperous futures—just as Father would have wanted.

As she followed the crowd she wished more than ever for Thomas to be at her side. She wanted to tell him what she'd finally learned and how it had changed her in a matter of seconds. It would be almost impossible not to tell him, though over the course of time she could—just, not indulging him with the details of *how* she came to this knowledge.

Her conscience pricked and Eliza's stomach once again became home to a pillow's worth of tickling feathers. It was time to return home. She'd received what she'd gone to the rally for, the personal revelation she'd been seeking. If she left now she would be back before they'd discovered her disappearance. God had kept her safe thus far. Better not to try His goodness.

It would be unwise to stay any longer.

Eliza shook her head and brushed aside the nagging voice that throbbed in her ears. She had to stay, just a bit longer. What could a few more minutes do? No harm would come.

She would watch the crowd at the courthouse, and *then* she would go home.

Chapter Twenty-one

Kitty's excellent cooking pleased Thomas immensely on most occasions. Tonight, he couldn't even chew. The worry that bit endless holes in his stomach continued its monotonous gnawing.

Kitty retired only moments ago and Thomas made her promise to tell him if Eliza was unwell.

He paced in front of the dying fire, certain she would come down within seconds. He couldn't shake the probing feeling that something was wrong even though he'd checked on Eliza an hour ago.

As seconds turned into minutes his tension rose and fell. Then did so again, and again.

He'd done his best to ignore the fact that the rally was today. The cheering of the crowd reached their home from the small town some distance away. He was relieved Eliza had ceased her absurd pleadings to attend. No doubt the crowd was enormous and could even be dangerous for a petite and innocent woman—not to mention the countless soldiers that no doubt fringed the excited patriots. Good thing the three of them were safe within the walls of their proverbial fortress.

"Thomas!"

Kitty's shrill cry struck like a javelin in Thomas's gut.

"Thomas, come quickly!" she screamed.

All the fears that had pricked him through the evening now stabbed. He raced up the stairs. Once in the room he stared, trying to distinguish the confusing scene before him.

Eliza was not there—only Kitty stood at the side of the bed, a corner of the quilt in one hand, the other covering her quivering mouth. A length of pillows lined the bed where Eliza usually slept.

Kitty began to weep. Her terrified eyes gorged him. "What's happened, Thomas? Where is she?" she questioned, both hands now covering her cheeks. "Why would she leave us? How could she have left without us knowing?"

Thomas's blood stalled. The rally. But why would she do it? He'd warned her of the dangers and yet she had ignored him.

"Kitty. Listen to me. I must go after your sister. I know where she's gone." He walked toward the trembling young woman and rested a comforting hand on her shoulder. "You must promise me not to leave this house no matter what happens. I will return soon and I'll have Eliza with me."

Kitty looked at him, her face as white as the flakes outside.

"Do you promise?" he said, praying she'd not do anything as rash as her sister.

Kitty only nodded, the lines in her forehead deepening.

He forced an encouraging smile. "I'll be back soon."

"Where is she Thomas?"

He stopped in the doorway, silent for a moment, before looking over his shoulder. "She went to the rally."

Kitty's hands flew to her cheeks. "The rally?"

"I'll bring her back, Kitty. I will."

Thomas flew down the stairs.

Greatcoat. Scarf. Gloves. Hat. Boots.

Once ready for the elements, Thomas bolted out the door. He covered his face with the scratchy woolen scarf, attempting to mask his appearance more than shield himself from the cold. Truth be told, he felt nothing of the snow and freezing air.

The task before him gathered like a hostile storm. Where was she? Had she been caught?

Oh, Eliza, what have you done?

Once in town, the sheer magnitude of the crowd overwhelmed him. How could he ever find her amongst such a multitude? *Dear Lord, open my eyes.*

He scanned the rustling current for any females as the group marched toward the courthouse. There were only a few women, and none of them Eliza.

Then a terrifying thought struck his mind. *She's dressed like a man!* How would he ever find her now?

Suddenly, at the opposite side of the crowd a small fray ensued between two soldiers and a large man holding a flag. Thomas rose on his toes to see above the animated men.

Four more Tory's came forward, taunting the small group in front of them, causing tensions to rise. A few more patriots rushed to the aid of the victim.

Thomas' blood heated as a powerful urgency racked him. Memories of the Boston Massacre flashed in his mind and he prayed that God would help him find Eliza. Now.

A small figure wearing a familiar hat and coat streaked across his vision and his lungs froze. He tried to trace the hat amongst the group as the person pushed their way past the tumultuous crowd.

Could it be . . . ?

He struggled to keep his gaze upon the bobbing individual that weaved and dodged through the group.

Blast!

He lost track. His eyes trailed along the unfamiliar faces and through the rising flags and torches, desperate to locate the person he'd seen.

God be thanked, there it was again. This time the figure moved dangerously close to the isolated feud. At that moment one of the soldiers shoved the man in front of him causing the other men behind him to rock and stumble about. One large man bumped into the figure Thomas had been watching, causing the small person to topple. After righting again, the person looked up, locking eyes with Thomas.

His muscles flexed, his breath dammed in his throat.

Eliza.

More soldiers flooded the scene to see what had caused the ruckus. Thomas had to get her out now or they stood a grievous risk of being caught.

Eliza slowed, negligent of the row that ensued around her. She stared at Thomas, her large eyes wide, her delicate mouth open in shock. Did she really think he wouldn't come for her once he knew she was gone?

What Thomas needed now was wings. He needed to fly atop the tremulous sea of men, and pluck Eliza from them, bringing her to safety. Pressing through the thick group, Thomas shoved his way to Eliza—consumed with the need to rescue her from this dangerous expanse of men. He kept his gaze fixed. He would *not* lose her again.

Without warning, she too started her way through the crowd. A momentary wave of relief flitted through his chest, but quickly receded. She didn't move nearer to him—she moved away! A frantic look filled her doe-like eyes as she pushed to the back of the throng.

He wanted to call to her to make her stop, but doing so would only increase the risk they already suffered. Shuffling against the tide as the distance between them lengthened, Thomas's heart drummed against his ribs, powering him to a frantic pace.

Thomas kept moving, pushing. Eliza worked her way through with remarkable ease, then popped out the back of the group, and ran.

Wild urgency ripped his muscles and he charged against the wave of solid shoulders and unforgiving elbows. He broke through the barrier and sprinted after her, reaching her in a few pounding strides.

Yanking her arm, Thomas led her to the nearest alley between two vacant buildings, out of sight of any curious soldier. He pressed her body against the side of the building, holding his solid grip over her heaving shoulders. Thomas jerked the scarf down from his face, ready to boil her for such recklessness. She had no idea what might have happened, or more important, how his heart would break if she were taken from his life.

Not even the innocent regret that shimmered in her eyes could assuage the fear that continued to ripple through him.

They were not out of danger yet.

Eliza shrank under Thomas's oppressive hold. His usual calm, inviting eyes launched a hundred daggers into her chest.

"What in heaven's name are you doing, Eliza?" he seethed, through gritted teeth.

No wonder he was upset. She'd done exactly what he'd warned her not to. The sight of him amidst the crowd had all but socked the air out of her chest. It took no time at all for her to recognize his striking blue eyes. The guilt that struck her had also robbed all good judgment from her mind. She'd tried to get away and run home before he could reach her, and before she caused either of them to be caught. She prayed no one had witnessed the scene.

"I'm so sorry, Thomas," she said between huffs. "I only wanted to—"

"I know what you wanted to do, Eliza." His grip tightened.

"Please Thomas, you're hurting me."

He released immediately and took her by the hand, leading her through a maze of quiet streets, past the backs of empty buildings, around Shawme Pond and far away from the excited band of patriots.

The darkness in the air softened as the snow reflected the night's minuscule light.

A safe distance from the fray and only a few long strides from the house, Thomas whirled her around. The color in his eyes testified of both his anger and relief. He yanked the scarf even further from his face, revealing his chiseled features before beginning his heated rebuke.

"It's no small miracle, Eliza Campbell, that neither of us were seen. Did you not notice the small feud that erupted only feet away from you? You could have been caught. I warned you against such a thing. It was remarkably foolish, Eliza. I never thought you capable of such a thing."

Eliza stiffened at his remark. He spoke to her as if she were a child, not a grown woman. "Nothing happened. I planned ahead, did I not?" Her volume began to rise, but Thomas cupped his hand over her mouth.

His masculine face contorted and his stance indicated he held back most of his rage. "No you did *not* plan ahead. Do you have any idea what that crowd could have done to you? Do you have any idea what would have happened had you been caught?"

His reprimand sliced through her thin armor, making her earlier excitement deflate. Soon a warm splash of pride coated her chest. She would not stand here and be punished like a schoolgirl. She whirled away from him and walked in the direction of the house.

"Eliza!" He called after her, his quiet tone loaded with anger. "Eliza!"

She quickened her pace.

Instantly, he was behind her again and yanked her around to face him. Her fury ignited.

"Unhand me, Thomas!" she snapped, in the loudest whisper she could produce and wrenched from his strong fingers. "I'm going home."

"Not yet. I'm not done giving you the tongue lashing you deserve."

She straightened and pursed her lips. "*Mr. Watson*, I am going home and if you'd like to lash me there you may, but I'll not stand another minute in this cold, my toes are becoming icicles! "

Eliza tromped through the muddy snow, trying hard not to stumble. She pumped her arms in the long heavy sleeves and puffed white clouds of air as she mumbled under her breath. All the while Thomas marched behind her. Her discontented thoughts rattled in her brain. Suddenly, she stopped and circled around to face Thomas, unleashing a scourging of her own.

"I had a grand plan Thomas, until you decided to come searching for me. No one would have recognized me in these clothes!" She moved her hands up and down in front of her. "Then you had to make a scene!"

He jerked the hat off her head, his hot words flying through gritted teeth. "You think this disheveled, ill-fitting mess you call a disguise would make you invisible to those around you?" He patted the tricorne back on her head with a scoff.

"Yes, I do! You saw the crowd, Thomas, there were hundreds upon hundreds of people—there is no possible way I could have been spotted, let alone recognized by anyone. Frankly, I cannot understand your anger."

Thomas shook his head and the muscles tightened in his jaw. "It was a fool's errand, Eliza."

She exhaled a sharp breath, and squared her posture. "It was not. I learned a great many things. Very important things. I'm glad I went!"

Tilting her chin upward, Eliza slammed her hands on her hips. "How did you even know I was gone? I thought of everything. My plan was flawless."

This time he threw his head back and laughed. "Not in the least. If it had been flawless, I'd never have known you were gone."

"How *did* you know?"

The features of his face relaxed. "I noticed you weren't in your regular spot by the fire like you usually are that time of evening. I got worried." He gazed at the house. "I asked Kitty where you were and she said you'd retired early, which you never do.

That also heightened my concern. When Kitty went to bed, well, I'm sure you can figure out the rest." A mocking tone echoed in his voice.

Looking at the sky, Eliza stomped her foot and growled. "Why couldn't you have left it alone, Thomas? I would have made it home safely and you would have never known about any of this." Suddenly, the bottled frustration she'd held on to for weeks bubbled to the surface. She leaned forward and pointed a finger at his chest. "And tell me, when have you ever really noticed me, or where I am, or where I sit? You never look at me. You avoid me like I'm the pox!"

Her volume reached new levels and she had to force herself not to yell up into his face. She spoke through her teeth to keep her voice low. "You've done your best to keep us safe and help me learn what I've needed to know about Father—and for that I will be forever grateful, but you can't honestly pretend that you care!"

Thomas captured her shoulders again and pulled her in front of him with a jerk, making her hat fall to the ground. The glowering look in his eyes simmered and Eliza turned her head away. Taking a hand from her shoulder he wrapped his strong, gentle fingers around her chin, compelling her to look at him.

The low resonance in his rich voice was both imposing and tender. "I notice everything about you."

Eliza tried to pull away, her heart beating against her lungs. "I don't believe you. You're actions say otherwise."

Thomas huffed and glanced away before locking eyes with her again. "I've tried to keep away from you, to keep from developing feelings for you, Eliza. I know you have a life in Boston and I've only ever brought you trouble . . . but I can't dictate my heart."

He brushed his calloused fingers against her cheek. Eliza closed her eyes, relishing the feel of his tenderness. It was too wonderful to be real.

"I couldn't bear to see you hurt again, Eliza. That's what caused my anger. Not the fact that you went to the rally." His honey voice softened. "If anything had happened to you, I would never have forgiven myself, and not because it's my duty to care for you, as you think. Because I love you."

Eliza's breath hitched, and her heart thumped at the sparkle of surprise in his eyes, as if he hadn't meant to speak the tender words. But from the way his gaze roamed her face, it seemed he didn't regret saying them.

She looked up with parted lips, soaking in the sweet dew of his affections as he stepped closer. As if unwrapping precious china, he unwound the scarf that still circled her hair and let it drop to the ground near the hat. He smoothed his fingers around her ears, cupping her head, and directed her face toward his. All the world disappeared, the surrounding trees and shadows melting together and closing around them like a celestial dream.

He stepped closer and her knees turned as weak as the wilted blades of snow-covered grass at her feet. "What are you doing?" she whispered, trembling under his touch. An unmistakable hunger swirled in his gaze, reaching out and expanding the longing of her own.

The heat in his low voice stole her breath. "I'm doing what I've wanted to do for a very long time."

He leaned toward her, but she put a hand on his chest to stop him, her heart slamming against her ribs.

His dark eyebrows crunched down. “What is it?”

Eliza swallowed, trying to keep her voice even. “Last time you kissed me, you avoided me as if I were a poison. I don’t want that to happen again.”

A quiet, rumbling laugh escaped him. “You are anything but a poison, Eliza.”

He cradled her face in his hands, tilting it upward and nuzzled her cold nose with his. She closed her eyes and inhaled in a ragged breath as his warm lips moved across the corners of her eyes, her cheekbones, her ear. Delicious shivers sprayed down her skin and she clung to his chest to keep from falling. His hands brushed down her neck and shoulders—one resting behind her head, the other at her back, as if he wanted to keep her safely next to him forever.

Dear Lord, I love him.

In that moment, she gave her heart to him, and no matter what, she never wanted it back.

Thomas relished in the sound of Eliza’s ragged breathing as he moved his mouth around her soft skin and inhaled the delicate scent of her hair. Slow, deliberate, he lowered his mouth toward hers as he surrendered to the desire that possessed him. Their lips caressed, soft at first. She let out a tiny mewing sound, expanding his driving need for her closeness. He pressed her against him and deepened the kiss as she looped her gentle arms around his neck. Raking her fingers through his hair, she gripped tight as she returned his passion.

His blood raced at ferocious speeds, driving his

imagination to places he couldn't yet go. Not until they were married. He had to stop, before the need for her overwhelmed his reason. With Herculean effort he eased away, gazing at her through hooded eyes.

Her own eyes remained closed, and her mouth slightly open. He could see her chest moving up and down at a rapid pace as she breathed.

As if waking, she opened her eyes, blinking. A worried expression crept across her delicate features.

"Why did you stop?"

Her innocence humbled him, and despite the danger, he pulled her to him, resting her head against his chest. He remained quiet, unable to answer as he tried to force his surging emotions to settle. But such a task was impossible.

"What do my actions tell you now?" he whispered.

She made no sound, only looked up and stroked his face with her delicate fingers. Her endless eyes shimmering back with such love, his heart swelled until it nearly stopped his lungs.

"Eliza?"

"Yes?" she answered, a husky sound to her voice.

"I want you to be my wife." The words toppled out of his mouth and he bit his tongue. He hadn't intended to ask her, but apparently his inner desires, no matter how suppressed, could no longer be ignored.

She pushed away and looked up at him, disbelief painting her face. "Your wife?"

He tucked a long strand of hair behind her ear. "What do you say?" The muscles in his shoulders tensed. Maybe she did truly love Samuel. "Will you accept me?"

She must have seen the emotions he attempted to disguise. Her slender fingers moved over his dipping eyebrows and the sweetest of smiles graced her enticing mouth. "There's no need for your brow to furrow so. Of course I accept you."

Joy rose in his heart like a surging sea. Thomas moved his hands further around her waist, hoping such closeness would erase all other men from her mind. "You're not wishing you would have accepted the man who asked before me?"

An impish grin chased across her mouth. "Never. You've surprised me, that is all. I couldn't be happier."

"So you do accept me?" he asked.

A petite laugh escaped her. "Have I not already answered? What do my actions tell you, Thomas?" Her delicious tone tantalized him.

A small chuckle of his own bubbled in his chest.

"Eliza," he whispered. "If we're going to be married I need to tell you something." The burden of his knowledge of Samuel weighed on him like a heavy chain. He knew he must tell her before she found out by some other means.

"Aren't you cold?" she said. "Do you want to go inside?"

"Not yet. How could I be cold with you in my arms? Can your toes survive a few minutes longer?"

"My toes?" She leaned on his chest and laughed. "After that kiss I'm warm as a summer's day, Thomas."

He pressed her closer and reveled in the feel of her body against his. Pensive, Thomas struggled to place his words in his mind before speaking them. "Eliza, the man who proposed to you—"

"Samuel?"

"Yes."

She looked up at him, a teasing grin opening her lips. "Are you going to ask if he kissed me?"

He hadn't planned on it, though the thought had crossed his mind. Now that she mentioned it, he most definitely would ask. "Did he?"

She moved her hands up to the cravat that peeked out from his greatcoat. "Would it make a difference if he did?"

Yes, I'll break his jaw. "I don't know. Maybe."

Her eyes twinkled. She looked far too amused. "Well, if it does matter I might have to keep such information from your knowledge."

He took her by the shoulders and extended his arms to their full length. "Don't toy with me, Eliza Campbell. Now you *must* tell me," he said, trying to sound more playful than he felt.

"Alright." She moved close to him again. "Yes. He did."

Thomas's muscles stiffened. He'd hoped she would say no, although he'd doubted it. Rotten scoundrel.

"Often?"

"No. Not often. Only when he proposed."

"Good, because from now on the only person you'll be kissing is me." And Samuel had better stay as far away as possible.

"I'm pleased to hear it, Thomas Watson. I don't want to kiss anyone else." She rose up on her toes and pressed her mouth against his, so light and gentle it turned his insides to liquid.

"Now," she said. "What was it you wanted to tell me?"

He swallowed and licked his lips. *Lord, give me strength to say what needs to be said.* "Eliza." He rested his hands on her arms. As hard as it was, he knew it was now or never. "You know the British were using me for information?"

"Yes. They were blackmailing you, of course. I'm still horrified by it."

Thomas inhaled deep and expelled a loud breath before spitting out the bitter words. "The man who blackmailed me was Samuel Martin."

Chapter Twenty-two

Samuel worked his way through the thick mass of patriots. His gut twisted into a tangle of knots at the fight that had ensued in front of the popular tavern. The Boston Massacre had been a living nightmare and he wanted to stop a similar disaster from occurring.

"What's happened here?" he yelled, reaching the group as the men exchanged fists and fighting words.

No one answered. Donaldson approached the group from the other side.

The row escalated and several of the men lost their balance, tumbling into the crowd behind them.

That's when he saw her.

Eliza!

His heart crashed into his ribs. The world slowed. *She's alive!* Her clothes were large and sloppy, but he knew it was she without a doubt. All these weeks, the quiet words that whispered to him was truly the echo of her voice, calling for him to save her.

"Eliza! Eliza!" He reached for her, pushing against the dozen or so men that separated them. His blood blistered in his veins and he growled at those in his way. "Move! Move!"

She pushed her way through the massive gathering. Peering behind her, she looked more frantic as she neared the back of the crowd. His vision dusted over the men and his heart stopped when he saw the reason for her haste. A large man pursued her at great speed. He knew right away it was Watson though only the man's eyes were exposed to view. Rage pulsed through Samuel as he watched her run from Watson and away from the crushing crowd.

She was trying to escape.

When she ripped out the back, Watson followed and stormed after her, grabbing her from behind and yanking her toward the empty shops.

Samuel stalled. He turned to Donaldson and yelled over the hats of the men in front of him. "Donaldson! Come with me. I've found Watson!"

Donaldson's features jumped and he instantly plowed into the group toward Samuel. "Where?"

"Follow me!"

"Martin!" Curtis's voice rose above the crowd. "Where are you going? Come back. We need you here!"

Samuel turned, fire exploding out of every pore. "I'm making an arrest!" He ignored Curtis's demands and focused on his mission.

He and Donaldson forced their way through the resistant group. Once out of the jumble, both men halted and looked around them, trying to find which way they'd gone.

"You saw him?" Donaldson asked, whipping his head around. "Can you be sure?"

"I saw them both," Samuel said, still searching and taking a few steps to one side then the other.

No. No!

He'd lost them.

He swept his gaze over the snow-sopped ground, hoping to recognize their tracks. But with the rally-goers stomping every which way, it was impossible to distinguish one footprint from the next.

"There! Could that be them?" Donaldson pointed to two figures arguing near a small home amidst the towering trees way beyond town.

From such a distance it would be hard to tell, and the darkness didn't help. He squinted, his breath racing. It had to be them!

Samuel ran. Donaldson followed. As they neared, he skidded to a halt.

The scene unfolding before his view seemed surreal. Though he was close enough to see them clearly, their voices only teased him, he couldn't make out their exact words. Watson grabbed Eliza and pressed her against him, kissing her square on the mouth. Samuel clutched the pistol at his side. He froze with utter shock, unable to make his heavy legs move from their spot.

His stomach lurched to his neck and wedged there like a chunk of lead.

No! This cannot be happening!

Samuel tried to read Eliza's reactions. Was Watson forcing himself on her? The longer they kissed, the more he realized how real her reaction was. The way she moved her arms around him, and pressed into him answered his question.

She wanted it.

He snapped his head at Donaldson who stared, with the same look of shock that owned every inch of Samuel's soul.

He looked again at the entwining forms. "Get out of here," he said to Donaldson in a low tone.

"But, Captain—"

"Leave me be!" Samuel whispered as he whirled and shoved the soldier away, causing him to stumble backward.

Donaldson's eyes thinned and he pinched his mouth tight as he looked from the kissing pair back to Samuel. "As you wish."

Samuel looked back at Eliza and Watson, still holding each other close.

His heart burst in his chest, sending a thousand nails scraping through his veins. The terrible scene before him began to swirl. He clutched his mouth, stifling a groan.

He moved behind the trunk of a large tree. Shaking his head and rubbing his eyes, hoping his fears somehow invented the sight.

When he looked again, her hands were still around Watson and her face tilted upward as she spoke to him.

That errant devil must have some wicked hold upon her to make her act in such a way. Eliza loved *him*. They were to be married. All these years he'd dreamed about her as his wife. They'd talked of their future together, and at great length. She couldn't—wouldn't—throw all of that away.

It took every ounce of fortitude not to shoot Watson where he stood. He glared across the distance as Watson continued talking. Eliza stepped back, losing her balance. Her hand shot to her mouth as a small yelp escaped her. Thomas reached for her and held her to him. He brushed his hand along her back, trying to soothe her. She shook her head then looked up at him as if what he'd said caused her considerable pain.

Samuel lurched forward, ready to race ahead and sweep Eliza away from her captor.

But he stopped, as Eliza reached up and stroked Watson's cheek, then took his hand and kissed it tenderly. Watson pressed his lips into her hair and circled her in his arms as they moved toward the small home several yards away. She held herself next to him as they walked, her lilting voice floating on the air, baiting him.

Watson opened the door, motioning for her to enter. He brushed her cheek, followed her in, and closed the door behind them.

Samuel's lungs collapsed and the snowy earth around him spun.

Staggering, he tried to stable his pulse. He couldn't breathe, couldn't see, couldn't feel. Samuel turned to the tree in front of him then punched it over and over again, slicing his frozen skin on the rough bark, then sunk into the snow beneath him and looked at his bleeding knuckles.

Tears burned his eyes. How he wished it were Watson he'd mangled and not some innocent timber. Yes, Thomas was vile, horrid—pure evil to take away his bride. To bewitch her into showing such intimate affections was a crime worthy of death. Torture first. Then death.

Samuel flew to his feet and slammed his knuckles into the waiting tree again and again.

This moment was both his greatest dream and worst nightmare. He'd located his beloved, but found her in the arms of his greatest enemy.

His lungs heaved. He pushed away from the blood-spattered tree and looked back at the house, so quiet and peaceful His hands trembled as blood trickled down his fingers and dripped into the snow.

He would have Eliza for his own, no matter the cost.

She belonged to him.

The chastising that erupted from Kitty upon Eliza's return sucked all breathable air from the room.

"You risked all of us to attend that rally! How could you do such a thing?" Kitty cried, swinging her hands in the air. "You could have been caught, or hurt. Or worse!"

"Kitty, I'm so sorry. Please forgive me." Eliza's stomach rolled to the floor. She fixed her stance and straightened her shoulders as she pointed all her strength to not fainting. Her voice quivered. "I should never have lied to you. My reasons for going were selfish, you're right, I see that now. I would never want to do anything that would hurt you."

This, coupled with the terrible revelation about Samuel was too much to bear. She tried to smile, attempting to lighten the mood. "Not to worry, Thomas has just now put me in my place. Such antics will not be repeated, I assure you."

Eliza sent a brief glance to Thomas. No emotion could be seen on his face, but the kindness in his eyes was obvious, if only to her.

Kitty didn't seem interested in quitting her castigation. "Liza, I have been very patient during these weeks, listening to you and Thomas discuss these issues, but I cannot keep these feelings inside me any longer."

Eliza shook her head. "What feelings?"

Features tight, Kitty quivered as if she used every measure of strength to stay calm. "How could you possibly do this? Our lives have been completely uprooted and destroyed because of what Father did."

She stared a moment at the floor, gritting her teeth. A shadow darkened her brow. "Even so, I have been able to forget that, to put it to rest knowing there is nothing we can do to change the past."

She peered at Eliza again, the flame of fury blazing in her blue-green eyes. "Because of his actions we were narrowly arrested and could have even been killed. We've had to stay in hiding, leaving our lives behind us, never knowing when we can return. Now, after all of that, you choose to put us all in danger by trying to learn more about why Father did what he did? You're actually interested in learning more about such a cause? I cannot believe my own sister would leave the safety of our upbringing. I am ashamed."

The blood in Eliza's limbs retreated to her heart, taking with it her last reserves of strength. She found the closest chair and sat, gripping the cushioned seat, only vaguely aware of Thomas standing behind her.

Eliza tried to ignore the lump that clogged her throat as a pressing guilt took form. She was supposed to care for Kitty, protect and love her. And here, she'd risked everything with her foolish actions. *Dear Lord, what have I done?*

"Forgive me, Liza, but you must know how I feel." Kitty went on. She paced back and forth, wringing her hands. "I cannot believe you would be so deceived. Where is your faith? You cannot tell me that God wants fighting and discord. He wants peace and charity between His children." She halted in front of Eliza, her voice calm but clouded. "I love you, Liza, and I refuse to stand by and watch you entangle yourself in this vain and evil pursuit."

Tears stung the backs of Eliza's eyes and spilled over her cheeks. *God, please help me know what to do, what to say.*

Thomas stepped forward, placing a calming hand on Eliza's shoulder. His fingers injected reassurance and his tone deepened. "Kitty, there is no sin in what Eliza has done."

Kitty didn't move, acting as if she hadn't heard him. "The more educated you become, the more unsettled you are. Liza, you must distance yourself from such things. Father was misguided, you must see that."

Eliza could think of no proper response. Her mind was like a dense autumn fog. She opened her mouth, hoping some words—any words—would join together, but Kitty continued before she could speak.

"It's not a woman's place, Liza! For that matter, it's no one's place." She snapped her head toward Thomas. "We should do whatsoever we are asked by our beloved king. King George will lead us. He will keep us safe. We must follow Christ's example of brotherly love and submission to our leaders. You must stop this foolishness, Liza. Now."

Eliza rested her forehead in her palm. Her sister was wrong. But how to convince her of it?

When it appeared Kitty had finished her verbal lashing, Eliza pressed her hands in her lap and attempted a calm response despite her fraying emotions. "Kitty, do you believe we should sit by and do nothing while King George abuses and robs us? You cannot deny that he is—"

"He is not robbing us. That is a lie!" Kitty pinched her mouth tight and looked away as if she regretted the outburst. She cleared her throat. "It is our duty to pay such taxes, and we should count it an honor to do so for the good of the Empire. And I will tell you, Liza, though you will not like hearing it, Father was wrong. He was a traitor to our great country. His actions changed our lives forever. And not for the better!"

Utter confusion and despair left Eliza's heart desolate and cold. The room wobbled as she struggled to stand and took Kitty's hands in hers. *Lord, let me help her see the truth. Don't let her despise me.*

"Kitty, everything Father did was for our benefit. His actions did change our lives, but I'm glad—I'm glad for what's happened. And our lives *are* better no matter what you may believe. What's happened has been a great blessing. You will see, I promise."

"It's a blessing for you." Kitty's chin quivered. "You have a dashing man to love and care for you. But what have I? Nothing!" She pulled back her shoulders and spoke quick as if to try and hide the waver in her voice. "While your world culminates in beauty, mine is barren."

Eliza reached for her sister, but she backed away, shredding the remaining fortitude in Eliza's chest. She tried to keep her voice from catching. "Kitty, please. We must trust God—"

"*I* trust God," Kitty shot back, tears tumbling over her cheeks. "God wants us to submit to Him and be peacemakers, not willfully stir contention and malice. It's you who must trust God. You are going against his will, Eliza, and you must stop it!"

The daggers of her words made Eliza drop again into the chair behind her, this time placing her head in her hands. Was Kitty right? Was she going against God's will? She thought of her Father's confession and the vision she'd beheld during those difficult weeks of recovery. Nathaniel's rousing speech played again in her mind, and how his words had moved within her, awakening a sleeping belief. She needed to be alone, to drop on her knees and pour out to God the confusion that weaved within her spirit.

Eliza wiped her hands down her face before clenching her knees. "Kitty, I'm so sorry. I'm sorry for what's happened and that you're hurt and confused—"

Kitty's voice spat arrows. "I'm not confused, Liza. You are. You cannot possibly appreciate the gravity of what you are doing. You must quit this foolish quest and stop your political involvement. You must repent and follow God's will."

Thomas stepped forward and raised his voice. "That's enough, Kitty. It's not your place to call your sister to repentance. You speak of things you do not understand."

"I understand more than you think," she said, raising her chin and staring at Thomas. Kitty squared her shoulders. "I've sat quietly and listened to the two of you long enough. You speak of righteous indignation, the proper role of government and laws, but our lives are good, even though it may be difficult for some. It will only be more difficult for everyone if we push against the one man who keeps us truly safe."

"And who is that, Kitty? Who is the one man that truly keep us safe?" Thomas baited.

"King George, of course."

"You're wrong." Thomas's rich voice rang clear and strong. "He who keeps us safe is God alone."

Kitty's face reddened. She pursed her lips and turned away. "You mistook my meaning, Thomas. Of course I know it's God. Don't play with my words!"

Without another glance, Kitty tromped up the stairs and slammed the door.

Eliza rested her head in her hands as the sound of Kitty's muffled cries tiptoed back down and pranced around her. The tides of her emotions ebbed higher until they breeched her carefully laid barriers of courage. She wept into her palms.

Thomas knelt in front of her, stroking her hair, helping to abate the sudden storm of pain.

"Thomas, I've done it again," she said between tears. "I made a decision, and it was the wrong one. I've pushed Kitty away from me. I've made her miserable. She's never raised her voice at me. I never knew she felt any of this."

Her weeping increased and she crumpled into his shoulder.

"You didn't cause her reaction. It would have happened at one time or another. Don't blame yourself. Kitty was wrong to keep it clamped inside. She should have told us her feelings long ago. Don't place blame where it isn't due."

Eliza knew his words were intended to be encouraging, but so far nothing could assuage the remorse that clawed through her. She kept her head down, self-conscious of her mussed looks and runny nose. Thomas handed her a handkerchief and she buried her face in it again, inhaling the masculine fragrance of him the fabric carried.

Looking up, Eliza folded and unfolded the soft fabric again and again in her hands as she gathered her thoughts. Thomas crouched in front of her, his thumb making little circles on her knee.

"Thomas, I know she's wrong. I can't put my feelings into words, but I *know* it." She stopped, remembering the revelation that had come to her at the rally. "Even though it was foolish to go, I did learn a great deal. I am beginning to see what my

Father meant for me to know, and why he believed what he did. Why he risked his life for such a cause. He always said to love and honor our King. And now I know he meant God the King. He never lied to us. How can I help Kitty see that?"

Thomas met her weak gaze with a powerful one, a contemplating stare in his ever-blue eyes. "There is not much you can do for Kitty but continue to love her, and continue to follow the path God is showing you."

"Do you really think God is leading me?"

"I don't just think it, I know it." Thomas took her hands in his and helped her to rise with him as he stood. "And I also know God led you to me, of that I have no doubt. I believe he meant for us to be together. For you to be my wife and love me forever the way I love you."

A flood of warmth filled the once cold cavern in Eliza's heart. She opened her mouth to answer him, then immediately closed it. The pain of moments ago renewed itself at her words.

"What shall we do about Samuel? What if he finds us? I'm afraid of what he might do, Thomas. Whatever shall I say to him?"

Thomas held her close, cupping her head against his hard chest. "Don't worry about that now, my love. We must stay vigilant a while longer, 'tis true, but I don't believe that Samuel will ever find us now."

Chapter Twenty-three

Why can I not formulate a decent plan?

Samuel growled at the ceiling. He had to stay focused, but the memory of Thomas holding Eliza—kissing her—infiltrated his thoughts, making it difficult to breathe.

He couldn't sleep. He ate nothing and drank only a few sips of ale after returning to his quarters at Newcomb Tavern.

A knock sounded at the door.

"Enter," Samuel grumbled.

"How are you, sir?" Donaldson came into the room they shared and closed the door behind him.

Samuel shook his head and turned away.

"If you truly love this woman, as you profess to, you will want the best for her. And from what I saw she didn't look like she was under any kind of duress. I suggest you let it go—"

Samuel launched from his place on the thin mattress and grabbed Donaldson around the neck. "Let it *go*?!" Samuel pushed him onto the bed and gripped harder as Donaldson choked for air. "Never! Eliza is *mine*!"

After another shove, he let go. Donaldson gasped for air and rubbed at his throat, coughing.

Samuel's chest heaved as he stared at his subordinate. "We will find a way to get her back. She loves *me*. That man has forced himself upon her, I know it!"

His vision darkened and his arms shook as his need for Eliza pulsed through him with the strength of the entire British Army.

Donaldson pushed off the bed, still massaging his neck. "You're on your own. I will help you no longer."

Samuel jerked back, his nostrils flaring as his hot breath seethed through his nose. "So be it," he said, opening the door. "You've been no help to me anyway. Get out."

Donaldson turned as he stepped into the hall. "You're digging your own grave, Martin."

Samuel leaned forward until their faces were only inches away. "When I bring her back, you will accompany me to Boston whether you like it or not. If you choose not to, I will personally see to your professional demise. I know how you need every cent for your pitiful mother and sisters. I suggest you obey orders."

Samuel shoved him into the hall and slammed the door, then pounded it with the side of his fist.

He shook his head. *I can do this on my own.* Pacing the length of the tiny room, he used every parcel of shrewd thinking left within his brain.

Time was precious. He rehearsed possible scenarios through the long night and mapped their location with precise detail in his mind. There were no guards at the small house, at least none that he had seen. No reason for him to have any trouble removing Eliza and her sister.

Yet, his thoughts stalled at every possible course. What if they were no longer there? What if they'd suspected his coming and left?

He shook his head and ran his fingers through

his hair, brushing away the thought. No. The house looked settled. They were there to stay.

Why could he not think of what to do? How to save her? How difficult could it possibly be?

After the long night ended, and as the first fingers of sun crested over the rooftops an idea, flawless and simple rose in his mind as pure and bright as the sunrise. For the first time since seeing Eliza again, his muscles relaxed and renewed strength charged through his veins. She would be safe and in his arms within the hour.

Heedless of his soldiering duties, he crept out of the boarding house in silence and paced down the street, taking the back way to Watson's hideout, just as he and Eliza had done the previous night.

A wild excitement pushed him over the frozen ground. His shoulders and arms buzzed with anticipation.

Do not worry, Eliza. Our nightmare is almost over.

The morning's sunrise sprinkled bits of pink and orange on the waiting horizon. Eliza noted how the evening's snowfall blanketed the outside world, the glowering clouds of last night having floated away as they slept. And with their welcome departure, a parcel of her own oppressive load vanished forever into the sorrowful past.

She smiled at the beauty of God's daily handiwork and splashed a handful of cold water onto her face, then patted it dry with her apron. She peered past her reflection in the north window that overlooked the small barn, getting lost in blissful visions of the future. There were no animals in the building now, but soon—once they were free from hiding—Eliza and Thomas would settle this small farm and make it their home, filling the barn with animals and their home with the fruit of their love.

She rested her head against the window pain, a smile tugging at her mouth. Her usual distress over important matters—such as marriage—never surfaced. The decision to marry Thomas came as natural as breathing. Where Samuel had wanted to make all her decisions for her—as easy as that would have been—Thomas allowed, even prompted her to think for herself. Thomas valued her thoughts and opinions. He valued *her*.

At the memory of Kitty's rebuttal, her heart pinched.

She exhaled a misty breath into the cold glass. If only Kitty would speak to her—like she used to. Kitty's eyes still glistened with love, but since last night something deep started to take root within her, and Eliza feared there was nothing she could do to make amends.

Now she could see why her Father had insisted that Kitty never know about his involvement—and that she was young, if not in age, in understanding. Somehow he had known she would react with anger and keep her heart closed to the truth.

Securing her bun in place, Eliza continued her meditative moment, then grabbed her cap from the table and fastened it on her head. It didn't matter. All would be resolved in God's time—Father, Kitty and Samuel—so long as she relied on Him with all her might and strength.

As she peered out the frost-framed window once again, a streak of crimson flashed around the door of the barn and disappeared. She jumped. Her hands began to tingle. Squinting her eyes, Eliza tried to see against the glare of the morning sun.

Gasping, she clasped both hands over her mouth.

Samuel!

It couldn't be. But it was.

His familiar face poked out from an opening in the barn door and his pointed gaze shot musket rounds through her chest. How had he found her? He held a finger over his mouth as if he wanted her to remain quiet. Her throat thickened and the hairs on her arms stood on end. Fear pierced its pointed nails into Eliza's pumping heart.

Lord in heaven, what do I do?

She whipped around to see if Kitty had returned to the room, but she was alone. Blessed be. She turned again toward the nightmare in the barn, hoping by some chance she'd imagined it.

Her limbs went numb. No. He was still there. She gripped her arms around her chest as her entire frame began to tremble.

He motioned to her to come to him, but kept his finger over his lips. *He doesn't want Thomas to know he's here.* She placed a shaking hand over her mouth and tried to breath.

A million frightening scenes pelted her brain like a destructive hailstorm. After learning of Samuel's behaviors with Thomas, she knew Samuel must have ill intentions. What would he do?

She stood glued to the floor beneath her feet, sorting out the tempest that wailed in her chest. A little voice chimed in her head. *You've only ever known Samuel to be gentle and sincere. He may have made mistakes, but there must be good in him.*

Looking again at the bedroom door, Eliza

struggled to calm her racing thoughts. Perhaps she could convince Samuel of Thomas's goodness, and plead with him to stop the hunt and allow them to live in peace, leaving all of this heartache behind them.

She looked back again at the window. It was worth a try. Didn't Thomas deserve that much?

Samuel continued his beckoning, waving his arms with more vigor. He looked around, as if wary of being seen.

I have to do this. Lord, please help me.

Eliza waved then raised a finger and pointed to the door. Samuel nodded before disappearing around inside the barn.

Grabbing her shawl, Eliza ran downstairs.

When she reached the front door she stopped, rested her hand on the cold metal and looked around for either Thomas or Kitty. The sounds from the kitchen and the pleasing morning aromas announced her sister was busy with her favorite chore. Where was Thomas? She almost called for him, went looking for him, to explain the danger that lurked just outside the house.

A clamorous warning rang in her ears. Thomas would never allow her to do what she planned. She flicked away the caution. This way she could keep him from possible harm, and maybe even convince Samuel to leave them alone for good.

She breathed in deep and slow, placing a hand over her middle.

No. Better not to worry Thomas. Samuel would listen to her. He would understand all that had happened. Besides, if he truly loved her, he would see the error of his ways.

Careful to stay silent, she slipped out the door

and tip-toed across the hard, sparkling snow.

Once inside the hollow barn she clutched the thick shawl around her shoulders. “Samuel?” No response. For a moment she breathed easier and her fingers relaxed. Perhaps she’d simply imagined it after all.

“Samuel?” she called, this time quieter, taking another cautious step into the cold, dim emptiness.

In an instant, strong arms came from behind and dragged her into the farthest, darkest corner. Eliza squealed in fear, but a rough hand covered her mouth and muffled the sound.

Samuel turned her to face him with a violent twirl. He released his hold on her mouth and traced her with an intimidating stare. His rough hands molded into her arms. The usual gentleness she’d come to recognize in his pale eyes had been replaced with raw anger, turning their light-blue into the color of his steel blade. His frenzied gaze narrowed as his fingers gripped tighter.

“Eliza!” he said, pulling her to him with crushing strength. His voice was quiet and the words poured from him. “Eliza! What happened to you? You were gone. Then I thought you were dead. I nearly died myself with worry for you. Are you all right? Are you hurt?”

He moved his hands along her back and kissed the top of her head.

Overcome with his tenderness, Eliza hugged him back. *Maybe there’s nothing to be afraid of. He was merely sick with worry.*

“I’m fine, Samuel. I’m fine,” she said, as he pressed her head against him. “There is much I need to say—”

Before Eliza could stop him, he cut off her words as he pulled her chin upward and kissed her mouth, grunting and moving his arms around her back in a way that made her stomach sick.

She squirmed, and tried to push away, but his mouth still covered hers and her words were mumbled. "Sa-uel—lease! Sto—!"

He kissed her harder. Panic surged through her muscles as she fought against him, hitting her fists against his solid chest.

Finally, he released her with an angry push. His clouded features hardened. "No, Eliza, I can't stop!"

His chest heaved and his knuckles turned white as he clenched his fingers. "I have done nothing but search for you all these many weeks. I've worried day and night over you. I love you. You're to be my wife! Will you not kiss me back?" He shook her by the shoulders. "What's happened to you? What has Thomas done to you?"

His eyes searched her face then grew wide and flashed with venom. "Has he defiled you? I'll kill him! Is that why you push me away? You think I won't have you? It doesn't make any difference to me, I'll love you just the same—"

"No! No, Samuel, please. It's nothing like that." Her fingers trembled as she held tight to his biceps hoping he could read the sincerity in her eyes. "He's done nothing to me. He's protected us from the beginning—"

"He kidnapped you!" Samuel seized her arms with iron fingers.

"He rescued us." Eliza whispered, hoping Samuel would follow her example and quiet his voice. "The soldiers were coming, what else was he to do? I . . . we . . . there's much to explain, all you need know is that Thomas got us to safety, Samuel. If we had been caught . . ." She looked away wondering if she should reveal all she knew. "Because of the threats placed upon his family it was necessary for us to stay in hiding until we knew all was safe." She paused and reigned in her remaining fears. "You should know plenty about that, Samuel. It was your doing."

She held her breath, waiting to see how her declaration would be received.

Samuel's face warped and he balked. "If you believe for a moment that I did anything less than my duty to the king you are mistaken."

"Your duty?" Eliza spat, as bursts of indignation blasted in her chest. "It was your duty to threaten the lives of innocent people? And for what purpose?"

He lifted her to her toes, and bent his face only inches from hers. "It is my duty to defend the king by whatever means necessary. The members of that traitorous group will get nothing less than they deserve."

"And what is that, Samuel? What do they deserve?" she said, thinking of not only Thomas, but of Father. What would Samuel have done to him?

Samuel didn't answer. He set her down, his features melting. He brushed her cheek with the back of his hand. "Something's happened to you, my love. That odious man has treated you wrongly, I have no doubt, and filled your mind with his vile rhetoric. I'm so sorry, Eliza. You must get away from here and back to your home where you can recover and begin to think properly again. I'm ready to take you away this instant."

Eliza shook her head and tried to answer but he stopped her with his finger on her lips. His eyes narrowed and his wounded tone carried fire. "I saw him kissing you."

The blood drained from her face and settled at

her feet. The dark barn began to spin. "What?" she breathed.

"I saw you at the rally. I saw you running from him."

Bile crept up her throat.

Samuel continued. "I tried to get to you, but Watson was there first. I followed you . . . I saw everything." A pitiful hurt knit his face.

Oh, Dear Lord, what have I done

He came closer to her and stroked her arms. "I know you love me, Eliza. We're meant for one another. I can only assume he's forced himself upon you and that's the reason you refuse me, but I don't want you to worry. When you and I—"

"You're wrong Samuel! He's done nothing but help and protect me."

He continued his gentleness, tracing her face with his eyes and stroking her arms. "I heard you'd been hurt—stabbed. Is that true? Did he do it because you tried to escape him?"

Eliza's nerves pricked. How much did he know? How long had he been watching them?

"No . . . yes . . . no!" The words wouldn't come quick enough. "I was hurt, very badly, but it wasn't Thomas who did it. It was the sailors, we saw them . . ." She shook her head and waved her hands in front of her. "It's too long to explain, but Thomas rescued me. Samuel, he saved my life!"

Samuel's eyes brimmed with emotion. "And for that, I will always be grateful."

His arms encircled her and he brushed his nose against her ear, his lips tracing along her jaw.

An icy chill wriggled over her spine as she tried to push away. "Stop, Samuel! Don't!"

He stilled, then stepped away and dropped his

lifeless hands at his sides. His features went slack and the muscles in his face ticked.

"I care for you Samuel." Eliza straightened, pulling the shawl back around her shoulders. "But I do not love you. I'm sorry. I don't believe I ever really did. And how could I marry you now, knowing what you've done?" She lifted her chin and straightened her posture. "I love Thomas. We're to be married."

His face twisted and flooded with red as he stepped forward. Eliza recoiled as his shoulders heaved from his heavy breathing

"No. Never! You're mine, Eliza!" His voice boomed as he spoke through his clenched teeth.

He took a step closer reaching his hands toward her, a wicked desperation spinning in his gaze. "I know you are frightened to make such choices in your life. You could never come to a decision this easily. He's forcing you to do these things. You don't have to marry him, Eliza. You're acting so different from the woman I know and love, and it pains me to see it. I will take you away and help you think clearly again."

"I am thinking clearly!" Eliza leaned into her words and clenched her fists, holding her arms rigid at her sides. "Samuel, I love Thomas and I *am* staying with him. I *will* be his wife! I'll not go anywhere with you!"

Samuel's face turned to stone. "Yes. You. *Will.*"

Eliza charged for the barn door, but Samuel overcame her and held her waist with iron muscles as she struggled to get free.

He wrenched her around and gripped her body against his. "Thomas will be killed for what he's done, make no mistake. And you and Kitty are coming with *me*!"

Her knees buckled. She stopped moving and peered into Samuel's cold stare. "Samuel, I beg of you. Don't hurt Thomas. I love him. And if you love me, truly love me, you'll leave us alone and allow us to live our lives in peace. You can end all this, tell them to stop looking for him and allow his cousin's family to return back to their home." Hands trembling, she gripped his crimson jacket. "Please, Samuel!"

He held her too close and too tight. He stroked her face with one hand and kneaded her back with the other. "I do truly love you, Eliza, more than you'll ever know. I can see what you cannot. And because of that, I will rescue you and take you back to Boston where you and I will marry, and *we* will live *our* lives in peace."

Eliza's blood turned to fire and she pulled away. "Never!"

Samuel leaned forward and jabbed a rigid finger into her chest. "Thomas will die, Eliza. There's nothing you can do to stop it from happening."

The room whirled. Her legs melted. She fell to her knees and pressed her hands against her chest. Suddenly, she sucked in a sharp breath as a repulsive yet powerful idea possessed her mind.

After a moment of pressing silence, she stood, keeping her voice void of the emotion that threatened to steal her strength. "If I come with you, if I vow to return to Boston and marry you, will you promise not to kill him?"

Samuel wrenched his neck and looked toward the house through the opening of the barn door then turned back to her as a wicked smile tilted his mouth. "Of course, my love. That's what I'd hoped you'd say."

Chapter Twenty-four

Thomas worked with the last few buttons on his waistcoat and marveled at the events of last night. God had given him a miracle by turning ashes to beauty. A cursed situation had been changed to a glorious blessing in his life.

He slipped on his dark brown jacket and pushed his feet into his boots. A smile slid over his face and a reassuring peacefulness settled over his shoulders.

Eliza loved him. She had accepted his proposal and was to be his wife. Thomas could handle anything—even farming—so long as Eliza was by his side. The thought of it made his insides light as the sparse clouds in the stark blue sky.

He left his room and entered the parlor. The regular clanking of utensil on pan drifted through the house along with the mouth-watering fragrance of fresh baked bread. Kitty must be at her usual post.

But where was Eliza? Most mornings, if she wasn't cooking the morning meal with Kitty, she cleaned or mended.

He explored upstairs and checked the kitchen, his shoulders growing tighter with each passing second.

"Kitty, have you seen Eliza?" he said, entering the warm, sweet-scented room.

Kitty looked up, her hands covered in flour. "I

don't know where she is. Let's hope she hasn't disappeared again." She stared for a moment. "Thomas?"

"Yes?"

Lowering her chin, she spoke quiet. "I do hope you can forgive me for last night. No matter our differences, I want you to know—"

"Kitty." He walked around the table and wrapped her in his arms. "You and I shall be brother and sister from now on. And though we may believe differently about certain things, our affection for one another will never be dimmed."

"What?" Kitty shot out of his arms, her bright eyes round and her mouth open. "Eliza didn't say anything about it—that's marvelous news—you're engaged! I'm so happy for you both. I suppose I did see that coming." She raised her shoulders with a chirping giggle.

Thomas smiled, tamping down the worry that pushed into his gut. Eliza hadn't mentioned it? Odd. Well, perhaps after their argument Eliza planned to announce the happy news when they were in better spirits.

The click of someone opening the front door reached Thomas. He spun toward the main room from his position in the kitchen doorway. He expected Nathaniel sometime today with his regular bi-weekly visit, but it was far too early for that.

Thomas rushed forward as frustration pierced him like a falling icicle. Eliza must be returning from wherever she'd been, and oh how she would get another earful from him. Now. He still hadn't recovered from the thought of almost losing her. After her escape last night, he wanted to know where she was at all times, and she'd promised him she wouldn't do anything impetuous.

Eliza came into the room as expected, head bowed. She kept her eyes at the floor and gripped her shawl with both hands. Thomas pinched his brow as worry skidded across his spine. Why did she look so solemn? He walked toward her and stopped in his tracks.

His lungs ceased to function, and the blood in his limbs refused to move. Entering the room behind Eliza, was the devil.

Once inside, Samuel closed the door quickly behind him, and reached a gentle hand to grab Eliza's arm. She looked up at Thomas for only a moment before looking down again. Her eyes were circled with red, her cheeks wet from tears. What had Samuel done? How had he found them?

Thomas's muscles refused to obey any command as he tried to make sense of what he saw. His peaceful, joy-filled world now broke into a devastating war, destroying everything around him.

"What are you doing here, Martin?" Thomas kept his tone cool despite the fury that blazed through his veins.

Samuel reached his arm around and tugged Eliza close. He nuzzled his nose into her ear, but she kept her eyes at the ground. Thomas's stomach wanted to revolt at the sight. His biceps twitched with the desire to unleash the full measure of his strength, but he refrained. Doing so might put Eliza in more danger and he'd rather die than bring her any harm.

"Would you like to tell him, my darling?" Samuel said. "I think it will be much better coming from you, under the circumstances." He looked at Thomas, a vile grin clawing up his face.

A paralyzing anxiety unleashed itself within

Thomas's gut as Samuel's fingers whitened around Eliza's arm.

Eliza inhaled deep before she spoke and raised her chin. Her voice was quiet, but a look of stoic resolve wound over her features. "Thomas, I wrote to Samuel. I told him everything that happened and he understands it was nothing more than a grievous miscommunication."

Her words were relaxed and calm, a dichotomy to the language that showed in her body. "I told him how miserable I've been. I asked him to come take Kitty and me back to Boston. He's promised to allow you to go free. Also, Daniel and his dear family. All is well. Is not that wonderful?"

Thomas's gaze jumped between the two of them as he tried to piece together the alarming puzzle. This wasn't right. She was lying. How could she have sent word to Samuel without him knowing of it?

Somehow he found his voice. "Eliza, don't be afraid to tell me the truth," he said, hoping she would sense the urgency in his stare.

Eliza pursed her lips and blinked as if straining to stay composed. She rolled her shoulders and lifted her chin, but not her gaze. "Samuel has renewed his sentiments to me, Thomas, and I've accepted him. The truth is, I love him. I always have."

The words slammed into Thomas with such force he took a step back. Impossible. Then again . . . the detached look on her face unraveled every tightly woven emotion around his heart. His breathing became ragged and he reached for the chair at his side.

Samuel drew Eliza closer and tilted her face upward, kissing her on the mouth as only a man in love can do. She didn't resist, didn't try to pull away.

Thomas's stomach lurched and his heart hammered his ribs until he thought his bones would break. She didn't love Samuel.

She couldn't. Could she?

His mind raced. Last night when he'd proposed to her, she'd said she would marry him, but never that she loved him. And she'd never even told Kitty the news of their engagement. He'd believed her response to his admiration was real. Had he wished something into existence that was too good to be true?

Eliza clearly did not want to look at him. She kept her gaze at the floor. It was so unlike her. His skin began to crawl. Samuel appeared calm, but the deep shadow over his face told Thomas he was angry enough to kill.

At that moment Kitty emerged from the kitchen, towel in hand. "Samuel! What are you doing here?" She looked between Samuel, Thomas, and Eliza as she wiped her white hands on her apron.

Samuel released his hold on Eliza and reached out to Kitty as one would to a little child.

"I've come to take you and Eliza home. There's no need to hide any longer. The danger's past."Kitty rushed forward, hugging him around the neck as he lifted her off the ground. "Thank you, thank you, Samuel! We've been waiting so long!"

Thomas stared at Eliza, praying she would look at him. She didn't. An endless abyss forced its way down Thomas's middle. He tried to swallow the lump of painful realization that swelled in his throat.

Eliza didn't love him.

"When can we leave?" Kitty asked, as Samuel set her on her feet.

"Right now, if it pleases you." Samuel shot a sinful

smile at Thomas, but Kitty didn't seem to notice.

She went to embrace Eliza, as if she expected her sister to be just as merry at the news, but instantly froze. "Are you . . . are you staying here, Liza?"

Eliza inhaled a choppy breath. "No, I'm coming with you. Samuel and I are to be married." The crack in her voice pulled at Thomas's heart. Perhaps she *was* being forced?

"What?" Kitty pulled back, her brow crinkling and she shot a look to Thomas. "But I thought—"

"Go gather your things." Samuel cut her off with a tap on her arm. "And would you be so kind as to gather Eliza's as well?"

Kitty's lips pinched, and she shook her head. She straightened her arms at her sides. "I don't understand, Samuel. Eliza and Thomas—"

"Please, dear Kitty." Standing straighter, Samuel's voice deepened. "We must be going."

"Of course." Kitty's tone remained heavy as she tossed a few concerned glances between Thomas and Eliza before doing as commanded.

Thomas still could not move, his feet were heavy as ships anchors, but he couldn't take the silence another moment. He walked straight toward her and moved to touch Eliza, but Samuel slapped his hand away.

"Don't you dare touch my future wife. You've done enough damage," he seethed.

Eliza whipped her head at Samuel, speaking through her teeth. "Let him be, Samuel."

Thomas clenched his fists. His arms ached to pull her away from the vile soldier. "Eliza, why are you doing this? I know you're lying. You don't love him." *Please say it. Say you don't love him.*

Eliza finally lifted her lashes and showed him her

distant brown eyes. "I'm not lying Thomas. I've told you the truth. I'm sorry for what's happened between us, truly I am, but I've made my decision." She stopped and turned her eyes away for less than a second before locking with his gaze. "I'm going to marry Samuel. I love him. This is what I want."

Her words burned a gaping hole in his chest. Thomas straightened and leaned toward her. She could *not* be speaking the truth. "Don't do this. Let me help you."

"She doesn't want your help!"

Samuel pressed a powerful hand into Thomas's shoulder and tried to push him away, but Thomas stood stronger. Samuel's fist raced through the air. Thomas deflected it and raised his own, ready to slam it into his enemy's jaw when Eliza rushed in front of him.

"No!" she pleaded. "Thomas, don't!" Her volume rose as she blocked his aim. She stood straighter and resolve owned her features as Thomas lowered his arm. "Thomas, you must believe me. I don't want to be with you. If I did, I would stay. I'm sorry. I'm going away with Samuel and you must stay here. Don't come after me."

"That's enough, Eliza," Samuel said, pulling her back.

Her words slapped Thomas with dizzying compulsion. He stepped away and continued curling his fists as he tried to make the room stop swaying around him. He flinched when the door flew open again and spun to see who was now invading his home.

Nathaniel. His shoulders slumped as relief bathed him. At least he'd have someone on his side.

Nathaniel entered, his stance stiff. He glared at

Samuel then looked at Thomas, his brow dark. "Good morning."

Thomas tilted his head toward Samuel and kept his words even. "We have a visitor."

"So I see." With his hand still on the door, he continued. "Is everything all right?"

"Aw, if it isn't the bold and daring Dr. Nathaniel Smith," Samuel said, stepping forward. "I spoke with you regarding Eliza's accident. You said she'd died. But as you can clearly see, she is alive and well."

Nathaniel stepped into the room and closed the door with reserved force. "This is true."

"You lied to me." Samuel approached him, stopping only inches away.

Squaring his posture, Nathaniel's eyes shot arrows. "You blackmailed my friend. Therefore, you didn't deserve the truth."

A sinister grin scratched at Samuel's mouth, and he took a step back. "It's too bad you gentlemen don't understand what it means to be a traitor to the Crown. I could have you both arrested." He looked back at Eliza and smiled, then turned to them again. "But, I've a good heart. I'm willing to let your actions remain in the past. And I really should be thanking you. Without that rally of yours I would never have found Eliza." He moved back and slipped his poisonous arms around her, placing another kiss on her temple. "I have my future bride with me, that's all that matters. I will take her back to Boston and the two of you can go on with your *very valuable* lives without any additional interference from us."

Thomas couldn't stop his muscles from twitching and flexing, or his pulse from pounding in his ears. What did that rat think he was doing? Thomas shared a glance with Nathaniel. His friend seemed to understand every emotion that played over Thomas's body and stepped closer to him, touching his flexed arm.

Samuel moved to the stairs and called up to Kitty. "Come Kitty, we must away."

"Coming." Kitty called, her steps growing louder as she descended. Her gaze landed instantly on Nathaniel and a pained smile graced her lips.

Samuel took the bag from her hands. "Say your goodbyes."

Thomas's heart lurched to a stop. *Dear Lord, help me find a way to keep Eliza from going with him.*

"Not the gowns, Kitty," Eliza said, as Kitty stepped into the main room, the evening gowns draped over her arm.

"Oh . . . of course." Kitty laid them over the back of the chair where Thomas stood. Eliza stroked the silk for a moment, before pulling her fingers away and wrapping her waist. She continued to survey the floor beneath her feet. Did that mean she didn't want to leave?

Thomas stepped forward, needing to be as close to her as possible. "Eliza, please," he said, lowering his voice. "I know you, Eliza. And I *know* you don't want this. You don't have to go with him."

A frantic thread laced Kitty's voice. "Thomas, what are you talking about?"

Samuel stepped forward and growled, pushing him away again. "Let Eliza make her own decisions, Thomas. Stop trying to manipulate her."

"Samuel, what's going on?" Kitty faced him, her mouth tight.

"This is not your affair, Kitty." Samuel moved to grab her arm, but Nathaniel smacked it away.

"Don't touch her."

The muscles around Samuel's eyes twitched as he stared at Nathaniel. "Come ladies, we're leaving."

Thomas held his arms rigid at his side to keep from tightening his fingers around Samuel's weak neck. If anyone manipulated Eliza it was Samuel.

Eliza raised her head and turned her face to the beast beside her, her lips stretching in a tight smile. "Do not worry, Kitty. All will be well."

Thomas's heart dried up in his chest. "Eliza, *are* you making your own decision?"

Her gaze lifted, but landed only at his chest. "Yes," she said, too quickly. "I'm ready to go, Samuel. I'll just be outside."

She pulled her cloak off its hook by the door and fled outdoors as if escaping a deadly fire. Kitty followed close behind. Then Samuel.

Thomas's knees weakened. He checked his stance to be sure he could remain erect. Nathaniel's grip tightened around his arm.

His vision blurred. This could not be happening. This morning all was well. Last night they were in love and eager to be wed. Now, in a matter of minutes, his life was upside down and the woman he loved was leaving in the arms of the man who'd made his life a living hell. All of Thomas's energy collapsed to the floor and he placed a hand on the back of the chair at his side. She hadn't said goodbye—hadn't even looked at him.

Thomas shot a desperate glance to Nathaniel who tilted his head toward their common enemy, his eyes narrowing. Thomas had seen that look before. Nathaniel wanted to stop Samuel and end this madness. There were two of them, and only one measly Redcoat. Thomas closed his eyes and shook his head in refusal. This was Eliza's choice and he couldn't compel her to stay, even though he wanted nothing more. He loved her. And if this was what she wanted, then that's what she would have.

"Must you leave so soon?" Nathaniel asked, moving out the door and standing next to Kitty. He cupped her elbow and peered back at Thomas as if pulling him out of the house with invisible ropes.

Somehow Thomas found his strength and followed them into the cold. His emotions bled out, pooling on the snow-dusted ground beneath him.

Kitty froze, and looked between all of them before her gaze rested on Nathaniel. "This is all very sudden, I know . . . I'm not sure what to make of it."

Samuel stepped forward, his icy eyes narrowing. "Eliza is very eager to be home, and I don't wish to detain her in a place where she's been so unhappy." He hugged Eliza across the shoulders. "These girls need to get back to Boston *where they belong*." He emphasized the last words and directed his glare at Thomas.

Kitty's eyes shimmered and her voice wavered. "Thomas, I . . . I don't know what to say."

Calling upon strength from God, Thomas tried to keep his own voice steady. "I'll always be here for you. Both of you," he replied, loud enough for Eliza to hear. She stood with her back toward him and made no indication she'd heard.

Samuel turned around a last time. He nodded in parting as he nudged the girls forward. A sour smile hinted across his ugly face. He took Eliza under his arm and Kitty shuffled alongside as the three of them walked toward town.

A dragon raged within Thomas, but he was helpless to bring an end to his living nightmare. Eliza would stay if she wanted, wouldn't she? If she were in danger she could have said something, knowing both he and Nathaniel would defend her.

She had made her choice, and the agony of it cracked his bones.

He walked a few steps forward and watched, paralyzed. Samuel released his hold of Eliza's shoulders and turned his attention to Kitty.

A whispering breeze sliced through Thomas as his gaze followed their waning figures. His heart shrunk with every advancing step Eliza took.

Thomas kept his eyes on her, knowing she would look back. Though she may not feel the same horrid loneliness that dominated him, they had shared so much. Surely she would acknowledge him before leaving his life forever.

The three of them rounded the far corner that led into town. Thomas's eyes burned and his throat seized.

She never looked back.

Chapter Twenty-five

The bleakness of the suppressing night compressed Eliza's already crushed heart.

"Well, what have we here?" Samuel sat higher on the saddle. "Seems as though the gods have provided us with the perfect resting place. We'll make camp here."

Why did he have to pick this spot? Eliza groaned as she stared at the familiar cave and blinked back the rush of tears. They'd traveled all day on horseback and Eliza's legs and backside ached from sitting sidesaddle in front of Samuel. Why he refused to take the highways and stay in the warm boarding houses along the way she would never understand. It wasn't as if they were being pursued. Though she had a feeling Samuel believed otherwise and had chosen this as a way to avoid any unwanted company.

She glanced beside her at Kitty who shared another horse with Donaldson. Her shoulders slumped and she rocked forward. Donaldson reached with a gentle arm and held her steady.

"You can sleep in a few moments," Donaldson said, his gentle voice waking Kitty enough to keep her upright.

Samuel pulled on the reins and slipped off the horse, then reached up to help Eliza down. She shuddered as his hands slithered around her waist. Bile inched up her throat again, as it had all day and she took a deep breath to keep it down.

"Are you feeling well, my love?" he said, before kissing her forehead.

"How do you imagine I'm feeling?"

A satisfied grin laced his mouth. "I imagine you're eager to wed, as I am."

"You can believe that, if it gives you pleasure." She glared and walked toward her sister.

Donaldson dismounted and helped Kitty onto the muddy ground. The two girls walked together into the rocky dwelling. Kitty leaned into Eliza as if ready to sleep on her feet. Eliza found a smooth spot on the ground and helped her sister onto the dirt. Warm memories of their first visit to this rocky shelter flickered to life in Eliza's mind, but she stamped them away, knowing if she entertained such images her heartache would be too much to endure.

"I'll start a fire," Samuel said, coming up behind Eliza and brushing her shoulder with his hand. "Donaldson, grab those bedrolls and bring them here. We don't want these women to catch a chill."

Eliza stood and looked into the beckoning forest. She wanted to run, to escape into winter's blackness. Her throat closed, clogged with surging emotions. She brushed at her eyes to hide the evidence of tears.

Donaldson entered, two rolled-up blankets under his arms, just as Samuel managed to start the meager fire. Without a word, Donaldson set the blankets on the hard cave floor and handed one to Eliza.

"I hope these bedrolls will be enough for you. Your sister was quite chilled as we rode. I suggest wrapping this heavy one around her and staying close to share the warmth of your bodies. Do you need anything else, Miss Campbell?"

"No." Eliza took the blanket, and found it easy to smile at his kindness. "Thank you, sir."

A deep smile crossed the man's handsome face, before he cleared his throat. "Well, if you do need anything—either of you—don't hesitate to ask." He bowed at the waist and turned to assist Samuel.

Eliza draped the blanket around Kitty, then covered herself with her own and snuggled awkwardly next to her sister for warmth while the men stayed busy on the opposite side of the cave. Sleep would not bless her with its company no matter how she willed it. How else could she suppress the wrenching guilt that plagued her? Without sleep she could not flee the memories of the man she loved—and how she'd hurt him.

Thomas, I'm so sorry.

The very thought of him made fresh tears scorch her eyes, and she squinted, burying her face in her cold hands under the scratchy covering. The image of Thomas's sorrow-covered features wove into her heart until it threatened to stop beating. She hadn't been able to look at him—except to try and convince him that she loved Samuel. Doing so had caused her such dizziness she nearly collapsed, but her motivation to keep Thomas safe rose above all else. She recalled how his blue eyes lost their deep color and the blood seeped out of his perfect face. If she'd let her eyes trail over him or allowed herself to be pulled into his gaze, she might not have been able to protect him. Giving away her true feelings would have made him follow her, she knew it, and that was a risk she couldn't take. Knowing Thomas was alive and could someday lead a normal, happy existence was her ultimate motivation. She loved him more than her own life and prayed with all her strength that somehow he would know it.

I know you're a talented little actress, Eliza, Samuel had said. *You must make Thomas believe you don't want him, that you want me instead. Because, deep in your heart I know that's what you want. Don't try to warn him or send him any kind of message. I'll be listening. If he so much as follows us, he's dead.*

Samuel's words swirled like a whirlpool, pulling every remaining hope into its endless spiral.

She prayed she'd done well enough—that Thomas had believed her charade and would leave them be. She wondered if his heart ached as fierce as hers. Walking away, and not looking back was the cruelest moment she'd ever endured. Making her legs step one in front of the other had been like walking through thigh-deep mire. How she managed it, she still didn't know.

A slight east wind lacerated her cheeks as it swept into the cave and her body shook again. This was her future now. She must accept it.

How could life change so quickly from greatest joy to the greatest of sorrows?

On the long ride, Samuel informed her that they would be married a week from tomorrow. He loved her so much, he said, he didn't want to waste time.

Seven days.

Pulling the blanket over her head to shield herself from the icy breeze, Eliza bit her cheek so hard she tasted blood. Her life was coming to an end, and worst of all, she was to blame. If she had taken Thomas's wise counsel and stayed away from that formidable rally, then none of this would have happened. Samuel might never have found them and she and Thomas could have lived and shared their love to the end of their days.

Forgive me, Lord, for what I've done. I tried to make things right—to make a proper choice and learn why Father did what he did. But now, I see I have failed yet again.

Eliza rolled on her side toward the fire, and writhed on the hard ground, her bones pressing her flesh into the unforgiving bed of solid earth.

Samuel fussed with the small fire and humphed, grumbling curses under his breath.

Eliza moved back the blanket and peeled her eyes when he rose and walked to the other side of the cave. In the dim light she could only distinguish a faint outline of both men. Donaldson stood over the fire, warming his hands and appearing to ignore Samuel's presence.

"Eliza and I will be married tomorrow week."

Donaldson turned a disinterested eye at Samuel, then gazed again at the growing fire. "So you said."

Samuel approached him. "I have one more task for you."

"I told you, I'm no longer your pawn."

Samuel's voice lowered even more and Eliza strained to hear above the popping of the fire. She peeked quickly at Kitty. Thank the Lord she'd found peace in sleep.

Samuel leaned into Donaldson, heat searing his words. "If you want to continue your military career you will do as I say. Your sister's medicines need to be paid for, and if I remember correctly, you supply the money, do you not?"

Donaldson cranked his head sideways, his tone low and heavy with malice. "So you'll blackmail me as well?"

"I wouldn't have to, if you would simply do as I

ask."

Eliza couldn't see his face, but Donaldson's stance showed his rage. "What is it?"

"Once we get back to Boston and Eliza and I are wed, you will return to Sandwich. Burn Thomas's house, his barn—everything."

Dear God! No! Eliza slapped a hand over her mouth to shelter her gasp.

Donaldson whipped toward Samuel and grabbed his collar. "Never."

Samuel shoved Donaldson into the spiny cave wall."You have no choice! I suggest you follow my orders."

"You're the devil," Donaldson seethed, shoving Samuel at the shoulders.

Eliza clenched her eyes and bit her lip again until the familiar taste of blood trickled over her tongue. She choked on the lump in her throat and clenched her arms around her stomach, trying to keep down the acid that surged in her belly.

Oh, Lord what have I done?

"You have to go after her, Thomas." Nathaniel sank into the Windsor chair across from Thomas at the lonely table in the kitchen. "You're a fool not to."

The dark sky outside grated on Thomas's thin nerves and matched the despair that swirled within him. Eliza had been gone for more than fifteen hours, but it seemed to him like three lifetimes.

"Perhaps I am. And yet, I cannot do it." Thomas ground his teeth together, picking at the day-old bread Eliza had made.

Nathaniel's face curled. "You know she loves you."

"She never said she loved me."

"Did she have to?"

Thomas sat back and wiped his hand across his mouth, trying to erase the memory of her kisses. Uncompelled, images of her walking away from his life slipped into his pain-clouded mind and rested there like an unwanted guest. "She never looked back at me, Nathaniel. She never said goodbye. If she wanted me to help her, to rescue her—if she wanted to stay here, she could have found a way."

Nathaniel pushed out of his chair and walked to the back of it, resting one hand on the upper rail and pointing with the other. "That man is a . . ." He snapped his jaw closed and shook his head. "And you're even worse if you believe she is such a woman—to love you one moment and desert you the next."

Thomas jerked up and clenched the bread in his fingers. "I don't know what to believe Nathaniel." He stared at the bits of mangled bread. "How can I live a full life without her?"

Nathaniel let out an exasperated groan and raised his hands in the air. "You don't have to live without her—why can't you see that?"

Thomas grunted and pushed away from the table. "Quiet, Nathaniel, or I'll be forced to throw you out."

He moved from the kitchen into the parlor, reliving the times they'd read to one another, talked, and shared memories. Thomas closed his eyes and could almost feel the slope of her waist, the velvety texture of her skin. He could smell the rose in her hair and taste the sweetness of her lips. The refrain of her gentle voice rang in his mind like the far away bells of a church steeple.

Nathaniel exhaled and sat in the largest chair in front of the fire. "If I know you as well as I know anyone, and I do, then I know you'll come to your senses and decide to go after her before too long."

Thomas's frustration crested. He pulled his fingers through his thick hair and growled, stomping his heel into the floor. "Nathaniel, I told you, she didn't want me to go after her. Didn't you see her? Did she act like a woman in love to you?"

"Yes she did."

"Are you mad?" Thomas said, ire and confusion melding into poisonous fumes in his chest. "She refused to meet my gaze. Didn't say a word to me, except to explain she loved Samuel and couldn't wait to get out of my sight and back to Boston. That doesn't seem like something a woman in love would do."

Nathaniel rested one ankle on top of his leg, fixed his eyes on Thomas and played absentmindedly with the buckle on his shoe. "Then I'm afraid you don't know much about love."

Thomas cupped his hand over his mouth and exhaled through his fingers. It appeared as though he didn't, yet his heart ached with such raw pain he believed he knew plenty about love.

He knew it could kill a man. A slow, horrifying death.

Nathaniel went on. "I didn't see as much as you did, Thomas, but from what I witnessed, the truth was clear. If she didn't care, she would have been able to look at you and bid you a civil farewell, if nothing else. It pained her too much to do so. Don't you understand? I've been around the two of you enough to see the starry-eyed longing in her eyes when she looks at you. She's protecting you. Somehow Samuel is making her do what she's doing. You must see that."

Could he be right? Could Eliza really have been trying to protect him?

No. Thomas shook his head. "You think very highly of yourself, Nathaniel, but in this case you're wrong. She wanted to rid herself of me. In the end, it's better for her that way."

Nathaniel launched out of his seat and planted himself in front of Thomas, glaring. "I'll say it again, Thomas." His angular features hardened. "I know you are distressed about your past—you've had a rough one, but you must leave it at the feet of God. You've done much good for many people. Eliza most of all. You've done your best with a wretched situation and no one could ask for more. Leave your disquiet behind."

Thomas kept his jaw hard as granite. "Are you finished preaching?" He curled his fists and breathed from his nose. How dare his friend advise on issues in which he had no business?

"No, I'm not finished preaching, but I'll stop there." Nathaniel paused and shared a caring smile. "I will bid you good evening."

He grabbed his cloak and hat, opened the door and turned to Thomas. "Think about what I said. I know you'll find bits of wisdom, even though I won't expect you to admit it. And you know where to find me . . . when you come to your senses." He tapped his hat on his head and stepped into the dark.

Thomas closed the door, and exhaled loud and harsh, still feeling the heat of their exchange. The revelatory truth of Nathaniel's words seeped into his mind and trickled into his chest. He slumped into the largest chair and sat motionless as the painful emotions slithered over him like hungry snakes. Thomas closed his eyes. The thought of Eliza being forced to do anything against her will made his muscles cramp—especially when it was at the hands of Samuel. Nathaniel might be right when it came to his past, but he couldn't be right about Eliza.

She'd made it clear she didn't want his help. Hadn't she? He growled and slammed his fist against his knees. He didn't know. Staring at the ceiling, he dug his fingers into his legs. No, she would have told him. Somehow she would have given him a sign that she needed him.

Yet she had done nothing but walk away—with his heart in her grasp.

"Thomas! Thomas! I'm so sorry." Eliza wept into her hands, her petite frame trembling as she sobbed. "I only wanted to protect you. I love you."

Thomas's eyes shot open and he grabbed the arms of the chair. With a quick shake of his head he tried to flick away the sleep from his mind and grasp the scope of what he'd dreamed. The popping fire ignored him, lending the only sound in the deserted home. He brushed a quivering hand over his jaw and tried to calm his shaky limbs. Staring into the dying flames, he blinked.

Not a dream. A nightmare.

Eliza, in a gold and cream gown, sat crumpled on the floor in the front room of her Boston home, weeping and calling out his name.

It was so real he could have reached out and touched her, wiped away her streaming tears.

He rubbed his hands over his head, gripping his hair by the roots and tried to press away the gnawing anxiety that bored into his gut.

She needs you. She loves you. Go to her.

The words were vivid and clear, Thomas jerked and looked around, expecting to see Nathaniel in the doorway. But no one was there. Silence enveloped the darkening room. He lay his head back against the chair and exhaled, expelling a storm of pain as he stared at the shadowed ceiling.

He closed his eyes and tried to fight away the recurring images from his nightmare that pervaded his mind. Eliza's tragic cries and declaration of love wove into his soul, causing his eyes to burn and his heart to seize with longing.

You have done much good, my son, and are of great worth to me. You have a righteous desire, pursue it. Eliza needs you. Go to her.

Slowly, like a drink of warm cider, the words filtered down through the maze of his mind and settled in the center of his soul, melting away the doubt and confusion. Every nerve in Thomas's body sprung to life. His mind cleared in an instant and a powerful energy shot down his spine.

It was not a nightmare he'd seen, but a vision. God was telling him to go after Eliza. She loved him—needed him. Blast it all, Nathaniel was right. Putting his past, his doubts, his pride and troubles at God's feet would bring Thomas new life. The life he wanted with Eliza. But he had to rescue her first.

His heart burst from his chest. How could he have been such a blind, selfish fool? *Thank you, Lord! Forgive me for not seeing it before. Forgive me for being afraid, for not believing you. Help me to get to her in time!*

After flying into his greatcoat, Thomas rushed across town and slammed his fist on Nathaniel's door, refusing to stop pounding until it opened.

Nathaniel came to the door fully clothed, and yanked his hat from the peg. "I thought it might be you."

Thomas didn't wait a second before speaking. "We're going to save Eliza."

Pulling his dark cloak over his shoulder, a broad smile painted Nathaniel's face. "Well. It's about time."

Chapter Twenty-six

As she stepped into her childhood home, Eliza felt as if she'd fallen into the arms of God. Safety enveloped her and she sank into the large chair in the center of the room, while Kitty made her way upstairs. Though the familiarity of the surroundings allowed Eliza to breathe deeply again, it failed to release her of the crushing grief that had become her constant companion.

She peered around, remembering that fateful night those many weeks ago when they had left in the dead of night, fleeing for their very lives. And though she'd missed these consoling walls, they no longer held such a powerful claim upon her heart. It was Thomas and his home that she longed for. It was in Thomas's home, in his arms, where she belonged.

Donaldson stomped in behind her and went immediately to the hearth, working to create a warm blaze in the cold and forlorn fireplace.

"Are you going to be alright, my love?" Samuel said, in a gentle tone when he finally entered the house.

Her voice refused to work, as her rising emotions thickened her throat. *No.* Her heart had been all but cut from her chest. She would never be the same again.

Samuel knelt in front of her and rested a hand on her knee. "You'll see in time, Eliza," he said, taking her hand in his. "This is the right way. I love you and I'll take care of you. You are simply in shock. You've gone through a horrifying ordeal. You need to rest. I promise, you'll feel much better in a few days."

He pushed off his knees, then walked around the room as Donaldson went back outside, the fire now blazing. "I came here many times after I'd found you were gone. I arranged the furniture again, as you can see, and replaced the broken glass." He ran his fingers over the back of Father's favorite settee. "Coming here made me feel closer to you."

Eliza moved her eyes to where he paced in front of the now roaring flames. Samuel's brow grew pensive. "I know I said we would marry at the end of this week, but I've decided on tomorrow instead. I have already asked a friend of mine, Reverend Edmonton, to officiate."

"What?" Eliza found her voice in an instant, and it resonated much stronger than she expected. "But you said seven days!"

Samuel spun on his heel, a determined stare possessing his features. "I'm sorry to disappoint you, Eliza, but we must not postpone. We can wed tonight if you'd rather." He winked as if she would find his eagerness amusing. "I've arranged for our wedding to be here. I'm sure you won't mind. We can have a special celebration sometime afterward, with our friends and family in attendance of course."

What friends and family? "Why are you doing this?" She choked on her words, her eyes burning.

He tilted his head toward the ceiling and sighed.

"Because we love each other, my darling. Your mind has been temporarily clouded. After we are man and wife you will be grateful for what I've done for you—for us."

Her mind raced, trying to find excuses and reasonable ways to delay. She cleared her throat and forced her voice to sound sincere, hoping that perhaps, such compliance would win her a few more days of freedom. "Samuel, I have no gown. Our wedding should be cherished, not rushed. There are things to prepare. Things to do before—"

"What is there that can get in the way of our love? Frivolous things such a gowns are unnecessary. Vowing before God to love and honor one another until death is enough. Besides, it's already been arranged. Tomorrow at six o'clock in the evening. Wear that gold and cream gown I love so much. It accentuates your already shining beauty."

Eliza trembled and clapped a hand over her mouth, sure she would cast-up what little food she had in her stomach. She stood to try and take a deep breath to suppress the wave of nausea. Once it receded, she faced Samuel who came to stand in front of her. He moved her hand away from her face, and held her by the shoulders, leaning closer until his lips rested on her head. She cringed as he tasted the line of her hair, her jaw, until he reached her mouth. Samuel released her before she had time to push him away. He laughed low in his chest and gave her a lecherous smile. By the way his eyes coursed over her body, she knew his errant thoughts.

With another deep chuckle, he took a step away. "We'd better use caution, Eliza, and leave the rest for tomorrow evening."

The mere mention of it caused her to sway, but he

caught her and helped her into the chair.

He chuckled again and kissed her cheek. "The excitement of it is simply overwhelming."

Eliza cringed and closed her eyes, fearing if she opened them the tears would flow without end.

"I'll be staying here tonight," Samuel said. "Just in case we have any unexpected visitors. And don't worry, Donaldson will be with us until after the ceremony. I won't ravish you until then."

The cold night air seemed to champion Thomas's cause and the very trees around him whispered "God speed."

Nathaniel had many good friends among his patients in town, one of whom had promised the use of his horses should the need ever arise. Thomas had never been more thankful for anything in his life. They could easily cover the sixty miles on horseback, saving themselves enormous amounts of time.

"Do we have everything we need?" Nathaniel asked as he tightened his saddle before mounting.

Thomas reined in his spirited animal and sat tall in his seat. He gripped the leather in his gloved hands and tried not to kick his horse until his friend was ready. "I believe so."

Nathaniel mounted and brought his horse alongside Thomas's. "Let's ride."

The strong stallions heaved and grunted as they galloped at full speed across the rock-solid ground. Thomas sped across the darkened path, not knowing how he would find Eliza, but believing that his Father in Heaven would lead him safely to her.

The vision replayed without end, Eliza's cries echoing again and again. How could he have let her go? He kicked the animal once more, but the horse was already racing headlong into the night. The memory of Samuel's prideful grin and possessive hold turned Thomas's muscles to stone and he leaned into the wind as it whipped past his face.

When he found her, how would he bring her to safety? What if he were caught? That would only secure her wretched future . . .

The rhythmic beat of the horse's hooves faded as a familiar voice whispered past the drumming. Robert's voice. *The pursuit of your righteous desires is worth every sacrifice.*

Squeezing the leather reins, Thomas held his jaw tight as the statement seemed to move the ground faster under the horse's hooves. No doubt Robert was right beside him, ready to help him bring his daughter to safety—and to the home where she belonged.

Eliza twisted and squirmed under the heavy quilt. When the moon hit the top of the sky, she sat up and propped a plethora of pillows behind her back. Kitty slept beside her, snuggled in her usual curled position. Sighing, Eliza tucked the covers around her sister's back. At least Kitty hadn't asked too many questions, though Eliza had seen the worry behind her sister's mask of acceptance. Kitty appeared happy to be home. That was all that mattered.

If only Eliza felt the same.

She pulled her knees to her chest as a squall of

bittersweet memories buried her heart and endless tears tumbled down her face. Eliza could bear the pain no longer. She had to leave the room before her tears woke Kitty. She lit a tall candle, wrapped a familiar shawl around her shoulders, and emerged from the room.

Tip-toeing downstairs, she absorbed the comfort of the intimate surroundings in the parlor, inhaling the scents that reminded her of happier times. A slight glow emanated from the fireplace, casting a golden light about the room.

From behind, Father's office beckoned her, as if it reached out and tapped her on the shoulder, drawing her near with invisible arms. She'd not dared go in since his death, knowing it would awaken precious and wrenching memories. But now, she could not hold back. She walked down the small, quiet hall until the large door towered in front of her. Her fingers twisted the cold handle and she pushed it open. The candle in her hand cast a haunting glow along the many rows of books that lined the walls. His desk, still covered with opened anatomy diagrams and papers, looked just as he'd left it.

She walked toward his large chair behind the desk, brushing her hand along the oak as she went, feeling closer to him than she had since his spiritual visit.

His thick medical journal lay open. She placed the candle on the scattered diagrams behind the book, turned to page one, and began to read.

She read of his treatments, and the patients he'd cared for, his times of success and times of sorrow. Surprisingly, mixed among his medical records were notes about personal matters. Page after page she saw not only his day-to-day happenings as a father and a doctor, but how he'd felt about the politics in Boston—and how those feelings changed over time.

Eliza gripped the shawl tighter and scooted to the edged of the chair, savoring every precious word. *Father, how did I not know this about you before?* And yet, it was as if she knew it already. As the hours passed, the light of clear understanding illuminated her mind, and her throat thickened. She recognized things she could never have comprehended if not for her time spent with Thomas. What he had taught her, and what she was now reading—words written in Father's own hand—fit together like the tiny pieces in a colorful mosaic.

Father kept all of this a secret, both for his protection as well as theirs. But he'd taught her all the things he believed, though she'd never recognized it.

"Always serve your King, Eliza."

"You must remember you have but one King—you must honor and serve him."

"Give your all to the King. He will protect and keep you."

Her vision blurred. Father had loved both her and Kitty, of that she had no doubt. And now, she knew without question that Father had never truly kept them in complete darkness. She had simply not been able to see everything for lack of knowledge, for lack of understanding. If only Kitty could see it too.

Eliza's heart swelled and cleansing tears streamed over her face. She continued to flip and skim, still reading, still learning, until she reached the last entry dated July 1, 1773.

> *My life is slipping away. It is not long now before I will once again see my beloved Mary, Peter,*

and rest in the arms of my Redeemer. I often wonder if I should confess my secrets to Eliza. Kitty shall not ever know—or if she does she must be older. She will not take it well. Eliza may be surprised, but I see a level spirit within her, and I feel it a sin not to disclose my activities to her knowledge.

How I wish I could have been alive long enough to see Eliza and Kitty wed and experience the joy their children will bring.

I have prayed many nights that Eliza will someday see the truth of Samuel—he is not the man for her. I have treasured Thomas Watson these many years now—I feel as if he is my son—and I hope that he and my dear daughter will meet. They are of the same cloth and I believe they would be very happy as husband and wife. But, I will leave such things in God's hands.

I hope Eliza and Kitty will know how much I love them, and that all I have done was done for their good. God will guide them, protect them, and lead them on the path of peace, so long as they trust in Him. I pray they will.

Large tears flowed, plunking onto the pages below and bleeding over his words just as her heart bled with new pain. Father had wanted her to meet Thomas. In fact, he wanted them to marry. She wept harder at the realization. God *had* led them from the beginning. He *had* brought them together just as Father desired, and now, because of what she had done, her future of endless happiness would never be.

Oh, how she wanted to see Father at this moment—to hold him tight and tell him she loved him, to thank him for his sacrifices and ask for his forgiveness for attending that ill-fated rally.

She folded her arms over the journal and pressed her head into the crook of her elbow, attempting to muffle her sobs. How she wished Thomas would feel her need for him and come to her and take her away from her self-inflicted grief, but he must hate her now, after what she'd done. The thought of her actions and his stone-like features ripped at her heart and she cried all the harder.

Two words moved back and forth in her clouded mind. Trust God. Trust God.

She must trust God. And she did. But she feared that despite her trust in Him, the life she'd dreamed of had come to an end, and it was all her doing.

The door to Father's study creaked, and she jumped to her feet, wiping her cheeks.

"Samuel." She swallowed and wrapped her arms around her middle, trying to hide her curves. The way his hungry gaze poured over her nightgown compelled her to take a step back. Without the usual red coat, his shirt accentuated his muscular frame and his hair had been fastidiously pulled into a queue as if he'd been up for some time.

"Good morning," he said, coming close and sitting on the desk in front of her.

It was then she noticed the light pink sunlight drifting through the window. She'd read all night.

Once again, his eyes combed over her and his breathing stuttered as if he were thinking of things he should not. "Today is the day I have been dreaming of these many years." He pressed his hands around her waist and pulled her close.

"You've been crying." He moved his thumb over her cheek and tucked a stray hair behind her ear.

"Are you alright?"

She nodded, if only to stop him from asking. *How I wish you were Thomas.*

He caressed the side of her head with his nose and whispered in her ear while his hands explored her back. "I understand you've been through a harrowing ordeal, Eliza, and the shock of it all must be terribly overwhelming. You will have a great deal of sorrow to battle, but I will battle it with you. You have no need to fear."

She choked on the rock that hovered in her throat. He had no idea how she feared her future with him. Her mind never stopped working, searching for something she could do to make Samuel understand they were not the match he believed them to be.

Her eyes flew open when a vital truth ignited in her memory and she pushed away from him. How could she have forgotten this? It might be her saving grace.

"Samuel," she said. "Before we're married there's something I must tell you."

He straightened and his mouth tightened as if she might bear bad news. "Anything, my love."

"My Father was a member of the Sons of Liberty. He was not the Tory we all believed him to be."

"I know." Samuel rested against the desk, pulling her closer. "That doesn't matter to me."

Eliza's heart dipped at his casual acceptance, but she wouldn't surrender. "Samuel, I don't believe my Father was wrong in what he did. In truth, I feel the same as he."

Samuel bristled and pushed Eliza away before scooting off the table. He rolled his shoulders back and clenched his fists by his sides. "Here you go again, talking of things about which you know nothing. There is much happening in politics and the issues are far too elaborate for you to even begin to understand."

"But I *do* understand!"

"No you don't!" He yanked her arm. "Anyone who goes against the king *does not understand*. I forbid you to ever speak of such treason again!"

Eliza shoved him away, her limbs tingling as she gained strength. "I will not remain quiet. I will say what I feel, no matter how it offends you. Christ is my only King, Samuel, and there is nothing you can say or do to make me believe otherwise."

He snatched her to him again, holding tight to her arms with unforgiving fingers. "Even Christ said to render unto Caesar that which is Caesar's. We should serve our leaders and be obedient citizens." He released her and pivoted, running one hand through his hair. "You should know all this Eliza. King George needs our devotion."

Blood pumping, Eliza lifted her chin. "He doesn't need anything from us, Samuel. If you had only served God with half the zeal you serve your king—"

"Don't quote Shakespeare at me, Eliza!" He spun toward her with venom in his eyes. "When we are man and wife you will do as I say. You will *never* speak of this again!"

Samuel came forward and loomed over her, his thick breath clouding the air in front of her face. "When you are mine, you will obey me."

"I will not be your wife. I refuse to marry a man who is dishonest."

"I have never been dishonest with you."

Fresh malice boiled in Eliza's belly. "You said you would not harm Thomas if I promised to return here and marry you, did you not?"

"I did."

"So why did you tell Donaldson to burn Thomas's property *after* we were married? I refuse to be your wife, since you have rescinded on our agreement."

A monster unleashed before her. Samuel shoved Eliza against Father's rows of books, their hard covers stabbing into her back just as Samuel's eyes stabbed into her chest.

"If you do not marry me, not only will his house burn, but Thomas will as well."

Eliza's blood escaped her face and she braced herself as the room twisted around her. "You wouldn't."

Samuel's eyes narrowed into small black slits. "I would."

Her bones wanted to crack under the weight of his words and her voice refused to work, but somehow she found her ability to speak. "If I find that you have done anything to him after we are married I will do everything in my power to leave you, make no mistake."

Samuel relaxed his numbing grip, a wicked laugh rumbling in his chest. "You can't leave me, Eliza. Not after everything I've done for you."

"I can, and I *will*!"

Samuel roared and without warning slapped her across the face, causing her to tumble sideways. She hit Father's chair and landed in a rough heap on the floor.

He rushed to her, panic lighting his features, as if it had been someone else who had struck her. "Eliza, I'm so sorry. I don't know what came over me. Are you hurt?"

A trickle of warm liquid ran down her cheek. He

tried to touch her face, but she slapped his hand away.

"Don't you dare touch me."

His face drained of all color and he sputtered as he spoke, his voice quiet. "I'm so sorry, Eliza, I—"

"Thomas would have never dreamed of hitting me, Samuel." She straightened to her full height, breathing in deep heaves. "He lets me speak my mind and ask questions. He believes that what I think matters. He *loves* me!"

Samuel lowered his brow and his tone rumbled in his chest as he shook her shoulders. "You will never speak of Thomas again. Today we will be married, and you will be mine forever and you will love *me*! As far as you are concerned, Thomas never existed."

The finality of his statement sluiced over her, causing her knees to buckle. She gripped the row of books behind her to steady her stance.

"So be it, Samuel Martin," she said, filling her voice with razors. "But know this, there is only one man that I will ever love—dead or alive. And it will never be you!"

Eliza's words stripped Samuel of every bit of hope still clinging to him.

She bolted from the room as if he were some kind of thief, ready to steal her very innocence. He couldn't stop his hands from shaking and the fury in his gut consumed every ounce of his body until his limbs grew weak.

Samuel righted the fallen chair and sat. His shoulders slumped and his features dropped. He stared ahead of him into the rows of books and cringed as if they derided him for his weaknesses. He replayed Eliza's murderous statement over again in his mind. *There is only one man I will ever love—dead or alive. And it will never be you.*

The recollection burned him anew and a powerful rage bubbled in his already boiling blood. He scratched his fingers through his hair and grabbed at his scalp squinting his eyes so hard the muscles in his face began to cramp. *How could she?* After all he'd done for her, after the love they had shared.

He clenched his fists and ground his still wounded knuckles into one another, grinding his bones until the cracks in his skin peeled and oozed blood. The pain helped him to think clearer. To think harder.

She still loves, me. I know it. She has been brainwashed. Once we are married, and I have a chance to show her the full measure of my affection, when I can clear her mind of Thomas, then she will remember how she loved me.

Samuel sat straighter and rubbed at the blood on his hands. Once they were married. Yes. Once they were married and Thomas was dead, she would have no choice but to accept him and love him the way he knew she could.

That would be tonight.

Chapter Twenty-seven

Dressed in the gold and cream brocaded silk as Samuel requested, Eliza sat before the dressing table mirror while Kitty styled her long brown hair. The emptiness that swirled made her nauseous.

Suddenly Kitty smacked the brush on the table and dropped her arms. "Liza, I can't stand it any longer. What's going on? Why are you marrying Samuel? This is madness. You love Thomas and he loves you."

How I wish I could tell you! Eliza could not open her mouth for fear that both the few bites of food she had eaten, and an uncontrollable wailing would erupt. She wrapped her hands around her stomach.

Kitty's mouth tightened into a straight line. She looked into the mirror and met Eliza's wet gaze, her face softening as she gripped Eliza's shoulders. "That mark on your cheek. How did you get it?"

Kitty's words struck Eliza's crumbling defenses and she cupped her hands over her face and tried to stop the flow of tears.

"Liza, please tell me!" Kitty knelt at her side with her hands on Eliza's knees. "If you are unhappy, you don't have to do this. It rips at my heart to see you hurting. Why won't you tell me—"

"There's nothing to tell, Kitty." Eliza sucked in a ragged breath and wiped her nose with a clean handkerchief. "I'm simply over tired, and wishing Mother and Father could be here, that is all. Please don't worry about me."

Eliza studied her reflection. Swollen eyes, splotchy cheeks, a red gash on her face. Not the picture of beauty that a bride wishes to be on her wedding day. The mar on her cheek represented the beginning of a life filled with the pain of regret and wounds that would never heal. And it was all her doing.

Eliza rested her face in her palms again and breathed through her fingers. *Father in Heaven, please deliver me!*

Slowly, Kitty rose to her feet and squeezed her sister's shoulders. She blinked, shedding large tears and her soothing voice wavered as she kissed the top of Eliza's head. "I love you, Liza. I hope you know that."

Blotting at her own eyes, Eliza tried to smile. "I know."

"If this is what you really want, then I know you will be happy. Samuel loves you deeply, I'm sure of it." She looked away, and her grip grew tighter. "And I . . . I hope you can forgive me for my outburst. I want you to know I hold no ill feelings toward you, even though you and I cannot agree on certain things . . ." Her voice trailed away as her lips pulled down.

The tenderness in Kitty's voice clamped around Eliza's fractured heart. She spun on her seat and flung her arms around Kitty's middle. "Oh Kitty, I love you. Please forgive me for causing you pain. I would never want anything to come between us."

Kitty fell to her knees again, clinging to Eliza, clutching ever harder as she cried. “Forgive me for being so angry. No matter what you believe, I will always love you.”

Before too long, Kitty pulled away. She tilted her head and smiled through tight lips as if trying to be happy for an event that she knew Eliza didn’t want. “I suppose we better finish your hair. There isn’t much time left before the reverend arrives.”

Eliza nodded as her heart stopped beating. No, there wasn’t much time left. Not much time before her world ended.

While Kitty placed the last curls atop Eliza’s head and worked the cream colored ribbon through her hair, Eliza prayed. She prayed more earnestly than she’d ever done. Though it seemed her prayers would float no higher than the top of her mirror. Had God forgotten her?

With her coiffeur complete, she stood to examine her appearance. Kitty came forward and rested her head on Eliza’s shoulder. Eliza set her cheek on Kitty’s head, relishing in her last moments of freedom. She had chosen this path to keep Thomas alive, but even that was no guarantee. She could do nothing to protect him from what awaited after she and Samuel were wed.

Surely, God in his wisdom could find a way to protect her dearest Thomas, even if He would not deliver her.

“You are more lovely than I have ever seen you, Eliza,” Kitty whispered.

Eliza blinked slow, ignoring the shallow sensation that wedged its way into her middle. “I suppose that’s thanks to you, dear Kitty.”

A knock sounded on the door and Samuel pushed

it open. His eyes grew wide and trailed over her, possessive. "You look like a dream, Eliza."

A familiar rolling nausea surged upward and Eliza had to force a smile as she swallowed it away.

"I've come up to tell you the reverend has arrived."

"Already?" Every muscle flexed and the bit of hope she'd clung to, that maybe God would still provide a way to deliver her from such torture, died instantly. Her legs twitched with the need to run from him—from her future. But she couldn't. Thomas's life depended on this night.

Samuel bobbed his head and a demanding grin possessed his lips. "He's waiting downstairs, and since you are ready, we may as well begin." He motioned toward the door in a quick, soldierly movement after a nod of acknowledgement to Kitty.

When she didn't instantly move, Samuel took her arm. "Are you feeling alright my dear? Here, let me escort you downstairs."

Eliza's legs were heavy as sacks of flour and she was forced to lean upon Samuel as he helped her walk down the stairs and into the parlor.

The reverend greeted her, bowing, and offering a gentle smile. "Good evening, Miss Campbell."

She blinked and tried to calm the whirling cyclone in her chest. "Good evening."

Donaldson and Kitty moved to the side of the room, silent, mouths tight. Each held a look in their face that told Eliza they were ready to flee and fight all at the same time. Was her distress so obvious?

With hands outstretched, the reverend stepped forward. "Shall we begin?"

From that moment on, the room grew fuzzy, and the voices around her seemed to be coming from some great distance. The Reverend's mouth moved, but Eliza couldn't concentrate on anything he said. The walls swayed, a little at first, until the floor beneath her feet threatened to give way. She had no choice but to hold on stronger to Samuel to keep from toppling. He gripped her tighter and whispered in her ear.

"I love you too, my darling. Now, you will be mine forever."

It seemed as though the reverend droned on for hours though it could only have been minutes. *How much longer must I endure this?*

A loud crash echoed in the room and Eliza almost jumped out of her shoes as the front door burst open. Three unfamiliar soldiers filed into the front room, their faces grim.

Samuel spun toward the door, keeping his voice low as if trying to maintain the reverence of the moment. "What's the meaning of this? I told you not to bother me under any circumstances, did I not?"

The largest soldier took a step forward with a hand on the sword at his side. He bowed slightly at the waist before speaking. "Captain, there's a massive crowd gathering at the Old South Meeting House. All available soldiers are requested to gather in town until further notice."

Samuel shot a frantic glare at Eliza and the others in the room before he turned back to the three strangers. "They are rioting?"

The tallest soldier took a step forward and answered in a thundering timbre. "No, sir. They are peaceful, but it's the sheer numbers of them. Many thousands have gathered. We're needed right away. It's believed the members of the Sons of Liberty are behind this. We fear they will do something with the three tea vessels in the harbor. We understand the sensitive nature of your engagement this evening, but we have our orders."

"Are there not plenty of soldiers already in Boston? I refuse to leave. This is my wedding!"

"I'm sorry, sir," the leader of the three said, "but I have my orders."

Samuel's nostrils flared and his chest pumped. "I will not leave. Not until we have finished here!" He shot a fiery look at the reverend. "How much longer will this take?"

The old man shook his head and gripped the Bible in his hands. "These things cannot be rushed if they are to be done properly."

"I don't care about it being done properly—"

"Please forgive Captain Martin, he is understandably frustrated." Donaldson moved toward the door, his hand stretched toward the soldiers. "We will leave directly." He aimed a fierce glare at Samuel. "You can finish this later."

Knees trembling, Eliza shook her head as the room began once again to take shape. Had God heard her pleas? Perhaps, somehow, their wedding could be delayed long enough for her to think of a way to escape—or at least change Samuel's mind—anything to keep her from marrying him.

The muscles along Samuel's jaw ticked and his face reddened. "Cursed patriots." He turned to Eliza and brushed his thumb across her chin, his voice soft. "I'm so sorry, darling. I won't be long."

She gripped her dress to keep her hands from trembling. "Do what you must. I understand, truly."

After giving her a quick kiss, Samuel flipped his cloak around his shoulders.

"I will come as well," the reverend announced,

snatching his weathered hat and greatcoat. "I wouldn't miss this for the world."

Samuel's eyes thinned as he glared at the old man. "Stay with me, preacher. I'll not have you shirking your duty here. You'll return when I do."

Eliza kept her gaze on Samuel, yearning for the moment he walked out the door. But he stopped and took Donaldson aside as the others bounded down the few front steps and mounted their waiting horses.

"I will go with the rest of the men and see what needs to be done. You must stay here and guard the house."

"Excuse me?" Donaldson jerked his own cloak around him and glared. A blatant hatred rose off him like a foul steam.

"I don't want anything getting in the way of my marriage. I don't trust Watson," Samuel continued. "And when Eliza is finally my wife, you will go to Sandwich and follow through on my previous orders, but make sure that Watson does not escape. He deserves to burn for what he's done."

All the air sucked from Eliza's lungs. She reached for the table at her side and tried to keep steady. Kitty rushed to her side.

Eyes narrowing, Donaldson growled. "Go to Hell." He shoved out the door, slamming his shoulder against Samuel as he went.

Samuel stood in the open doorway pointing and yelling at Donaldson's back. "You will obey my orders, Donaldson! Or your sister's will feel what it's like to die in the streets!"

Eliza's body shuddered as she worked to keep her composure. She turned her head toward Kitty, hoping to detect whether her sister had caught the dreadful command. Kitty's eyes were round, her face pale. She *had* heard. *Thank you Lord, I needed her to know, to bear this burden with me.*

Samuel spun out the door and called to Eliza over his shoulder. "I'll return as quickly as I can, my love."

The door slammed shut and the house went instantly quiet. The pounding of hooves rumbled away leaving Eliza and Kitty alone.

Alone except for Donaldson. Eliza could see him pacing in front of the house from the large front window.

Kitty faced Eliza. "There is more I should know, I can see it in your eyes. Tell me."

Eliza shuffled to the nearest chair and sat, resting her head behind her on the striped upholstery as a smothering defeat blanketed her shoulders. "Kitty, Samuel was the one who blackmailed Thomas."

Kitty clapped a hand over her mouth. "What?"

"I had just learned about it myself, the night of the rally. I saw him in the barn the next morning. I didn't know how in heaven's name he found us. I could tell he wanted me to meet him, so I did, thinking I could help us all. We argued. I told Samuel that I planned to marry Thomas, but that only infuriated him more. Finally, I told Samuel I would come back to Boston and be his wife if he promised not to hurt Thomas. He agreed."

Kitty slid to her knees in front of Eliza, her brows folding down. "So why did he just tell Donaldson—"

"He lied," Eliza said, her voice shaking. "Kitty, I love Thomas. I don't know what I am going to do if he's killed! Samuel said I had to convince Thomas that I wanted to leave, that I didn't love him so that Thomas wouldn't follow us . . ."

Kitty stared forward, brushing her hand along Eliza's back. "I can't believe it, Liza. It's too horrible to be true."

"But it is true, and it is all my fault." Eliza wept, clutching tighter to her sister's petite shoulders.

The two remained in each other's comforting arms until the swell of grief receded enough for Eliza to pull away.

Kitty pushed out a rough sigh. "I can't understand how Thomas would just let you go. He loves you just as you love him." Her volume escalated as she rose to her feet. "This entire tragedy is—"

"Kitty, please. I didn't want Thomas to come after me. It is too dangerous for him. You must see that." Eliza reached out and squeezed her arm. Her sister needed a distraction before the weight of their adversity overwhelmed her, too. "I'm feeling a bit weak, would you be so kind as to make me a bit of something?"

"Of course, Liza." Kitty stared at the floor for a moment before nodding. "I shall prepare a small platter."

"Thank you."

Kitty kissed the top of Eliza's head and walked past the large fireplace toward the darkened kitchen. "Care to join me?"

Eliza shook her head and spoke slowly to keep her voice from wavering with the emotions that pressed ever upward. "No. I need be alone for a while."

A look of understanding streaked across Kitty's face. She lifted an extra candle off the table and illuminated the pathway into her favorite room in the house.

Once alone, Eliza slumped to the hard floor, and sobbed.

Her King had forsaken her.

Samuel rode back to the Campbell's on his steady gelding, the winter air striking his nose and neck as anger rusted his heart. If only he hadn't allowed the over-zealous reverend to come along—he and Eliza could have been married as planned. He should have known the man would get lost among the crowds. Samuel should never have trusted him.

He squeezed the reins in his hand. Those ruthless Sons of Liberty had foiled his designs yet again, just as they had done at the beginning when Watson had taken Eliza. The memory still plagued him and twisted in his gut like a cold dagger. He squirmed in his saddle. There had been no need for Samuel to go to the church. The minute he'd seen the menial ruckus and how *polite* the patriots were, he knew there was nothing he could do. Besides, their behavior was nothing but repulsive and he wouldn't sit through hours of watching them destroy such valuable merchandise. Thousands of pounds worth of tea destroyed! And by men in Indian dress, no less. Despicable. If Samuel hadn't had Eliza waiting for him, he would have gladly stayed and found a way to punish at least one or two of those wretched traitors. There would be hell to pay!

Even with the dramatic events at the wharf swimming in his mind, a ghostly shadow seemed to follow him as he rode. He shifted once again and kicked his horse to move faster. He could never rest until he knew Thomas was dead. The man was sly and conniving and Samuel could only imagine what he was capable of, considering the ploy he'd already pulled with his future bride.

As he put more distance between himself and Boston proper a persuading voice echoed in his head.

You and Eliza were mere minutes from being man and wife. You had simply to say a few words and you would have been united. Take her as your wife this night as you planned, how could she object to that?

He sat taller. *Yes. Why not*? He'd waited these many years and after all he'd done for her it was the just reward he deserved. Once he poured his passion upon her she would love him back, he knew it.

A stimulating desire set him aflame and he flicked the reins, kicking at his horse to move at a blistering speed.

He smiled.

Eliza was waiting for him.

Chapter Twenty-eight

The familiar dirt road that led to the Campbell's home resonated under the pounding hooves of Thomas's stallion and mimicked the pounding of his heart. It would be only a few more minutes of riding before they reached Eliza's home.

Only a fragment of the moon shone in the December sky. The horse's breath plumed into large white clouds as it exhaled into the brisk air. Thomas yanked on the reins and Nathaniel rode up next to him.

"Is this it?" Nathaniel asked, looking at the tree-dotted landscape around them.

"No, we're still a half-mile away. But I want to leave the horses here—we'll be able to keep silent and stay out of view of any soldiers if we travel the remaining distance on foot. We can go around the back." Thomas slid off his horse.

Nathaniel nodded. "How many guards do you suppose Martin will have posted?"

"I don't know."

Thomas moved quickly as a stinging urgency flashed through his body. He secured his horse next to a towering oak and Nathaniel did the same then fastened his pistol and a small dagger around his middle.

"I have no idea what to expect." Thomas glanced

around him, clutching his own weapon in his fingers. "I don't even know for certain if she will be here, but it's the most logical place to check first."

"I'm right behind you."

Thomas took Nathaniel around the back, the same way he and the girls had left in early October. The house rested, quiet and dark. Only a few candles glowed through the windows in the parlor, and another flickered in the kitchen.

Cautious of every movement, Thomas crept toward the house, crouching low. Knowing he may be close to Eliza made his pulse surge.

The modest window by the backdoor provided the needed view. He rose slow, and peered into the dimly lit parlor.

"I don't see any guards inside," he whispered into the glass as Nathaniel knelt beside him.

"That doesn't mean they aren't around the front."

"Right. Let's check there first, before we try and go in."

"I can do that. You stay here," Nathaniel said.

Thomas ducked down and shook his head. "No, I'll come with you. It will be safer if we move together." He didn't want his best friend stumbling upon a group larger than he could take on himself.

They crept in silence around two more corners of the house until the front came into view. A lone soldier paced back and forth a few feet from the doorstep, wearing a long black cloak. His arms were folded around his middle as if trying to keep warm. He didn't seem to be interested in keeping watch. His musket was propped by the front door and his sword was lounging on the front step behind him. When he turned in their direction, his gaze at the ground, Thomas squeezed his pistol's wooden handle so hard he could have produced sap. A guard out front *had* to mean Eliza was inside.

His memory pricked to life.

"I know him," Thomas said. "He's the one that was after me and the girls the night I came to rescue them."

"He'll be an easy one to bring down." Nathaniel's mouth twitched upward.

Thomas's arms and legs cramped. Only this man stood between him and Eliza. But where was Samuel? Inside? There wasn't time to be worried about that now. "Follow my lead."

Nathaniel gave him a quiet smack on the shoulder. "I'm right behind you."

The blow to Donaldson's head was quick and hard and Thomas moved back to let Nathaniel close.

He checked the soldier's pulse then rolled him onto his back. "Nice hit, Thomas," he whispered.

"Nathaniel, I need you to keep watch here and alert me the minute anyone arrives." Thomas lodged his pistol at his side. "I'm going in for Eliza."

Muscles buzzing, he opened the front door, careful to be silent as he closed it behind him should the enemy still lurk within.

As he tip-toed, the scene before him struck like a falling beam and he froze where he stood. Eliza, wearing a gold and cream gown, crouched on the floor weeping and calling for him. Tears glistened against her fair skin as her skirts billowed around her. The anguish in her voice drove into his chest, stealing his breath with the pain of it. His vision!

His heart bled and he rushed to her.

Eliza propped herself up with one hand and wept into the other. The tremendous load she'd carried, poured from her with all the power of a flooded waterfall. Her muscles cramped and her eyes burned. Even after all her efforts, Samuel would kill the man she loved, and she was powerless to stop it.

"Thomas, I'm so sorry. I only wanted to protect you. I love you."

"Eliza."

She gasped and shot her eyes in the direction of the voice of the man she cherished. It couldn't be . . .

Her lungs heaved. "Thomas?" She blinked, not believing the sight before. The dark coat he wore accentuated his broad shoulders and matched the mid-night color of his hair. Pure love poured out of his dark-blue eyes and circled around her quivering heart.

He rushed forward and knelt in front of her, cupping her cheeks in his strong hands. "Did you not believe I would come for you?"

"Are you real?" she said, almost unbelieving. But the feel of his cold hands against her skin, and the way his eyes mapped her face made reality crash into her chest. "Oh, Thomas! I wanted you to come. I wanted to tell you—" Suddenly the blood drained and her heart flogged her ribs. Struggling, she rushed to get up. "You must leave. You can't be here it's too dangerous!"

Bending down, he helped Eliza to her feet before pulling her against his strong frame. His solid arms formed a protective shield she never wanted to leave. The sound of his heartbeat made Eliza cling to him all the more. Crooking his finger underneath her chin, Thomas tilted her head upward, folding his soft lips into hers with a quiet moan. All her strength evaporated like mist in the sun and she pressed into him, gripping his thick hair at his neck. His warm mouth roamed hers and an audible sigh escaped her throat as a thrilling tingle splashed over her.

Slowly, he moved his hands to her shoulders and he pushed her away, his breath heaving as much as hers.

Thomas's deep gaze traced her figure as if assessing her condition.

"Are you alright?" His eyes narrowed as he focused on the cut on her cheek. He brushed it with gentle fingers and his voice hardened. "What's happened, Eliza? What did he do to you?"

Her hands trembled and her leg muscles ticked. She placed her hands on his chest. "Thomas, I told you not to follow me. Samuel will kill you if he finds you. You have to leave. Now!"

Instead of acknowledging her statement, he tucked his fingers into her hair and smiled. "What love can do, that dares love attempt."

She pushed away from him as her love and desire for him to live surpassed her own need to be at his side. "I beg you Thomas, you must go. Please! I told Samuel I'd marry him as long as he promised not to kill you, but I overheard him saying he would kill you regardless. You have to get away from here. I couldn't bear anything happening to you. You must leave now!"

Thomas's eyes widened, then his brow dipped low. "You sacrificed yourself again. This time for me." He shook his head and pulled her to him once more. "I knew something was wrong when you left. You should have told me."

"Thomas, I love you, and that's why you must go. He'll kill you the moment he sees you and I have no idea when he'll be back."

Thomas looked as if her admonition meant nothing. "I won't leave you again."

The backdoor burst open and Eliza's heart shot to her throat. She pressed a hand to her chest and pushed out a quick breath of relief when Nathaniel entered. "Heavens, Nathaniel! What are you doing here?"

"Hello, Eliza." He quickly shut the door behind him and motioned to the front. "We have trouble."

"What is it?" Thomas asked.

Nathaniel gripped tight to a pistol. "He's here."

Both Eliza and Thomas snapped their heads in the direction of the front door as it flung wide and Samuel entered with iniquitous strides. Clinging to Thomas's thick bicep, Eliza felt it flex when their enemy drew near.

Samuel's eyes melted through Eliza then made their way through each person in the room.

"I figured you would be foolish enough to come." Samuel's voice was flat.

"You would have been foolish to figure otherwise," Thomas answered. He rolled his shoulders back and strengthened his grip around Eliza.

"I'm surprised it took you this long," Samuel sneered. "*I* never would have let her go."

Thomas stiffened.

"I have you and your Sons of Liberty to thank—once again—for ruining my plans." He slammed the door shut.

"How do you mean?" Thomas asked. Eliza could

almost feel the bristles of anger poking through his jacket.

"You haven't heard?" Samuel baited. "If it weren't for your friends in that traitorous group of yours Eliza and I would already be married."

Eliza lifted her eyes to Thomas. The muscles in his jaw ticked. "Do explain."

Samuel shifted his weight to his other foot and removed his long black cloak, laying it over the chair next to him. "They're destroying thousands of pounds worth of valuable tea by dumping it into the water at Griffin's Wharf. Had they not done so, I would not have been called to duty. And If I'd not been called to duty, Eliza would even now be my wife." He stopped and turned his eyes to her. "In more ways than one."

Thomas lunged, but Eliza pressed him back.

Samuel's smile exuded wicked pleasure before his expression changed and his glare compressed into tiny slits. "Where's Donaldson?"

No one answered. Eliza looked between Nathaniel and Thomas, but neither man so much as blinked.

"No one wants to tell me what's happened with an innocent soldier? Sounds suspicious to me." He took a step further, his eyes boring holes into Eliza's skull.

The men exchanged fleeting glances, but none spoke.

Samuel drew his sword from its sheath and Thomas's muscled flex around her.

"The charges against you are piling to the sky, Thomas," he said, fondling the hilt of his weapon with feigned indifference.

Nathaniel took a step toward Samuel. Thomas flung him a halting look and he stopped mid-stride.

"Tell me where he is," Samuel demanded through clenched teeth.

"I'm right here."

Every head jerked in the direction of the voice.

Donaldson staggered in through the back door, rubbing his neck and trying to stand straight.

"Some guard you are. You fool!" Samuel said, the red in his face mirroring the color of his coat.

Samuel marched forward and backhanded him across the jaw. "Get out, Donaldson! I'll deal with you later. I can handle these traitors on my own."

Donaldson extended his hand. "They struck me from behind, sir. I had no way of knowing—"

"Enough! Find your way to the wharf and make yourself useful somehow—*if* that's possible. Now!"

Donaldson strode away sending a quick look to Thomas, then slammed the front door closed behind him as he left.

Thomas's breathing quickened as he exchanged communicative glances with Nathaniel.

Samuel, still brandishing his sword, took on an even more domineering stand. "You know you can do nothing to me. Nothing." His chuckle oozed malice as he returned his long sword to its sheath. "I'm a soldier in His Majesty's Army. If anything happens to me you'll both be hanged and what would happen to dear Miss Campbell then?"

"What's going on, Liza?" Kitty's clear voice echoed through the crowded room. "Thomas . . . Nathaniel. What are you doing here?"

Eliza turned, her heart exploding behind her ribs. *Lord, don't let anything happen to Kitty.*

Kitty stood at the doorway of the kitchen, a tray of bread and cheese in her hands. Her wide eyes darted between Eliza in Thomas's arms, to Nathaniel and at last to Samuel. Eliza moved a step toward her, but stopped when Samuel's demands broke the fragile silence.

"Upstairs with you, Kitty. This is not your affair," he barked.

Kitty slammed the tray on the table beside her, her features tight as she marched to stand beside Eliza. "Absolutely not, Samuel. Don't think I am still ignorant of your wicked ways."

"Do as he says, Kitty." Eliza forced her voice to stay even.

Samuel pointed to the stairs. "Listen to your sister."

Undeterred, Kitty lifted her chin. "You don't frighten me. I'm staying with my sister."

Nathaniel's resonating voice billowed in the heated room, his pleading eyes pinned on Kitty. "Kitty, please I don't want you hurt."

"Nathaniel, I—"

"Quiet!" Samuel moved toward Eliza, hostility dripping from his stare as he walked. "You told him to come. Somehow you told him!" Samuel spat when he spoke keeping only a few feet between them.

"Samuel, I promise I didn't tell him to come here—"

"Silence!" Samuel bellowed, the veins in his head and neck bulging.

Thomas pushed Eliza behind him, gripping his pistol at his side.

"Your quarrel is with me, Samuel," Thomas said. "Don't release your anger of defeat on Eliza just because she refuses to be with a man like you."

"A man like me?"

Samuel's mouth coiled and he swiped his pistol from his side, pointing it at Thomas's chest. Thomas and Nathaniel stepped back and swung their weapons at Samuel the same instant.

"No!" Eliza screamed and tried to move in front of Thomas, but his solid arms kept her back.

"Drop your weapons now! Kick them to me!" Samuel demanded.

No one moved.

"There's nothing to stop me from shooting you if you kill him," Nathaniel said, widening his stance. "I'm not afraid to hang."

"But are you afraid to bleed?"

In one swift movement Samuel pivoted. Thomas lurched forward, gun extended. Both Kitty and Eliza screamed as the sound of three pistols exploded with an earsplitting crack. Nathaniel hit the ground shouting and clawing at his shoulder, but Thomas and Samuel stood motionless. Eliza almost collapsed.

Thomas kept his eyes on Samuel, but his voice was directed at Eliza. "Are you hurt?"

"No." Eliza's heart slammed against her ribs.

"Nathaniel!" Kitty bolted for him as he writhed on the floor, scooting his way to the fireplace, leaving a dark smear of blood as he went.

Samuel yanked Kitty back, but she jerked her arm from his grip. "Let go of me!" Dashing to Nathaniel's side, she spoke quiet as she attended to his wound.

With the one round used, Samuel tossed his useless weapon on the ground. "I warned you. Both of you!" he yelled, slinging his sword from his side and waving it in front of Thomas as he stalked closer. "Eliza needs me to care for her. She needs someone to think *for* her, Thomas, not *force* her to think for herself."

Thomas wrenched his neck to look behind his shoulder at Eliza, and spoke so calm it was as if nothing terrifying had happened. "Help Kitty with Nathaniel. Samuel and I will put an end to this."

As much as her muscles willed her to stay next to Thomas, she obeyed, leaving her heart behind her.

Nathaniel sat against the wall next to the fireplace. He probed his own wound and gritted his teeth as he searched for the musket ball. Kitty stared at him, her own face so warped with worry it was as if she experienced the pain with him. Blood gushed from the dark hole in his flesh and Eliza breathed through her lips to keep from vomiting.

"What do you need me to do?" Eliza asked.

She tried to focus on the task in front of her but her peripheral vision strained for any glimpse of what was happening behind her.

"Stoke the fire," Nathaniel said, his face pale but his eyes steady.

"What?" She couldn't have heard right.

"Stoke the fire."

Eliza winced and shot a questioning glance to Kitty. Was Nathaniel's wound so terrible he was already delirious?

She glanced to her left, toward the fireplace. The flames wobbled over the dilapidated logs. "I'll take care of that after I—"

The fire poker!

She stopped mid-sentence and her mouth opened upon recognition. Nathaniel nodded. Thomas needed a weapon—something, anything to defend himself against Samuel's sword.

She squashed the escalating panic that surged upward from her toes and moved toward the fire.

Lord, I can't do this without you, please help me!

Eliza looked between Samuel and Thomas, leaving her eyes on her hero a second longer, hoping he would somehow sense what she was about to do. Thomas closed his lips and dipped his head ever so slight.

"I've been dreaming of this day you know," Samuel said. "Eliza was mine long before you ever knew her."

Thomas took a step back. "God doesn't want people to be forced or coerced. Let her decide the future that she wants for herself, Samuel."

Eliza grabbed the poker with two hands, fearing her trembling fingers wouldn't perform the needed calling. *Dear God, guide this from my hands to Thomas's.*

Chapter Twenty-nine

Thomas's muscles flexed as he gauged his adversary's every move. Samuel proceeded gracefully, with the same reserved strength of a tiger, ready to pounce.

Thomas kept a careful side-glance on Eliza. His body wanted to heave forward and snatch the weapon, but he used every measure of resistance to wait for just the right moment.

"She made her own choice, Thomas. Or don't you remember?" Samuel said. He straightened an inch. His face lit with mock surprise. "Oh! That's right. She chose me!" His hissed the last words as the muscles around his mouth contorted.

Now!

Thomas gave a slight nod, still locking eyes with his foe. The poker soared in a perfect arch. He reached out his hand and the heavy, impromptu weapon landed directly in his waiting palm.

Samuel recoiled in momentary surprise, then lunged. Thomas parried the attack, the sound of metal on metal clanking in the air. Samuel repositioned with lightning speed and swiped downward. Thomas dodged to the right before he could be sliced in two. He swung the poker against the sword with a powerful smack.

His muscles throbbed, raw energy pulsing

through him as Samuel's fight grew desperate. He slammed the sword over Thomas, but Thomas held both ends of the poker above his head to shield himself from the hit. He released one hand and held to the poker with the other, vaulting it through the air in a perfect arch, forcing the sword away from him.

Samuel reared back and poised for another strike.

The room around Thomas blurred. All that existed was the man who subjected him to years of blackmail. All that existed was the man who had taken Eliza against her will. All that existed was the man who wanted him dead.

"Give up, Thomas! All this dancing around is only postponing the inevitable. I *am* going to kill you." Samuel lunged again. The sound of his slashing blade ripped the air.

Seeing the half-second opening, Thomas moved in. He gouged forward with his two-pronged poker. Samuel weaved to the side. Thomas jumped. He dropped his weapon and lunged at Samuel's hand. Thomas gripped the sword, using both of his arms for added stability. The men wrestled for control, grunting and shaking.

Thomas worked all his muscles and wrenched Samuel to the side, smacking his wrist against the wall.

A hollow roar cut the air and Samuel dropped the sword, but pushed into his aggression and launched forward. He plowed his shoulder into Thomas's gut and wrapped his arms around his back.

Thomas fumbled backward. He slammed into the table beside him as he fell to the ground, sending the burning oil lamp crashing onto the floor.

The air popped from his lungs as he hit the solid

wood beneath him. Samuel released his hold then jumped on top of him, jamming his elbow into Thomas's exposed ribcage.

Thomas's vision blurred as the bones in his chest cracked, sending a stabbing sensation into his back. He battled for air and blinked to clear his sight when another blinding pain sliced into his jaw.

As if from a tunnel, Eliza's panicked voice reached his ears. "Stop, Samuel! You'll kill him!"

"That's the point, my dear." Samuel grunted, as he molded his iron-like fingers around Thomas's neck.

Ears ringing, head pounding, the taste of blood trickled into his mouth.

Suddenly, Eliza's scream climbed two octaves. "Fire! The house is on fire!"

All his senses collaborated in a second. The acrid smell of burning wood filled his nose and his ears honed in on the crackling that grew ever louder. The flames devoured the wood and made their way across the floor toward the walls.

Powerful reservoirs of strength flooded into Thomas's arms and legs. He thrust his knees into Samuel's chest, shoving him to the side. His assailant's grip loosened and Thomas pried Samuel's hands away from his neck. He leaped to his feet and took an aggressive stance, ready for another attack.

Eliza tried to beat the spreading flames with a cloak while Kitty helped Nathaniel to his feet.

"Get out of here, all of you!" Thomas yelled. "Get out now!"

Samuel ran toward him, snarling and sweating. Thomas jabbed his knee into Samuel's groin sending him writhing backward.

Eliza dropped the cloak as Kitty and Nathaniel made their way out the back, her face twisted with worry, before escaping into the freedom of the field.

Thomas turned to Samuel just before another blistering punch to his stomach bent Thomas at the waist.

The charring smoke swirled around him, burning his lungs. His muscles ached for air, forcing him to take deep breaths of the soot-clogged gasses.

Samuel launched again, this time bellowing and clawing. Thomas deviated Samuel's aggressive arms and landed a fist in the center of his face. Blood splashed from Samuel's nose, but the pain he must have felt only seemed to heighten his ferocity. Samuel attacked again and again, releasing a kind of demon into his continuous blows.

The flames licked up the walls as several portraits fell to the ground. Thomas shielded his eyes from the vicious heat. "Samuel, quit this! We must get out of here before we're burned alive!"

"Burned alive? So be it." Samuel wiped another stream of blood from his nose and streaked it up his face.

Perspiration dripped from Thomas's every pour and trailed over his muscles. The oppressive heat drained the remaining reserves of strength in his weakening limbs. The flames consumed the room at terrifying speed and the smoke annihilated the breathable air.

Thomas stepped backward to dodge another fist when his foot knocked something hard.

The sword.

In one quick motion he bowed to pick it up, but instantly tossed the scorching metal aside. The sword flew, lodging the handle in an open crevice between the wall and the floor. The blade stuck out into the room at a forty-five degree angle only inches from where they fought.

Samuel plowed his fist into Thomas's jaw. He reeled backward, shaking his head to make the smoky orange room stay still.

"Thomas! Samuel! Get out of there!"

Both men turned at the sound of Eliza's voice. She stood in the opening of the back door while the dangerous blaze swayed fatally close to her skirts.

Rage split Thomas's skull. "Eliza, what are you doing—"

"Thomas, look out!"

He whirled around to see Samuel charging toward him, screaming like a mad man with the fire poker raised above his head. With less than a second to react, Thomas jumped to the side and shoved Samuel away before the poker met his chest.

The following seconds moved slow, dream-like. The sword, still jammed in place, glowed from the reflecting flames. Samuel pitched and slammed onto the waiting blade. It popped through him with sickening ease, splattering blood into the air. His body went immediately limp and heaved forward.

He was dead.

"Samuel!" Eliza's shrill cry stabbed through the smoke and ravenous flames.

Thomas stared at the gruesome sight, heedless of the fire that threatened to consume him.

"Thomas! Thomas, get out!" Eliza's voice called to him again.

He twisted toward her, his lungs shriveling from smoke, his limbs quaking.

"Eliza, get out of here *now*!"

She hesitated before disappearing outside. Once convinced of her safety, he turned and weaved through the hungry fire. He pushed through the front door and tumbled out just as Nathaniel and the girls rushed from around the back of the house.

Thomas careened from the burning building and rested on all fours. Coughing and choking, his lungs devoured the clean night air.

Eliza flew to his side and brushed her hands along his body. “Are you hurt?”

He raised his throbbing head and tried to give an encouraging smile, but none would surface. “I’m fine.”

Large tears flooded her dark gaze and spilled over her cheeks. Their eyes communicated what their voices could not.

The unbelievable had happened.

Nathaniel sat next to Eliza, then laid flat on his back still clutching at his shoulder. Kitty perched at Nathaniel’s side, brushing his hair away from his face, and pressing a wad of cloth to the hole in his shoulder.

The heat from the inferno throbbed against their bodies as the flames consumed the screaming wood. A towering cloud of smoke rippled through the air, lending a vile smell that burned his nose and throat.

Eliza’s soft voice cracked, her eyes shimmering. “It’s all my fault, Thomas. I should never have gone to the rally. I should have listened to you.”

“It isn’t your fault—”

“Look what’s happened! Father’s home, all our memories are gone. And Samuel’s dead!”

Thomas’s throat thickened. “We can talk about all this later, my love.”

She nestled her head into his neck and cried harder, gripping tighter to his back.

Kitty moved closer and tugged on Thomas’s arm, her large eyes swimming with tears of her own. “We must get Nathaniel some place warm, some place we can treat his wound."

Thomas nodded. "Of course, we'll go at once." He wrapped his arms tighter around Eliza and helped her to stand. Her arms were freezing. They needed to find shelter and fast. He knelt by Nathaniel and helped him to stand, lacing his arm around his waist and allowing his friend to lean into him.

"It is a fair distance to my cousins, but I'll walk beside your horse while you ride, Nathaniel. The girls can both ride mine. Do you think you can walk to where we left them?" Thomas's tone carried more worry with it than he intended, but the pale look of Nathaniel's face caused his gut to harden.

Nathaniel huffed tiny breaths through gritted teeth before he nodded and rested the bulk of his weight into Thomas. "Remind me not to come with you on your next adventure."

Thomas couldn't help but chuckle. At least he hadn't yet lost his sense of humor.

Eliza came to the other side of Nathaniel. Kitty followed and rested a caring hand on his forearm.

"Samuel was right, you know," Nathaniel croaked. "He's dead, and we look strangely suspicious. It's only a matter of time . . ."

Thomas flashed his eyes at Eliza. From the tight form of her lips and the roundness of her eyes, she had already surmised as much. Thomas stiffened. What terrifying implications awaited them now?

A resounding crash thundered and the four of them whirled toward the tumbling house. Massive plumes of smoke and ash exploded and raced for the stars as the house crumpled into itself, the flames still devouring the victim within its grasp.

Kitty wailed and flung herself into Eliza's

embrace. She cradled her sister's head as tears plummeted down her own cheeks.

It wouldn't be long before the far away neighbors came rushing up the road. The flames could likely be seen from a great distance. And with them, would come the sealing of their fate.

"We must face whatever comes," Thomas said. "It was I who fought him, so I shall take the blame."

Eliza pressed her hands to her mouth, a chirping kind of sob escaping her lips. She released Kitty and grasped his arm. "No, Thomas, please. There must be a way to—"

"You need not worry."

A shadowy figure emerged from the trees. Eliza gripped tighter and sucked in a frightened breath. Thomas gripped around her small waist as his blood congealed in his veins.

"Donaldson. What are you doing here?" He kept his voice strong, not wanting to show how his knees had turned to jelly.

Donaldson moved forward, looking casually between them and the fire. He stopped within a few feet of the group, one hip cocked as he pressed the center of one hand into the pommel of his sword.

As if knowing what might happen, Nathaniel moved away and rested against Kitty's much smaller build, allowing Thomas unmitigated access to the approaching foe.

Thomas straightened, fists clenched at his sides. His reserves of energy renewed at the thought of an impending battle, but Donaldson waved his hand.

"I'll not fight you."

Thomas jerked to a halt and his brow dove toward his nose. He relaxed his rigid fingers, though his heart still pounded against his lungs. "What do you want?"

Donaldson took a step forward, his hands raised in front of him, showing his desire for peace. He looked at the raging blaze and pointed. "'Tis a tragedy. I've been serving with Martin for a while now and I've worried for him."

Thomas flinched back. He turned to Eliza who gave a slight shake of her head. Confusion dribbled over him, and he maintained his defensive stance.

The soldier talked to the ground as he dug in the dirt with the toe of his boot. "He hasn't been himself of late. I just never thought he would take his own life . . ." He looked up and stared, as if hoping Thomas would understand his meaning. "A terrible tragedy."

Thomas's jaw fell to his knees and when Eliza's fingers twined with his, he gripped tight.

What is he saying?

Donaldson nodded as his eyes flowed over the ragged group. "I'm sorry for what's happened, Miss Campbell, Miss Katherine. Having to witness someone lose control of themselves in such a way is terribly distressing. I'll report to my superiors the details of this evenings events and I can promise you will have no trouble from us."

Eliza folded into Thomas, her tone clouded with emotion. "Thank you, Lieutenant."

At that moment, the sound of voices and stomping hooves echoed through the night.

"What's happened here?" The first rider approached and hopped down. Two more followed close to him, buckets in hand. "Is everyone well? More help is on the way." He looked at the home, immediately assessing the damage. "It appears there's nothing our buckets can do now. I'm sorry."

Donaldson came forward, assuming an air of authority. "Yes, it will burn out soon enough. Thank you gentlemen, for your willing assistance. All is well, it's simply a terrible accident." He looked at Thomas and nodded as if to say they were free to go their way.

A wave of relief whistled through Thomas's still tense muscles. "Come, let us find some place warm."

Eliza and Kitty huddled together, absorbing the unreal scene before them for the last time. The glow of the fire reached into Eliza's soul and burned her very heart. Kitty turned her head into Eliza's shoulder and wept.

She stroked her sister's hair and cooed whatever encouraging words she managed to assemble in the barren desert of her brain. All of their family treasures, gone. Father's precious journal, a heap of ash. That thought alone pushed a hard sob from her chest. The rooms and halls where she'd run and laughed as a child, where Father's tender voice still echoed, were ascending to heaven as spirits of smoke.

The surreal moment bathed her with unquenchable grief. The gruesome picture of Samuel's hunched and bleeding body jumped out from its hiding place in her mind and slapped her. She cupped her mouth as another cry made its way to her lips, but it stopped just short of release. There was nothing that could have been done. He'd gone mad, and only God could sort that out now.

Lord, what would you have me do? Where are Kitty and I to make our futures?

Suddenly, she stopped as God's voice pierced

through the smoke of her smoldering grief.

Where do you think, my child?

Her breath caught. She turned and looked toward Thomas as he helped Nathaniel down the muddy path. A blossom of hope opened in her heart as she clutched the soft lace at her chest.

Thomas had come for her. He was her future now!

God had led him to her. God had helped them both. She pressed her hand to her mouth as the realization broke through her veil of sorrow. Her King had delivered her! He had not forsaken nor forgotten her in the moment of her greatest need.

Eliza held to Kitty even tighter, smiling toward heaven.

Thank you, Lord! I've found my path of peace.

January 23, 1774
Sandwich, MA

Thomas shuffled his feet and played nervously with the lace cuffs that stuck out from his blue-gray jacket. He tugged on his coral colored waistcoat and fussed with his cravat for the thirtieth time. Again, he checked the clock. Only two minutes had passed since the last time he checked though it felt like twenty. Why did women take so long?

Not that Eliza was late. She wasn't. In fact, the wedding ceremony wouldn't start for another fifteen minutes. But as far as Thomas was concerned, those minutes could have been years.

In the other corner of the room, Reverend Charles talked with Daniel and Clara, their new babe swaddled and tucked in her arms. The other two children sat quiet and well behaved in the upholstered chairs in front of the hearth. Daniel looked up from the conversation to pass Thomas a telling grin as he raised one brow. He moved his eyes to the stairs and back before winking. Thomas smiled, and shook his head at Daniel's teasing.

Both his cousin and Clara had insisted on coming to Sandwich when they'd learned of the impending nuptials the night of the fire. Thomas and Eliza were guilt ridden at the thought of them traveling all those many miles, with their three young children on wintery roads. But Daniel and Clara were stubborn. They'd come three days ago, and Clara had helped Eliza prepare her dress, the meals and other celebratory accouterments for the joyous day. Kitty had spent many a happy hour doting on the children and appeared to be more joyful than Thomas had seen her in weeks. As for now, Kitty was upstairs assisting his future bride.

Nathaniel came from behind and tugged on Thomas's elbow, keeping his volume low. "I hope you've come to your senses in allowing the Williamses and Kitty to stay at my home this evening. You and Eliza need a proper wedding night."

Thomas's heart pattered at the anticipation, but he did his best to keep his voice calm. "That's not necessary."

A sly grin slid up Nathaniel's mouth and he bobbed one eyebrow. "Oh, I believe it is. I will have it no other way."

"No other way? Who made you king?" Grinning, Thomas brushed his hand down the front of his waistcoat. He'd wanted an evening alone with Eliza, but didn't want to seem over-eager. "You're very generous, thank you."

"Of course. That's what I do best." Nathaniel chuckled.

Thomas stood taller and straightened his jacket, smiling at his friend's good humor. "Well, when the time comes for you to enter into matrimonial bliss, I shall do my best to find a way to offer you a similar gesture."

"I can't say such *bliss* is in my near future." Nathaniel cleared his throat, and looked toward the stairs. His breathing slowed and a dreamy look captured his features for less than a second before he shook it away. "I've got plenty of women to keep my attentions, why settle on one?"

Thomas chuckled. "Whatever you say." Running his fingers over his head, he tightened the ribbon that held his hair in place before he looked at the clock. "What's keeping them?"

Nathaniel laughed and leaned his back against the mantel. "I've told you before, a woman's toilette is a mystery, Thomas. You can look forward to waiting, just as you are now, many times over in your life from this day on." He grinned with a mocking slide to his mouth and slapped him on the back. "She'll be down soon enough, and looking perfect no doubt. You must have patience."

"Patience?" Thomas chuckled and rubbed the cleft in his chin, feeling the evening whiskers peeking through his skin. "You know I've heard from my Uncle George."

"Have you?"

"Seems he's besotted with a Southern woman, and wants to leave the press. He asked if I would like my supplies . . ."

Pushing from off the mantel, Nathaniel's face brightened. "Please tell me you said yes."

"Of course I did. I can't wait to get my fingers black again. I think I might have gone mad as a farm—"

At that moment, Kitty entered the room, and all conversation ceased, bathing the room in silence. The emerald gown clung to her feminine figure and her countenance beamed as if she were the happy bride herself. How beautiful she looked. So much like her sister. Thomas snuck a glance at Nathaniel, whose round eyes were sweeping over her from head-to-toe and up again.

Thomas couldn't hold back and leaned toward Nathaniel's ear. "No *bliss* in your future?"

The glare that shot from his friend's eyes seared Thomas's mouth shut, but it didn't stop his smile, or the mocking chuckle that rumbled in his chest.

Thomas's heart drummed. Where was Eliza?

And then he saw her.

His breath stalled in his lungs as she moved toward him, floating over the ground like a pink angel from heaven. The dusty-rose gown she'd worn that infamous night hugged her luscious curves, giving him ample fuel for his imagination, but he pushed those thoughts away for the moment. They would be man and wife soon enough. Never had he seen such beauty, or known such grace. *Lord, help me be the kind of man she deserves.* He glanced to heaven. *Robert, I shall do my best to make you proud and give your daughter the best of my days.*

A quiet voice brushed behind his ear, and Thomas stilled as Robert's familiar tone made his heart swell. *I know.*

In that moment Eliza's dark eyes found his, and she smiled, lifting Thomas from the ground. Her cheeks darkened to the same rosy hue of her gown as she neared.

Nathaniel chuckled deep and low. "You're a lucky man, Thomas."

Nodding, Thomas couldn't move his eyes away from his bride. "I know."

"Good evening." She reached his side and curtsied low.

"Are you ready?" he whispered, cocking his elbow.

Eliza peered at him through her long lashes, a perfect smile gracing her lips. "I am."

The young reverend looked at them and nodded. "Let us begin."

Eliza sat alone at the modest dressing table Thomas had given to her as a wedding present. She had told him it was too much but he insisted, and she loved him all the more for it. Contemplating the day's glorious events, she brushed her long hair, a permanent smile gracing her face.

She gazed at her reflection in the expansive mirror. God had given her more than she'd ever imagined. He certainly did know how to give good gifts to His children.

As she worked through her tumbling locks, her gaze fastened upon the brown book resting on the table—Father's book. Placing the brush down, she picked it up. This was the last remaining thing he'd touched, the only tangible thing she had left to remember him.

Her throat swelled and she held it to her chest. How she wished he were here. How she yearned to tell him what she'd learned and most of all—that his own wish had come true. She and Thomas had found each other, and were united as husband and wife. How happy he would be. She replaced the book and went to the window to close the curtains. Staring at the fabric, she drew them together and paused. Somehow, Father knew. She felt it. He'd watched over her from the beginning, just as he had promised, and with God's help, everything had knit together into a beautiful pattern of love, trust and truth.

A light knock sounded on the door and her hands

went numb. She tugged at the sleeves and lacy collar of the nightgown Clara had given her, making sure it draped her just right, and pulled a shawl around her shoulders.

"Come in," she said, trying to hide the nervous crack in her voice as she went back to her seat at the table.

The door creaked and opened. Thomas filled the doorway, still wearing the magnificent blue-gray jacket and breeches he'd worn at their wedding—the same suit he'd worn when they'd first tasted of the love that bloomed between them. His broad shoulders filled the fabric and his dark hair and shaven face beckoned her to touch. She was powerless to look away.

Giving her a sideways smile, Thomas entered, removed his coat, and laid it on the edge of the white bedding. A light glow from the two candles resting on her table sent a pleasing pattern across his angled features. He began to unbutton his waistcoat and suddenly Eliza couldn't swallow. The shirt he wore exposed the outline of his muscular form, leaving little to her imagination.

Thomas remained casual, and looked at her with an endless sparkle in his blue eyes as he continued his task.

"I hope I gave you enough time . . . I didn't know how long you'd need," he said, an unmistakable teasing refrain in his voice.

Eliza cleared her throat and focused on her words. "Not very long. I'm . . . I'm finished as you can see." She gripped the buttons on the neck of her nightdress. Her mouth went dry.

Thomas slipped out of his waistcoat and tossed it next to his jacket, his eyes squinting as a royal grin swept over his face. "I can see."

Eliza's head tipped backward as he came forward and stood directly in front of where she sat. Restless butterflies swirled in her middle, and her breath caught in her throat. He took her hands and helped her to stand.

She kept her gaze down, and moved her arms around her middle then dropped them to her sides. Her white nightgown, though modest, draped over her unreserved curves leaving her remarkably exposed.

He moved his hands around her waist, pulling her close. Eliza wiped her clammy palms on her gown, while his hands were warm and wanting through the thin fabric.

"Thomas?"

"Hmmm?"

"I, uh . . ." Her voice cracked again.

Thomas raised his hooded eyes. Pure desire possessed his gaze and he kissed her mouth with a kind of passion she'd never known possible. He pulled her against his body, letting his lips and hands wander where they may. Her heart rapped wildly against her ribs and her breathing heated.

Dotting feather-light kisses against her cheek and ear, he broke away but kept his forehead against hers. His breath was heavy and hot, his voice quiet. "You were saying?" He moved his lips down her neck, while his hands wandered over her back and pressed her harder against him.

Eliza tried to calm her runaway heart, but his breath against her skin sent the most tantalizing tingles down her shoulders that every thought escaped her. "I don't remember."

"Good," he said, a husky timbre to his voice.

In one swift movement he scooped her into his arms. Eliza released a nervous giggle, wrapping her arms around his neck. He whispered into her ear as he moved toward the bed.

"Welcome home, Eliza Watson."

Author's Note

Dear Reader,

I can't thank you enough for taking part in Thomas and Eliza's journey. It was a blessing to write, and I hope it has been a blessing for you to read. If you enjoyed the story and would like to recommend it to others, I would be very honored if you would take the time to write a quick review and post it on Amazon.com or another review site of your choosing, and let other readers know what you thought about it. (I'm sure Thomas and Eliza would be honored by that, too. *wink *)

These character's experiences, though fictional, are not unlike many colonists who lived in and around Boston at the time. The political world was in turmoil and many people, like Eliza, were confused about what was right and what they ought to believe. Others, like Thomas and Nathaniel, dove into the conflict, strongly convinced of what needed to be done—and *why* it needed to be done. Then of course there were Tories like Kitty, who believed the cause was wrong and refused to get politically involved.

Today, like then, we live in a time of serious turmoil. We must "find the truth", just as Robert instructed Eliza to do, and decide for ourselves what side we will take in the battle for our freedoms—both spiritually and politically. We are surrounded by people who fall into the same categories that these characters did—there are people like Eliza and Kitty, and Thomas and Nathaniel all around us. I believe we can be a powerful force for good when we embrace the truths that God has shown to us and share those truths with others who might still be unsure about what it is they believe.

~

Founded only seventeen years after the pilgrims landed in Plymouth, Sandwich is Cape Cod's oldest town. It simply bursts with colorful history and is arguably one of the most picturesque places on the Cape.

I first visited there in 1997, and it has illuminated my imagination ever since. I knew I wanted to set my story there, but had no idea how absolutely perfect it would be.

Sandwich was a hotbed of political unrest in the years before the Revolution, as were all of the towns and provinces surrounding Boston. In 1775, a political gathering was organized by Doctor Nathaniel Freeman—the figure I fashioned my own Nathaniel Smith after. I was enthralled with that piece of history, and knew I needed to include something similar in my novel.

As much as I love American history and the colonial era, I am not a historian. I did my utmost to collect information and facts to make this story as accurate as possible—leaving room for literary license, of course. Please forgive me for inaccuracies or mistakes I may have overlooked.

In book two—Kitty and Nathaniel's story—you will get to know even more about this marvelous city and the rich history it holds.

I have loved bringing these characters, and this marvelous town to life and I can't wait to do again, and again, and again.

Acknowledgements

I hardly know where to begin . . .

To my Lord and Savior—my Heavenly King—I will praise You all the days of my life. My soul is full of gratitude for all You have done for me, and I will strive to be worthy of that love with every breath.

What would I do without my loving husband and children? I'm so blessed by your kindness and patience as I worked through the years to bring this book to life. You three are my greatest friends and I love you endlessly.

Muzzy Arbon—the greatest Editor-In-Chief there ever was—I shudder to think what this book would be like without your knowledge and wisdom. You are a master!

Sandra Orchard, you saw this "diamond in the rough" when it was nothing more than a tangle of words. You pushed me to greater strides with every version and I can't thank you enough.

To Barbara Gill, Janell Hoffman and those at the Nye Homestead—thank you for your patience, support and for taking the time to share with me the majestic history of your town.

And of course where would I be without my critique partners and my fabulous group of beta readers? Thank you to Renee Gustin, Tammy Francis, Jen Bullock, and Kent Arbon for helping me see the ways I could improve this story.

Jennifer Major! You are fast becoming one of my dearest friends, and I am beyond grateful for the sacrifices you made to help make this book shine!

Tina Radcliffe, you have blessed my writing life in many ways! I've learned so much from you and I can't thank you enough for being so patient with my many emails.

I cannot forget to thank you, Professor Benjamin Carp. Your expertise about the city of Boston and the Boston Tea Party was invaluable to me and I'm grateful to you for your help in making sure my facts were correct.

Julie Lessman—you are truly my surrogate sister! You have always been so generous with your time, compliments and encouragement. My life is greatly blessed by you—thank you!!

Joanne Bischoff! You are an inspiration to me. I will be forever blessed by your humble generosity and how you never failed to answer my many questions, no matter how silly they were.

To my other marvelous author-friends Laura Frantz and MaryLu Tyndall—your friendships are priceless!! Laura, I love your Christ-like spirit and the way you always see the good in others—I want to be more like that. MaryLu, you have always been a great friend and I am honored to have you in my life.

To Tekeme Studios: the book cover is a dream come true and my website is simply wonderful, I love them both!! Thank you so much for all you did in my behalf.

Danyell Diaz, your photography is fabulous! I love the work you did for the cover and I couldn't have been more thrilled to be a part of it.

Lynnette and Castle Bonner--you are an answer to prayer!! I thank you with all my heart for formatting this story into something beautiful and for answering my endless questions. Working with you has been a joy! Your willingness to help and your giving spirits are a blessing to me!

Without all these marvelous people, this book would never have made it into print. God bless you all for everything you have done for me.

Amber Lynn Perry is a historical romance novelist, focusing on her favorite time in American history--the Revolutionary era. She received a Bachelor's degree from Portland State University and currently lives in Washington state with her husband and two daughters. She loves to hear from readers and you can contact her through her website, www.amberlynnperry.com or through her Facebook page, www.facebook.com/amberperrywrites.

Made in the USA
San Bernardino, CA
08 May 2014